'THE BOOK OF [ ]
INDEPEND[ ]

'A beautiful tale of how we live now'
ELIZABETH DAY

'RAZOR-SHARP ... MAGNETIC'
OBSERVER

'Twists that made me gasp out loud'
MADELINE MILLER

'COULD NOT BE MORE NECESSARY'
LENA WAITHE

'EXCEPTIONAL' SUNDAY TELEGRAPH

Praise for *Such a Fun Age*

'Unleashes a reckoning with issues of class, money and race . . . A firecracker debut' *Guardian*

'What a joy to find a debut novel so good that it leaves you looking forward to the rest of its author's career . . . A tantalisingly plotted tale about the way we live now' *The Times*

'Marks the arrival of a serious new talent' *i*

'A cracking debut – charming, authentic and every bit as entertaining as it is calmly, intelligently damning' *Observer*

'A witty and incisive debut . . . Joyously funny' *Financial Times*

'Sensational on every level' *Daily Mail*

'Wry yet nuanced . . . An accomplished and, above all, extremely enjoyable debut' *Sunday Telegraph*

'A biting tale of race and class . . . It's witty and subversive and leaves you feeling impressively uncomfortable' *Sunday Times*

'A gripping first novel, peopled by wholly believable and engaging characters' Booker Prize Judges

'*Such a Fun Age* is a satire of white saviour syndrome, woke culture and virtue-signalling motherhood. That it manages this balancing act with such political finesse and humour is testament to the powers of its author' *Spectator*

'A dazzling slice of contemporary literature' *Independent*

'So ingeniously plotted and observed that my heart pounded as though I was reading a thriller . . . Kiley Reid is the writer we need now' Chloe Benjamin

'Funny, piercing and satirical, it explores everything from race and prejudice to getting things wrong when you're trying to do the right thing . . . Brilliant' *Stylist*

'A dangerously, gaspingly funny novel' Emma Donoghue

'The hit novel . . . Reid delivers with a glorious fluidity and wit, and often devastating relatability' BBC.com

'Refreshing, funny and brilliant' Refinery29

'A bullseye of a debut' Emma Straub

'Makes for urgent, timely reading' *AnOther Magazine*

'Kiley Reid's sharp, spiky, funny debut delves into questions of race, class and privilege and comes up with some uncomfortable, complicated answers' *Sunday Express*

'Fresh, urgent . . . A thought-provoking, challenging but funny reflection on modern life' *Red*

'Reid constructs a plot so beautifully intricate and real and fascinating that readers will forget it's also full of tough questions about race, class and identity' *Washington Post*

'Hilarious, uncomfortable and compulsively readable' *TIME*

KILEY REID earned her MFA from the Iowa Writers' Workshop, where she was awarded the Truman Capote Fellowship and taught creative writing with a focus on race and class. Her short stories have been featured in *Ploughshares*, *December*, *New South* and *Lumina*. *Such a Fun Age*, her first book, was both a *Sunday Times* and *New York Times* bestseller and was longlisted for the 2020 Booker Prize. She lives in Philadelphia.

kileyreid.com | @kileyreid

KILEY REID

SUCH A FUN AGE

BLOOMSBURY PUBLISHING
LONDON · OXFORD · NEW YORK · NEW DELHI · SYDNEY

For Patricia Adeline Olivier

BLOOMSBURY PUBLISHING
Bloomsbury Publishing Plc
50 Bedford Square, London, WC1B 3DP, UK

BLOOMSBURY, BLOOMSBURY PUBLISHING and the Diana logo
are trademarks of Bloomsbury Publishing Plc

First published in 2019 in the United States by G. P. Putnam's Sons,
an imprint of Penguin Random House LLC
First published in Great Britain 2020
This edition published 2020

A catalogue record for this book is available from the British Library

ISBN: HB: 978-1-5266-1214-4; TPB: 978-1-5266-1215-1; eBook: 978-1-5266-1217-5;
PB: 978-1-5266-1216-8

4 6 8 10 9 7 5 3

Book design by Laura K. Corless
Printed and bound in Great Britain by CPI Group (UK) Ltd, Croydon CR0 4YY

To find out more about our authors and books visit www.bloomsbury.com
and sign up for our newsletters

"We definitely wait for birthdays. Or even an ice cream. Like [my daughter] has to earn it. Yesterday we promised her an ice cream, but then she behaved horribly. And I said, 'Then I'm sorry, ice cream is for girls who behave. And that's not you today. Maybe tomorrow.'"

—RACHEL SHERMAN,
Uneasy Street: The Anxieties of Affluence

PART ONE

One

That night, when Mrs. Chamberlain called, Emira could only piece together the words ". . . take Briar somewhere . . ." and ". . . pay you double."

In a crowded apartment and across from someone screaming "That's my song!," Emira stood next to her girlfriends Zara, Josefa, and Shaunie. It was a Saturday night in September, and there was a little over an hour left of Shaunie's twenty-sixth birthday. Emira turned the volume up on her phone and asked Mrs. Chamberlain to say it again.

"Is there any way you can take Briar to the grocery store for a bit?" Mrs. Chamberlain said. "I'm so sorry to call. I know it's late."

It was almost astonishing that Emira's daily babysitting job (a place of pricey onesies, colorful stacking toys, baby wipes, and sectioned dinner plates) could interrupt her current nighttime state (loud music, bodycon dresses, lip liner, and red Solo cups). But here was Mrs. Chamberlain, at 10:51 p.m., waiting for Emira to say yes. Under the veil of two strong mixed drinks, the intersection of these spaces almost seemed funny, but what wasn't funny was Emira's current bank balance: a total of seventy-nine dollars and sixteen cents. After a night of twenty-dollar entrées, birthday shots, and collective gifts for the birthday girl, Emira Tucker could really use the cash.

"Hang on," she said. She set her drink down on a low coffee table and stuck her middle finger into her other ear. "You want me to take Briar right now?"

On the other side of the table, Shaunie placed her head on Josefa's shoulder and slurred, "Does this mean I'm old now? Is twenty-six old?" Josefa pushed her off and said, "Shaunie, don't start." Next to Emira, Zara untwisted her bra strap. She made a disgusted face in Emira's direction and mouthed, *Eww, is that your boss?*

"Peter accidentally—we had an incident with a broken window and . . . I just need to get Briar out of the house." Mrs. Chamberlain's voice was calm and strangely articulate, as if she were delivering a baby and saying, *Okay, mom, it's time to push.* "I'm so sorry to call you this late," she said. "I just don't want her to see the police."

"Oh wow. Okay, but, Mrs. Chamberlain?" Emira sat down at the edge of a couch. Two girls started dancing on the other side of the armrest. The front door of Shaunie's apartment opened to Emira's left, and four guys came in yelling, "Ayyeee!"

"Jesus," Zara said. "All these niggas tryna stunt."

"I don't exactly look like a babysitter right now," Emira warned. "I'm at a friend's birthday."

"Oh God. I'm so sorry. You should stay—"

"No no, it's not like that," Emira said louder. "I can leave. I'm just letting you know that I'm in heels and I've like . . . had a drink or two. Is that okay?"

Baby Catherine, the youngest Chamberlain at five months old, wailed in the receiver. Mrs. Chamberlain said, "Peter, can you please take her?" and then, up close, "Emira, I don't care what you look like. I'll pay for your cab here and your cab home."

Emira slipped her phone into the pouch of her crossbody bag, making sure all of her other belongings were present. When she stood and relayed the news of her early departure to her girlfriends, Josefa said, "You're leaving to *babysit*? Are you fucking kidding me?"

"Guys . . . listen. No one needs to babysit me," Shaunie informed the group. One of her eyes was open and the other was trying very hard to match.

Josefa wasn't through asking questions. "What kind of mom asks you to babysit this late?"

Emira didn't feel like getting into specifics. "I need the cash," she said. She knew it was highly unlikely, but she added, "I'll come back if I get done, though."

Zara nudged her and said, "Imma roll witchyou."

Emira thought, *Oh, thank God.* Out loud, she said, "Okay, cool."

The two girls finished their drinks in one long tip as Josefa crossed her arms. "I can't believe you guys are leaving Shaunie's birthday right now."

Emira lifted her shoulders and quickly dropped them back down. "I think Shaunie is leaving Shaunie's birthday right now," she said, as Shaunie crawled down to the floor and announced she was taking a quick nap. Emira and Zara took to the stairs. As they waited outside for an Uber on a dimly lit sidewalk, Emira did the math in her head. *Sixteen times two . . . plus cab money . . . Fuck yes.*

Catherine was still crying from inside the Chamberlain house when Emira and Zara arrived. As Emira walked up the porch stairs, she spotted a small jagged hole in the front window that dripped with something transparent and slimy. At the top of the landing, Mrs. Chamberlain pulled Briar's glossy blond hair into a ponytail. She thanked Emira, greeted Zara the exact same way she always did ("Hi, Zara, nice to see you again"), and then said to Briar, "You get to hang out with the big girls."

Briar took Emira's hand. "It was bedtime," she said, "and now it's not." They stepped down the stairs, and as the three girls walked the three short blocks to Market Depot, Briar repeatedly complimented Zara's shoes—an obvious but unsuccessful ploy to try them on.

Market Depot sold bone broths, truffle butters, smoothies from a station that was currently dark, and several types of nuts in bulk. The store was bright and empty, and the only open checkout lane was the one for ten items or fewer. Next to a dried-fruit section, Zara bent in her heels and held her dress down to retrieve a box of yogurt-covered raisins. "Umm . . . *eight dollars?*" She quickly placed them back on the shelf and stood up. "Gotdamn. This is a rich people grocery store."

Well, Emira mouthed with the toddler in her arms, *this is a rich-people baby*.

"I want dis." Briar reached out with both hands for the copper-colored hoops that hung in Zara's ears.

Emira inched closer. "How do you ask?"

"Peas I want dis now Mira peas."

Zara's mouth dropped open. "Why is her voice always so raspy and cute?"

"Move your braids," Emira said. "I don't want her to yank them."

Zara tossed her long braids—a dozen of them were a whitish blond—over one shoulder and held her earring out to Briar. "Next weekend Imma get twists from that girl my cousin knows. Hi, Miss Briar, you can touch." Zara's phone buzzed. She pulled it out of her bag and started typing, leaning into Briar's little tugs.

Emira asked, "Are they all still there?"

"Ha!" Zara tipped her head back. "Shaunie just threw up in a plant and Josefa is pissed. How long do you have to stay?"

"I don't know." Emira set Briar back on the ground. "But homegirl can look at the nuts for hours so it's whatever."

"Mira's makin' money, Mira's makin money . . ." Zara danced her way into the frozen-food aisle. Emira and Briar walked behind her as she put her hands on her knees and bounced in the faint reflection in the freezer doors, pastel ice cream logos mirrored on her thighs. Her phone buzzed again. "Ohmygod, I gave my number to that guy at Shaunie's?" she said, looking at her screen. "He is so thirsty for me, it's stupid."

"You dancing." Briar pointed up at Zara. She put two fingers into her mouth and said, "You . . . you dancing and no music."

"You want music?" Zara's thumb began to scroll. "I'll play something but you gotta dance too."

"No explicit content, please," Emira said. "I'll get fired if she repeats it."

Zara waved three fingers in Emira's direction. "I got this I got this."

Seconds later, Zara's phone exploded with sound. She flinched, said, "Whoops," and turned the volume down. Synth filled the aisle, and as Whitney Houston began to sing, Zara began to twist her hips. Briar started to hop, holding her soft white elbows in her hands, and Emira leaned back on a freezer door, boxes of frozen breakfast sausages and waffles shining in waxy cardboard behind her.

Briar Chamberlain was not a silly child. Balloons never sent her into hysterics and she was more concerned than delighted when clowns threw themselves on the ground or lit their fingers on fire. At birthday parties and ballet class, Briar became sorely aware of herself when music played or magicians called for screaming participation, and she often looked to Emira with nervy blue eyes that said, *Do I really have to do this? Is this really necessary?* So when Briar effortlessly joined Zara and rocked back and forth to the eighties hit, Emira positioned herself, as she often did, as Briar's out. Whenever Briar had had enough, Emira wanted her to know that she could stop, even though sweet things were currently happening to Emira's heart. For a moment, twenty-five-year-old Emira was being paid thirty-two dollars an hour to dance in a grocery store with her best friend and her favorite little human.

Zara seemed just as surprised as Emira. "Oop!" she said as Briar danced harder. "Okay, girl, I see you."

Briar looked to Emira and said, "You go now too, Mira."

Emira joined them as Zara sang the chorus, that she wanted to feel the heat with somebody. She spun Briar around and crisscrossed her chest as another body began to come down the aisle. Emira felt relieved to see a middle-aged woman with short gray hair in sporty leggings and a T-shirt reading *St. Paul's Pumpkinfest 5K*. She looked like she had definitely danced with a child or two at some point in her life, so Emira kept going. The woman put a pint of ice cream into her basket and grinned at the dancing trio. Briar screamed, "You dance like Mama!"

As the last key change of the song started to play, a cart came into the aisle pushed by someone much taller. His shirt read *Penn State* and his eyes were sleepy and cute, but Emira was too far into the choreography to stop without seeming completely affected. She did the Dougie as she caught bananas in his moving cart. She dusted off her shoulders as he reached for a frozen vegetable medley. When Zara told Briar to take a bow, the man silently clapped four times in their

8

direction before he left the aisle. Emira centered her skirt back onto her hips.

"Dang, you got me sweatin'." Zara leaned down. "Gimme high five. Yes, girl. That's it for me."

Emira said, "You out?"

Zara was back on her phone, typing manically. "Someone just might get it tonight."

Emira placed her long black hair over one shoulder. "Girl, you do you but that boy is *real* white."

Zara shoved her. "It's 2015, *Emira*! Yes we *can*!"

"Uh-huh."

"Thanks for the cab ride, though. Bye, sister."

Zara tickled the top of Briar's head before turning to leave. As her heels ticked toward the front of the store, Market Depot suddenly seemed very white and very still.

Briar didn't realize Zara was leaving until she was out of sight. "You friend," she said, and pointed to an empty space. Her two front teeth hung out over her bottom lip.

"She has to go to bed," Emira said. "You wanna look at some nuts?"

"It's my bedtime." Briar held Emira's hand as she hopped forward on the shiny tile. "We sleep in the grocery store?"

"Uh-uh," Emira said. "We'll just hang out here for a little while longer."

"I want . . . I want to smell the tea."

Briar was always worried about the sequence of upcoming events, so Emira began to slowly clarify that they could look at the nuts first, and then smell the tea after. But as she began to explain, a voice cut her off with, "Excuse me, ma'am." Footsteps followed and when Emira turned around, a gold security badge blinked and glittered in her face. On top it read *Public Safety* and the bottom curve read *Philadelphia*.

Briar pointed up at his face. "That," she said, "is *not* the mailman."

Emira swallowed and heard herself say, "Oh, hi." The man stood in front of her and placed his thumbs in his belt loops, but he did not say hello back.

Emira touched her hair and said, "Are you guys closing or something?" She knew this store would stay open for another forty-five minutes—it stayed open, clean, and stocked until midnight on weekends—but she wanted him to hear the way she could talk. From behind the security guard's dark sideburns, at the other end of the aisle, Emira saw another face. The gray-haired, athletic-looking woman, who had appeared to be touched by Briar's dancing, folded her arms over her chest. She'd set her grocery basket down by her feet.

"Ma'am," the guard said. Emira looked up at his large mouth and small eyes. He looked like the type of person to have a big family, the kind that spends holidays together for the entire day from start to finish, and not the type of person to use *ma'am* in passing. "It's very late for someone this small," he said. "Is this your child?"

"No." Emira laughed. "I'm her babysitter."

"Alright, well . . ." he said, "with all due respect, you don't look like you've been babysitting tonight."

Emira found herself arranging her mouth as if she'd ingested something too hot. She caught a morphed reflection in a freezer door, and she saw herself in her entirety. Her face—full brown lips, a tiny nose, and a high forehead covered with black bangs—barely showed up in the reflection. Her black skirt, her slinky V-neck top, and her liquid eyeliner refused to take shape in the panels of thick glass. All she could see was something very dark and skinny, and the top of a small, blond stick of hair that belonged to Briar Chamberlain.

"K," she exhaled. "I'm her babysitter, and her mom called me because—"

"Hi, I'm so sorry, I just . . . hi." From the end of the aisle, the woman came forward, and her very used tennis shoes squeaked against the tile floor. She put a hand to her chest. "I'm a mom. And I heard the little girl say that she's not with *her* mom, and since it's so late I got a little nervous."

Emira looked at the woman and half laughed. The sentiment felt childish, but all she could think was, *You really just told on me right now?*

"Where . . ."—Briar pointed to one side of the aisle—"Where these doors go?"

"One second, mama. Okay . . ." Emira said. "I'm her sitter and her mom asked me to take her because they had an emergency and she wanted me to get her out of the house. They are three blocks away." She felt her skin becoming tight at her neck. "We just came here to look at the nuts. Well, we don't touch them or anything. We're just . . . we're really into nuts right now, so . . . yeah."

For a moment, the security guard's nostrils expanded. He nodded to himself, as if he'd been asked a question, and said, "Any chance you've been drinking tonight, ma'am?" Emira closed her mouth and took a step back. The woman next to him winced and said, "Oh, geez."

The poultry and meat section came into view. There, the Penn State shopper from earlier was very much paused and attuned to Emira's conversation. All at once, on top of the surreptitious accusations, this entire interaction seemed completely humiliating, as if she'd been loudly told that her name was not on a guest list. "You know what—it's cool," she said. "We can just leave."

"Now wait a minute." The guard held out his hand. "I can't let you leave, because a child is involved."

"But she's *my* child right now." Emira laughed again. "I'm her sitter. I'm technically her nanny . . ." This was a lie, but Emira wanted to imply that paperwork had been done concerning her employment, and that it connected her to the child in question.

"Hi, sweetie." The woman bent and pressed her hands into her knees. "Do you know where your mommy is?"

"Her mom is at *home*." Emira tapped her collarbone twice as she said, "You can just talk to *me*."

"So you're saying," the guard clarified, "that a random woman, three blocks away, asked you to watch her child this late at night?"

"Ohmygod, no. That's not what I said. I'm her *nanny*."

"There was another girl here a few minutes ago," the woman said to the guard. "I think she just left." Emira's face checked into amazement. As it seemed, her entire existence had become annulled. Emira felt like raising her arm as if she were finding a friend in a large crowd, with a phone to her ear, and saying, *Do you see me? I'm waving my hand.* The woman shook her head. "They were doing some . . . I don't even know . . . some booty dancing or whatnot? And I thought, okay, this doesn't feel right."

"Ummm." Emira's voice went high as she said, "Are you serious right now?" Briar sneezed into the side of her leg.

The Penn State man came up and into view. His cell phone was raised and recording in front of his chest.

"Ohmygod." Emira shielded her face with chipped black nails as if she'd accidentally walked into a group photo. "Can you step off?"

"I think you're gonna want this filmed," he said. "Do you want me to call the police?"

Emira dropped her arm and said, "For what?"

"Hey, big girl." The security guard got down on one knee; his voice was gentle and practiced. "Who's this right here?"

"Sweetheart?" the woman said softly. "Is this your friend?"

Emira wanted to bend down and hold Briar—maybe if Briar could see her face more clearly, she'd be able to deliver her name?—but she knew her skirt was gravely short, and now there was a cell phone involved. It suddenly seemed like her fate was in the hands of a toddler who believed broccolis were baby trees, and that placing yourself underneath a blanket made it difficult to be found. Emira held her breath as Briar stuck her fingers in her mouth. Briar said, "Meer," and Emira thought, *Thank God*.

But the guard said, "Not you, honey. Your friend right here. What's her name?"

Briar screamed, *"Meer!"*

"She's saying my name," Emira told him. "It's Emira."

The security guard asked, "Can you spell that for me?"

"Hey hey hey." The man behind the cell phone tried to get Emira's attention. "Even if they ask, you don't have to show your ID. It's Pennsylvania state law."

Emira said, "I know my rights, dude."

"Sir?" The security guard stood and turned. "You do not have the right to interfere with a crime."

"Holup holup, a *crime*?!" Emira felt as if she were plummeting. All the blood in her body seemed to be buzzing and sloshing inside her ears and behind her eyes. She reached down to swing Briar into her arms, placed her feet apart for balance, and flipped her hair onto her back. "What crime is being committed right now? I'm *working*. I'm making money right now, and I bet I'm making more than you. We came here to look at some nuts, so are we under arrest or are we free to go?" As she spoke, Emira covered the child's ear. Briar slipped her hand into the V of her blouse.

Once again, the tattletale woman took her hand to her mouth. This time, she said, "Oh man, oh shoot."

"Okay, ma'am?" The security guard widened his stance to match hers. "You are being held and questioned because the safety of a child is at risk. Please put the child on the ground—"

"Alright, you know what?" Emira's left ankle shook as she retrieved her cell phone from her tiny purse. "I'll call her father and he can come down here. He's an old white guy so I'm sure everyone will feel better."

"Ma'am, I need you to calm down." With his palms to Emira, the security guard locked eyes with Briar again. "Okay, honey, how old are you?"

Emira typed the first four letters of *Peter Chamberlain* and clicked on his bright blue phone number. Against Briar's hand, she felt her heart bounce underneath her skin.

"How many are you, honey?" the woman asked. "Two? Three?" To the guard she said, "She looks about two."

"Ohmygod, she's almost three," Emira muttered.

"Ma'am?" The security guard pointed a finger at her face. *"I am speaking to the child."*

"Oh right, okay. 'Cause she's the one to ask. BB, look at me." Emira forced a gleeful expression into her lips and bounced the toddler twice. "How many are you?"

"One two fee four fie!"

"How old am I?"

"Happy birfday!"

Emira looked back to the security guard and said, "You good?" In her cell phone, the ringing stopped. "Mr. Chamberlain?" Something clicked in the earpiece but she didn't hear a voice. "It's Emira, hello? Can you hear me?"

"I'd like to speak to her father." The security guard reached out for her phone.

"The fuck are you doing? Don't touch me!" Emira turned her body. At this motion, Briar gasped. She held Emira's black, synthetic hair against her chest like rosary beads.

"You don't wanna touch her, dude," Penn State warned. "She's not resisting. She's calling the kid's dad."

"Ma'am, I am asking you to kindly hand over the phone."

"Come on, man, you can't take her phone."

The guard turned with a hand outstretched and yelled, "Back up, sir!"

With her phone pressed to her face and Briar's hands in her hair, Emira screamed, "You're not even a real cop, so you back up, son!" And then she watched his face shift. His eyes said, *I see you now. I know exactly who you are*, and Emira held her breath as he began to call for backup.

Emira heard Mr. Chamberlain's voice at the top of her cell phone. He said, "Emira?" and then, "Hello?"

"Mr. Chamberlain? Can you please come to Market Depot?" In the same controlled panic that started her night, she said, "Because they think I stole Briar. Can you please hurry?" He said something between *What* and *Oh God*, and then he said, "I'm coming right now."

Emira hadn't anticipated that the heated accusations would be favorable to the silence that followed. The five of them stood there, appearing more annoyed than justified, as they waited to see who would win. As Emira began a staring contest with the floor, Briar patted the hair on Emira's shoulders. "Dis is like my horsey hair," Briar said. Emira bounced her and said, "Mm-hmm. It was very expensive so please be careful." Finally, she heard the glide of an automatic door. With quick footsteps, Mr. Chamberlain emerged from the cereal aisle. Briar pointed with one finger and said, "That's Dada."

Mr. Chamberlain looked as if he'd jogged the whole way—tiny

beads of sweat on his nose—and he placed a hand on Emira's shoulder. "What's going on here?"

Emira responded by holding out his daughter. The woman took a step back and said, "Okay, great. I'll just leave you guys to it." The security guard began to explain and apologize. He took off his hat as his backup arrived.

Emira didn't wait for Mr. Chamberlain to finish lecturing the guards about how long he had been coming to the store, how they cannot detain people without reasonable cause, or how inappropriate it was that they question his decisions as a parent. Instead she whispered, "I'll see you tomorrow."

"Emira," he said. "Wait. Let me pay you."

She waved no with both hands. "I get paid on Fridays. I'll see you at your birthday, Bri." But Briar had begun to fall asleep on Mr. Chamberlain's shoulder.

Outside, Emira jogged around the corner, in the opposite direction of the Chamberlain home. She stopped and stood in front of a closed bakery with cupcakes on display behind a gridded security gate; her hands were still shaking as she texted no one. Breathing in through her nose and out through her mouth, Emira scanned through hundreds of songs. She shimmied her hips and pulled her skirt back down.

"Hey hey hey." Penn State appeared at the street corner. He made his way toward her and said, "Hey, are you okay?"

Emira slumped her shoulders in a miserable lift that said *I don't know*. With her phone in front of her stomach, she bit the inside of her cheek.

"Listen, that was super fucked up," he said. "I got the whole thing on tape. I would turn it in to a news station if I were you and then you can—"

"Oof. Yeah . . . no," she said. She pushed her hair out of her face. "No way, but . . . thanks anyway, though."

He paused and ran his tongue over his front teeth. "Okay, that guy was a dick to you. Don't you wanna get him fired?"

Emira laughed and said, "For what?" She shifted in her heels and put her phone back in her purse. "So he can go to another grocery store and get some other nine-dollar-an-hour bullshit job? Please. I'm not tryna have people Google my name and see me lit, with a baby that isn't mine, at a fucking grocery store in Washington Square."

The man exhaled and held up one hand in surrender. Underneath his other arm was a Market Depot paper bag. "I mean . . ." He put his free hand on his hip. "At the very least, you could probably get free groceries for a year."

"Oh, right. So I can stock up on kombucha and shit?"

He laughed and said, "Fair."

"Lemme see your phone." Emira jiggled her ring and middle finger as she held out her palm. "You need to delete that thing."

"Are you sure you want to do that?" he asked carefully. "I'm serious. This would definitely get you an op-ed or something."

"I'm not a writer," Emira said. "And I don't mess with the Internet, so give it."

"Wait, how about this?" He took out his phone. "It's your business and I'm happy to delete it. But let me email it to you first, in case you ever change your mind."

"I won't, though—"

"Just in case . . . here. Type your email in."

Because it seemed easier to share her email than convince him otherwise, Emira held the strap of her purse in one hand and began to type with the other. When she saw the email address in the From section, reading *KelleyTCopeland@gmail.com*, she stopped and said, "Hold up, who the fuck is Kelley?"

He blinked. "I'm Kelley."

"Oh." As she finished typing her email, Emira looked up and said, "Really?"

"Alright, alright." He took the phone back from her. "I've been to middle school so you can't really hurt me."

Emira smiled. "No wonder you shop here."

"Hey, I don't usually shop here." He laughed. "But don't make me feel worse. I have two types of kombucha in this bag right now."

"Uh-huh," she said. "Did you delete it?"

"It's gone." He showed her the screen and scrolled backward. The most recent photo was a man she didn't know with a Post-it stuck to his face. She couldn't read what it said.

"K." Emira pulled a string of hair from the gloss on her lips. She gave him a sad *I don't know* grin, and said, "K. Bye, then."

"Okay, yeah, have a good night, take care." It was clear he hadn't seen this exit coming, but Emira didn't care. She walked toward the train while texting Zara, Come over when you're done.

Emira could take a cab—Mrs. Chamberlan would certainly pay her back—but she didn't because she never did. She kept the future twenty-dollar bill and took the train to her Kensington apartment. Just after 1 a.m., Zara buzzed from downstairs.

"I can't handle any of this." Zara said this from Emira's toilet seat. Emira wiped her makeup off and locked eyes with her friend in the mirror. "Okay, because like . . ." Zara raised both of her hands up by her face. "Since when is the Running Man considered booty dancing?"

"I don't know." Emira removed her lipstick with a washcloth as she spoke. "Also, we all talked about it?" She said this with an apologetic wince. "And everyone there agreed I'm a better dancer than you."

Zara rolled her eyes.

"It's not a competition or anything," Emira tried again. "It's just that I'm the winner."

"Girl," Zara said, "That could have been *bad*."

Emira laughed and said, "Z, it's fine," but then she put the back of her hand to her mouth and silently started to cry.

TWO

Between 2001 and 2004, Alix Chamberlain sent over one hundred letters and received over nine hundred dollars' worth of merchandise. These free products included coffee beans, Luna Bars, makeup samples, scented candles, putty to hang posters on the walls in her dorm room, magazine subscriptions, sunscreens, and face masks—all of which Alix shared with her roommates and the other girls on her floor. While she majored in marketing and minored in finance, Alix did product reviews for a student newspaper during her sophomore and junior years at NYU. In her senior year, she quit the newspaper to become a beauty intern at a tiny publication, but she didn't stop sending letters. On thick, textured stationery and with dreamy cursive handwriting, Alix asked nicely for the things she wanted, and it became a rare occurrence when she didn't receive them.

Over the next four years, Alix wrote letters to Ray-Ban, Conan O'Brien, Scholastic, Keurig, Lululemon, the W Hotel, Smartwater, and hundreds more. For the most part she sent requests accompanied by affirmation and praise, but there were often tactful complaints and suggestions for improvement. Alix had a knack for taking high-quality photos of the free merchandise she often received, and she posted these items and the letters that prompted them onto her blog. It was a project she'd started on a whim, but it gained her a small Internet following. Around this time, she met Peter Chamberlain.

Alix met Peter in a bar at age twenty-five, and if she were honest about it, she'd admit that she thought he was much taller until he stood up at the end of their conversation. But in addition to her height he matched her personality. Peter did all these enchanting things that were fancy but not showy, like put mint in his water and privately tip thirty percent. What Alix immediately liked best about Peter was that he treated her side project like an actual job. Alix had a self-deprecating way of describing her letters: "Well, I . . . I write letters and reviews and I have this blog . . . but it's tiny, it's not a big thing at all." Peter told her to try that again, but this time, to pretend like it was. Peter was a journalist-turned-newscaster who was raised in up-state New York. He was eight years older than Alix, he didn't think it was strange to wear makeup on camera, and he firmly believed in building your brand. When Alix married Peter at age twenty-eight, the party favors, her shoes, and the white wine at her wedding were all items she'd received free of charge from hand-writing gorgeous letters and promising glowing reviews. On a honeymoon in Santorini, Peter helped her write each rave.

Alix worked in student recruitment at Hunter College when a friend—a high school English teacher at Columbia Grammar and Prep—asked her to give a cover-letter-writing workshop to one of her classes. One of the attending students was seventeen-year-old Lucie, a senior with unrealistically white teeth, light pink hair, and an Insta-gram following of 36K. Three months after the workshop, Lucie posted a picture to her account featuring the cover letter and essay she'd drafted with Alix on top of acceptance letters from UC Irvine, UC Santa Barbara, Fordham, and Emerson. *I owe all of my acceptances to Alix*, she said in her caption. *Honestly never would have applied to half these schools if she hadn't made my application so bomb. #allyouhave-todoisask #writealetter #LetHer.* Lucie's post received more than 1,700 likes, and, seemingly overnight, Alix Chamberlain became a brand. Her propensity for receiving free merchandise quickly turned into a philosophy about women speaking up and taking communication back to basics. In the middle of the night, Alix changed her Instagram bio to #LetHerSpeak. Peter suggested she do a rebrand of her website, and to not forget him once she became famous.

During the year she turned twenty-nine, Alix quit her job at Hunter College. She held cover letter and interview-prep workshops at halfway houses, leadership retreats, sorority houses, and career-night events. Students signed up for her sessions at college-recruitment fairs and her inbox became loaded with *Thank you!*s, and *I got in!*s. Alix was also contacted by a high-end paperie to help design a new line of office stationery geared toward women in the workplace. The paper was ivory, the pens dark blue, and Alix made her second print debut since NYU, this time in *Teen Vogue* magazine. It didn't hurt that Alix's large blue eyes and surprisingly long legs were extremely editorial. The picture on her new website under *About Alix* showed her sitting and laughing at the edge of an office desk, two stacks of letters in overflowing mail bins at her feet, and her thick, sand-colored hair gathered on top of her head in a charming, exhausted heap.

Peter believed in her; he always had. And the impact of her work was palpable in the gracious testimonials her new interns organized and photographed for her blog, but Alix was often shocked at the generous trust that organizations placed in her capacity. Alix was asked to speak on panels next to small-business owners on topics like

"Hospitality in the Workplace" and "Designing Leaders for Creative Change." She participated in feminist podcasts that discussed sustainable workplace cultures for women in tech and engineering. And once, Alix spoke at a workshop titled "Making the First Move" as two hundred single women drank champagne out of clear plastic cups inside a lecture hall. Alix loved writing letters and thought she was good at it, but it was consistently the confidence and excitement of the people around her that made the ideology of LetHer Speak bloom.

It was during a morning brunch—as she spoke to a small group of educators about the importance of teaching cursive in schools—that Alix felt such an urgent wave in her gut that she thought to herself, *I better not be pregnant.* She was, and two weeks later, Peter cried on the corner of University and 13th when she confirmed the news. He immediately asked, "Should we move?" Moving back to Philadelphia, Alix's hometown, had been a distant plan since they'd met four years prior. She'd wanted a backyard and children to put inside it; she'd wanted them to one day ride their bikes in a familiar cul-de-sac, or a street where no one was selling counterfeit purses or pulling down a large grate as they locked up a bodega. But at the height of her new career, one that she never knew was possible, Alix backed away from Peter. "No no," she said, "not yet, not yet."

Briar Louise was born. Alix's world became a place defined by Pack-'n-Plays, white noise machines, chafed areolas, and grapes cut in half. Her days were suddenly marked with third-person speech ("That's Mama's earring." "Mama's on the phone."), referring to ages in months rather than years, putting the term *big girl* in front of everything to spark domestic excitement (big-girl naps, big-girl spoons, big-girl jeans), and accepting openmouthed, wet kisses from a tiny drooling person who only recently existed outside her body.

By then, Alix had a team consisting of one editorial assistant, two interns, and an "office space" that overflowed into the kitchen in their Upper West Side apartment. Peter wanted to move. His vision of becoming a news anchor in New York City had been hit by reality: he appeared on television five nights a week to a Riverdale audience of no more than eight thousand, doing stories of charity dog marriages, toys being recalled, and Times Square tourists completing obstacle courses for the chance to win Best Buy gift cards. Several seasoned journalists in Philadelphia would be retiring soon, and their salaries matched Peter's in Riverdale. There were also rumors of their current apartment potentially going co-op. Philadelphia had always been the plan, but Alix Chamberlain was just getting started.

Alix's revamped blog, detailing the success of other letter-writing promotion-receiving getting-what-they-want women, had six thousand hits a day. She was partnering with a hospital for a weeklong charity with a love-letter-themed fund-raiser. And in long dark gowns and caps, Alix spoke at two all-girls high school graduations to rows of keen, eager faces. In addition to her career, for the first time since college, Alix had a group of girlfriends. Rachel, Jodi, and Tamra were bright, sarcastic women with careers and young children of their own, and having a baby never seemed too scary with a group text of women who were doing it, too.

But then, seemingly all at once, Briar started talking.

Funneled by two massive front teeth, Briar's voice consumed everything in its path. It was loud and hoarse and never stopped. When Briar slept, it was as if a fire alarm had finally been turned off, and Alix's head throbbed with what she remembered was peace and quiet. Alix's girlfriends assured her that their toddlers had done the same thing, that they were just excited to be able to communicate. Still, this seemed extreme. Briar was constantly asking, singing, rambling, humming, explaining that she liked hot dogs, that she once saw a turtle, that she wanted a high five, that she was not tired at all. When Alix picked Briar up from Peter's mother's apartment in Midtown, the woman opened the door with a desperate velocity Alix had come to know well. She could always hear her daughter's voice from the elevator, even before she reached the proper floor. Alix was managing her business, savoring pockets of silence, and pitching book proposals to literary agents, when one day, as she picked up Briar's rocking chair, she realized she was, once again, pregnant. Peter's reaction, in the kitchen of their home, was filled with more confusion than joy.

"I thought . . ." He shook his head. "I thought that wasn't supposed to happen while you're breast-feeding."

Alix pursed her lips with a face that said, *So did I.* "It's rare, but it's not impossible."

"Alix . . . We can't do this." Peter referred to the kitchen table turned receptacle for a current LetHer Speak project including Polaroid pictures and bulky brown craft paper. Sippy cups were drying on paper towels lined against the windowsill, and casserole dishes held extra recycling. That morning, Peter had come downstairs to an intern who hung her head upside down to put her hair into a ponytail. He then made his coffee as she and another intern put on white event polos with *LetHer Speak* embroidered on the pockets. "We don't have enough pots to put a second child in," he said. And two days later, after a letter arrived from the corporation that would be purchasing their apartment complex, Peter announced, "I'm calling a broker in Philadelphia."

What was she supposed to do, say no? There was a gap in New York housing so large that it would have been insane to suggest buying their place or renting a bigger one. Yes, she now made more money than she ever had, but no, it wasn't enough to comfortably house two children in their current West Side neighborhood. And sure, she could look into Queens or New Jersey, but then she might as well just move to Philadelphia. Alix *did* work from home. Philadelphia wasn't that far away. And more than anything, this was the person Alix had framed herself to be when she met Peter in that bar. "I think I've got like three years left in me for this city," she'd told him. "Every time I sit in someone else's butt sweat on the train, it goes down by about two weeks." This was one of the things Peter had liked most about Alix: that she didn't need to be at every event, that she liked getting out of the city, that she was an excellent driver, and that she wanted her children to trick-or-treat at houses, rather than apartment lobbies and Duane Reade.

So she had to move. Alix and her family would be moving out of New York City. But the timing couldn't have been worse. Alix had been busy writing a very important letter of her own to the campaign team of Secretary Hillary Clinton, who had just announced her run for the presidency. This was a cause that mattered to her, Hillary's feminist platform completely matched her brand, and a link to Hillary could keep Alix relevant even when she wasn't living in the most relevant city in the country. Luckily, Alix's dear friend Tamra knew a woman who knew one of Secretary Clinton's campaign advisors. After four drafts and constant switches from *Always, Alix* to *All My Best, Alix*, she pressed Send on a volunteer proposal that she hoped would become a paying gig. Weeks went by and she heard nothing back from the campaign advisor or the agents she'd queried.

Abruptly, everything was packed, but Alix hadn't allowed the tempo of her calendar to decline. She loved all of it: sitting on panels and listening to brilliant women in oversized shift dresses and dramatic lipstick, teens emailing her success stories of entry-level job offers they had accepted. But there was still no word from the Clinton campaign, or the six agents who received her book proposal. In the middle of fund-raisers and brunches, as she shook hands with earnest high schoolers, Alix thought, *Is this it? Is this as far as I'll ever go?*

But on the morning of her last talk in New York City—she was speaking on a panel at an event called Small Business Femme—Alix decided, in a quick and incomplete thought, to not use her breast pump. She called one of her interns in, the one with the most babysitting experience, and said, "How would you feel about having Briar on your lap during the panel?"

On a stage in a SoHo theater space, Alix positioned herself between two male panel members, a podcast host and a reality TV show father who had quintuplet girls. Seated across from a crowd of three hundred, the panel discussed reproductive care and empowering books for girls as Alix's breasts—particularly the left one—ached with expansion. Finally, after the audience laughed at a joke made by the host, Briar stirred and opened her eyes.

Briar hummed and asked why Mama was up there and if the intern had any Cheerios and if she could get down. Alix held a finger to her lips toward her daughter in the front row. Her intern motioned to the door and mouthed, *You want me to take her out?* Alix shook her head. She waited until she was asked another question.

"I think that women are often just asking for a seat at the table," Alix said. The microphone attached at her collar bounced her voice to the back of the house. "But what's heard is 'I want *special* treatment,' when that's not the case. And the fact that . . . Actually?" Alix's heart raced as she pushed forward. "I'm sorry to interrupt myself and the conversation." Was she really doing this? *Yes*, she told herself. *Yes she was.* "I have a lot more to say on this topic, but my daughter is the very fussy person in the front row because she took a very long nap, and if it's alright with everyone, I'd like to . . . well, I'm not really asking." She stood and talked with her hands as she made her way to the front of the stage. "I'm going feed my daughter as I participate because I can definitely do both."

Whoops and cheers went up from the crowd. Alix bent her knees sideways as she reached for Briar, who was immediately met with *awww*s as she gripped her mother's neck. "Will you throw me that shirt?" Alix motioned to her intern for the pastel pink T-shirt that had been given to her in a goodie bag. She threw it over her shoulder and walked backstage.

The host of the show, a giddy graduate student, said, "You go girl!" into her mic. She looked backstage and whispered, "Should I just keep going?" But Alix was right on time. She emerged from backstage, Briar attached firmly to her left breast. The pink T-shirt was slung across her shoulder and blocking Briar's head from sight. Briar's shoes hung adorably at Alix's right arm as she sat back in her seat.

"Okay, now we're in business. That didn't take too long, right?" Alix turned back to the host and said, "I'm happy to pick up where I left off." Alix did pick up where she left off, and when she finished, the swooning host thanked her doubly for her answer and candor. Just as Alix had predicted, the host then asked for her daughter's name and age. Alix made sure her words were clear. "My client here is Briar Louise. She is two years old and she's *very* good at it." Alix's smile practically dared the audience to bat an eye at the age of her daughter suctioned to her chest.

The photographers for the event swarmed the foot of the stage. They backed up into the aisle to get a clear shot of Alix, crossing her ankles, breast-feeding her child above a pregnant stomach, and speaking between two suited men. At one point, a photographer whispered, "Can you adjust the shirt so that the logo is showing?" Alix laughed and said yes. She smoothed out the shirt against the side of Briar's head and let the bottom hang flat. Blocking her daughter's face were black letters spelling out *Small Business Femme*.

That day, Alix earned another thousand followers. Small Business Femme posted a picture of the moment on their Instagram account, the caption reading *Find You A Woman That Can Do Both*. Two baby magazines wanted to interview her about child-led breast-feeding, and the stigmas and benefits that come along with it. Alix paid her interns double to stay an extra hour to answer the emails, calls, and interview requests. A representative from the Clinton campaign phoned her cell. They were so sorry they'd missed her email, but they'd love for her to participate in some events later this year. Two of the agents Alix had queried also returned her emails. Within ten days, Alix sold her book to an editor named Maura at HarperCollins, a woman with children of her own and an alarmingly fast email response time.

The buzz from her center-stage breast-feeding carried her over the Pennsylvania state line, into her new home, and through her third trimester. Before she left the city, Alix took lots of pictures with her assistant and interns at the tiny good-bye party in her packed office, but she never posted them online. She never mentioned her departure from New York on her blog, on her social media accounts, or to the Clinton team. Instead, she'd take the train in when they needed her. She'd pretend like she was there while she wrote her book. She'd come back more when the girls were older.

And then, in Philadelphia, after five short hours of labor, Catherine May was born, and her face immediately took the shape of her mother's. Alix looked into her teeny, squishy, confused face and thought, *You know what? Things will be okay here.*

And they were. All of those non–New York things came back to her in small bright moments. She had a car to put groceries into. A ticket to a movie wasn't fourteen dollars, it was ten. And she lived in a three-story brownstone (seven minutes' walk from Rittenhouse Square) on a leafy, shaded street. The house had a massive, marble-floored entryway and a charming kitchen on the second floor. The kitchen counter space was ample, and a table for six underneath a chandelier looked out to the street through a curved wall of windows. In the morning, with pancakes and eggs on the stove, Alix and her children could sit at the window seats and look down at people walking their dogs or watch the trash collectors go back and forth. Upon seeing these things and realizing their worth, Alix immediately felt a tiny pang of amusement, but then a painful longing to show them to just about anyone. Her girlfriends. Her LetHer Speak interns. A stranger standing across a filthy platform in a New York City subway.

Before Philadelphia, Alix had never hired a regular babysitter. Peter's mother was always available, and with three friends who also had small children, there was an implied sharedness when it came to watching one extra toddler while Mom ran to the dentist or mailed a package. Several girls were recommended by Peter's new colleagues at the station, which led to interviews of Carlys and Caitlyns, camp counselors and resident assistants, on the bar stools in Alix's new kitchen. They told Alix what fans they were of LetHer Speak, how they wished she'd been around when they applied to college, and that they had no idea she'd moved to Philadelphia. These girls, Alix knew, would never work.

Alix had a knack for acquiring merchandise back in New York, and searching for a babysitter in Philadelphia was no different. Her girlfriends would never do this, but she created a profile on SitterTown.com and began to scroll through photos of caretakers. The whole thing felt very simulated and impersonal, but Alix had found two of her three

Manhattan apartments from sketchy ads on Craigslist, and like the steals she lived in during her twenties, Emira Tucker's profile did not come with a picture. Her description said she was a Temple University graduate, that she knew beginner sign language, and that she could type 125 words per minute. Alix said, "Huh," and clicked Request Interview. They talked once on the phone before Emira came to the house. And when Alix opened the door and saw Emira for the first time, she found herself once again thinking, *Huh*.

The other girls had asked Alix how her book was coming along and if she was having another child and if she'd gotten to meet Hillary Clinton yet, but Emira didn't say much at all. Briar immediately saw this as a challenge and verbally attacked the twenty-five-year-old woman with stories about her new backyard and all the worms she was not allowed to touch and how floaties are only allowed in the pool. When Briar finished speaking, Emira bent down and said, "Okay, miss, what else you got?"

Most importantly, Emira Tucker had never heard of LetHer Speak.

"So it would be Monday, Wednesday, and Friday." This was the sixth time Alix had explained the schedule to a potential sitter. "From noon to seven. Sometimes I'd take Catherine with me—she's a super-easy baby—and sometimes I would just be writing at a coffee shop nearby."

"Okay." Emira sat at the kitchen table with Briar and handed her a piece of Play-Doh. "Is it work writing or is it fun writing?"

"I have my own . . ." Alix leaned on the counter separating them. "I'm actually writing a book right now."

Emira said, "Oh wow."

Alix felt hollow and impatient as she waited for Emira to ask what her book was about, or who her publisher was, or when the book would officially be out. "It's more of a compilation of old letters . . ." she said in the silence.

"Oh, okay." Emira nodded. "Is it like a history book?"

Alix fingered her necklace. "Yes, exactly." She bent her elbows onto the counter and said, "Emira, when can you start?"

Three times a week, Alix got to sit in the sun for hours—Catherine often slept next to her in the shade—as she read all the things she would have never been caught with in Manhattan. *Us Weekly* and *People* magazines. A tell-all from a recent Bachelorette who was known for sleeping with four of her male suitors. On one special Friday, Alix laid out her laptop, her writing schedule, and pages of her book proposal, only to watch three episodes of *House Hunters International* in the corner of a rooftop restaurant patio. Catherine only fussed when she was hungry, and Alix lifted her to say, "Hi, lovey," before she slipped her underneath a complimentary nursing shawl. The fantasies of using Emira's quick typing became quickly laughable, because Alix would have to have things to write down in order for them to materialize. In bed one evening, Peter said, "You just look so much happier here."

Alix couldn't tell if she was happier or if she just cared less. She had definitely gained weight on top of the baby weight. She wrote much less than she had in New York and she slept much more than when Briar was born. But at 10:45 p.m. on a Saturday night in September, eggshells smashed against the front window of her home and brought her out of a deep sleep. The sound didn't register right away, but when Alix heard, "Racist piece of shit!" it was like she came online. She reached out and touched her husband. Alix and Peter rushed to the top of the stairs and watched egg yolks break and splatter against their front window. Just as Peter said, "I told you," two large eggs broke the barrier. Splintered glass, eggshells, and a long string of yolk and mucus flew into the Chamberlain house. The sound and surprise made Alix's chest seize. She breathed again when she heard boyish laughter, sneakers running away, and someone saying, "Oh shit! Go, go!"

Catherine cried out and Briar said, "Mama?"

Peter said, "I'm calling the police," and then, "Fuck. I *told* you this would happen."

That morning, Peter's co-anchor Laney Thacker had introduced a segment on the creative ways students were asking their dates to a dance: a sweet homecoming tradition at Beacon Smith High School. Peter echoed her enthusiasm with, "Misty is on campus for the romance right now." Clips of students were shown with Misty's voice narrating. Teachers were interviewed, students were filmed next to huge balloon displays, and the volume at a pep rally turned to screams as a freckled girl was led to the half-court line. A football-jerseyed junior appeared with a box of pizza. He opened it to reveal words inscribed on the box's lid: *I know this is cheesy, but homecoming?* Pepperonis were positioned as a giant question mark below.

The segment ended with a five-foot-tall student with a flattop of thick hair above a white mask marching toward a group of girls. He set down a boom box and pressed Play. His masked friends helped clear the space for a dance to begin, and the girl in question covered her mouth as her friends took out their phones. After spinning on their heads and doing intricate shapes and patterns with their fingers, the group ended by revealing a white flag with *Homecoming?* written in Sharpie. The black teen in front removed his mask and held out a rose.

Over the cheers of the girl's acceptance, Misty turned the camera back to Peter in the studio.

"Whoa!" Peter said.

"That was *very* impressive," Laney agreed. "I was definitely never asked to a dance like that."

"Well." Peter shook his head. His teeth showed as he winced at the camera and said, "Let's hope that last one asked her father first. Thanks for joining us on WNFT and we'll see you tomorrow morning on Philadelphia Action News."

The backlash was immediate.

In the comment section underneath the video—which was now available online—criticisms and questions popped up in between praise.

Ummm, why would the black guy need to ask her dad, but the white guys don't?

That's a bit sexist. Is this the 18th century?

WTF? Why would he even say that?

Alix was working at a coffee shop, which had turned into a smoothie, mimosa, and participating in the group text with her girlfriends in Manhattan. She told Peter that it was one high school, that it wasn't that terrible, and that no one would even remember it. (In a weak champagne buzz, Alix caught herself thinking, *If it didn't happen in New York, honestly who cares?*) But Peter was mortified. "It just came out," he said. "I don't even know why I . . . it just came out." Alix assured him that it really wasn't that bad.

And suddenly it was. After the crash, Alix took her youngest daughter from her crib with such speed that Catherine practically bounced out of her arms, but Alix's world moved underwater. *What if Peter got fired?* Peter had gone straight to the producers of the show to apologize for his fumble, and they'd chalked it up to something between "things happen" and "you're still the new guy." But what if the students were so angry that it made them reconsider? Once again, Alix peeked out over the stairwell and saw flecks of glass strewn across the tile floor and stuck in ooze. *Would the Clinton campaign find out about this, and would they think her husband was sexist? Or even worse, racist? How did she even get here? And how was she this fat right now? Whose house was this anyway?*

Peter carried Briar, who secured both her hands to her ears. "I don't like that noise," she said. "I don't . . . I don't like it loud, Mama."

"Shh shh shh," Alix said to Briar for maybe the hundredth time that week. She turned to Peter and said, "I'm gonna try Emira." Peter nodded with his phone to his ear.

And when Emira arrived fifteen minutes later in a tiny faux-leather skirt and strappy heels that she walked remarkably well in, Alix handed Briar's little wrist toward her thinking, *Wait a second, who is this person? Oh God . . . does she know what Peter said?* All at once, it was somehow much worse to think of Emira knowing what Peter had said, rather than the hopeful first female president of the United States.

As Peter gave two policemen a statement, Alix scooped up the glass with a hand towel in the glaring light from the chandelier. In between long, sad strokes, she told herself to wake the fuck up. To write this book. To live in Philadelphia. To get to know Emira Tucker.

35

Three

There's a town in Maryland called Sewell Bridge, where 6.5 percent of the population (5,850 people) are hearing impaired. This is the town where Emira Tucker was born. Emira had perfect hearing, the same as her parents and younger siblings, but the Tucker family had a proclivity toward craftsmanship that was so dogged that it leaned into religious territory, and Sewell Bridge served this philosophy well. The Tucker family worked with their hands.

Mr. Tucker owned a bee store with a long rooftop where the buzzing beehives were often kept. Despite hiring several deaf employees over the years, he didn't waste any time training his fingers to do anything that wasn't related to bees. Mrs. Tucker bound books in a shaded screened room attached to the front of the Tucker home. She made baby albums, wedding books, and Holy Bible restorations, and her worktable was consistently covered in leather swatches, needles, bone folders, and closures.

Twenty-one-year-old Alfie Tucker won second place in the National Latte Art Competition in 2013. He was invited to serve as an apprentice at a roasterie in Austin, Texas, where he trained other baristas, wearing an apron made by his mother. And nineteen-year-old Justyne Tucker sewed. She had an active Etsy shop where she took orders for Halloween costumes and flower girl attire. Upon graduating from high school, Justyne was hired by a community college to create the costumes for upcoming productions of *Our Town* and *Once on This Island*.

Because the interests of her family members had come so naturally to them, and because university seemed like an acceptable place to wait for her hands to find themselves, Emira became the first person in her family to attend a four-year college. It was Temple University where she met Zara (in line to take her student ID photo), where she got drunk for the first time (she threw up into the side pocket of her purse), and where she purchased her first weave from the funds she saved working in the library in between classes (long and black and wavy and big).

Emira tried to make her hands find formal sign language at Temple, but it was surprisingly difficult to unlearn the conversational slang she grew up with back in Sewell Bridge. Emira also tried transcription, which seemed like a career path and narrative that made sense. In her senior year, Emira typed lecture notes for two deaf students for thirteen dollars per class. This was more or less the reason she ended her five years at Temple with a major in English. Emira didn't mind reading or writing papers, but this was also mostly the problem. Emira didn't love doing anything, but she didn't terribly mind doing anything either.

After graduation, Emira went home for the summer and desperately missed Philadelphia. She returned with a stern suggestion from her father: to find something and to stick with it. So Emira enrolled in transcription school, and she absolutely hated it. She wasn't allowed to cross her legs. Memorizing medical terminology was insufferable. And when a key on her steno machine broke, instead of fixing it (which would have cost hundreds of dollars), Emira gave it up completely and applied to a part-time job she found on Craigslist. In a small office on the sixth floor of a high-rise building, in a large cubicled room labeled *Green Party Philadelphia*, a white woman in a T-shirt and jeans named Beverly asked Emira if she could really type 125 words per minute. "I can," Emira said, "as long as you don't mind if I cross my legs." In a tiny corner with squishy headphones, on Tuesdays and Thursdays from 12 to 5 p.m., Emira transcribed text from speeches and meetings. When things got slow, Beverly asked her to cover the phones.

Temple University had been kind to keep Emira as an on-call transcriber for the two years following her graduation, but they wanted to keep entry-level employment open to current students, and gave her fair warning that she'd have to move on by summer. Emira hadn't told her parents about her departure from transcription school. She wanted to be able to replace it with something, rather than a passionless negative space. In a quiet panic, Emira changed her availability on SitterTown.com to Mondays, Wednesdays, and Fridays, and two days later, she met Alix Chamberlain.

Briar was a welcome break from Emira's constant concern of what to do with her hands and the rest of her life. Briar asked questions like, "Why can't I smell that?" or, "Where is that squirrel's mama?" or, "How come we don't know that lady?" Once, after Briar tried zucchini for the first time, Emira stood in front of her high chair and asked the toddler if she liked it. Briar chewed with her mouth open and looked all over the room as she articulated her response. "Mira? How, how . . . because—how do you know when you like it? Who says when you like it?" Emira was fairly certain that the caregiver-approved answer was something like, *You'll figure it out*, or, *It'll make sense when you're older*. But Emira wiped the toddler's chin and said, "That's a really good question. We should ask your mom." She honestly meant it. Emira wished that someone would tell her what she liked doing best. The number of things she could ask her own mother were shrinking at an alarming rate.

Emira hadn't told her parents that she was babysitting and typing for a living, which meant she couldn't tell them about the night at Market Depot. Not that they would have any insights she hadn't heard before, but it would have been nice to safely share her frustrations. In the fourth grade, a white classmate had marched to Emira's lunch table and asked her if she was a coon (upon hearing this, her mother had promptly picked up the phone while asking Emira, "What's his name?"). Emira was once followed by sales associates in Brooks Brothers while she shopped for a Father's Day gift (her mother had said, "They ain't got nothin' better to do?"). And once, after a bikini wax was completed, Emira was told that because she had "ethnic texture," the total came to forty dollars instead of the advertised thirty-five (to this, Emira's mother had responded, "Back up, you got *what* waxed?"). It would have been nice to talk to her parents about the night at Market Depot because it was honestly the biggest thing to happen to Emira in a while, and it involved her favorite little person. Emira knew that she should have been mostly disturbed by the blatant bigotry of the altercation. But more than the racial bias, the night at Market Depot came back to her with a nauseating surge and a resounding declaration that hissed, *You don't have a real job.*

This wouldn't have happened if you had a real fucking job, Emira told herself on the train ride home, her legs and arms crossed on top of each other. *You wouldn't leave a party to babysit. You'd have your own health insurance. You wouldn't be paid in cash. You'd be a real fucking person.* Taking care of Briar was Emira's favorite position so far, but Briar would someday go to school, Mrs. Chamberlain didn't seem to want Catherine out of her sight, and even if she did, part-time babysitting could never provide health insurance. By the end of 2015, Emira would be forced off her parents' health coverage. She was almost twenty-six years old.

Sometimes, when she was particularly broke, Emira convinced herself that if she had a real job, a nine-to-five position with benefits and decent pay, then the rest of her life would start to resemble adulthood as well. She'd do things like make her bed in the morning, and she'd learn to start liking coffee. She wouldn't sit on the floor in her bedroom, discovering new music and creating playlists until three a.m., only to put herself to bed and think, *Why do you do this to yourself?* She'd try out a new dating app, and she'd have more interesting interests to write about: activities other than hanging out with Zara, watching old music videos, painting her nails, and eating the same dinner at least four nights a week (a Crock-Pot meal consisting of shredded chicken, salsa, and cheese). If Emira had a real job, she'd look at her wardrobe full of clothes from Strawberry and Forever 21 and decide it was past time for an upgrade.

Emira constantly tried to convince herself that she could find another child, a little girl with nice parents who needed her full-time. They'd keep her on the books and she could say she paid taxes. They'd take her on vacations and consider her part of the family. But when Emira saw other children, anyone who wasn't Briar Chamberlain, she felt viscerally disgusted. They had nothing interesting to say, their eyes had dead, creepy stares, and they were modest in a way that seemed weirdly rehearsed (Emira often watched Briar approach other toddlers on swings and slides, and they'd turn away from her, saying, "No, I'm shy"). Other children were easy audiences who loved receiving stickers and hand stamps, whereas Briar was always at the edge of a tiny existential crisis.

Underneath her constant chatter, Briar was messy and panicky and thoughtful, constantly struggling with demons of propriety. She liked things that had mint smells. She didn't like loud noises. And she didn't consider hugging a legitimate form of affection unless she could lay her ear against a welcoming shoulder. Most of their evenings ended with Emira paging through a magazine while Briar played in the bathtub. Briar sat with her toes in her hands, her face a civil war of emotions, singing songs and trying to whistle. She'd have private conversations with herself, and Emira often heard her explain to the voices in her head, "No, Mira is *my* friend. She's *my* special friend."

Emira knew she had to find a new job.

Four

The next morning, instead of setting Briar in front of a children's program about colorful fish and animals in the ocean, Alix strapped her children into the double jogging stroller. There was so much more room to run in Philadelphia. She didn't have to jog in place at stoplights to keep her heart rate up, and she didn't have to make it to the highway to see more than one hundred steps ahead. Just after mile three, which felt more like the twenty-sixth, both of her children had been rocked back to sleep. Alix stopped in a coffee shop, asked for a latte, and took it to a bench outside.

I need a conference call immediately, she texted. No death or sickness but very urgent.

Alix had said the names *Rachel*, *Jodi*, and *Tamra* so many times that there was no other way to say it. She hadn't texted her group of girlfriends this way since her move—most of their recent conversations concerned other women they knew, product advice, articles and books they were reading, and complaints about their husbands—so seconds after this text was sent, it was met back with two Are you okay? texts and one Tamra, can you start it?

Jodi was a children's casting director who had two redheaded children—ages four and one—who often appeared as crying extras on TV shows and movies. Rachel, proudly Jewish and Japanese, managed a firm that designed book covers while she tried to get her son to be not-so-good at soccer, because who the hell knew it was so intense? He was only five years old. And Tamra was the principal of a private school in Manhattan. Twice a year, the four women gorged on the wine, cheese, and hummus packages sent by parents trying to boost their children's admission applications or keep their problem child enrolled. Tamra had two girls with inch-long dark afros, a two-and-a-half-year-old and a fully literate four-year-old who spoke beginner French. Tamra's children referred to her as Memmy.

With her knees spread wide on the bench and cold sweat at her temples, Alix told them everything.

Rachel gasped and said, *"What?!"*

In an overly enunciated tone, Tamra said, "They wouldn't let her *leave?*"

Jodi said, "All of this happened in one day?"

"Jesus Christ, that would never happen in New York," Rachel said. "Hudson, get that out of your mouth! Sorry, we're at soccer."

Alix's heart sped up to the same sickening point as it had the night before, when Peter returned without Emira and said, "Okay, everyone's fine," before he explained. Alix couldn't help but ask what sounded like uselessly generic questions as soon as they left her lips. *Was she crying? Was she mad? Did she seem really upset?* If Alix had been asked about Emira and her mental state for all the Mondays, Wednesdays, and Fridays in the last three months, she wouldn't have had an answer. Most days, Alix practically threw Briar into Emira's arms on her way out the door, calling over her shoulder that Briar hadn't eaten lunch or hadn't really pooped. The Tuesdays and Thursdays without Emira included swimming lessons at the Y, where Briar swam so hard and desperately that she ended up taking three-hour naps. These naps were followed by a movie on Netflix, and by the ending credits, Dada was walking through the front door. This pattern had sustained Alix so well that she had no idea if her babysitter was the type of person to cry, sue, or do nothing at all.

Tamra clicked her tongue. "You gotta call that girl right now."

"I'm Googling Peter's clip," Jodi said. "Okay, five hundred views . . . that's not awful."

"Did anyone get a video of this?" Tamra asked.

"You guys could probably help her sue the store," Rachel said.

"I don't know. I'm freaking out." Alix placed her elbows at her knees. "I've been terrible to her. She's so good and she's so on time . . . Briar adores her and I feel like I'm gonna lose her because of some stupid fucking grocery store cop." Alix removed the side of the seat belt from Briar's sleeping mouth, and looked around to make sure no one had heard her say the F-word in front of her children. "I've just been so sloppy with everything lately that it all feels like a big punishment. I'm late with my book, I'm gaining weight, and I have a dozen of Peter's colleagues coming over today for Briar's birthday, which Emira was supposed to help with. But the thought of losing her forever is making me physically ill. I'll never be able to finish this book without her."

"Hey." Rachel cut her off. "You will finish this book no matter what. You're a badass and you finish things, but right now, Emira is the first priority."

Tamra said, "One hundred percent."

"Prudence?" Jodi took her mouth away from the phone. "You have to share with your brother, is that understood?" Then, closer to the receiver, she said, "I agree with everything that was just said."

"Of course. I get that. And I know I need to call her," Alix said. "But what . . . how do I go about this?"

"Don't tell her to write a letter," Rachel mumbled.

Jodi said, "Rachel, this is serious," in the same mom-ish way she spoke to her daughter.

"Honestly," Tamra said, "she might not even answer. And you need to be prepared for that."

Next to Alix, the bell attached to the coffee shop door rang as a couple came outside. The woman said, "I bet we can rent it on Amazon," and the man replied, "But 3D was the entire point." Alix dipped her head and sweat fell off her nose. "I'm literally gonna be sick."

"Hey, if she does answer," Tamra said, "just tell her that you're *so* sorry that this happened, and that you support her in whatever she needs, whether that means lawyering up or doing absolutely nothing."

"Yeah, just don't get emotional," Rachel told her. "Not that you would, but make it all about her. Hudson, it's okay, bud!" Rachel could be heard clapping her hand to her thigh. "You wanna go home? No? Okay, fine."

Alix knew that this probably wouldn't have been so daunting if it wouldn't be the longest conversation she'd ever had with Emira. She took a deep breath and said, "Is this my fault for sending her there?"

"Oh honey, no," Jodi said.

"I would have called her too!" Tamra said.

"It's your fault you moved to Philadelphia," Rachel said. "I'm sorry, but again, this would never happen in New York City. When I pick Hudson up from anywhere they literally don't trust that he's my kid. But when Arnetta goes, they're like, 'Here ya go! He's allergic to nuts, bye!'"

"Pru?" Jodi called. "I'm gonna count to three, young lady. One, *two* . . . Thank you, ma'am."

Alix sat back and her sweaty top clung to her shoulder blades. In front of her, in her sleep, Catherine's bootied feet ran somewhere in her dreams. Tamra said, "Go call her," and Alix said, "I know."

"Alix?" Jodi beckoned. "I love you. And you're beautiful, you always are. But I'm being a good friend right now and asking how much weight you've gained."

Alix looked down toward her neon orange shorts. A mushy pudge made up of baby weight, a gym membership she'd never gotten, and sugar-based smoothies consumed in the sun poked out over her waistband and underneath the damp tank top. Alix sighed. "I'm afraid to check."

"Oh, *God*," Tamra said. "Why didn't you say something earlier?"

"Okay . . . sweetie?" Jodi said. "You need to get your s-h-i-t together because you are *not* this person. You are so good at confrontation, and you breast-feed in front of audiences, and you are going to write a very successful book. You need to hang up the phone, beg your sitter to stay, tell Peter to watch his mouth, and get a Fitbit or something, okay?"

"Yeah, she's right, A," Rachel added. "'Cause when your book comes out your photo is gonna be everywhere and book covers add like seventeen pounds, I am *not* kidding."

"Consider this an intervention," Tamra agreed, "but a very kind and very supportive one."

"Do they have juice there?" Rachel asked. "Should I send you a cleanse?"

"I think they have juice, Rach." Jodi laughed. "It's not like she's in Montana."

Emira didn't answer her phone, so Alix took a shower and tried her again. This time she answered, and Alix delivered all the things her friends had suggested, mentally checking off each point. But as she said the words "It's completely your call," Emira replied, "Wait . . . am I late?"

Alix heard Zara's voice in the background say, "Who is calling you so early?" Alix looked at her watch. It was 9:14 a.m. Emira, Alix realized, was half asleep.

"No, you're not late!" Alix assured her. "The party's still at noon, or eleven forty-five, if you can come early . . . but you don't have to, but I'd love for you to come. *We'd* love for you to come. But it's up to you."

"No, I'll be there," Emira said. "I'm coming, don't worry."

"No, Emira, I wasn't checking up on you. I mean . . . I'm checking *on* you," Alix struggled. "But just to see how you are. But okay. I'll see you at noon? Or eleven forty-five?"

"Mm-hmm."

Zara's voice, now more awake, said, "Would you get a bagel if I ordered one?"

Alix said, "See you soon!" and Emira hung up the phone.

I called. Alix texted Tamra. It seemed like she didn't want to talk about it.

Tamra responded, That's her choice. Is she coming?

Yes.

Okay, be cool, Tamra texted back. Drink lots of water. No pasta. But you're allowed to eat cake because your baby is three.

KILEY REID

Alix looked to Briar, who was playing with two combs on the floor in her bedroom. "Bri," she said. "Happy birthday, lovey," to which Briar very seriously responded, "Is it happy birfday pretend?"

If the decision had been Briar's, the theme of her party would have been glasses because the toddler savagely wanted glasses, and to touch everyone else's glasses, and to see how she looked in all of the glasses. But Briar also loved airplanes and pointing at them and the sounds they made, and Alix felt that this, out of all of Briar's other interests (smelling tea bags, other people's belly buttons, touching the soft skin on Mama's earlobe), should be openly encouraged.

Alix pushed the furniture in the living room back against the walls and then evenly spread out white balloons that covered the towering ceilings. Hanging at the bottom of each twenty-foot string was a blue paper airplane with curved edges and wheels. Next she set up a snack table with a cloud-covered paper tapestry; by the door, she hung up soft aviator goggles meant for toddlers to take and wear. There were mini cupcakes dyed the color of the sky, and party favors were lined up in bright blue bags with tiny white propellers that could spin. Alix took close-up photos of the propellers and the cupcakes to post on her Instagram (so close-up that they could have been taken anywhere, particularly Manhattan). Peter brought a few of the balloons outside and taped them around the jagged hole in the window. When Alix peeked her head outside, he said, "Is this dumb?" She shook her head and felt a warm and sad affection for him. She knew he hadn't meant what he said on the news. "No," she said. "It's not dumb."

Upstairs, Alix put on a loose-fitting denim jumpsuit and straightened her hair. Peter was singing "Baby Beluga" to Briar and Catherine, who lay on the bed as he secured his belt and buttoned his shirt. Between *Way down yonder* and *Where the dolphins play*, he stuck his head into the bathroom. "She's still coming to help out, right?"

48

Alix looked at him through the mirror as she applied mascara to her bottom lashes. "She said she was."

Emira arrived at eleven forty-five.

She had her own key, and when the door closed downstairs, both Peter and Alix looked at each other above their children's heads. Briar was finally in her birthday outfit, a hunter-green jumpsuit that made her resemble a *Top Gun* cast extra, and Catherine was cuddled in a cloud costume. Alix handed Peter a gold winged pin and said, "Give us a minute," before she bolted down two sets of stairs. There was Emira hanging her backpack on the wall, in dark jeans, a loose braid down her back, and chunky black eyeliner.

In her first week of babysitting for the Chamberlains, Emira took Briar to a painting class. She'd been wearing an oversized knit cardigan, the kind that paint would never come out of, and Alix offered her one of her many white LetHer Speak polos. "I actually have tons of these and you're the same size as my old interns," she'd said. "Well, they might be a bit big on you, but you're welcome to wear one anytime." This became Emira's uniform. Three times a week, Alix came downstairs to find Emira slipping a white polo over her head. She hung it up on the coatrack just before she left. And suddenly, as Alix walked through blue ribbons hanging from the balloons above, the tenderness of this tradition made her throat start to close. She made it to the bottom step as Emira said, "Hey," and pulled her braid out of the back of her collar.

"Hey. Hi." Alix stood in front of Emira and held both her elbows. "Can I . . . can I give you a hug?"

This promptly felt like an ignorant response. Alix didn't want this to be their first hug, but she had offered and she had to commit. In her arms, Emira smelled like body butters, burnt hair, nail polish, and cheap perfume.

"First of all"—Alix backed away—"you do not have to be here today."

"Oh no. I'm here. It's cool." Emira turned to her backpack and took a ChapStick out of the front pocket.

Alix crossed her ankles and arms as she stood. "I'm not going to even pretend to know what you're feeling right now or how you felt last night because I never truly will, but I just want to extend my support in whatever way you need it. If that's a lawyer or . . . a civil action suit . . . or . . ."

Emira smiled. "A what?"

"Emira," Alix said. She realized her shoulders were up by her ears, and she tried to bring them down into her back. "You could sue that entire store. Seeking legal action is completely within your right."

"Oh no." Emira pressed her lips together and sealed the lid of her balm. "I'm not tryna get into all that."

Alix nodded. "And I completely respect that. We just want you to know how sorry we are and—"

Another voice from outside said, "Alix?"

Behind Emira, the door slid open two inches. Emira reached for the knob and revealed two little boys and their mother: a family from Briar's swim class.

"Ohmygod, hi," the woman said. "I know, I know. We're so early. Hi! I'm sure you're not even done setting up. But we can help and we won't be any trouble. You look so cute!"

Alix ushered them in with *hi*s and *how are you*s. The boys rushed the snack table and one of them took off his shoes. As the woman began to remove their jackets, Alix whispered to Emira, "Let's talk about this later."

"It's okay," Emira said. "It's honestly fine." As she said this, Emira dug into a paper bag that she'd set beneath her backpack. She pulled out a small bowl with an orange ribbon around the rim, holding a bright yellow goldfish inside.

"Oh, wait. Emira." Alix put her hand to her heart. "Is that from you?"

"Yeah." Emira placed the bowl on the mantel next to a little paper airplane that read *Presents Land Here!* As she turned the bowl so that the ribbon faced forward, Alix remembered. Yes. Emira had asked if she could get Briar a fish for her birthday. She'd asked both Alix and Peter days ago. Alix hadn't considered it would be a real one, because she hadn't really been listening, but here it was, gold and wiggling. Emira had curled the ribbon around the tiny bowl, but it had bent and flattened in transit and now hung bitterly around the rim.

Two minutes into their earliness, the first guest's three-year-old threw up in the space next to the toilet seat, and he began to cry in an embarrassed whimper. By the time it was cleaned up and apologies had ceased, a group of Peter's co-workers from WNFT had arrived. Alix turned on some music, went to the door, and said, "Hi, I think we met once before, I'm Alix." (When she met people for the first time, Alix overpronounced her name—ahh-*lix*—with a strong emphasis on the second syllable.)

Peter never seemed like he was eight years older than Alix—his waist was trim and his light haircut was boyish—but when she found herself in a room of his peers, Alix suddenly felt as if she were attending a gathering of her parents' friends and counting down till she could retreat to her room and watch music videos. Peter's female co-workers arrived in floral fit-and-flare dresses, wedges, and pumps. Even the one black woman there arrived with her hair teased, bobbed, and highlighted. These ladies wore massive statement necklaces with costume-ish gems and beads. The men looked like grown-up Ken dolls in khakis and golf shirts.

The most popular point of conversation was the sharp hole in the foyer window. Before she'd learned of the incident at Market Depot, as she waited for the police to finish their report, Alix had worried that Peter's co-workers possibly felt the same as the juniors at Beacon Smith High. That Peter's career in Philadelphia had possibly ended before it began, and maybe they'd take him back at Riverdale . . . which would have been kind of amazing if it meant she'd be back in New York. But WNFT's reaction to the toothed hole in the window was a strange home-court pride mixed with backslapping joy. It was as if Peter, the new guy in town, had been properly and jokingly hazed. They wanted to know the story. They laughed and said, "Don't worry." They clinked their beers to the top of Peter's and said, "Welp, welcome to Philadelphia!"

No one at Briar's birthday party had heard of Alix or LetHer Speak. As she sipped on a club soda underneath a playlist of Kidz Bop and Michael Jackson, Alix decided to consider her anonymity a research-based challenge: to develop a clear elevator pitch that might appear on her book's dust jacket, one of the many tasks she hadn't yet started. But none of her descriptions seemed to work.

"Ohhh, so you're not exactly *writing* the book," one woman said. "It's like . . . what was that thing called, PostSecret? Do you remember that? And it was like . . . super raunchy?"

"We saw some wacky movie called *She*, no, it was called *Her*, *Her*?" Another wife looked to her husband for confirmation, but when he didn't give any, she still went on. "Maybe it was *Them*. But anyway—this guy's job is to write love letters for people. People he doesn't even know. It was so strange, is that what you do?" Alix pretended to hear Catherine crying and politely excused herself.

Laney Thacker, Peter's co-anchor, arrived with her four-year-old daughter, Bella. She also brought yellow roses, a bottle of wine, a mason jar filled with cookie ingredients and a recipe, and wrapped presents for both Briar and Alix. She greeted Alix with outstretched hands, and a look that said, *It's finally happening.* "Ohmygosh, I just feel like I know you so well," she said. "Gimme a hug. You're Philly Action family now." Twice, Alix thought their hug had reached its limit, but Laney hummed as she kept her hold. She gently rocked Alix from side to side. Bella went to Briar and rocked her back and forth as well.

Back in Manhattan, Alix went to birthday parties at least twice a month with Rachel, Jodi, and Tamra. They sat in corners drinking wine from paper cups and took turns dancing with the children. They whispered about obnoxious extravagances like chocolate fountains or complete toddler makeovers, and they rolled their eyes at mono-grammed favors and the hired Disney princess look-alikes who were always from New Jersey. But the guests attending Briar's very simple birthday party seemed to be trying twice as hard. The women dressed as if they were pretending to live on the Upper East Side, not as if they actually did, or as if they'd actually been there. There was no way they were comfortable standing in pumps, and why wasn't anyone wearing jeans? Alix felt out of place and uncomfortably large.

But Peter had smiled through Alix's luncheons and parties and conventions. He'd stayed up late, next to his wife, stamping five hundred letters that high school girls had written to their future selves. He'd put the children to bed when workshops ran late, after convincing Briar that her mother would come in and kiss her the very second she got home. Alix tried to remind herself of this and find someone she could relate to, someone she wouldn't mind coming over to plop her kid in front of the TV with Briar, someone she could go to yoga with. But these women were as pleasant and sweet as they were old-fashioned and disconcertingly uncool. Peter's co-anchor, Laney, fondled the wrap on Alix's jumpsuit affectionately. "I always want to try one of these," she said, "but I could *never* pull it off." She leaned in to laugh and ask how Alix could pee in that thing anyway.

Then it was apparently time for gifts. Children in Manhattan never opened presents at a party. Gifts were put in cabs and trunks, or in large, clear plastic bags to be taken home with leftover cake. If you remembered, you could hide a few in a closet and save them for a plane ride distraction, or for when your child peed in the proper place. But as Peter and Alix talked to a WNFT staff member, her five-year-old child came and clung to her knees. "When are they gonna do presents and cake?" he whined.

Peter looked at Alix. "Should I set up a chair?"

Briar sat on Alix's lap while Emira handed them presents. After the second gift, Briar became overwhelmed, flapped her arms, and said, "I don't like it I don't like it." Emira and Peter soothed her as Alix unwrapped each gift.

In between a Make Your Own Jell-O Princess Mold and a tiara that reeked of toxins and plastic, Alix retrieved her cell phone from her pocket to text Rachel, Jodi, and Tamra. Kill me, she typed. I hate everyone here. Every present given to Briar was completely ridiculous, borderline sexist, or horribly clichéd. The three-year-old received a silver Fendi snowsuit, a white and pink Little Ladies Tea Set, an Edible Arrangement (had they ordered this online?), and a "birthday cake" scented Yankee candle with a Build-A-Bear gift card attached to the lid. At Alix's feet, Emira stuffed wrapping paper into a large recycling bag. Briar held up a gift in confusion, a frilly blue apron with matching bonnet. Emira said to her, "That's for you, birthday girl." Alix wanted to grab Emira's shoulders, both of them, and say into her face, *This party is not me.*

Alix's home was filled with the types of mothers she often saw in airports and had come to completely despise. Women with full faces of makeup, way too much luggage (Vera Bradley carry-ons and Lilly Pulitzer passport cases), cork wedge sandals, and plastic bags with souvenirs that took up all the room in the overhead compartments. They noisily called their husbands as soon as they landed or to let them know they'd made it to the next gate. They held up the line to get off the plane ("Do you have everything? Because we *cannot* come back"). In bathroom stalls, they detailed their activity of papier-mâchéing the seat with toilet paper, rather than doing what Alix always did: chalking up public bathrooms to exercise and just squatting over the bowl.

Alix didn't even own a stroller until she was pregnant a second time. She was an incredible packer, often only brought a backpack on weekend trips, and frequently found herself texting Peter that she'd jumped on another flight that got her home quicker. So as she looked around her living room, Alix wondered how she would ever call Philadelphia home. How she could keep her dexterity as a mother and small-business owner while surrounded by the type of woman who halted security check flow because she'd forgotten to remove her jacket.

Alix stood by the door as parents struggled to squeeze shoes back on their children's feet and the toddlers began to rummage through their favors. She said, "We have to get the kids together," about four times as her cheek was kissed and her hands were squeezed.

Again, Laney made her way to Alix for a heartfelt moment of connection. "I'm just so glad you guys are here," she said. "We gotta do some cocktail time after the babes fall asleep."

It was clear that Laney was being very friendly, but also assuring Alix that while she sat next to her husband every day, she was a girl's girl, and that there was no funny business going on. This had never even crossed Alix's mind, and she felt guilty that it hadn't. Laney had an embarrassing laugh, a disproportionate gum-to-teeth ratio, and she often said things like, "Holy moly." Laney was the definition of sweet, and as Alix hugged her, she thought, *I want to like you. Why is this so hard?*

Over Laney's shoulder, Alix watched Emira bend down to help a little boy into his jacket. "We didn't play my favorite game," the five-year-old told her.

"Oh yeah?" Emira pulled the sleeves down onto his hands. "What's your favorite game?"

He turned around to her and said, "My favorite game is called I'm a Murderer!"

"Cooool." Emira stood up and walked to the next room, calling out, "Hey, Briar? Come hold my hand real quick."

After Alix finally closed the door behind Laney and her family, she pulled out her phone again. Correction, she texted her friends. I hate everyone except for my sitter.

You better give that girl a raise, Tamra said.

Or an Edible Arrangement! Rachel replied.

That night, Briar went to bed with her new fish on her nightstand, one of the few gifts Alix didn't place in a donation bag. Newly three-year-old Briar promptly named the fish Spoons, and watched it swim in circles until she fell asleep.

Five

Just as Emira decided to distance herself from the now three-year-old girl, to check Craigslist and Indeed every day, and to only apply for jobs that hired adults and offered very adult benefits, Mrs. Chamberlain stepped in hard. The night at Market Depot had done something to her, and she tried to right the night's wrongs with a forced casualness that made Emira quite cagey. Since that night, Mrs. Chamberlain started returning home at six forty-five, sitting down across from Emira, and referencing conversations that they'd never had. "Emira, remind me what you majored in?" "Tell me where you live again?" "Did you say that you had any allergies?" The timing couldn't have been worse. These were the questions you asked at the beginning, and not at what Emira was trying to make the end. But for a part-time gig, the money was decent, making it difficult to get excited about potential jobs that offered less money and zero Briar. Every other Friday, Alix handed Emira an envelope with six hundred seventy-two dollars inside.

Two weeks after the night at Market Depot, this envelope felt particularly fat. On the front porch, underneath a flushed sunset, Emira peeked inside the envelope flap to reveal twelve hundred dollars in cash. A small note on thick card stock was paperclipped to the hundred-dollar bills with Alix's brilliant handwriting on one side. *Emira——*, it read.

> *This is for the past two weeks, Briar's birthday, and the awful*
> *night when you completely saved us. Thank you for everything.*
> *We love having you and we're here for you.*
>
> *Xo P, A, B&C.*

Emira looked down the street. She laughed, whispered "Fuck," and immediately purchased her first leather jacket.

The subway was packed. Emira was pleasantly late to meet Zara, Shaunie, and Josefa for a dinner, followed by drinks, followed by all the other practices of twenty-somethings in the nighttime. Everything she wore looked shiny next to her new jacket. It was black with asymmetric zip fastening and was cropped just above her hip. The belt hung effortlessly at her sides, and she let the silver zippers sit open at her forearms. Emira's jacket came in at two hundred thirty-four dollars, making it the biggest purchase she'd ever made other than her bed frame and laptop. With one hand holding the subway pole, and the other texting Zara that she was on her way, Emira found it both funny and sad that she could feel so cheap in the most expensive thing she owned. She turned her earbuds up loud and balanced into the subway's turns.

Behind Emira was a family of six, very much not from Philadelphia, and the mother was calling out, "The next stop is ours. Does everyone hear me?" Underneath her music, she listened to the conversation to her left, where a man in a suit was saying he needed an excuse to not attend a family function. The woman next to him said, "I don't mind if you blame me." Emira's hip bones were prominent beneath her black leggings, and when she caught a flash of her gold multi-chain necklace, she flattened it out against her chest in the window reflection of fast-moving concrete and darkness. She smoothed her bangs and the dark waves at her shoulders, and in the space between one song ending and another beginning, she heard someone call her name.

Emira turned to see *KelleyTCopeland@gmail.com*. Over baseball hats and ponytails and shoulders, he said her name again, but this time he said, "Emira Tucker." Emira readjusted her grip on the subway pole and found herself remarkably nervous.

He was cuter this time around, partially because Emira wasn't babysitting or being accused of a crime, but he was also just cuter on his own. Kelley Copeland had dark hair and eyes; a long, pale face; and a big, strong-looking chin that for some reason implied he'd played sports all through college. Emira smiled from one side of her mouth, and Kelley said, "Excuse me," as he inched his way toward her.

"Do you remember me? Of course you do, hi." Kelley laughed as he answered his own question. "I probably shouldn't say this, but I've drafted about six emails to you and I've never sent them." He paused. "I've gotta know if you quit or not."

Emira was still startled by his very tall and friendly presence. She crossed her standing legs and said, "Sorry, what?"

"Sorry," he said. "I was curious if you quit your nanny job."

Kelley Copeland was so tall that he could press his hands flat against the top of the subway car, which was what he did in front of Emira. Emira thought this was both a painfully obvious show of masculinity and also insanely attractive.

"Ohh, sorry," Emira said. "Well . . . I'm actually not a nanny."

"Wow," he said. "So you did quit. Good for you."

"Oh no, I'm still working." Emira switched her purse strap from her right shoulder to her left. "But yeah, I'm just a sitter. I'm not a nanny."

"Can you tell me what the difference is?" Kelley asked. "I'm not trying to be weird, I honestly don't know."

The subway car stopped and Emira stepped out of the way of a man with four shopping bags as he exited the train. Kelley motioned the empty seat to her, and Emira sat down. "Nannies are full-time," she said. "They're salaried and they get bonuses and vacations. And babysitters are part-time and they do like . . . date nights and emergencies."

"Okay, gotchyou," Kelley said. "Sorry, I thought I heard you say you were a nanny at the store that night."

"No, yeah, I said I was a nanny so that guy would leave me alone," Emira explained. "Which obviously worked really well."

"Right." Kelley gave her the kind of goofy, annoyed look that passengers exchange when there's a loud, drunk person on a train, or when the conductor keeps announcing that there will be more delays. "Well, if you stayed you obviously had a reason to. But I'm hoping you got a raise at the very least."

Emira swiped a strand of hair out of her lashes and the zipper at her sleeve jingled delightfully. She smiled and said, "They took care of me."

Kelley leaned both of his hands on the bar above Emira's head. "Where are you going right now?" he asked.

Emira raised an eyebrow. She looked up at him and couldn't help but think, *Really?* It was Kelley's casual determination mixed with the sight of twelve uncreased hundred-dollar bills that gave her the spirit to think, *You know what? Yeah, okay. Fuck it.* She pursed her lips and said, "Dinner with some friends. And then Luca's. Why?"

"Luca's." He put out impressed lips and said, "That's very fancy."

Emira raised her shoulders in a sweet *I don't know* motion.

"What if I buy you a drink real quick?" he said. "Then we can go our separate ways. I'm meeting friends tonight, too." The train stopped and a woman pushed past Kelley to claim the seat next to Emira.

Emira feigned reluctance; she was enjoying this as much as he was. She was counting down to the last time she would see him tonight, and from what she could tell, it would be around two a.m. "I'm already late," she said. "You could buy me a drink at Luca's, though."

Kelley laughed. "Yeah, I'm never gonna get in there."

Emira looked down at his shoes. They were laced and brown, beneath dark jeans and an expensive-looking gray hoodie. "You're dressed okay," she assured him. "You should be fine."

"I didn't mean my clothes, but thank you, I am now brimming with confidence," he said with a grin. "It's just I've heard they don't let you in that place unless you're with a woman."

Emira's stop was next, and as the train started to slow, she stood up in the space next to him. "Well, you have my email. Just shoot me a note and I'll come outside."

Kelley pulled his phone out. "Wouldn't it be easier to text you?"

Emira exhaled in a laugh. "You can email me, son."

"Right, totally." He put his phone away with an obvious *duh* expression. "I was gonna say the same thing. Email. Cool."

Emira said, "Mm-hmm," and stood by the double exit doors.

Kelley sat in Emira's previous spot, which looked much too small for him and his frame. He rested his hands between his knees and smiled aggressively at Emira. She raised her eyebrows again and dropped her eyes down to her phone.

"That's my girlfriend," he said loudly to the woman sitting next to him. The woman looked up from the book she was reading and said, "Hmm?"

"That's my girlfriend right there." Kelley pointed at Emira.

The woman's face came into curiosity. She looked to Emira, who shook her head and said, "Umm, that's not true."

"She does this," Kelley said, keeping his eyes on the woman to his right. "It's cute, she plays this game when we're on the train where she pretends like she doesn't know me."

"Ohmygod." Emira placed three fingers to her forehead.

"When we get home she goes, 'Wasn't that funny, babe?' And then we laugh about it. It's hilarious."

The woman laughed and said, "That's really romantic."

The train stopped and Emira said, "*Bye.*"

Kelley called out, "See you at home, honey!" and the doors slid shut behind her.

At Luca's, Shaunie requested a booth on the balcony and bottle service, to which Zara said, "Excuse me, bish?" and Shaunie replied, "What? It's on meee." In a plush booth with white leather seats, the four girls sipped their drinks and bounced to the music. Shaunie ordered a second bottle, and when it arrived, Josefa held up her phone to announce to Snapchat, "We havin' a blessed motha-fuckin' night, *okay?*"

Shaunie's parents were as rich as Shaunie was generous. Her family's money came from a southern chain of drive-through Laundromats, and Shaunie's bigheartedness stemmed from a deep belief in karma, as well as inspirational quotes found online. Ever since they'd met (Zara had come to Emira after class and said, "This light-skinned girl offered to take us to a concert and she might kill us but it also might be dope"), Shaunie was constantly offering up her wardrobe, a first round of drinks, and the other half of her queen-sized bed. When Emira spent the night on Shaunie's couch, she'd wake up sweating beneath a blanket that Shaunie had applied sometime in the night.

Josefa, Shaunie's roommate, was as inconsistent as Shaunie was reliable. She either stayed at home, glued to her phone and new memes and videos, speaking to her sister and mother in Spanish via FaceTime, or she wanted to rally and drink until sunrise. Josefa went to Boston University and was now a research assistant and fellow at Drexel. Her parents said they'd support her financially as long as she was in school. She currently was in the process of getting her second master's, this one in public health.

"I invited this guy here but I don't think he'll come." Emira said this to Zara as they danced in front of their booth, behind the railing that looked down to the first floor. "I met him on the train, but it's whatever."

"He got friends?"

"That's what he said."

Zara nodded that she'd understood, and then put her leg on the table so she could twerk to the side.

Shaunie leaned her ear in to say, "Boys are coming tonight?"

"No no." Emira shook her head. "Probably not."

Zara pushed Shaunie's shoulder as she danced and said, "It doesn't matter, 'cause *you have a boyfriend*."

Shaunie raised her hands in defense. "I was just asking!"

Josefa announced, "I want a picture." In the reflection from her phone's screen, the girls were in order from lightest to dark. Josefa with her thick brown hair and glossed pink lips, Shaunie with her curls and honeyed round face, Zara with her freshly done twists and massive smile, and Emira at the end with her waves on her shoulders. They held on to the railing and looked into the flash.

Emira kept checking her email. As she waited for messages to load, she'd think, *Why did you try to be cute with this dumbass email thing?* But when she saw that she had no new messages, she'd think, *No, it's good he didn't come. He'd probably like Shaunie. It would have been weird.*

But when she saw him walk onto the second floor of Luca's, Emira saw why Kelley had not emailed her to get him at the door, and why he did not need her help getting in. Around eleven p.m., Kelley arrived with four friends, and these friends, to Emira's indisputable surprise, were all black. Kelley looked like he was being filmed for the intro of an extremely problematic music video. One of the men was wearing sunglasses. Two of them were wearing Timberlands.

When Emira went to make introductions, she saw that Josefa had put her phone away. Shaunie had draped her curls over one shoulder, and Zara just squinted hard at her friend. One of Kelley's friends announced that they were getting drinks, and what did the ladies want. Together, the men went down to the bar, and when the last of their heads disappeared down the stairs, Zara said, "Umm, *really bitch?*"

"Okay, you know what? It's whatever. I'm in a good mood." Emira blushed and sat down in the booth next to Shaunie. Josefa scooted into her right hip and the girls' heels clunked together beneath them.

"Donchyou *whatever* me." Zara held up a pointer finger from the other side of Shaunie. "'Cause lemme get this straight . . . it's okay when you do it? Is that right?"

"Ohhh." Josefa started to laugh and pointed at Zara. "'Cause you went home with redhead guy from Shaunie's party?"

Shaunie remembered this and said, "He was so nice!"

Zara placed a hand to her chest. "Apparently I can't swirl but you can? You get a leather jacket and you better than everybody?"

"Okay, okay." Emira laughed. "I get it. I'm *sorry*. But you know what I meant. That guy you fucked with had a compass tattoo."

"That boy went down for a whole EP." Zara twirled one of her twists in her hands. "I ain't seen or care about no tattoos."

Shaunie sat up so she could see over the railing to the bar. "Okay, but for real? Emira, that boy is *fine*."

Emira followed Shaunie's gaze down to the first floor, where Kelley put both of his hands on the bar and leaned over it to talk to a blond bartender. Already, Emira was madly jealous. "It's not a big deal," she said. "We met that night at the grocery store and I just saw him on the train tonight. I did *not* think he'd roll up like this."

Zara leaned in closer. "That's the guy who filmed you that night?!"

"Girl, yes."

"Why you so sneaky?"

"I didn't think he'd come!"

Still looking over the railing, Shaunie asked, "Is he wearing an Everlane sweater?"

Emira rolled her eyes. "Why are you acting like I know what that is?"

Zara matched Shaunie's posture as she eyed Kelley and his friends. A new song came on and Kelley began to nod his head and mouth the lyrics. "He's like that one white guy at every black wedding who's like, *super* hyped to do the Cupid Shuffle."

"Ohmygod," Shaunie said. "I fucking love the Cupid Shuffle."

"This is weird though, right?" With a drink in her hand, Josefa trailed on. "I mean . . . he's rul cute or whatever, but does someone wanna tell me why all his friends are black?"

Emira, Zara, and Shaunie rolled their heads toward their friend. "Ummmm . . ." Emira put a fist under her chin. "I don't know, Sefa, why are yours?"

"First of all, rude." Josefa put a hand in Emira's face. "Second of all, I just got my 23andMe results back and I'm eleven percent West African, *thank you very much.*"

Zara scrunched up her face and asked, "Why you tryna play one-drop rule right now?"

"And *third of all*," Josefa said, "I'm serious. I hope he doesn't have a fetish or something. When I was on Match all these old white guys were tryna touch my feet. Asking me to call them *papi* and shit."

"I hope he does try to touch some feet. Well done, sister." Zara high-fived Emira. "I'm gonna support you in this because unlike *some* people, *I* am a good friend. I'm also gonna grind up on his friend with the fade."

Josefa and Zara began to go back and forth over who would get to pretend like it was their birthday. Zara won the best two out of three in rock, paper, scissors, so when Kelley and his friends returned, they sang to her as she danced and blew out Josefa's lighter. Shaunie generously accepted the attention from two of the four men (one of whom actually was celebrating his birthday) and Josefa got another to arm-wrestle her on the table. An hour later, Kelley tapped Emira and said, "Okay, miss. I owe you a drink."

Kelley followed Emira downstairs and stood while she sat at the bar. Emira could tell that her teeth and lashes were glowing pink from the lights that bordered the counter's edge. Kelley purchased Emira's fourth drink of the evening, and then clinked his glass to hers. "Cheers to you," he said, "for having reserves of patience I have never known." After she thanked him and took a sip, Kelley said, "Tell me you aren't in college."

Emira crossed her legs. "No, I'm not in college."

"You must be a dancer, then, right?" Kelley set his glass back on the bar. "You must be classically trained to do moves like . . ." He brushed his shoulders off with pouted lips.

"Oh wow, it's like that." Emira laughed. "That was a very special occasion. The kid I babysit, someone egged her house. Her mom wanted me to take her while they dealt with the police . . . so I could go to the grocery store and see more police. Get it?"

"I got it," he said. "And that guy wasn't a real cop, but okay. So what do you do when you're not babysitting?"

Emira rested her elbow on the bar and grinned. "Are you gonna ask me what I do for fun next?"

"Maybe."

"That's *super* lame."

"Okay, but it's way better than asking how many siblings you have."

"Fine, well . . ." she said. "I work as a transcriptionist and do some clerical work at the Green Party Philadelphia office uptown."

"Really?" Kelley said. "You don't strike me as a Green Party person."

"I just type things."

"How fast can you type?"

"I do 125."

"Words per minute?!"

"Mm-hmm."

"Are you serious?"

Emira smiled. "Deadass."

"Damn. I could definitely hook you up if you're looking for more work," Kelley said. "My office pays a shit ton for transcription."

"Maybe I make a shit ton right now." *Ooo girl, you drunk*, Emira told herself. The jacket on her back and hundred-dollar bills in her purse were giving her bravadoes she couldn't contain.

Kelley held his hands up and said, "Fair."

"What's up with that, do you work in HR or something?" she asked. "The night I met you, you were like, 'You should write an op-ed.' Like, yeah, okay sure."

Kelley leaned on the bar and stared upward at the bottles and bitters. "I did say that . . . Huh." He squinted at Emira, and asked her quite honestly, "Am I an asshole?"

"You? Oh, for sure." Emira nodded. "I mean . . . I don't know from experience but like, just statistically speaking? One hundred percent. But it's chill."

"It's chill?" He grinned.

"Yeah, kinda."

"I think we should get a cab." Kelley said this into her ear. It came out in a strangely offhanded way that sounded very hilarious in Emira's haze. It was as if he were saying, *I think you're gonna need some stitches*, or, *Unfortunately, your card was declined.*

Emira laughed and picked up her drink. With her straw in her mouth she said, "You're lit."

Kelley folded his hands and said, "So are you, miss."

In the elevator up to Kelley's apartment, Emira checked her phone. OH OKAY BYE BITCH, Zara texted. Trap trap trap trap get that l.l.bean dick gur. At the other side of the elevator, Kelley watched her with his back against the railing. Then he stood up straight and said, "Can I come over there or what?"

Inside, on a couch that felt pricey and firm, Emira sat facing Kelley on his lap as he held the back of her thighs. The space smelled boyish and also like laundry done with detergent that was marked *Unscented*. Above Kelley, hung tightly against his living room wall, was a massive framed blueprint of Allentown, Pennsylvania. Emira kissed him in the glow from an opened window until he pulled back and whispered, "Hey hey hey."

Emira said, "Hmm?"

Kelley rested his head on the back of the couch. "You're not like, twenty years old, are you?"

"No. I'm twenty-five."

"Yikes, okay." He put his hands behind his head. "I'm thirty-two."

Emira stood up to remove her pants. "Okay."

"That's seven years older than you."

"Uh-huh." Emira laughed once as she moved forward to undo his belt buckle. "You're like . . . really smart."

"Okay, miss." Kelley laughed. "I'm just making sure."

In between strokes and kisses, Kelley pulled out a condom and placed it on the couch cushion to his left. It sat there like a peace offering or a panic button; a plastic symbol of consent. At one point, he lifted her hips and told her, "Sit up for me," before he pressed her pelvic bone to his mouth. Emira said what she recognized as a very white expression, "Oh, you don't have to . . ." By this she meant, *I'd rather not return the favor when you're done.* Kelley seemed to understand her appeal. He laughed and said, "I know," before he took her in his mouth again. He stopped once more to say, "Unless you're not cool with it," to which Emira quickly replied, "No, I am." She balanced her hands and one knee on the back of the couch. For the second time that night she thought, *You know what? Fuck it*, and she took hold of the back of his head.

On her way back down Emira reached for the condom. That she stayed on top seemed implicit and implied.

Later, she was still quite drunk as she pulled out her phone and texted Zara, Where you at. Kelley had put on shorts and a T-shirt, and he brought a glass of ice water to her on the couch. He went back to the kitchen to drink his own as he looked at her across an island counter. The clock on his microwave read 1:10.

Emira reached for her shoes. "May I please have an Uber and a snack?"

Kelley reached for his phone. "You may have an Uber. But you get a snack when I get your number."

Emira laughed. To her right, next to the record player, was a milk crate full of albums. "Why do you have the *Waiting to Exhale* sound-track?" she asked. Other titles Emira could see were Chaka Khan and Otis Redding.

Kelley sighed, his eyes on his phone. "Because I have the music tastes of a middle-aged black woman," he said.

Emira rolled her eyes, but Kelley didn't catch it. Maybe Josefa was right and he did have a fetish. Emira almost asked him how many times he'd used that line, but instead she said, "You have nice things." She was loose and tired and delighted. She looked around the room and took in the record player set, a chair that looked like it wasn't from IKEA, a black coffeemaker on the kitchen counter that looked like it was from a wedding registry, and a bike and a tire pump leaning against the wall. Her head rolled to her left. "You have nice, adult things in here."

"You don't seem like a thief but if you are, you're terrible at it. Hassan will pick you up in three minutes."

"Allentown," Emira said. She stared, upside down, at the name of the city above her head and blinked as the letters went in and out. "Who do I know from Allentown?"

"You know me from Allentown." Kelley made his way over to her, placed a bag of popcorn in her lap, and said, "Let's start with your area code."

Emira gave Kelley her phone number as she snacked on popcorn, her right arm draped deliriously over her head. On the blueprint behind her, two streets over from where her pinky hung, was the place Kelley Copeland completely ruined Alex Murphy's senior year. Back in the spring of 2000, before she became Alix Chamberlain.

PART TWO

Six

In the vestibule of the Chamberlain home sat a small, teak table near the front door. On top was a porcelain cup that collected change, a wooden trough holding three sprouting succulents, and an upright phone charger from CB2 that was plugged in to the wall behind it. In the past few weeks, Alix had developed what she knew was an awful and invasive habit of returning home, closing the door quietly behind her, bending at the hip, and looking at Emira's phone. The small entryway was protected by another door that entered into the main foyer, which made Alix feel as though she wasn't quite at home, and that she wasn't exactly looking *through* the phone. She didn't know the passcode and she would never use it if she did, but the lock screen of Emira's phone was always filled with information that was youthful, revealing, and completely addicting.

She never took Emira's phone off the charger, and she rarely pressed any buttons (messages and notifications would light up on their own), but three times a week she scrolled with her middle finger as she listened to Emira cook dinner upstairs and tell Briar to blow in case it was hot. A month had gone by since the night at Market Depot, and in that time, Alix had developed feelings toward Emira that weren't completely unlike a crush. She became excited to hear Emira's key in the door, she felt disappointed when it was time for her to leave, and when Emira laughed or spoke without being prompted, Alix felt like she had done something right. The times when this happened were few and far between, which was why Alix kept peeking at her sitter's cell phone. She would have just checked Emira's social media channels instead, but from what she'd gathered from searching, Emira didn't have any.

Emira had a group text titled Siblings where her brother and sister sent songs, memes, and trailers for upcoming movies. Emira was constantly texting Zara, labeled Kween Zara, who would often reply in clipped messages, one right after the other (No. Stop. Don't you dare. I cannot). Zara and Emira went out nearly every weekend, and many of their texts discussed the logistics. One afternoon, Emira must have just placed her phone on the charger moments before Alix arrived, because it sat unlocked and waiting. Alix didn't even have to scroll. Emira had texted What are you wearing, to which Zara replied Slut, and Emira had responded, Cool, same. When Alix went upstairs, Emira was playing on the floor with Briar and saying, "Okay, now you have to tell me your *second* favorite vegetable."

Sometimes there were no conversations available for Alix to read, but there was always paused music. Some of the names Alix recognized, like Drake and Janet Jackson, OutKast and Usher, but most of them were strangers like J. Cole and Tyga, Big Sean and Travis Scott. Alix ended up Googling things like *Is Childish Gambino a person or a band? How do you pronounce the name SZA?* One evening, Alix memorized the name of a song and later Googled it in her room. Alix listened to the first verse in her headphones, which began with *Hoe you ain't wanna see up all this Birkin / Tear a nigga's face off, watch me be a surgeon.* Alix's eyebrows rose up into her forehead. She looked over at Catherine next to her and whispered, "Whoops."

But out of all the information she'd gathered in the past few weeks, what was most intriguing as a future point of connection was the fact that Emira was definitely seeing someone new. Someone she'd labeled in her phone as Kenan&Kel. One afternoon—Alix saw this on her way out—he'd said, Maybe next time let me know that you don't drink coffee, weirdo. On a Wednesday evening he'd said, Is basketball something you'd be interested in? And one time, Emira had sent a screenshot of her conversation with him to Zara, to which Zara replied, That boy doesn't play. The messages between Emira and this new person were of that cool and careful variety that only exists at the beginning of something, as you try to exude spontaneity and effortless humor, and space out responses to appear busy and even-keeled. Alix was dying to ask Emira about him, to know if his name was Kenan, Kel, or neither. She wanted to cross a threshold where Emira would offer up information on her own, and more importantly, trust Alix to keep it. And tonight, after seeing Emira's newest message (Excited to see you tonight, Miss Tucker.) inside her dirty and rubbery pink phone case, Alix decided to make this happen.

Alix walked upstairs into the kitchen. Briar looked up from her drawing and said, "Mama? Mama this is not a scary ghost, okay?" Alix put her purse on the counter and realized that the room had turned very sweet and warm. That morning, she had put out pumpkins and gourds at the center of the table and hung fall leaves (collected from the backyard) over the windows that looked out onto the street. Briar colored a picture of a very friendly ghost next to a plate of cucumbers, garbanzo beans, and plain pasta. On the fridge were new art projects: a googly-eyed witch made out of felt, and a purple paper that read *BOO!* The letters were colored in so nicely on one side that it was clear Emira had "helped" Briar complete it. Alix took off a drapey cardigan sweater, kissed Briar's cheek, and received Catherine from Emira, who was already holding the baby up.

"You guys have a good day?"

"Yeah." Emira picked at dried food on the knee of her jeans. "I think we did pretty good, huh, B?"

Briar held up a crayon and said, "You do it."

Emira sat down next to her. "I do what now?"

"Let's say 'please,' Bri," Alix said. "Emira," she added, "do you drink wine?"

Emira carefully accepted a crayon from Briar. She blinked and said, "I mean . . . yeah."

Alix took two glasses from a cupboard and thought, *Yeah, you do.* She sat down, and with a bottle of wine in between her legs, she somehow managed to uncork the bottle while holding Catherine. When Catherine looked up at her, Alix said, "Hi. Did you miss me or what?"

Alix told Emira she could take the wineglass into the bathroom with Briar, that she did it all the time. She hadn't eaten since lunch (she'd lost five pounds since her very loving and supporting intervention) and as she sipped her glass of wine, cleaned up toys from the kitchen table, and listened to Emira give Briar a quick bath, she sensed those lax and wonderful feelings of decorum leaving her body. She lit two candles on the kitchen counter. She turned on a playlist with Fleetwood Mac and Tracy Chapman. And as she turned off the bright kitchen lights and left the chandelier blushing over the table,

Alix recognized that she was very much courting her babysitter. But the evening reminded her of Fridays with Rachel, Jodi, and Tamra. She hadn't poured a glass of wine for another woman in months.

Emira emerged with a few picture books beneath her arm, a glass half full, and Briar in tow, changed into her pajamas and wrapped in her tattered white blanket. Emira stopped at the kitchen counter and took another sip of her wine. "This is really good," she said.

"I like it too." From the table, Alix held up her glass and looked at the color. In her other arm, Catherine was receiving a bottle, which Alix administered with one hand. "Are you a wine person or no?"

"I mean, I like it," Emira said. She set her glass at the other end of the table, then took the books from underneath her arm and set those down too. "But I'm used to drinking like . . . boxed wine, so yeah, I'm no connoisseur."

There were moments like this that Alix tried to breeze over, but they got stuck somewhere between her heart and ears. She knew Emira had gone to college. She knew Emira had majored in English. But sometimes, after seeing her paused songs with titles like "Dope Bitch" and "Y'all Already Know," and then hearing her use words like *connoisseur*, Alix was filled with feelings that went from confused and highly impressed to low and guilty in response to the first reaction. There was no reason for Emira to be unfamiliar with this word. And there was no reason for Alix to be impressed. Alix completely knew these things, but only when she reminded herself to stop thinking them in the first place.

"Well, I used to be a boxed wine fan myself," Alix said, "but you know I didn't buy this, right?"

Emira sat down and settled Briar on her lap. "Hmm?"

"Oh yeah, I don't really buy wine anymore. Or a lot of other things." Alix took another sip. "I've been doing this for years. I just write a wine company and say that I'm doing an event and I'm testing out wines. And then they send me a few bottles for free. This one is from"—she turned the bottle's label toward her—"Michigan, I think."

"So does that mean you have an event coming up?"

"When my book comes out, I will." Alix winked.

Emira laughed and said, "Dang, okay."

"I read dis now!" Briar announced, lifting up a board book. "I read dis one."

Emira said, "Okay, go for it."

Briar tolerated being read to during the day, but Alix's child was the only toddler she knew of who didn't enjoy partnered story time before bed. Instead, Briar liked to be held as she "read" to herself before her eyes cast a sleepy focus on the pages in front of her. She constantly shushed the person holding her, even when they hadn't said a word. Alix tried to hold her voice at a smooth level to keep Briar happy and keep her sitter talking.

"Are you doing anything fun tonight?"

Emira nodded. "Just going to dinner."

"Do you know where?"

Emira crossed her arms over Briar's lap. "This Mexican place called Gloria's."

"Gloria's?" Alix clarified. "Is that the one that's BYOB? And really loud?"

"Mm-hmm."

"I've gone there. That's fun. Oh, you should take this with you." Alix flicked the wine bottle. "I can't have more than a glass since I'm still pumping."

When Emira said, "Really?" Briar looked up at her and said, "Shhhh, no Mira, no no."

Emira placed a finger in front of her mouth, and Briar turned the page. Emira mouthed, *Thank you*, and Alix said, "Of course."

This is good, Alix thought. *We aren't there yet but we're getting there.* Alix knew that her aspirations for a relationship with Emira were possibly too high because of what she'd seen with her girlfriends and their sitters. Rachel and her nanny, Arnetta, often discussed their divorces, their least favorite children in Hudson's class, and the most attractive fathers. Tamra once took the day off from work and allowed her kids to skip the first half of school to watch their beloved sitter, Shelby, have a speaking role on a daytime soap opera. And Jodi was always picking up scarves and lotions because her sitter, Carmen, wore things like that, or she might want to try them. Alix didn't know what Emira liked, or what she didn't like, or how she stayed so skinny, or if she believed in God. It wouldn't happen all at once, but she had to keep trying, even if it meant being the first to speak at every silence, and with Emira, there were many.

"Are you going there with girlfriends?"

Emira smiled and shook her head no.

Alix let a cartoonish, gossipy expression go into her eyes. She said, "Ooohh," and Emira laughed. Her lips came together in a flirtatious secrecy. "Well, come on. Is he cute?"

Emira nodded in thoughtful consideration. She took one of her hands up next to her face and made her fingers flat as she whispered, "He's really tall."

"Yesss," Alix said. Emira laughed again. Alix felt like Emira's laughter was still backed by a small token of toleration, but she didn't care. This conversation was better than any of the ones she'd had with

Peter's co-workers. She rocked Catherine and said, "Where'd you meet him?"

"Umm . . ." Briar slammed the first book shut and moved to the second. Emira ruffled her bangs. "We met on the train."

"Really? That's cute." In her arms, Catherine had started to fall asleep, but her lips continued in a furious rhythm for a now-empty bottle. Alix placed the bottle on the table and stuck her pinky in her daughter's mouth. "Is it your first date?"

"That's for the horsies," Briar said into her book. "We need a map."

"It's like . . . the fourth?"

"Shhh, Mira," Briar said.

"Okay, shh," Emira whispered back.

Alix shook her head and rolled her eyes. "Sorry."

Emira mouthed, *It's fine.*

There was a very small window of time where Catherine would fall right asleep in her crib, and Alix knew that this was it, but she didn't want to break the moment just yet. She couldn't ask what his name was. That would make her sound so old. And she couldn't ask what she really wanted to know, if Emira had slept with him yet, or if sleeping with someone before they were together was a thing Emira did, if sleeping with someone, for her, meant anything at all. It was officially six minutes after seven o'clock, the latest Emira had ever stayed. Alix knew she could ask one more question before she had to let her go. "Do you think it could be serious?"

Emira slumped and laughed. "I don't know," she said. "He's cute. But I'm not tryna get like . . . wifed up anytime soon."

This sentiment made Alix squeal inside.

She wanted to ask Emira when her mother had gotten married and tell her that her own mother had been twenty-five. She wanted to know if Emira had had serious relationships before, and what this new guy did for a living. But Briar's whispers had turned into nods, and Emira placed a hand on the child's forehead so she wouldn't bang it into the table. Phil Collins started pouring from the speakers. Both of their glasses had turned transparent and empty.

Alix did two long nods and said, "Good for you." She touched the wine bottle, stood with the baby in her arms, and said, "I'm going to put this by your bag."

Seven

There was a two-story Starbucks near the Chamberlain house where freelancers and college students camped out for hours. After babysitting, Emira typically walked to the second level—seemingly to meet other classmates and friends—and changed her clothes in the single bathroom. Tonight, over jeans, she changed into a white T-shirt, oxblood-colored booties, and Shaunie's maroon varsity jacket with a textured letter *S* on the front left side. Emira applied lipstick in the mirror, put her hair into a ponytail, and texted Kelley, I'm late I'm sorry I'm running.

Gloria's was always at max capacity. There were permanent Christmas lights on the walls along with hanging sugar skulls, roses, and dense patterned blankets. Emira stepped through couples and groups waiting outside and past a hostess calling, "Reuben, party of six!" When her eyes adjusted inside, she saw Kelley seated in a corner.

"I'm so sorry."

"You're fine, you're fine." Kelley touched her elbow and kissed the side of her face. When he pulled back he smiled and said, "Is it weird if I say you smell like a bath?"

Kelley Copeland was born in Allentown, Pennsylvania. He had an older sister who had one child, and two younger brothers who worked at the same post office his father had worked at for twenty-eight years. Kelley made a huge effort to avoid screens after ten p.m. He read only print books, and before bed, he wore embarrassingly large, orange-tinted glasses that were called Blue Blockers. He spent half his day staring at a computer, coding and creating interfaces for gyms, yoga retreats, physical therapy sessions, and spin classes that required their participants to sign up using apps with campy copy and push notifications. Emira knew that Kelley had broken his collarbone twice, that he became "irrationally furious" when people didn't hear their names being called out at coffee shops, and that he was grossed out by the thought of drinking whole milk, but what she didn't know was what it was like to sleep with him a second time.

Four days after their night at Luca's, Kelley asked Emira if she could get coffee before she went to work. Emira screenshotted his request and sent it to Zara, who replied, I can't tell if you're getting hired or dumped rn. Coffee with Kelley felt strangely formal. It was as if they were pretending that they hadn't had sex the last time they saw each other, that she hadn't repositioned his hands away from her hair (he'd said sorry twice and she'd said it was fine), and that he hadn't very cutely removed the remote control he'd sat on, placed it on the side table, and said, "Sorry. As you were." In a very trendy place with lots of natural light and four-dollar cold brews, Emira kept expecting Kelley to give her a promotion, or ask her about a time when she had to be part of a team. But he asked her about where she was from, who the most embarrassing person she followed on Instagram was—she didn't have an Instagram account; his was a pet raccoon—and if she ever, while doing something very ordinary in her day, suddenly remembered a dream she'd had the night before.

If Kelley had ever met Emira's mother, she would have said something along the lines of, "That boy likes to talk." Kelley definitely did that thing where he asked her questions with the intention of explaining his own answer afterward. But he did plenty of listening on his own, and Emira didn't mind. Kelley was silly in a way that wasn't loud or obnoxious. He once initiated a game of guessing what people were listening to on their headphones as they walked by. Another time, after passing two crying babies, he'd looked at Emira and said, "Breakups are the worst, am I right?" And once, as they were leaving a basketball game behind a small child singing "The Song That Never Ends," Kelley whispered in Emira's ear, "I will give you seventy-five dollars to take your Coke and dump it on that kid's head. But you have to do it right now."

Emira settled in across from him, removed Shaunie's jacket, and took him in. "I would have been very on time . . ." she said. "But my boss has been really into asking me questions and wanting to talk."

Kelley looked back down to the menu and used the candlelight to see. "Is she afraid you're gonna sue her for sending you to the whitest grocery store in Philadelphia?"

"I have no idea. Oh! But wait!" Emira reached behind her seat and into her bag that hung off the side. She retrieved the recorked bottle of wine that Mrs. Chamberlain had set near her charging phone. "She did give me this, though."

Kelley pulled out his phone and used the light to read the label. "Your boss just gave this to you?"

"She asked if I wanted some and then she was like, 'Take it.'"

"This looks extremely expensive," Kelley said. "Do you mind if I look it up?"

"No, go ahead." Emira reached for a chip and dipped it into salsa. "She didn't even buy it. She writes wine companies and tells them that she has an event coming up and then they just send her shit."

"Seriously?" Kelley's face lit up with the brightness from his phone. "What does she do again?"

"She's a writer," Emira said. And because she had recently Googled Mrs. Chamberlain and saw pictures of her with college-aged students, Emira added, "And maybe a teacher? I don't know. She's writing a history book that's coming out next year."

"Holy shit." Kelley looked at Emira and squinted. "This is a fifty-eight-dollar bottle of Riesling."

Emira said, "Damn," but she wasn't surprised. Mrs. Chamberlain had expensive tastes that she never openly acknowledged. Instead, she enjoyed telling Emira about the bargains she acquired. She'd divulge the exact price of a rug that was a "steal," or she'd say she "felt good" about finding a cheap flight for Christmas. Emira couldn't help but wonder why Mrs. Chamberlain couldn't feel good paying full price for things when she could obviously afford it. Emira often looked up the cost of things that came from Mrs. Chamberlain's home, suggestions, and lifestyle. In every one of her purses was a tube of mascara called Juice Beauty, which came in at twenty-two dollars each. She'd once stayed at a hotel in Boston that Emira discovered was three hundred sixty-eight dollars a night, on weekdays. And one day, when Emira explained that she'd bought Briar new shorts after she sat in mud, Mrs. Chamberlain dug into her wallet with an urgent apology: "Let me pay you for the shorts. Will thirty dollars cover it?" Emira had bought the packet of shorts at Walgreens, and they were

$10.99 for two. When Emira relayed this interaction to Zara, Zara was beside herself that Emira didn't accept the surplus. "The *fuck* is wrong with you?" she'd said. "You tell her, 'Yes. The shorts cost thirty dollars exactly. You are very welcome, good-bye.'"

"Well." Kelley handed the bottle of wine back across the table. "I brought beers because I thought that we were honest, working-class people, but if I'd known you were trying to seduce me . . ."

"Right. Uh-huh." Emira smiled around the chip in her mouth. This was another thing that she'd decided she would let Kelley get away with: considering himself working class. Kelley worked at one of those fancy offices where everyone sat in the same huge room with plush headphones on and there was unlimited cereal and La Croix. But instead of reminding him of this, and the fact that he lived above a CrossFit in Fishtown, she said, "Not gonna lie. It's the best wine I've ever had."

They ended up drinking the beers because Gloria's had a rule that you couldn't drink anything that was already opened. Emira slipped it back into her bag, and Kelley said, "We'll work on that later."

They talked about their days, but underneath it all, Emira kept thinking, *If you don't fuck me tonight I'm gonna be livid*. It seemed— and this was just her opinion that was backed by Zara's confirmation— that Kelley was still slightly hung up on their age difference. In the same way that white women were often overly accommodating to her when she found herself in specific white spaces (dental offices, Oscar parties in which she was the only black attendant, every Tuesday and Thursday at the Green Party office), Kelley was overcompensating for the implications of their age difference by taking Emira to places that were completely unsexy, and ending the night kissing the space next to her ear. Emira had been surprised by how rhythmic and chemical their first night together had been—this, in her opinion, usually took time—but after two dates of "Have you ever been to Europe?" and "What would you do if you won the lottery?" she was ready to go back to his place. On his couch, that first night, Emira hadn't thought of Briar, or her impending health insurance problem. Or even the fact that her rent would be going up by ninety dollars as soon as the new year began.

Kelley held his arms up behind his head, then quickly removed them as a waiter stopped by to deliver their plates. "So I think it's time you told me about the losers you dated before you met me," he said.

Emira laughed. "Oh, it's that time?" She set her beer back on the table.

"Mm-hmm. And also what they're doing now and how miserable they are without you."

"Oh wow, okay." She readjusted in her seat. "Well . . . I dated someone this summer for a few months, which was fine for a minute. But then he started to send me motivational quotes all the time . . . ? And I was like nuh-uh, I can't do this shit with you."

"I need to see at least one of them."

"I probably deleted them." Emira cut into her enchiladas and tried to remember. "But yeah, he'd text me all these pictures and quotes that were like, *Michael Jordan didn't make his high school basketball team*, and I was always like . . . okay, and?"

"Alright, so no quotes for you. Do you want another?" Kelley pointed to the bucket of beers and Emira nodded.

"I dated a musician for a year in college and that was fine but dumb. I think he's touring with some band now and tuning their guitars."

Kelley finished chewing and said, "Why do I feel like that band is like, the Red Hot Chili Peppers or something?"

"Please, I know who that is." Emira smirked. "And then I dated a guy for like, ten months from high school into college. But it was long distance for the second half so that was dumb, too."

"Huh." Kelley wiped his face with his napkin and set his hands on the table. "So you haven't had like, a long, serious relationship?"

Emira smiled as she chewed. "Well, I haven't had a long, serious life, so no. Is this you tryna tell me that you were married with kids or something?"

"No no no . . . why do I have the impulse to say, 'Not that I know of!'"

Emira faked a gag and said, "Please don't."

"I know. Ignore that." Kelley shook his head and started over. "My last girlfriend and I met in college but dated years after. She now delivers babies on a reservation in Arizona . . . I had a girlfriend for two years at the end of college, and we say *Happy Birthday* or *Merry Christmas* sometimes. I think she lives in Baltimore. I had a girlfriend for a little while during my freshman year. We're still cool. And . . . you went all the way back to high school so I guess I gotta play, too. When I was seventeen I had a girlfriend who was the richest girl in town."

Emira crossed her legs. "How rich are we talking?"

Kelley raised a finger. "I'll tell you how rich. We took a school trip to Washington, D.C.—she was in the grade above me—and like thirty of us were on the same plane ride. She was the first one on the plane and I was right behind her. And after she found her seat, she set her luggage down in the aisle, and then she just sat down. Without putting it away."

Emira's head dipped and her ponytail swung. "Did she expect you to do it for her?"

"No." Kelley leaned into the table. "She expected people on the *plane* to do it. I opened the overhead and she was like, 'Don't mess with the plane!' She'd never been on a plane where the staff didn't put your luggage away for you."

"Are there planes like that?"

"Evidently in first class."

"Oh shit," Emira said. "Does she own her own plane now?"

"Probably. I'm fairly certain she's in New York. I just remember that like, well, this sounds weird, but it was one of those loss-of-innocence moments where things kind of click, you know? And I had a *lot* of moments like this with her—that's another story—but I remember that most of my classmates had never been on a plane, and probably wouldn't again for a long time. And here's this girl who travels in first class and doesn't understand why there's no leg room. And my seventeen-year-old mind was like, 'Oh hey, people live very different lives.' Do you know what I mean?"

"Mm-hmm," Emira said. "Yeah. This is like, the opposite, but when I was little, I went to this girl's house for a sleepover, and when I went into the bathroom there were three huge cockroaches in the middle of the floor. I screamed, but this girl was like, 'Oh, you just shoo them out of the way.'" As she said this, Emira flicked her napkin gently in imitation, as if she were cutely herding very tiny sheep. "And I was like, *you do what*? And when I think back I'm like, okay yeah, that girl was mad poor. I think she and her sister slept in the same twin bed. But at the time the cockroaches seemed like a bigger deal. It shook me, I was like, 'You live like this?' And now I'm like oh, wait, most people live like this."

"Eeek, exactly. That's a really good one." Kelley wiped his mouth, cringed, and nodded. "Okay, yeah, I have another one. When I was little, my little brother loved that show *Moesha*. Do you remember that show?"

"Of course I remember that show."

"Yeah, that makes sense 'cause you're closer to my little brother's age."

Emira made a face and said, "Cool, Kelley."

"Sorry sorry sorry. So yeah, anyway . . . my whole family was sitting around the table at dinner, and out of nowhere my little brother, who was like six, goes, 'Mom, why is *Moesha* nigger shit?'"

Under the mariachi music that suddenly seemed quite loud, Emira's eyes went wide and her mouth twisted as if she'd found a hair in her food. Kelley went on.

"My mom was like, 'What?' And my brother goes, 'Michael's dad told me to turn it off because . . . ' Well, I'm not gonna repeat it, but he obviously had no idea what that meant. But I was older, so I did. And I saw this kid's dad all the time. And I was like, *Holy shit. You're a bad man, Michael's dad.* I'm looking at evil when I see you at school."

Emira stared at Kelley and her heart started to double.

The two of them had only discussed race once, and barely. At the basketball game, a group of black teens saw Kelley hand Emira her ticket, and one, very much wanting to be heard, said, "That's a damn shame." Kelley did a very cute half salute in their direction and said, "Okay . . . thank you, sir. Thank you for your service." When they made it to their seats, Kelley sat with his legs spread and leaned in to her ear. "Can I ask you a question?" Emira nodded. "Have you ever dated . . . " He trailed off, and Emira thought, *Oh Lord.* She crossed her legs, thinking, *It's whatever. Let's just watch the game.* "Have you ever dated," Kelley started again, "someone who wasn't . . . so tall?"

Emira laughed and shoved his shoulder. "Boy, stop."

Kelley raised his shoulders in mock-concerned defense. "It's a legitimate question. Would your parents be mad if you brought home a . . . tall guy?" Emira laughed again. She didn't call him out on stealing that joke from *The Fresh Prince of Bel-Air*. Maybe that was part of the joke. They never discussed it again.

Emira had dated one white guy before, and repeatedly hooked up with another during the summer after college. They both loved bringing her to parties, and they told her she should try wearing her hair naturally. And suddenly, in a way they hadn't in the first few interactions, these white men had a lot to say about government-funded housing, minimum wage, and the quotes from Martin Luther King Jr. about moderates, the ones that "people don't want to hear." But Kelley seemed different. Kelley Copeland, with his dadlike humor and exaggerated expressions and his affinity for saying the same word three times (*hey hey hey, listen listen listen, no no no*), could apparently acknowledge that he was dating a black woman, and that she could appreciate a good story over the need for decorum, but still . . . shouldn't he have said "the N-word" instead? Maybe save the whole thing for the seventh or eighth date? Emira couldn't tell. Sitting across from him, she wrestled with feeling moderately appalled that he had said the whole thing, with that painfully distinctive hard *r* sound at the end, but as she watched the veins in his hands move as he took a last bite, she settled on, *You know what? Imma let you get away with that too.*

"What did Michael's dad look like?"

"I mean, I'm sure he looks like most dads in Allentown." Kelley put his fork at the side of his plate. "But now when I think of him I picture him in a cowboy hat on a front porch with a—"

Emira reached across the table to stop him before he did another impersonation. She lowered her voice and asked, "Do you wanna go back to your place?"

Later, in Kelley's bedroom, he sat up in bed and said, "We forgot to drink the wine." He put shorts on and walked out to the kitchen.

In a T-shirt of his that read *Nittany* on the front, Emira got up to pee. She took a selfie in Kelley's medicine cabinet mirror and sent it to Zara, who replied, I can't stand you rn. It was 11:46 p.m.

Kelley retrieved two glasses and set them on the island counter at the center of his kitchen. Emira brought the bottle wrapped in a purple plastic bag and stood at the other side.

"'Little Lulu's Ballet Academy,'" Kelley read. He removed the bag and set the wine on the counter. "That sounds like a complete nightmare."

"It's not. I take Briar every Friday and it's like, my favorite thing."

"This is the one I saw at the grocery store?"

"Mm-hmm. She's terrible at it." Emira stretched her arms up over her head and felt the bottom of the T-shirt begin to reveal her behind. "All the other girls are very shy and graceful, but Briar is always yelling that she wants a grilled cheese and shit. Next week is our last class. It's a Halloween party and we're very excited about it."

Kelley poured the wine into the two glasses. "Will you be dressing up?"

"I will be a cat. And Briar will be a hot dog."

"Nice. That classic cat-and-hot-dog combination. Are you ready for this?" Kelley placed a glass in front her. "Oh wait, you already tried it. Am *I* ready for this? Yes. Yes I am."

With his eyes on Emira, Kelley did a very showy swirl of the wine in his hand. He took a sip, let it hit the back of his throat, and said, "Oh wow." He nodded as he placed it back on the counter. "Shit, yeah, this tastes like a country club."

"I told you. It almost makes me sad 'cause I'll probably never have it again." Emira leaned her forearms onto the counter. "Do you think your high school girlfriend is drinking this in first class right now?"

Kelley laughed. "Probably, yes." He eyed Emira before he added, "You wanna know how I broke up with her?"

"Yes."

"It's awful," he warned. "You can't leave after I tell you this. There was like, a lot of other bullshit involved with her and how she wrote me letters all the time and all this other stuff, but when I actually ended it, I said, 'I think it would be best if we went our separate ways, and that those paths never again connected.'"

Emira covered her mouth. Against her palm she said, "Noooo."

"Yep." Kelley took another sip and said, "I thought I was very cool."

"What is wrong with you?"

"I was seventeen years old."

"Yeah, I was seventeen once too, bro."

"Okay okay okay, I don't know. She wrote me all of these very flowery and poetic letters all the time, and I think I felt like I had to break up with her in the same elevated tone, but it did not go down that way. And I'd like to say that that was the dumbest thing I ever did in high school, but it most definitely was not."

Emira stood up straight. "What else did you do?"

"It wasn't exactly things I did but . . . things I thought? Like . . . you know how Valentine's Day was invented by card companies? What I thought I heard was *car* companies. Till college, I thought that like, Toyota and Kia invented Valentine's Day. Which I *did* think was odd, but still a thing that happened. Actually, no, wait. Even worse than that? I thought that the word *lesbian* had a *d* on the end? Like—*lesbiand*? And I thought it was a verb."

"Kelley." Emira covered her mouth again. "No, you didn't."

"I absolutely did," he said. "I thought that one woman could *lesbiand* the other. Till I was like, sixteen. Why am I telling you this?"

Emira laughed. "I honestly don't know. But tell me the breakup line one more time."

Kelley put both hands on the counter and cleared his throat. "'I think it would be best if we went our separate ways, and that those paths never again connected.'"

"That's really beautiful."

"Thank you."

Emira leaned against the counter with her hip bones first. She watched Kelley take the fifty-eight-dollar wine bottle and tip the remaining liquid into her glass.

"Do you want to call me an Uber?" she asked.

Kelley set the empty bottle on the tile. "Not really, no."

Emira nodded and said, "Okay."

Eight

Back in New York, long before Catherine was born, Tamra poured wine into three glasses. "Everyone has to share their most embarrassing moment."

"I love when Tamra drinks," Jodi said, "because she turns into an eleven-year-old girl."

The four women sat on wiry patio furniture next to plastic shovels, pails, and a kiddie pool covered in leaves in the ivy-surrounded space that was Rachel's backyard. Tiny white lights hung overhead. On the other side of the sliding glass door was a downstairs studio that Rachel used for guests. A queen-sized bed folded out from the wall where a very little Briar slept with her thumb in her mouth. Tamra's daughters, Imani and Cleo, slept next to her, on the other side of Jodi's daughter, who was soon to be a big sister (Jodi sipped a club soda with lemon). Rachel's son, Hudson, was in Vermont with his grandma. It was the first time the four women were together without the immediate presence of their children.

Rachel quietly closed the sliding door with her elbow and her slippery black hair whipped behind her. "My answer to this question is more of a time period, and it is defined by my son's penis." She set four white plates on top of the table, next to a large pizza with tomatoes, pepper flakes, and basil on top.

"Don't tell me this, la la la la." Jodi raised her hands to her ears. She'd learned three days prior that she was pregnant with a little boy, whom she would later name Payne. Her thick red hair glowed as she reached over a large bug-repellent candle for the same slice of pizza as Alix. She retreated and said, "No, Alix, you go first." It was Jodi whom Alix had first met in the waiting room when Briar had her four-month check-up. Jodi had introduced her to Rachel and Tamra, and Alix could still feel Jodi's sweet concern and the gestures she made to make Alix feel at ease.

Rachel sat back with her arms at the sides of the patio chair. "In the grocery store, in the line for coffee . . . 'Mommy, a penis is private.' 'Mommy, you can't play tag with a penis.' 'Mommy, I have a penis and our dog has a penis and you lost yours so you need to be more careful.'"

"Oh *God*," Tamra said. "Why is he being all Freud on you?"

"Okay, so these guys already know my embarrassing moment," Jodi said, turning to Alix. "But Prudence went to a church camp with her cousins last summer and one of her counselors called me in because Prudence had carefully explained that her mommy took little boys and girls into a room and put them in front of a video camera."

"Oh no." Alix laughed.

"And the children that cried?" Jodi leaned forward. One of her green eyes went wide and the other closed. "Those were the bad ones, and they don't get to come back again."

Tamra chuckled through her nose. "I remember this."

Rachel shook her head. "I fucking love that kid."

"*And*"—Jodi held up a finger—"only the good boys and girls got to come back, and Mommy puts them on camera more, and when you're on camera you have to do exactly what Mommy says, even if you cry."

Alix said, "I'm guessing she wasn't invited back to camp."

"I had to go in and everything." Jodi pulled a chunk of crust off her pizza and took a bite. "I was pulling out my business card, I pulled up my website. I became this crazy person sitting in a kid's chair way too small for my ass, telling them that I'm not a pedophile and that I cast children in *feature films*."

Tamra looked to Alix. "What does Briar think you do for a living?"

Alix picked up her wine and said, "Briar is fairly certain that I work at the post office," to which Tamra replied, "Okay, that's not so off."

"Hudson thinks I buy books for a living, which is sometimes pretty accurate," Rachel said. "Jo, what does Pru think you do now?"

"I think I just covered this. Mommy is a pervert."

The women laughed into their wine and mozzarella.

Alix looked to Tamra. "And what do Imani and Cleo think you do?"

Tamra put down her glass. "Oh, they know I'm a principal."

"Ohhhh, how *odd*." Rachel sighed. "Tamra's perfect children are perfectly aware of their mother's perfect job." As she said this, Rachel clasped her hands together at the side of her head as if she were an animated princess. Alix realized that Rachel was quite tipsy, and she felt an affinity for her, this group, this moment. She loved hearing their voices and seeing them take large bites of their pizza, and how the sun took so long to go down in the summer.

Tamra smiled beneath the cluster of dark freckles that gathered underneath her eyes. When she shook her head, her long, neat dreadlocks shimmied behind her elbows. She was the only one eating her pizza with a fork and knife. "Imani would disagree with you on the perfect-job part," she said. "But my most embarrassing moment was in college for sure. I started my period in a lecture hall on my second day at Brown. And I was wearing *white shorts*." Tamra said this slowly, hitting the *t*'s hard with a tight bottom lip. "A very nice girl gave me her jacket to tie around my waist, but this was after a bunch of people had seen. I didn't drop the class," Tamra congratulated herself, "but I sat in the back row all semester, and asked other students to go up and turn my tests in for me."

"Good for you," Jodi said. "I would have deferred."

"Alix's turn," Rachel said. "You have to say yours, and it's gotta be better than periods, penises, and pedophiles."

Alix had a tomato slice in her mouth. She spread her fingers and waved them in front of her chest. "Uh-uh." She swallowed. "Mine is . . . not fun."

"Okay, is no one hearing me?" Jodi raised her right hand. "Ped-o-phile."

"She has a point," Rachel said.

"Okay, okay," Alix said. "Mine was in high school."

In the summer before her junior year, Alex Murphy's grandparents died, two days apart. They were written about in the local newspaper, and their joint funeral, held in a tiny chapel on a Thursday afternoon, was standing room only. In public, Alex's father properly mourned the loss of his parents, but in private, Alex's parents rejoiced over a surprise inheritance of what came close to nine hundred thousand dollars. Grandma and Grandpa Murphy had plots picked out in a cemetery, side by side, and not far from Grandma Murphy's parents, but before the burial, the funeral home made a massive mistake. Grandma and Grandpa Murphy were accidentally cremated. Alex and her family went through with the funeral and pretended there were bodies in the closed caskets in front of them.

Rachel gasped and Tamra said, "Oh *God*."

"Yeah, it was a huge deal," Alix said. "So my parents used their inheritance to get this big-time lawyer, they sued for a shit ton of money . . . they won. And then immediately went insane."

Mr. and Mrs. Murphy, who looked shockingly alike with light hair, skinny legs, and round, paunchy bellies, moved Alex and her little sister, Betheny, from Philadelphia to Allentown. They wanted land. "Like, *land* land," Alix explained, and they purchased a seven-bedroom house on a rolling green hill; what Alix now recognized as a textbook McMansion. There were four digits to punch to open the front gate and enter the long stretch of driveway. There was a balcony off the master bedroom where you could spot the flagpole of Alex and Betheny's new high school. And there was a double staircase framing a fireplace where Alex and her sister would never end up taking pictures before they left for prom or graduation. "From day to night, my whole life changed," Alix said. "My mom got her eyeliner tattooed. We had a movie theater in our house. I'd never been on a plane before, and suddenly we were flying first class to Fort Lauderdale."

The Murphys also purchased the services of Mrs. Claudette Laurens. Claudette was a light-skinned black woman with curly gray hair who kept the home clean, cooked weekly dinners, and watched game shows with the Murphy girls when they were home sick. It was Claudette who taught Alex how to make a cobbler, how to sew a button, and how to drive a stick shift. Claudette was the only person in the world to whom Alix still signed her letters as *Alex*, but instead of going into her deep affection for Claudette, Alix told her girlfriends about the pointless purchases her parents had no business buying (self-portraits done by real artists, loafers with real gold coins on the tops, guitars and pianos once owned by rock stars).

"Alix, I feel like I'm learning so much about you," Rachel said. "So much of this makes sense."

Jodi agreed. "Is this why you hate clutter so much?"

"Well, yeah." Alix rolled her eyes. "When your parents become crazy, trashy rich people who put rhinestones and monograms on everything and get six—*six!*—Pomeranians, you end up throwing a lot of stuff away. At the time I was like, 'This is awesome! I can buy all the CDs I want!' but they weren't even that rich. It was ridiculous." Just speaking about it, Alix could smell the inside of her parents' home, the one they'd since had to give up to custody of the state. Outside were SUVs with vanity license plates and cheetah-print steering wheel covers. Inside was an overly air-conditioned blast with cardboard boxes containing new purchases constantly piled next to the front door. It perpetually smelled empty, like a model home, the kind you find in a ranch-style housing development where the kitchen drawers are glued shut and the sinks have never been connected to water. The Pomeranians roamed the house and left poop everywhere that looked like piles of moldy grapes.

"So anyway," Alix said. "My senior year, I got my first real boyfriend."

Kelley Copeland grew three inches between his sophomore and junior years, and Alex Murphy noticed. At five-ten, Alex felt the number of guys she "could" date were limited, but Kelley would have been an excellent option regardless. He was just so nice and casually funny, and he did this thing where he held the door for people with his arm above their heads. You got to duck down cutely beneath his elbow, and he'd say things like, "I gotchyou," or "No sweat." Alex and Kelley both played volleyball at William Massey High, and she managed to sit next to him on a three-hour bus ride to a tournament in Poughkeepsie. At the time, Alex felt very radical and progressive for dating a junior, when she herself was a very mature senior. "I think we only dated for about four months," she said, but Alix knew exactly how long they dated. It was officially from New Year's Eve, 1999, to April 12, 2000. "But still, we said 'I love you' and I went to all of his games . . . all of that stuff you think means something when you're eighteen."

Rachel widened her eyes and said, "I love you, but I'm waiting for the embarrassment."

"Sorry, okay." Alix sighed and sat back; the bottom of her chair squeaked beneath her. "So I kind of wrote him letters every week . . ."

Rachel snorted and Jodi said, "Oh, Alix."

"I know, I know. Obviously now I'd be like, 'Hey Al, pump the brakes on the letters,' but it seemed like a really good idea at the time. Until Kelley decided to show one of my letters, the worst possible one, to the most popular kid in school." This kid's name was Robbie Cormier. Everyone knew Robbie, and even though he was a bit of a class clown, teachers enjoyed having him in class because he'd loudly make up raps and rhymes to help himself memorize the material. He was very short but insanely attractive for high school and was crowned king at the prom that Alix never went to.

Jodi said, "Uh-oh."

"Well, come on, now." Tamra placed her fork on her plate and dusted her hands away from the table. "I'm going to need the original transcription of that letter. Spill, girl."

"I sent Kelley a lot of letters . . ." Alix stared up into the patio umbrella and shook her head. She remembered the feeling of using her pinky nails to slide the folded letters through the slats of Kelley's locker, and the light sound they made inside when they landed. "But this letter," she said, "was the absolute worst."

Rachel gasped. "Was it a sext? A LetHer sext. LetHer send nudes."

From across the table, Jodi touched Alix's hand. "You write beautiful letters for a living, so don't feel bad."

The women leaned forward and waited for Alix to describe the only letter she'd ever regretted sending. "The letter he showed to this kid," she said, "had my address, driveway code, and a map to my house. I literally made him an invitation including where, when, *and to which song* I'd like him to take my virginity." The map included two sets of curly lines representing water; one was labeled *Jacuzzi* and the other was marked *Pool*. Alex also drew the massive keyhole-shaped driveway, the basketball court, an arrow to where the fire pit was, and a heart above her bedroom. There was a box at the bottom for him to check *Yes* or *No*.

Tamra said, "Oh lord," and Rachel said, "Eeeekkk."

"I wanted to have sex!" Alix talked with her hands and said this over Jodi saying, "Oh, honey." "My parents were going to be out of town for the weekend. We could never fool around at his place because he had a bunch of siblings . . . and I just liked him so much and wanted to know it would happen."

Tamra poured more wine into Alix's glass.

"So Kelley shows this note to Robbie," Alix continued, "and Robbie, who I'd never talked to in my life, comes up to me and says, 'I heard your parents will be out of town this weekend. We want to come party at your mansion.'" At the time, Alex could barely register that Robbie was speaking to her. Alex and Kelley weren't outcasts, but they weren't exactly high on the social chain. Alex knew this because it happened twice; when people found out that they were dating, they'd go, "Really?" and then, "Yeah, that makes sense."

So when she remembered Robbie asking if he could come to her *mansion*, Alix remembered saying no in a more polite way than she should have. At the time, she was much more disturbed about the idea of him seeing the rest of the letter. Alix marched straight to Kelley, who denied receiving the letter altogether.

"Why would I show one of your notes to Robbie?" Kelley kept saying. Alex confronted him at his car while wearing knee pads and a ponytail. "I swear I didn't get that one. But if Robbie wants to come over . . . that would be kind of awesome."

"Kelley!" Alex screamed. "That letter was like . . . the most important one!"

On top of having to explain the contents of the letter, Alex remembered being equally annoyed at Kelley's fondness of Robbie Cormier and the five other athletes he was always seen with. They were stars on and off the field, loud and funny and cute. They were overly friendly with the high school custodians and they showily high-fived them when they passed in the halls. When any member of this group showed Kelley an ounce of attention, Kelley's neck went red as he tried to act both interesting and normal. It wasn't hard to picture Kelley showing Alex's note to Robbie in passing. Kelley thought he was "awesome" and their lockers were stacked near a frequently used water fountain.

But Alex wasn't about to have a party when her plan was to lose her virginity. She didn't know these people, Claudette would be spending the weekend at the house with Alex and Betheny, and she wasn't going to college as a virgin. It didn't take much for Kelley to win her back over. "Hey, maybe you dropped the note or something." He said this with his forearms on her shoulders. "But it's fine because you told him no. He's not just gonna come over. But . . . am I still invited?"

That weekend, with the Counting Crows playing inside her bedroom, and Claudette and her sister downstairs in the movie room,

Alex and Kelley had sex for the first time. It was exactly a week till prom. Alex felt very in love and less like a cliché. When they finished they spooned on her bed and watched reruns of *The Real World Seattle*.

It was around 10:30 p.m.—three episodes later—when Robbie Cormier and eight other students showed up. The security cameras later showed Robbie at the front gate, punching in the code to her driveway, which—as if Alex needed any more proof—confirmed that Kelley had in fact shown Robbie her note.

"You are lying," Jodi said. "What bad kids!"

"So suddenly all the coolest kids in school are at my house," Alix said. "And they're knocking on our windows and blasting music and demanding that we turn on the hot tub jets. As you can assume, most of them were wasted."

"I was bad in high school," Rachel said, "but I was never *that* bad."

"Sometimes," Tamra said, "I think about sending the girls to public school? And then I hear things like this and I'm like, no way."

Alix disagreed with this sentiment, but she went on and said, "It was a disaster." She remembered rushing to the window at the sound of a boom box turning on. Robbie was leading group jumps into her pool to the sound of "The Real Slim Shady" while another student pretended to hump an inflatable crocodile. From upstairs in her bedroom, Alex looked from her backyard to Kelley. "What am I supposed to do?"

Kelley slipped his shirt back over his head. "Alex, wait," he said. "Maybe . . . I mean . . . your parents *are* out of town."

Alex pushed the curtains back over her window and felt her mouth drop all the way open. Two hours ago, he was telling her he loved her, and asking if they should get a towel. But now Kelley proceeded to walk around her bed to locate his socks and shoes. Alex watched him assess the opportunity being presented to him downstairs: the chance to befriend the most popular athletes in school because he happened to be in the right place at the right time. She suddenly felt embarrassed; it was supposed to be *their* night. She crossed her arms and asked, "Are you kidding me?"

Betheny didn't knock. She opened Alex's door and said, "Alex, what is happening?" Claudette was behind her, a dish towel thrown over her shoulder. With a hand on the wall she said, "Should I call the police?"

Kelley began to lace up his shoes.

This was possibly the most authority Alex had ever held, all while her crotch still ached from her first time. It was the sight of her little sister, the wet towel on Claudette's shoulder, and the expectant energy of Kelley's silent social climbing that made Alex nod and say, "Yes, call the police."

"Whoa whoa whoa." Kelley stood up. "Alex, come on."

Betheny followed Claudette downstairs and Alex reached for her sweatshirt off the bed. "This isn't cool," she told him.

"Alex, wait wait wait." Kelley followed her downstairs, and Alex swore she saw him carefully look for windows, just in case anyone from outside could see him, so he would be prepared to duck. "This doesn't have to be a big deal. Robbie's cool. Just let them hang out."

"You don't even know them!" By this she meant, *They don't know you for a reason.*

Kelley, understanding the implication, replied, "I know them way better than you."

Someone outside yelled to turn up the music. Alex walked into the kitchen, where Claudette was hanging up the phone. "They're on their way," she said. Alex said, "Good." Kelley said, "Really, Alex?" He grabbed his backpack from the kitchen table and walked out the side door.

It wasn't like Alex would have pressed charges; she just wanted them to leave. Her parents would have been furious with her if they found out she'd had a party; they'd probably ground her for the weekend of prom. And the driveway was definitely long enough for the group to see the warning lights and flee. But when the police arrived, not everyone made it out of the backyard in time. After screams of, "Oh shit!" and "Five oh, five oh!" Robbie's friends hopped a fence and ran across the hills to safety. Robbie, however, had been in the middle of climbing a ladder that leaned against the Murphy house when the police were approaching. His plan had been to jump from the balcony into the pool. The police arrived and pointed their flashlights at him, and Alex heard one of them say, "Come down from there, son." On top of trespassing, Robbie Cormier was taken in drunk off PBRs and with a tiny bag of cocaine in a zipped cargo pants pocket. The combination of a popular black student athlete arrested on property that had plantation columns standing out front did not pan out well for Alex Murphy.

"It was like, 'Oh, the Murphy girl has this huge house and she doesn't even want to share it? What a bitch,'" Alix explained. "And any time my sister and I would dare venture outside, we'd be tormented. 'There's Princess Murphy.' 'Watch out, rich girl Murphy will have you arrested.' 'Robbie got his scholarship taken away 'cause you got him arrested, so good job.'" This wasn't the worst of it. That summer, Alex and her sister were referred to in public and private as *new money trash*. When she picked up her sister from an IHOP parking lot, a classmate asked if she was going swimming in the plantation pool. And once, Robbie Cormier bumped into her at a Jamba Juice. He greeted her with, "Good mornin', Massa Murphy."

"People would bow down and open doors for me like I was royalty," Alix said. "*Everyone* knew. And that is what capped off my senior year."

Somehow, even worse, that night at the Murphy house accomplished everything Kelley had evidently hoped it would. Alex learned that Kelley had left her house only to run into Robbie's fleeing friends on the street. He drove them to the precinct, where they waited all night until Robbie was released. Kelley was the one to drive Robbie home.

Kelley broke up with Alex on the following Monday, just after first period and five days before prom. It happened in between his homeroom door and the frequently used water fountain, which was used by three different students during his speech. He began the conversation by saying, "Hey, don't be mad . . . but I think I'm gonna go to prom with Robbie's cousin Sasha." Alex hadn't been sure how they'd make up—he hadn't returned her phone calls all weekend—but she hadn't seen this coming. Yes, things got extremely messed up that night, and maybe she'd made a mistake, but hadn't they just had sex? It seemed as if Kelley was saying another girl's name to make it appear as if he were choosing another girl, when he was clearly leaving Alex for Robbie. Alex had no idea what her classmates had in store for her (spitting on her car, calling her a Nazi), but Kelley's way of ending their relationship, by informing her of his updated prom plans, stung in the way only a first heartbreak can. Alex felt similarly to when she'd learned that her grandfather died, confusing sadness and the instinct to clarify, *Wait . . . you mean, we're not gonna hang out anymore?*

"I never meant for Robbie to get in trouble," she said to Kelley. She tried to say more before her voice began to crack. She managed to get out, "I just . . . wanted them to leave."

"I know. I'm sorry."

"Can we talk about this after school?" she asked. She knew she couldn't erase Robbie's record, but maybe she could think of something to say by then.

"I just . . ." Kelley sighed. "I think it would be best . . . if we went our separate ways? And that those paths never again . . . connected."

Tamra leaned into the table. "He said what?"

"That was the line he used, I swear to God," Alix said.

Jodi was sincere when she asked, "Was he a little bit off?"

Rachel rolled her eyes. "Sounds like *you're* better off."

Alix took a long pull of her wine and threw another slice of pizza on her plate. Tamra said, "Ooh, Alix, I'd have to kill that boy."

"I didn't think you could beat me," Jodi told her, "but you absolutely did."

Alix sat in front of Jodi, Rachel, and Tamra, trying not to be at 100 Bordeaux Lane, Allentown, Pennsylvania, 18102. She could still hear Robbie and his friends outside her back window, hooting and running away from police. Alex's sister had cried on the floor ("At least you get to graduate. I have to stay here and live with everyone knowing!") while Alex watched Robbie get handcuffed in her backyard. Claudette stared out the window next to her, whispering, "Devils," to herself and to them.

The last time she'd seen Kelley Copeland was at a Sunoco gas station the day before graduation. When he got out of his car, Alex theatrically removed the nozzle and sealed up the gas door, even though her tank wasn't even half full. "Alex, come on," he said. Alex saw that he was wearing Fila flip-flops and white tube socks, exactly like Robbie wore after his games. "I broke up with you," he said. "But that's it. And I'm sorry, but . . . you know? That's all I did."

By this point, Kelley was a key member of Robbie Cormier's clique, and Alex had been officially exiled from all high school activities. While Kelley sat at an elite lunch table and began dating a light-skinned black girl with braids, Alex ate her lunch alone in an empty art room, and she left last period five minutes early so she could get to her car without being harassed. Alex had been dreaming of a moment like this, where Kelley paid attention to her once again and they could try to talk it out. But she read his shitty concession as a move of self-fulfilling pity, and she couldn't keep her cool.

"That's *all you did to me*? No one forced you to go and share a private fucking letter! This was just as much your fault as it was mine, but *I'm* the one getting punished for it. I had to protect my sister and Claudette. What was I supposed to do?"

Kelley seemed genuinely confused as he said, "You had to protect your sister from *Robbie*?" Alex got into her car and drove off. She'd wasted six dollars of prepaid gas, which despite everything that had happened with her family still seemed like a large amount of money.

"I was supposed to go to Penn State," Alix said. "But I'd gotten into NYU and I begged my parents to let me attend. I took out loans to go, which"—Alix held up a finger—"my parents refused to pay for with their *millions* of dollars because they said it was stupid to pay that much for college when I could go in-state. But I was like, 'Nope, I'm going.' And I just waitressed all summer and moved." When Alix thought of her eighteen-year-old self, and feeling as though she were signing her life away by taking out tens of thousands of dollars in student debt, she wished she could go back in time. She'd tell herself that it would be okay, that she'd meet the best guy at a bar at the age of twenty-five, that he'd have a huge heart and a surprisingly large penis, and that before they got married Peter would pay off all her loans as if they were his, and as if it were nothing. He wouldn't judge her for the lack of grief she felt when her parents passed away, two months apart. He'd understand that for her, it felt more like relief.

"Well, technically," Rachel said, "we would have never met you if you hadn't become a Pennsylvania pariah."

Alix exhaled and whistled as if she'd barely caught her flight after running to the gate. "Pennsylvania is fine. But I will *never* go back to Allentown again."

From inside the partially cracked sliding glass door, Alix heard the familiar raspy voice of her only child saying, "Mama?"

Jodi sang, "Uh-ohh."

Alix stood. "Someone could tell I was having too much fun," she said.

Nine

On Friday morning, October 30, Spoons Chamberlain passed away peacefully at home, surrounded by his family, who had no idea. Alix discovered the floating body at 11:34 a.m. and softly whispered, "Shit." Briar was finishing a lunch of chicken and pears, and Catherine bounced in a Jumperoo in the corner. Alix placed a plant in front of the bowl and reached for her phone.

Briar's fish just died, she texted. Can I ask Emira to pick up another one?

JODI: Yes.

TAMRA: Yes.

RACHEL: One time Arnetta picked up a Plan B for me.

"You all done?" Alix asked Briar, who nodded with her mouth still full, and Alix set her on the floor.

"Mama?" Briar ambled over to Catherine. She swiped her sister's blond hair across her forehead, and Catherine beamed. "How does feathers get wet?"

"Umm, in the rain?" Alix said. "Or when birds take a bath? Let's be gentle with baby sis."

"But how—because . . . the feathers is . . . how the feathers get wet and fly away?"

"Bri, look." Alix picked up a pink ball from a bin of toys and tossed it down the hall. Briar gasped, overjoyed, and dutifully pumped her arms as she went running after it.

So it's not weird if I call her and ask her to grab it on her way over?

JODI: You are so funny, Alix. Not at all. She's on the clock.

TAMRA: Exactly. One time I had Shelby pretend to be me so I wouldn't have to talk to a salesman.

Alix texted: Was she mad about it?

Not at all, Tamra replied. She was very excited to do a British accent.

One time, Rachel texted, I had Arnetta tell this creep that I died.

Emira answered on the first ring. When Alix whispered that Briar's fish had died, Emira laughed and said, "Spoons?"

"I'm so sorry to ask, but can you pick one up before you come here today? I can text you a picture of it in case you forgot."

After a moment, Emira said, "A picture of a dead fish?"

"That's not weird, is it?" Alix bent to retrieve the pink and squishy ball Briar had returned to her. "There it goes!" she whispered to Briar, and she tossed it toward the girls' bedroom. "If it's a pet store I'm sure they've seen a lot worse."

"So . . . today is the Halloween party at Briar's ballet class? And if I go to the pet store I'll be too late to take her."

Alix placed a hand to her forehead and once again said, "Shit."

"I mean, you could take her. I could just meet you guys there and we can switch."

"I would but I can't," Alix said. "I have Laney Thacker coming over here at six and I need to grab some things."

"Who?"

"Peter's co-anchor."

"The one you don't really like?"

Had Alix said that? She'd said it to Rachel, Jodi, and Tamra many times (Jodi had replied that Thacker was not a real name, and in response to the Internet photo Alix had sent of Laney, Tamra had said, No way, and Rachel had said, That woman is not real. But had Alix revealed how she felt about Peter's co-anchor to Emira? Well, yes. In so many words. The day that Alix finished the thank-you cards to Briar's birthday party attendees, she'd licked the last envelope and said, "That was painful."

Emira had said, "I hate writing thank-you notes."

"I'm usually good at it, but most of those gifts were insane." Alix slipped the letters into her purse. "And I can't say, 'Thank you, Laney, for the toddler glitter and lipstick set, and insinuating to my daughter that her looks matter more than her mind.'"

Emira had laughed politely.

Slighting Laney had been the by-product, not the intention, of pointing out to Emira that these were not the items Alix wanted around her daughter. Emira *was* partially raising Briar. These gifts were a perfect moment to emphasize how Peter and Alix wanted Briar to think for herself, rather than think *of* herself. But adding Laney to the equation had been a mistake that wasn't apparent until now, with Spoons's dead body floating in the bowl. Laney Thacker discernibly wanted a friendship with Alix, and unlike Rachel, Jodi, and Tamra, Emira had witnessed this genuine longing in person. Laney checked in with Alix's face before she laughed or responded in group conversation. She'd sent a housewarming gift during Alix's first week in Philadelphia, including two pairs of what—she wrote in a gorgeous card—she hoped would become Alix's "good scissors." Gossiping about Laney was no longer dirty and fun. It felt like smacking a kitten in the face.

"Sorry, what?" Alix stalled. "Oh, Laney's fine. But does that sound okay?"

"Okay, so . . ." Emira said, "I'll go and pick up a fish, and then I'll come over, and Briar will miss the Halloween party at ballet?"

"Yes," Alix decided. She began to think out loud. "I'd rather that than have her asking questions about it all night long. And you know what? She doesn't have her costume on and she won't remember at all. She's going trick-or-treating tomorrow so she'll have more than enough Halloween."

Alix wasn't certain, but above the street noises on Emira's end of the line, she thought she heard Emira laugh, but not as if she'd heard a joke. "Of course I'll pay you for the fish," Alix said.

"Oh, no. It was like, forty cents. It's cool. I'll see you . . . whenever I get there."

"Okay, great. Thank you."

"Mm-hmm."

"And you'll get to leave at six today!"

"Oh, okay."

"But of course we'll pay you like it's seven."

"K."

"Okay, great. Thanks, Emira." Alix cringed and hung up the phone.

A text message from Laney was waiting on her phone. Is it okay if

Ramona and Suzanne swing by with me tonight? They have girls too and they're completely lovely. Feel free to tell me no if you just want one-on-one time!

Alix rubbed the back of her neck and thought, *Jesus fucking Christ.* With both hands she texted, The more the merrier!

Emira arrived at twelve thirty. When Alix met her downstairs, she didn't mean to, but she did a goofy *Did you get it?* face that she immediately regretted. With zero secrecy and without a word, Emira handed her a plastic bag with a goldfish swimming inside. Alix didn't know where Emira first purchased the fish, but she assumed it was one of those places with an overcrowded tank; hundreds of bulging bodies swimming frantically inside. Maybe they hadn't let her be choosy, because this fish both was smaller than the original Spoons and had black dots on its tail, but Alix still said, "Great," and exhaled, "Thank you." She wrapped it into the side of her sweater and headed upstairs to make the switch.

Whenever Alix was afraid that Emira was mad at her, she came back to the same line of thought: *Oh God, did she finally see what Peter said on the news? No, she couldn't have. She's always like this, right?* Emira came upstairs as Alix finished washing her hands. She said nothing when Catherine saw her and squealed, and she only smiled when Briar pointed and announced to the room, "Mira likes pants." Alix dried her hands and gently cracked her big toe on the tile floor. Was Emira really *that* mad over the fish? Had this been an embarrassing task? If anything, wasn't Alix giving Emira a little break? Alix had been to Briar's ballet class before. It was boring and tedious and the other mothers were hypersupportive in an uncomfortable way, seeing great promise in their three-year-olds as future ballerinas whereas Briar's doctor had recommended enrollment merely for balance and listening skills. Only a week had passed since Emira stayed late to have a drink with Alix, but their silent and secret agreement—that they'd had a nice time talking together, that they didn't always have to discuss the children, that they could possibly be friends—had lapsed back into a formal toleration. Emira sat on the floor next to Briar and adjusted the collar on the LetHer Speak polo.

Alix retrieved Catherine and strapped her into the Babybjörn. With a few clicks on the computer in the kitchen, the one Briar watched fish and pandas on, she found a Halloween-themed dog parade in a park nearby and wrote down the address and time for Emira. "I think this will be a fun thing for you guys. If it isn't, it's obviously your call. Have fun, Bri. You might see some doggies today."

Briar looked up from inspecting Emira's earring. "Doggies in my house?"

"No, honey. At the park. I love you."

"Is there doggies in the house?"

"No, Bri."

"Did their mamas get lost?"

"I love you, have fun!" Alix trotted down the stairs.

At the front door, Alix sealed herself into the front vestibule, one hand around Catherine's bootied foot and the other on the strap of her purse. As always, in the charger was Emira's blinking phone.

KENAN&KEL: Good luck at your Halloween ballet recital/pageant/ performance. I know how much you and (what's the kid's name?) have trained for this moment. Leave it all on the stage. Break a leg. Merde.

When Alix reached for the front door, something sparkled from Emira's purse, hung on the vestibule wall. Inside the front flap was a black headband with glittery cat ears. The price tag was still attached and read *$6.99*.

Peter texted to make sure this date with Laney was still happening. Alix had rescheduled twice so far, and this night was to prove that she had honestly just been very busy, that she supported her husband and his career, and that sure, Laney wasn't that bad. Alix purchased flowers, Halloween coloring books, sparkling water, bread, nuts, and cheeses. While Catherine slept in the bassinet she kept next to her bed, Alix rearranged the girls' room and set up her iPad in front of a row of sleeping bags and pillows. Alix considered calling Emira while she was at the park with Briar, speaking to her while Catherine napped, or peeking her head in as Emira gave Briar a very early bath. But the idea of possibly turning the second floor of her home into an even more awkward place seemed more terrifying than trying to fix the situation.

And at 6 p.m., when Laney, Suzanne, and Ramona arrived (Laney with her four-year-old, Bella, and Suzanne with her yoga mat), Alix was reassured that she had done the right thing. If she could go back, she'd still go to lengths to replace the fish, rather than telling Briar the truth. After canceling on Laney so many times, Alix felt the need to give her an extra pleasant evening, without the presence of a grieving, hyperinquisitive toddler.

When Briar was two, after learning that she'd bruised her vagina while riding a tricycle, Briar explained her diagnosis to every individual present at the playground, a sales associate at J.Crew, and three students in a mommy-and-me art class. Briar did the same thing when she learned the words *earwax*, *handicapped*, *pink eye*, and *Chinese*. On top of her daughter's unfiltered gregariousness was the general preciousness of Bella Thacker. Bella's cheeks were naturally blushed and her brown hair—there was an anomalous amount of it—hung down sweetly and curled at her shoulders (whenever Alix saw Bella and her thick mane, she couldn't help but think of the Orthodox women in New York who shopped in groups at Bloomingdale's and carried black strollers onto the subway). As Alix bent to thank Bella for coming over, Bella bowed her head and said, "Yes, ma'am." She wore a striped set of pajamas with a pressed collar at the neck.

Emira and Briar came down the stairs, hand in hand, as Suzanne told Alix how lovely her home was. Laney nodded and said, "Isn't it perfect?"

Bella said loudly, "Hi, Briar." She stepped forward to give Briar a theatrical embrace.

"Briar has been looking forward to this all day," Alix said. "Bri, do you want to show Bella your room?"

In purple leggings and a white T-shirt with a New York City taxi on the front (Emira couldn't have put her in cuter jammies?), Briar stepped back from Bella and revealed her two front teeth in confusion. She looked up at Alix with a face that said, *Do I know this person?* then looked back at Emira with, *Do I really have to do this?*

"They haven't been upstairs yet, Bri," Emira said. "You gotta show 'em around."

Bella was the first to hit the stairs and Briar followed. Laney, Ramona, and Suzanne said hello to Emira (Laney added how it was nice to see her again) as they followed the children up to the kitchen. Alix put her hand on the railing and called, "I'll be up in just a minute."

Emira placed her phone in her jacket pocket. There had been no text messages on it when Alix returned. Just a song called "Shawty Is Da Shit." Emira took her bag off the wall, removed her white LetHer Speak polo, and hung it where her bag had been.

"I can take that." Alix reached for it. "I'm washing everything this weekend. But Emira . . ." she said, "I feel bad about you and Bri missing ballet today."

There was a chance that this wasn't the thing bothering Emira at all. She had a life and family and friends of her own. But Alix told herself that she would never regret covering her bases with Emira. She'd never be sorry for apologizing.

Emira shook her head and made a face that implied she'd almost forgotten. "Oh, it's cool. You were right. She didn't remember."

Alix reached up to her head and adjusted her blond bun. "Just to be clear . . . I want you and Briar to do fun things together. And I definitely know how tedious children's things can be, so if you ever want to mix things up, just let me know. If there's a movie or a carnival or whatever it is . . . say the word and I'll leave money for you guys to change it up."

Emira placed her fingertips against the wall and held her balance as she stepped into her shoes. "Okay. That sounds good."

Upstairs, after a pop of champagne, Suzanne said, "Oof! I hate doing that." Laney was telling her daughter, "I don't know, sweetheart, we'll have to ask Mrs. Chamberlain when she comes back up," and Briar was explaining to Ramona that her fish had chicken pox on its tail. Alix glanced toward the purses and jackets left on the hooks, the ones belonging to her guests. Behind a camel-colored Coach purse was a velour black jacket. In cursive white and pink letters on the back was written, *Plank Now, Wine Later.* There was something about this sentiment, and the pink rhinestone letters it came in, that made Alix realize that Bella Thacker and Emira were the only people to call her Mrs. Chamberlain, despite the permission she'd given them to do otherwise.

"Are you doing anything fun tonight?" she asked Emira.

"Just like"—Emira released her hair from the inside of her leather jacket—"hanging out at my friend Shaunie's."

For a moment, Alix felt betrayed by Emira's cell phone. These were the first plans Emira had in the last month that Alix hadn't known about before she pretended that she didn't. She watched Emira's black, chipped nails feel for the doorknob.

"I'm sure Zara's included."

"Yep. She is."

"Tell her I said hi."

"Okay, I will." Emira stood still. The two women stared at each other in the tiny atrium, until Emira pointed at the envelope in Alix's back pocket. "Is that for me?"

"Oh God, yes. I'm sorry." Alix reached for it as she shook her head. "Been a long week."

Emira accepted the envelope and stuffed it deep into her bag. "That's cool. Okay. See you."

As she stepped onto the stoop stairs, Emira waved four fingers. Alix couldn't bring herself to shut the door behind her. Upstairs, someone said, "It's wine o'clock!" and someone else said, "Ladies' night!" Alix looked at the back of Emira's head, her fingers securing her earbuds in place, and she thought to herself, *Mira, please don't leave me.*

Ten

Between Emira's fourth and fifth knock, Shaunie's apartment door flung open and Emira jumped back. With her hands in fists at her collarbones, Shaunie hopped in place and screamed, "I got it I got it I got it!"

Shaunie's hair bounced and coiled around her face and across her open mouth. From the couch, Zara raised both of her hands and cheered, "Shau-nie, Shau-nie . . ." In a gray sweatshirt that read *BU* on the front, Josefa looked up from the grilled cheese she was making and said, "Heeyyy."

Emira stepped inside. "Hold up . . . you got what?"

"You are looking at . . ." Shaunie stepped into the living room as Emira set her purse on the kitchen counter. "The newest associate marketing specialist at Sony Philadelphia."

Emira blinked. "No waayy."

"Mira, I get my own office." Shaunie gripped onto the back of her neck, seemingly keeping her body from floating off the floor. She was still in work clothes—a gray pencil skirt and a baby blue button-down—the kind of clothing that Emira had once thought she'd definitely wear in adulthood. "It's 52K a year," Shaunie said, "and I get my own *fucking* office. Well, I share it with this other girl, but *still*!"

"Oh shit." Emira tried to make her face go into something that hopefully resembled joy. "That's amazing." Shaunie didn't notice her struggle. She was beginning to dance against the side of the couch.

"Go, Shaunie. It's your birthday." In dark blue scrubs, Zara started singing about Shaunie's new achievements. Shaunie dipped with her hands on her knees, and echoed each new triumph with, "Ayyeee."

"She got a new job."

"Ayyeee."

"She got an office."

"Ayyeee."

"401(k)."

"Ayyeee."

"Fuck it up, girl."

"Ayyeee."

From the kitchen, Josefa asked, "Emira, you want something to drink?"

Emira watched Shaunie dip it even lower as Zara clapped double time. "I'll literally take any alcohol you have," she said.

Shaunie's two-bedroom apartment had a kitchen with an exposed brick wall and a fire escape outside the window. Josefa lived there too, but Josefa never objected to anyone referring to the space as "Shaunie's." It was filled with Shaunie's things, and co-signed by Shaunie's dad. Emira recognized the dormy-twenty-something-isms about the space—the mess of cords leaking out from the TV stand, the IKEA best-seller couch, too many recent pictures fighting for space on the refrigerator—but Shaunie's place maintained an air of adulthood, and now her employment did too. Apparently, the management at Sony called Shaunie in at the end of the day. They told her how pleased they were with her performance, asked if she was happy working there, and then they offered her the promotion. On the seventh floor of a high-rise in South Philly, Shaunie toasted her bosses with sparkling cider in plastic cups as she did what she claimed was an ugly cry. And that was when she became the last of Emira's friends to no longer be listed on their parents' health insurance.

Emira accepted a glass of wine from Josefa. Across a cutting board, Josefa pressed a knife into her sandwich and ate a leaf of basil that slipped out the bottom. The plan for the evening had been to watch Netflix, drink wine, and maybe order Thai from the place down the street, so Emira was a bit confused by Josefa's meal. She also needed a few more minutes to accept this new information. Fifty-two *thousand* dollars a year?

"So what are we watching tonight?"

"What?" Without looking up, Josefa put the sandwich halves on a plate and licked crumbs off her finger. "Girl, we goin' out," she said. "You want a bite of this?"

"No, I'm fine. Since when are we going out?"

"Shaunie's 'bout to make it rain over here." Josefa pointed over her shoulder. At that moment, Zara collected the plastic fall leaves Shaunie had sprinkled to decorate the coffee table, and she threw them at Shaunie as she danced. Zara sang, "Make it clap, girl," and slipped one leaf in between Shaunie's waistband and her twerking behind. "If you need clothes," Josefa said, "you can just borrow mine."

"Man, okay." Emira pulled her hair over one shoulder. "I don't know. I'm kinda beat, though." This wasn't a lie, but the first of the month was also stupidly close. In two days, Emira would pay her rent and watch the entire contents of her white envelope disappear.

"Say what?" Josefa topped her own wineglass off. "I thought you only babysat on Fridays."

Emira held her glass with both hands. Josefa would never say something like this to Shaunie. She'd never say, *Zara, I thought you only nursed today.* For someone who was paid to go to school, Josefa had a strict opinion on what constituted a proper workday. But Emira wasn't about to defend a job she kind of wished she never had. "Yeah, but we just like . . . did a lot," she said.

"Well, I had a huge exam today, and I think I killed it." Josefa did a sign of the cross before she lifted her plate. "So I'm about to get real stupid."

Emira said, "Right," and "Good for you," but she didn't follow Josefa into her bedroom.

More than Emira hated the idea of going out, she hated the idea of Zara going without her. She knew this was a stretch, but if Emira wasn't there, Zara could possibly realize that Emira wasn't her closest friend, but rather the reason why the four women didn't do more things, like take tropical trips on summer Fridays or utilize gel manicure discount days or try exercise classes like stiletto workouts. Emira wished she also wore school sweatshirts (or scrubs, or button-downs that she considered "work clothes") that would give her periodic reasons to celebrate, or a valid excuse to say no and stay in.

Emira walked back into the living room and carried Shaunie's varsity jacket over her arm. She picked a piece of lint off the sleeve and said, "Hey, don't let me forget to give this back to you."

"Oh shoot, I almost forgot about that." Shaunie scrunched up her face cutely and tossed the jacket into her bedroom. With her other hand, she held her phone to her ear. "Or you can wear it again. Drinks on me tonight. I gotta work on getting Troy to come through, but Mira, just go through my closet. Take anything you want." Inside

Shaunie's bedroom, Zara plugged her phone into the speakers and Young Thug began to play. "Babe," Shaunie shouted over the first verse and into her phone. "Babe, guess what. You're coming out with us tonight."

Zara started to dig through Shaunie's closet, and in the next room over, Josefa began to paw through her own. Emira stepped into the adjacent bathroom and closed the door behind her.

Above the sink, Emira wondered if there was an appropriate amount of support and enthusiasm you needed to have for a friend, because if there was, then Shaunie was hitting her retainer. Every week it was something. Wasn't it so great that Shaunie got this internship? Wasn't Shaunie's new boyfriend so cute? Wasn't it so nice that we got free drinks from that old guy who loved Shaunie's smile?

And most importantly, why did Mrs. Chamberlain have to lie to Briar as if she couldn't fucking handle the truth?

At the back of Emira's calves, on the fabric of her leggings, were leftover white pieces of fur from a dog that leaned up against her at the park that afternoon. There were dogs dressed like celebrities and vegetables, and puppies fighting to get hats and capes off their shoulders. Briar kept pointing and screaming that there were in fact even more dogs, and that the dogs she'd seen before were still there, but every so often, she looked up at Emira as if she'd come into a room and already forgotten what she needed.

Emira couldn't tell if her annoyance with Mrs. Chamberlain came from the ingrained Tucker standard within her (*You start something, you finish it*), or if it was mostly to do with missing out on dressing up with Briar. Or maybe it had more to do with the fact that Emira had witnessed Mrs. Chamberlain being an outstanding mother, and was realizing that when she wasn't being one, it was by choice rather than default.

Emira once spotted Mrs. Chamberlain with Briar and Catherine at the post office on a Tuesday morning. She didn't say hi, but she watched Mrs. Chamberlain sing with Briar as she carefully placed Catherine into a complicated wrap. Briar was distracted and over-stimulated by the post office lights and boxes and people. But Mrs. Chamberlain kept her nearby with precious prompts to "stay here, big sis," to show Catherine how the wheels on the bus go round and round, to try and jump as high as she could. Mrs. Chamberlain did this all in gorgeous, expensive-looking jeans.

What bothered Emira was knowing that Mrs. Chamberlain had that mommy it-factor. Mrs. Chamberlain could tell when Catherine was about to cry. She gave Briar goldfish in a cup, never on a plate. She could be genuinely congratulatory when Briar successfully pressed the button on the stroller's seat belt, or when Catherine almost waved buh-bye. But only in the moments when she truly felt like it. As Catherine got bigger and cuter, and still very thoughtfully quiet, Emira noticed that these moments came further and further apart.

And another thing? Emira considered this as she pulled her pants down and sat on the toilet. Laney Thacker was actually super fucking nice. She'd offered to help Emira twice at the birthday party, and she'd tucked in Emira's tag at the back of her polo. And sure, she was extremely dorky and had a weird laugh and her makeup was a shade too dark, but coincidentally, not telling your child the truth about a first pet, just because you have people coming over, seemed like a very Laney Thacker thing to do.

Someone knocked on the door and Emira said, "I'm peeing."

From outside Zara said, "K," but she still let herself inside. Zara closed the door and leaned a hip on the sink. "I thought you'd be hanging from the shower rod."

This was Emira's favorite version of Zara. Long twists on her shoulders. Navy scrubs. Orange socks with white grips on the bottom. On a Friday, Zara looked like home. In addition to her annoyance with her employer and the fact that she'd bought stupid cat ears at Walgreens for nothing, Emira felt what she knew was a childish reaction to having to share her best friend.

Zara had two sisters, one of whom struggled with anorexia, and the other with depression, two conditions that Emira's mother believed black people didn't "get." On top of Zara's energy and humor and wit, Emira treasured her unfailing and nonjudgmental patience for her family, her patients, and Emira herself. Despite the fact that she'd known since she was little that nursing was her passion, Zara never discredited Emira, or the fact that Emira had no idea what she wanted to do with her life. Instead, Zara often covered Emira's coat check fees, which, for some reason, greatly annoyed Josefa. Zara randomly and privately Venmo'd Emira to cover a well drink or cover charge, and when Emira didn't feel well, Zara listened to her symptoms over the phone or via texts (she'd either respond with detailed advice or say that it was probably gas). Emira never doubted Zara's loyalty to her, but Shaunie and Josefa could offer Zara friendship *and* first rounds, when Emira often ordered appetizers as her meal.

Emira slumped as she listened to herself pee. "I'm sorry. I just had a shitty day."

"What happened?"

Emira placed her elbows onto her knees. What was she supposed to say? *The little girl I spend twenty-one hours a week with is definitely starting to get it. Every day I watch her grip tighter and tighter onto the feeling of being ignored by the person she loves the most. And she's this awesome, serious child who loves information and answers, and how could her own mother not appreciate the shit out of this? And in the bottom of all of my purses are all these old bags of tea. And sometimes when I grab my wallet some Earl Grey or Jasmine will fall out on the counter, which makes me feel like I need to leave this job, and that there's no way I ever could.* In moments like this, Emira also felt that if she wasn't careful—that if she brought Zara's mood down with trivial things like goldfish and tea—that Zara's patience would possibly run out. "No, it's dumb," Emira said. "I'll tell you later."

"Okay." Zara leaned forward at the waist and whispered, "But you need to check yourself and be happy for Shaunie."

Emira closed her eyes. "She is so extra right now."

"That girl is always so extra."

Emira opened her right eye to watch Zara's reaction. "I also kind of hate Troy." Whenever Shaunie's boyfriend came out, which was not often and took lots of coaxing and bribing, he claimed seats in clubs and bars where he could easily see the television. Whenever Emira talked to him, his eyes were half on her and half on a basketball game. He answered any and all comments with, "That's tight, that's tight."

"Girl, everybody hates Troy," Zara whispered. "You are not special, okay?"

Emira blew out through her lips. "I think . . ." she said, "I think I need a new job."

"Umm . . . fucking duh, bitch." Zara laughed. "You're mad depressed whenever you get done. But you need to either get a new one or keep the one you got because we are still going to Mexico for my birthday next year. I wanna go all out." Zara clapped once after *all*, and again after *out*.

As she was saying this, Emira was folding toilet paper in her hands. "I know, I know," she said. But unlike Josefa, Shaunie, and Zara, Emira didn't have vacation days or spring break. When she didn't work, she didn't get paid. Not only would her hourly paycheck be going toward hotels and Ubers (instead of her rent and SEPTA card), but she'd also be losing money every day she was gone, and Zara made her promise five days.

"Let's do this, then," Zara said. "Let me know when and we'll sit in front of the TV and fill out some job applications."

Emira pursed her lips. "Oh right, like tonight?"

"Girl, shush." Zara took her voice down again to say, "You need to buck up and be happy for Shaunie."

"Okay, okay." She stood and flushed.

As Emira washed her hands in the sink, the scent of Shaunie's soap, the organic kind she got at a weekend farmer's market, filtered up to Emira's face. Behind her, Zara pulled out her phone and leaned her hip against Emira's, which Emira had come to know as a very Zara way of making sure she hadn't been too hard on her, and that it came from a good place.

"See, this is why you need Instagram," Zara said. "You get to be nice to people and you don't even have to see them. Watch me . . ." Zara tilted the screen for Emira to see. In a monotone whisper, she quoted the words and symbols that she began to type. "'OMG Shaunie. Slay bitch. Exclamation point, star emoji, black girl emoji, cash bag emoji.'" Zara showed Emira as she clicked the word *Comment*. Then she liked Shaunie's photo—the one of her jumping in front of the Sony building—and a tiny heart flashed red. "Done," Zara said. "See? We have the technology."

When Emira came out of the bathroom, she grabbed Shaunie's forearm and said, "Let's do a shot." In the kitchen, next to the open window where basil and mint grew on the fire escape, Emira and Shaunie tipped two glasses back and made twisted faces as they sucked on lime wedges Josefa had cut up.

"Shaunie, congratulations," Emira said. She licked the last bit of salt off her hand. "For real. This is big and you deserve it."

Shaunie pouted in gratitude. She went in for a hug and said, "Thank you, Emira."

Emira never really understood hugging someone in the middle of a conversation, but this was Shaunie's night so she squeezed her back hard. She smelled the creams in Shaunie's hair, from products that had names like Beautifully Mixed and Half & Half. Shaunie stayed close after Emira backed away.

"And between you and me, well . . ." Shaunie looked toward Josefa's bedroom door. "You know what, I'm sure she already knows. But I'm probably gonna start looking for a one-bedroom or a studio."

"Oh, for real?" Emira was shocked, and then she was jealous, and then she wondered, *Is that what we're supposed to be doing right now? 'Cause if it is, I ain't there.*

"I've obviously loved living here . . ." Shaunie kept her voice down despite the fact that Josefa could be heard speaking with her sister behind her closed bedroom door. "But yeah," Shaunie said. "I just think it's time. But, more importantly, you should take my room. I want it to go to someone who I can come back and see. Besides Josefa obviously."

Emira currently lived with a classmate from Temple (a graduate student who stayed at her boyfriend's apartment from Wednesdays to Sundays) in a tiny fifth-floor walk-up where the rent was $760 each, soon to be $850 in 2016. She had a twin bed, and only one of the stove burners worked, but it was just fine for now. Shaunie's apartment was better on all accounts. There was a coffee shop nearby, the bedroom windows opened up to sky and not concrete walls, and it wasn't in Kensington, it was in Old City. But there were all these parts of Shaunie's apartment that made it Shaunie's apartment regardless of location, and those would all leave with her. The HBO her father paid for. The framed prints on the wall that were painfully commercial (bridges, sunflowers, a New York skyline). A spice rack that was alphabetized, and a flowery oven mitt that hooked onto the fridge. Shaunie had a stereo system in her bedroom and a record player in the living room. When Emira's roommate wasn't at her boyfriend's, the two of them played music in the kitchen from a bowl they called the "phone bowl." If they put it on top of the refrigerator, it seemed to echo best.

"That's a really amazing offer," Emira said. "What's your rent again?"

"Oh, it's not bad at all." Shaunie shook her head. "Only $1150 each. Plus utilities. Total steal. Oh shit, Troy's calling me. Babe, hi."

Zara emerged from Shaunie's room holding a slinky red dress against her shoulders. "I'm trying this on." Shaunie waved a hand at her and said into her phone, "Boy, I'm not taking no for an answer." Shaunie started undoing the buttons on her blouse in the living room and held the phone between her ear and her shoulder. "You know what? Imma send you a picture and *then* I want to hear you tell me no."

Emira finished the rest of her wine.

"Zara, will you take a photo for me?" Shaunie walked into her own bedroom.

"Girl, why you have to beg him like this?" Zara said. She threw the red dress onto Shaunie's bed.

"Just lemme change bras real quick, hang on."

Emira took a breath. She grabbed her phone from her purse, braced her hands against the wall, and crawled out the kitchen window. She hugged her elbows together on top of the fire escape and crossed her legs beneath her, careful not to kick the planted herbs. Kelley answered on the second ring.

"Hey, are you okay? Let me get somewhere quiet, hang on."

It was cold outside, but she wasn't about to climb back in for her jacket. In the receiver, Emira heard men's voices in the background above Earth, Wind & Fire. This was the first time she'd ever called Kelley.

"Hey, what's up?"

"Hi, sorry," she said. "Sorry, you sound busy over there."

"No, I'm just at the last event of this conference," he said. "It's just a bunch of tech guys drinking Long Island Iced Teas."

"Oh, gross. Okay."

"What's wrong?"

"No, nothing." Emira shifted so her socks covered as much of the grates below as they could. She leaned her back against the wall to Shaunie's apartment and looked down to the sidewalk, where a deliveryman repeatedly buzzed an apartment door. "Sorry, I don't really have anything interesting to say. I just had a really shitty day."

"No way," Kelley said. "I did, too."

"Really?"

"It was the worst. Tell me yours first, though."

Emira told him all about Mrs. Chamberlain, Spoons, and how she began her afternoon by showing a teenage clerk a picture of a dead fish. When she told him that they missed the Halloween party, that her days taking Briar to ballet were over, Kelley said, "Nooo! Not the Halloween party at Lulu's!"

Emira laughed. "I brought my cat ears and everything. It just pissed me off that she didn't want to talk to her kid and made her miss a party because of it."

"Well, any mom who misses the chance to dress her kid up like a hot dog sounds like a psychopath to me."

"Exactly. Thank you. And now"—Emira took her voice down—

"I'm at Shaunie's and she just got this huge promotion. So now she's all hyped and I know I should be happy for her . . . but I just wanna punch her in the face and go to bed."

"Easy, killer," he said. "Just buy her a drink."

Emira held on to the railing. "Now you tell me yours."

That day, Kelley introduced himself to who he thought was a tech lead named Jesse. The real Jessie was a woman, but Kelley had introduced himself to her male assistant, in front of her and her team. He'd also gotten salad dressing in his eye and thought he was blind for approximately two minutes. And he just hated Cleveland.

"I get back early tomorrow, though."

"Okay." Inside, Emira heard Shaunie and Zara call for Josefa. Josefa replied with an annoyed *"What?"* Emira bent to glance inside the kitchen and saw that she was still alone. "I'll let you go. Sorry," she said. She sidestepped and winced. "Sorry, I know this was weird."

"Why would it be weird? Wait—are you going out right now?"

"Yeah, I think I have to."

"Well, hey. Go sleep in my bed when you're done."

Emira laughed and said, "What?"

"I'll call my doorman and tell you you're coming. Sleep there and we'll do breakfast tomorrow."

This, Emira thought, was the most adult thing that had ever happened to her.

"Wait, no," she said. "Kelley, I can't do that."

"There's absolutely no reason you can't do that," he said. "It's a perfect opportunity for you to steal whatever you want. I'll call the front desk right now. Does that sound good?"

It sounded so good that Emira said, "Umm . . ."

Kelley said, "What do you mean, 'umm'?"

Inside the window, Zara yelled, "Bish, you need to relax your shoulders!" Emira looked up into the dark clouds and said, "Lemme think for a second."

"Emira, come on." Kelley laughed. She heard him take a breath before he said, "Are you gonna be with me or what, miss?"

She placed her hand to her forehead and grinned.

By the time she crawled back into the kitchen, she had a new text from Kelley. Frank knows you're coming. Bring your ID. Emira helped herself to another glass of wine as she heard Zara say, "Sefa, you gotta get closer, sweetie."

Emira pushed Shaunie's bedroom door open. Inside, Shaunie was topless and kneeling on top of her bed, cupping her breasts with one arm and hanging the other at her side. Josefa was holding a desk lamp above her head and saying, "I feel like you have to get even higher, Z." Zara stood on a chair with Shaunie's iPhone held out in front of her.

"Wait, Emira's better at this." Zara tossed Emira the phone. "I'll get down and hold your tits up, though."

Eleven

Alix didn't care that she was plateauing eight pounds above her pre-baby weight. She didn't notice that she and Peter hadn't had sex in almost three weeks. (To be fair, he didn't seem to notice either. He was getting insane camera time while covering the current snow-storm.) And she was also fine to ignore her editor's emails and calls, asking how the book was going, and if there were a few chapters she could read over the holiday. Everything could stop for just a second, because Rachel, Jodi, and Tamra were coming to Philadelphia for Thanksgiving. Even better, Alix would go back with them to New York City for five whole days. The Clinton campaign had finally reached out and asked her to attend a women's event. It would be her first time back in eight months, and Catherine's first visit to the city. And as Alix removed her gloves and hat in the front vestibule of her home, Emira's phone glowed with a text banner across the top. *We regret to inform you that flight WX1492 is no longer in service.*

Outside, snow raced so quickly that it seemed impossible that it would settle. But it did, burying cars and trees, slamming storefront doors shut, and then keeping them spread open like very used books. The top of the Chamberlain porch stairs had been the stomping ground for mud and ice for the past three days. Alix still made the trek to swim class in Ubers and cabs—she and the girls were often the only ones in the pool—because she was quickly running out of patience and indoor activities (games like *Let's look at pictures on Mama's phone. Let's play go underneath the blanket. Let's pull all the books down from the bookshelf and put them all back again*). But tomorrow was Thanksgiving, and this Thanksgiving was going to be different.

Alix and Emira hadn't been the same since Briar's fish died three weeks ago. On a Monday, Emira turned down the offer to take extra cookies home so that Alix wouldn't eat them. And on a Friday evening, when Alix offered her a glass of wine, Emira had said, "I'm actually okay, but thank you." This shift in their relationship haunted Alix in everyday places where she never would have imagined she'd ruminate about her sitter. In a bookstore, Alix found herself pondering what time Emira went to bed. While breast-feeding Catherine, she wondered if Emira had seen the movie *Pretty Woman*, and if she found it contentious. On the escalator inside Anthropologie, Alix imagined what Emira had said to Zara about her, and if Zara was the type to blindly agree or push back.

Alix also found herself reorganizing her lifestyle around Emira, despite the fact that she didn't have an explicit reason to. If Alix went shopping, she took the tags off clothes and other items immediately so Emira couldn't see how much she'd spent, even though Emira wasn't the type to show interest or ask. Alix no longer felt comfortable leaving out certain books or magazines, because she feared Emira eyeing her Marie Kondo book and subsequently thinking, *Wow, how privileged are you that you need to buy a hardcover book that tells you how to get rid of all your other expensive shit*. Sometimes, Alix found herself pretending—in front of Emira—that she was about to eat leftovers for dinner. In reality, she'd be thinking to herself, *Just order the sushi. Just text Peter and ask him what he wants. What point are you trying to prove by eating leftovers?* But still, she'd wait till Emira closed the door behind her to go to her computer, ask Peter if he wanted the usual, and place her order via Seamless.

In the beginning, Alix would search Emira's name on the Internet and Instagram, to see if she'd finally gotten an account (she'd convinced herself that this was a safety precaution concerning her children), but now Alix had taken to looking at her own Instagram account while imagining she was Emira and viewing it with fresh eyes. She'd slowly scroll through her own feed, and guess which pictures Emira would click on. Emira never hinted that she felt this way, because why would she, but Alix often felt that Emira saw her as a textbook rich white person, much in the same way that Alix saw many of the annoying Upper East Side moms that she and her girlfriends had always tried to avoid. But if Emira would only take a deeper look, if she gave Alix a chance, Alix knew that she would begin to think otherwise.

Alix fantasized about Emira discovering things about her that shaped what Alix saw as the truest version of herself. Like the fact that one of Alix's closest friends was also black. That Alix's new and favorite shoes were from Payless, and only cost eighteen dollars. That Alix had read everything that Toni Morrison had ever written. And that out of her group of friends, Alix and Peter actually had the smallest salaries, and that Tamra was the one who always flew first class. Alix often and unsuccessfully tried to drop these bits of information, but tomorrow, if things went Alix's way, Emira could see all this in person.

Rachel, Jodi, and Tamra would be taking the train to Philadelphia on Thanksgiving morning. Rachel was thankful to not spend the holiday alone (Hudson would be with his father); Tamra would be coming with her daughters, Imani and Cleo (her husband was traveling for work in Tokyo), and Jodi's entire family would be present (her husband, Walter; her four-and-a-half-year-old daughter, Prudence; and her one-year-old son, Payne). It was Thanksgiving that made Alix realize that her three best girlfriends hadn't yet met Catherine, who was almost seven months old. Had it been that long? Catherine, who looked more like Alix every day, and was so easily toteable and darling and unconcerned with crawling that she made Briar seem borderline manic. Her girlfriends had joked about Alix showing them a traditional Murphy Thanksgiving complete with very suburban décor, fluffy turtlenecks in warm fall colors, DIY Pinterest projects and table toppers, and the Macy's Thanksgiving Day parade on repeat. But this joke had turned into an ironic theme that Alix couldn't wait to execute.

Alix hired two caterers to pour drinks, hang coats, serve food, and remove plates. She filled the first floor of her home with pumpkins, gourds, wheat stalks, and acorns; a turkey piñata was waiting to be hung above the massive rented dining table set up in the stretch of the tiled foyer. With red twine, above a small table that held four different types of pies, Alix hung slips of brown craft paper where guests could write down what they were thankful for. She was delighted to consider the upcoming day, being around her three favorite women with a cheesy Thanksgiving scheme and tons of red wine, but just the idea of Emira being there too made her blush into her scarf.

Holding her last grocery store lot (bread, pink salt, butter, cookie dough, club soda), Alix said, "Hey!" and set the reusable bags on top of the counter. Catherine was drooling on a blanket while sitting in a Bumbo at the center of the room. Emira held Briar's hips as she stood at the window seat and pointed out onto the street.

Briar said, "Mama? The window is biting my fingers."

Emira turned and said, "I can't believe you went out in this mess."

Thank God for the weather, Alix thought. Most of her conversations with Emira in the last few days were fueled by weather management—if Briar should wear gloves, if an art class was snowed out, or if Emira needed to borrow an umbrella for her travels home. Alix rolled her eyes at her own actions. "It was insane, and kind of apocalyptic. I shouldn't have made you come out today."

"Nah, it's cool. It's only two days," Emira said. She turned back to Briar and said, "I'm not gonna see you for a little bit, B."

Briar's top teeth popped out in response. "No," she disagreed. "No, you see me."

"So I usually see you three times a week?" Emira explained. She held up three fingers and Briar grabbed onto them. "But this week is Thanksgiving so I'll only see you two."

When Emira put her ring finger down, Briar looked offended. "Nuh-uh." Briar shook her head. "No, you see me *three*."

"But then I'm gonna see you every day next week. Isn't that cool?"

"You're really saving me next week," Alix said. She opened the refrigerator door and the quickness of it made a loud suck of air. "Emira, I hate to say it"—she winced—"but you should really check on the status of your flight tonight."

"Really?"

"Just to be safe." Alix started moving containers and plates around in the refrigerator. "You can use the computer there."

Was this cruel? Trying to win a best supporting Oscar as she waited for Emira to learn her flight was canceled? Who cared, she'd make up for it anyway. The realization that Emira could have a seat at their Thanksgiving table made Alix practically high. Suddenly, the fourth Thursday in November wasn't just a holiday. It was four (or hopefully five or six) hours to finally make Emira family. It was a night to say through Malbecs and yams and candlelight and pie that Alix hadn't forgotten about that night at Market Depot. That she thought about it every day, multiple times. That she'd never go to that grocery store again, even if it was an emergency, even if it was snowing the way it was now, even if Emira wasn't her sitter. Emira moved to the computer and clicked and clicked as Alix prayed that Zara didn't have family in Philadelphia.

Emira put her elbows on top of the desk, touched the sides of her face, and said, "Well, shoot."

"Oh noooo," Alix said. She closed the refrigerator door. She couldn't overdo it, but she had to appear like this was in fact a tragedy. "Emira, my heart is breaking for you, I'm so sorry. I feel like I jinxed it."

Emira kept staring at the screen. She bit her bottom lip and took a deep breath as Briar crawled into a nearby chair. "No, sorry. Is it okay if I call my mom real quick? They bought my ticket so they might know about a later flight."

"Absolutely. Briar, get down."

Briar said, "Mama, you can't touch Mira's water," and as Alix set her on the ground, she said, "Okay, I won't. Thank you for telling me."

By the time Emira came back upstairs, Alix had turned music on low. Paula Cole played softly as Briar explained that even a snowman needs a nap sometimes. Alix picked up Catherine, who snuggled tightly into her chest. Emira sat down at the windowsill.

"Looks like I'm the last to know," she said. "The earliest flight I can get is tomorrow night, which would make the trip pointless."

"I'm so sorry, Emira." Alix turned Catherine around, the back of her head leaning into Alix's chest. Briar walked to Emira and began tapping on her knees. "Maybe it's better to find out now than at the airport?"

"Yeah, I went home last summer so it's okay. And there's nothing I can do, I guess."

"Emira." While she rocked her second daughter in front of her stomach, Alix walked over to her sitter at the windowsill. "I know it's not your first choice," she said, "but we would absolutely love if you spent Thanksgiving with us."

"Ohhh, wow, no no." Emira shook her head.

"Okay, 'cause Mira?" Briar interrupted. "I . . . I'm your first choice." Alix thought, *Yes, Bri, good girl.*

Emira laughed. "Well, I can't really argue with that," she said. She reached forward to pick up Briar from underneath her armpits and turned her around to sit her on her thighs. "That's extremely nice, but I'll be okay."

"Emira." Alix kept on bouncing, hoping it gave some coolness to her words, which she knew she had to deliver like a decent option rather than a desperate plea. "I'm telling you that the grocery stores are nuts. And I've been in my twenties and I've done Chinese takeout for Thanksgiving before, and it never made me happy. It made me really depressed and I swear it also made my face break out." It was still a thousand times better than spending the day with her own parents in a smelly nursing home, but that wasn't the point. "My three best girlfriends from New York are coming in. We are going to have way too much food, and we'd love to have you."

Briar reached up with six fingers and said, "How many is dis?"

Emira touched her hand and said, "That's six. Mrs. Chamberlain, I really appreciate it. But it actually looks like my boyfriend will be stuck here with me." She glanced at her cell phone. "He was supposed to meet his family in Florida but his flight got canceled too."

This was even better.

"We'd love to have him," Alix said. "Bring your boyfriend. Four o'clock on Thursday, and you won't be here as a sitter. No diaper changing or anything. You guys will just be here as guests."

Emira exhaled in thought.

"If you eat all your toes?" Briar looked back at Emira, and whispered, "Then, then guess what, Mira? No more toes."

Emira pressed the main button on her cell phone, smiled, and said, "Lemme ask him." As Alix prayed for the second time that evening, Emira wrapped her other arm around Briar's waist. "B, should I eat turkey here with you? I don't really like eating toes." Emira wore earrings with square copper plates, and instead of answering, Briar reached up for them and said, "I want to open dis."

"It doesn't open, mama," Emira told her as she texted. Hearing this pet name made Alix fidget and think, *Please o please o please come tomorrow.*

Emira looked at Briar and asked, "Should I come eat pie with you this week?"

"Yes," Briar decided. "But you can only have ten pieces."

"Only ten? That seems fair, I guess." Emira looked at her phone. She looked back up at Alix. "He said he'd love to come."

It took everything in Alix not to drop her daughter and hold her chilled cheekbones in her hands.

"Did you hear that?" Alix said into Catherine's ear. "Mira's gonna come eat turkey too!"

"Is that okay?" Emira reached over and squeezed Catherine's foot. "Can I come hang out with you on Thanksgiving?"

And then, Catherine May Chamberlain looked at Emira and said, "Hi."

Emira and Alix gasped. Alix felt her face flush and tears run to the corners of her eyes. She turned her daughter around and brought her face up high. "Did you just say hi?" she asked. "Did you say hi to Mira? Briar, did you hear your sister?"

"Mama?" Briar called. "Can you . . . you take a picture of Mira's earring? Let's take a picture."

Emira bounced her. "Your sister just said hi, big girl."

"Can you say hi again? No?" Alix swallowed. Catherine smiled sweetly and Alix held her little body close. She shook her head happily and said, "Emira, go home."

Emira laughed and said, "What?"

"It's insane out there, go home. And we'll see you on Thanksgiving."

"Oh, I can give Briar a bath real quick."

"No, no. Mira, go." The warmth Alix felt for her daughter's first word, and for the day she was about to have—it was almost too much to keep in one room. If Emira stayed much longer, Alix would risk accidentally saying *I love you*, or ask if Emira liked babysitting for them, or how old Emira thought she was. "Actually," she said. "Wait one second."

Alix set Catherine back down in the Bumbo, retrieved a Whole Foods bag from a bottom drawer, and opened up her refrigerator. She filled the grocery bag with two bottles of water, a frozen tortellini dinner, a can of soup, a can of chili, a pack of Briar's animal cookies, and a bottle of red wine.

Emira came into the kitchen. "Wait, Mrs. Chamberlain, what is this?"

"This is yours." Alix pushed it into her arms. "I'm sure you have food at home, but this is better than anything you will find at a grocery store right now."

"Whoa . . ." Emira adjusted the bag in her arms. "This is really, *really* nice."

"Just do me a favor"—Alix beamed—"and come very hungry on Thursday. And Emira, I mean it. You're not coming to babysit. You'll be here as *family*. Okay?"

Emira pouted a little in a way that made her look quite young. She pulled up the back of her leggings and said, "Okay."

Twelve

On Thanksgiving Day, at 4:06 p.m., Emira stepped out of a yellow cab in beige faux-suede boots. Kelley held the back of her arm as she spotted previously made footprints in the snow on the way up to the Chamberlain front gate. It was the first time all day the snow had stopped falling, and above their heads, it balanced an inch high on naked trees, wires, and window ledges. Emira stopped with one hand on the gate latch, and the other around a bouquet of purple and yellow daisies. Through the cold, she could see her own breath.

"Hey. Do we need a code word or something?" she said.

Kelley stuck his hands into his pockets and matched her low tone. "A code word for what?"

"If you're like . . ." Emira blushed. "If you're not having a good time and you want to leave."

"Ohhh, okay. How about . . . 'I don't want to be here anymore.'"

Emira shoved his chest and opened the gate. "Boy, stop."

"We'll be fine. I'm happy to be here," he said. "I am expecting excellent wine, though."

"I'm sure you won't be disappointed."

At the top of the landing, Emira went to take out her key, but today was different. She could already hear women's voices inside, along with multiple children who could speak in full sentences. Kelley stood next to her—so holiday handsome—in dark jeans, a red sweater, and a black coat that went down to his knees. They'd spent the last twenty-four hours together at his apartment having lots of sex, watching bad movies, and ordering in, and Emira felt more like an adult than she could have ever imagined. She looked up at him and whispered, "I feel weird using my key."

"Okay . . ." He placed his finger on the doorbell. "Wanna use this?"

Emira said, "Yes," and Kelley pressed the button. Together they waited and Emira held her breath.

"Hey." Kelley touched her waist as the doorbell chime sang. "What's your boss's name again?"

"Mrs. Chamberlain."

"Do I have to call her that? What's her first name, just in case?"

"Umm . . . it's like"—Emira adjusted her thick black braid on her shoulder—"Ellix?"

"Ellen?"

"No." Emira put her head to his shoulder. "It's Alex but it's weird. It's like, uh-*leeks*?"

"Emira." He grinned. "How do you not know this?"

"I do, it's just not what I call her. Just call her Mrs. Chamberlain. Shh!"

They readjusted and waited in silence.

In the painful pause, Kelley, once again, leaned toward Emira. "Is she European or something?"

"I don't know, maybe?"

"What do you mean *maybe*?"

"Jesus, Kelley. I don't know, she's *white*."

Kelley laughed into the top of his coat. "Okay, miss. Let me kiss you before they come."

Emira leaned into him, and she felt his lashes close on her face. They backed away as Mrs. Chamberlain opened the door.

"Emira, you made it!" Mrs. Chamberlain's blond hair was curled at the ends, and it flew with the gust of the door. Fumes of candlelight, pumpkin pie, and brandy came with her.

Emira said, "Hi, Mrs. Chamberlain, thanks so much for—" But then Mrs. Chamberlain said, "Ohmygod," with both panic and recognition, as if she'd almost walked into a very clean glass door.

Emira watched Mrs. Chamberlain's face go into the same warfare that her daughter's did when schedule did not go according to plan, or when Emira tried to read to her at night. With her hand on the door, Mrs. Chamberlain seemed to brace herself as if she were preparing to be hit, or as if she already had been and barely made it out alive.

Kelley seemingly woke up, blinked twice, and said, "Alex?"

PART THREE

Thirteen

Alix checked herself in the mirror (she wore a deliciously chunky oatmeal-colored sweater over tight jeans and brown boots). She walked downstairs with Catherine in her carrier (she whispered to Tamra, "I think she's here"), and then, as she swung the door open, she stepped back and tapped herself fifteen years into the past. In front of her stood both a grown man and a high school junior, and this person that embodied them both was saying, "Alex?" as if he knew her.

There, next to her babysitter, stood Kelley Copeland, William Massey High School, class of 2001. Alex Murphy's first everythings (blowjobs, sex, *I love you*, heartbreak), and a million insecurities in between. On top of his unbelievable presence on Alix's front stoop, the way he'd said her name had momentarily paralyzed her. *Alex.* It sounded whiny and pedestrian, and it felt like she'd discovered a vegetable deep in a refrigerator drawer, forgotten so long that the mold it gained had also started to gain mold. Her heart buzzed as she thought, *No, it's not possible*, but the more they stood before her, she thought, *Fuck fuck fuck fuck fuck*.

Emira laughed once and said, "Wait, what?" as she looked from Alix to Kelley.

Catherine started to squirm in the cold and Alix said, "Umm, come in, come in . . . it's freezing."

Emira and Kelley stepped into the vestibule, and Alix closed the door behind them thinking, *Kelley Copeland is in my house*. Past the vestibule door, Alix saw all the people she loved most surrounded by the campy Thanksgiving decorations she'd piled high in her trunk just days before, all glittering beneath a dumb fucking turkey piñata. It was all much akin to the over-the-top décor her parents would have paid for someone to assemble on 100 Bordeaux Lane, and for a moment Alix actually thought, *How fast can I throw all this garbage away?* It wasn't supposed to look like this. It was supposed to be a *joke*.

"Is this the wonderful Emira?" Jodi's beige poncho flowed past her elbows as she came forward. "We're so happy to meet you. I'm Jodi."

"Don't be scared." Rachel hugged Emira next. "We just feel like we know you already. Hi, boyfriend. I'm Rachel."

"Kelley. Nice to meet you."

Fuck fuck fuck.

Tamra came down the stairs appearing, as she typically did, presidential and important. She opened both of her arms to Emira as if she were a ringmaster at the top of the show, and said, "Emira? Bring it in, sister." She embraced Emira as Alix tried unsuccessfully to lock eyes with Jodi. "Happy Thanksgiving, girlfriend. Let's get you a drink."

The three women seized Emira and took her to the bar, where the bartender asked if she'd like red or white. Just outside the front vestibule where she'd read so many of his text messages, Alix stood with Catherine and Kelley. Catherine kicked her legs and chewed a sock she'd pulled off her foot. For the first time ever, Alix wished she hadn't strapped her daughter to her chest.

"You look . . ." Alix had no idea what to say or where to put her hands. "Very much the same."

Because he so heartbreakingly did. His tallness was still shocking and his hands seemed almost freakishly huge. This was Emira's boyfriend. This was Kenan&Kel. This was the guy Emira met on the train who'd told her that he was excited to see her tonight.

"Thank you." Kelley looked up at the chandelier above the table that stretched twelve places long, and the red and brown turkey piñata that swiveled slightly in the blasts of heat that came up from the floors. He was seemingly assessing the rest of his evening when he said, "I see nothing has changed for you either."

"Excuse me?"

But before he could answer, Peter was walking over and sticking his hand out to Kelley like it was a football on the first day of the season. He smiled and said, "Peter Chamberlain," the way he did on TV.

Walter joined Peter to alight on the only other male presence in the house aside from baby Payne, who was fast asleep. Rachel, Jodi, and Tamra were interrogating Emira with drinks in their hands, and nodding furiously at all of her answers. Alix removed Catherine from her chest and placed her in a playpen beneath a soft arch of hanging moons and stars. She paced halfway up the stairs, locked eyes with Jodi, and mouthed over the banister, "Come *here*."

Upstairs the kitchen was still. The counters were stocked with yams, mashed potatoes, bread rolls, and asparagus waiting on top of burners and under sweating foil lids. Next to the girls' bedroom, Alix stepped over a case of red wine on the floor and opened the door to the tiny laundry room, which was more of a substantial closet by New York standards. When she heard Jodi's footprints change from carpet to wood, she reached for her friend and pulled her inside.

"Jesus, honey, what are you doing?"

Alix said, "Shh!" and pulled the string above their heads. A single light bulb clicked on in the small square space. Alix realized she was about to say Kelley's name out loud, and her heartbeat double-timed. "Listen to me," she said. "Downstairs?" Alix put her hands on Jodi's shoulders. "That's Kelley Copeland."

"Okay . . ." Jodi smiled. "I don't know who that is."

"Emira's boyfriend? That's the guy from high school who took my virginity and broke up with me and told everyone where I lived and ruined my *fucking* life."

Beneath the shelves of guest towels, diapers, laundry detergent, and emergency batteries, Jodi's green eyes went big. "You are joking."

"Jodi, I don't even . . ." Alix backed up against the washer and dryer, which were stacked on top of each other. "I don't know what to do."

"You just found out?"

"Just now."

"How long have they been dating?"

"I don't know, a couple months."

"Months?!"

Alix said, "Shh!" and heard Rachel's voice say, "Hello?"

Alix opened the door and pulled Rachel inside.

"Are you two being bad?" Rachel held a glass of wine that Alix thought might be her second of the evening, the evening that hadn't yet begun.

Jodi grabbed Rachel's arm. "Alix knows Emira's boyfriend."

"From where? I thought you just met him. He's cute."

Alix fanned herself as Jodi went on and explained. When Rachel fully understood, she said, "Your ex-boyfriend is dating your *sitter*?" Jodi palmed Rachel's mouth and Alix said, "Shh!"

"Okay, okay, but wait . . ." Rachel removed Jodi's hand. "That's the fucktard you told us about?"

Alix nodded and placed her hand on her stomach. "I feel like I can't breathe," she said. "Ohmygod he's here and I'm still so fat."

Both women hissed, "No, you're *not*!"

Jodi tapped Rachel's elbow and said, "Go get Tamra." To Alix, Jodi said, "Okay, put your head between your knees."

Alix wanted to pace around, but she'd quarantined herself and her friend in this closet and everywhere she looked were light bulbs and Swiffer refills and canvas bins overflowing with tangled extension cords. The reality of how completely different this run-in was from the last fifteen years of Kelley Copeland fantasies came down on Alix and crushed her lungs. She was still eight pounds heavier than she'd been before Catherine. The current state of her home wasn't the modern, minimalist environment she'd worked so hard to achieve. And there were babies everywhere, not just the sleeping cute kind but Briar with her questions and Prudence with her naughtiness and Tamra's kids with their obedience that was somehow very pretentious. This wasn't how it was supposed to go. Throughout marriage, motherhood, and monumental career changes, Alix had always found herself forming ideal scenarios of how she would see a grown-up Kelley Copeland, or rather, how he'd see her. There were the cliché pipe dreams (seeing him after a particularly good blowout, running into him while wearing heels at the airport), but there were elaborate premises that took Alix entire showers and subway rides to fully flesh out the logistics of.

In one of these more elaborate illusions, Kelley was on vacation in New York with a short, brunette, picture-taking, Longchamp-toting girlfriend. After a frustrating morning of getting turned around on the train, they'd end up at the farmer's market in Union Square, and enter Alix: tiny Briar strapped to her front, both with messy and darling hair. She'd see them before they saw her, and she'd lift her sunglasses up onto her head (*"Kelley?* Ohmygosh, *hi!"*). And then Kelley's girlfriend would promptly fall in love with Alix as she gave them excellent directions and recommendations for cheap cocktails on rooftops in the city. Alix would wave ("Good luck! Have a great trip!"), and she'd be the one to walk away first. She'd be wearing something classic, like a white tee and red lips.

Alix had even dreamed Kelley into her future. She hadn't exactly finished her first book but maybe she'd write another, and this time, it'd be a book for young girls. A forty-six-year-old (hopefully pudgy or balding) Kelley would stand behind his daughter in line at the Barnes & Noble on 86th Street (they'd drive all the way from Allentown and stay in a hotel by the train in Astoria). Alix would open her book and sign the title page for the inspired tween. She'd look up at Kelley, smile, and say, "Did you know that I knew your dad?"

But here he was, nowhere near chunky or bald, explicitly reminding her of the night that ruined her high school career. And not only was he here, Kelley Copeland was dating Emira? *Her* Emira? The fact that he knew Emira at all seemed unbelievable. Could he tell when she was mad? Was he allowed to touch her hair? What did Zara think of all of this, did she approve? And then Alix touched her forehead, coming to what she knew was an adolescent realization, but nevertheless she thought, *Ohmygod. Kelley and Emira have sex. Simultaneously. With each other.*

With two-and-a-half-year-old Cleo in her arms, Tamra opened the laundry room door. Rachel came in behind her and the room seemed to meet its capacity. Tamra whispered, "What the . . ." as Cleo pointed upward and said, "Light, Memmy. Hot, hot."

Tamra said, "That's right. Don't touch."

Jodi rubbed Alix's back in slow, circular clips. "Okay, Tam? Here's the situation."

When Tamra was caught up, she nodded and said, "Okay. Alix? Hey." Alix stood up, her face flushed and her head throbbing. "It was high school, a very long time ago. This is going to be okay."

"I know it was a long time ago!" Alix wasn't anywhere near ready to be okay about Kelley Copeland. She placed her hands over Cleo's ears and said, "Would you be calm if your ex was *currently* fucking Shelby?"

Tamra reflected on this and said, "Okay, I get it."

Cleo covered both of her eyes and asked the room, "Where's Cleo?"

"How did this *happen*?" Alix said to no one.

"Babe, you are so red right now," Rachel said. "You gotta cool it."

Jodi's maternal instincts couldn't ignore Cleo. She tickled her side and said, "We see you, lovey." A child started crying downstairs and Jodi looked to Tamra. "Is that my kid or yours? I feel like it's mine."

"Okay, this looks bad. We gotta get outta here," Tamra said. "Listen. Just be cool. Pretend that you went to high school with him, and that is it." Tamra would have kept going, but her face turned. She looked at Cleo and said, "Did you just poop?" She lifted the child to smell her behind and then reported back, "No, we're good."

This gesture devastated Alix and she couldn't help but think, *Oh my God, my friends are such MOMS*. Alix found it remarkable how she could be both in love and embarrassed at so many things at once. There was the age and status of her friends (Rachel, divorced twice at thirty-five. Jodi, the mommiest mom ever, also thirty-five. And Tamra, though impressive in every other way, was quickly pushing forty). And then there were other numbers that suddenly seemed mortifying. The height of Alix's husband (the same as her, 5'10"), her own post-baby body (141 pounds), and most of all, the fact she'd lain in bed the night before and been so pleased as she counted in her head how many African American guests would be present at her Thanksgiving table. This number had totaled to five.

Rachel shook her head. "I wanna kill him."

Jodi said, "I think there was a *This American Life* where this happened."

Tamra nodded. "I know which one you're talking about."

Jodi asked, "Are you going to tell Peter?"

Peter wouldn't know what to do with this information in the context of the evening. Alix needed him to be his charming self and keep Kelley occupied with gracious hospitality. She said, "Not tonight."

Rachel waited a second before asking, "Are you going to tell Emira?"

This sent Alix back inside herself. She looked to Tamra and said, "Tam, what do you think?"

"You're not telling anyone anything tonight, okay?" Tamra decided this for Alix and for the rest of the group. "She and Kelley are probably having the same conversation we're having right now anyway. But listen, I'll take care of Emira. Peter and Walter are already taking care of Kelley. You went to high school with him and *that's it.* What a coincidence. How funny. That's *all.*"

"Okay . . . just a coincidence." Alix reached her hand into the neck of her sweater and tried to create space between her sweating armpits and her top.

"What a shame though, right?" Rachel took another sip of wine. "Their kids would be *gorgeous*."

Fourteen

When Mrs. Chamberlain had opened the front door, Emira had to stifle her laughter. Mrs. Chamberlain's face had landed at a similar bewilderment as it had the first time they met. Five months ago, Emira watched Mrs. Chamberlain swing her door open to reveal a person she'd created in her head, and *surprise!*, it was someone much darker. Mrs. Chamberlain was so graciously confused at the sight of Emira that she even apologized for herself ("Sorry, hi. You're so pretty! Come on in"), and her reaction to Kelley on Thanksgiving was much akin to this. But as Emira waited for her to apologize for herself, Kelley called her Alex. Emira's knowing giggles turned into nervous laughter and Mrs. Chamberlain's face curved down. Before she could get an answer, Emira was pulled into a Thankful Wonderland and ambushed by three other moms. The women shoved a glass of red wine into her hands as they asked where she was from and where she went to school and if she was caught up on a sitcom called *Black-ish*. When Emira said she hadn't seen it, Tamra touched her arm with a solid hold and said, "Oh Emira, you have to see it. It's a *very* important show."

After the three women all headed upstairs, Emira spotted Briar in the living room in a plaid and uncomfortable-looking dress sitting next to two other little girls, one with bright red hair and the other with a tiny afro held back by a flowered headband. Emira tapped Briar on the shoulder. "Hey, pickle."

Briar stood. She solemnly wrapped her arms around Emira's neck. "I don't like fancy shoes in the house."

"You wanna come meet my friend?"

Briar didn't say yes, but Emira picked the little girl up and walked back toward the front hall where Peter, Kelley, and another man were talking.

"This is my . . . this is mine," Briar said to the man Emira didn't know. "This is my friend."

"That's terrific," he said. He had huge cheeks, big shoulders, and looked like a young Santa Claus in a white sweater with knit swirls. "We haven't met yet. Walter. I think you already met my wife, Jodi. All the redheads you see are mine."

"Emira, nice to meet you." She smiled. "Hey, B. This is my friend Kelley. Can you say hi?"

Briar tucked her head into Emira's neck at what looked like a painful angle; she could still inspect Kelley even though her face was almost upside down. She stuck out two fingers and said, "I'm three."

Kelley turned toward the little girl and said, "No way. I'm three, too."

Briar eyed him and grinned. "Noooo."

"I'm just big for my age," he said. "Well, I'm actually three and a half." Emira's lips mushed against each other and she felt so pleased.

Of course he was completely wonderful and easy with children. Of course he had a scripted show of how to entertain new ones before they became familiar. But as Tamra came down the stairs, Jodi, Rachel, and Mrs. Chamberlain in tow, Kelley ended his routine early. He placed his hand to Emira's back and said, "Can we talk for a second?"

Emira said, "Hmm?" but Tamra interrupted their gaze.

"Briar, I know you're so glad your buddy is here today. Emira, can you lend me a hand in the kitchen?" She passed Cleo to Jodi and headed back upstairs. The woman's question sounded more like a command, and from the way she threw back her shoulders as she walked, it seemed like she very much expected Emira to be coming right behind her.

Emira set Briar on the ground. "I guess I'll be right back."

On top of the upstairs table was fancy silverware Emira had never seen before, and a pile of cloth napkins next to it. "I just need a hand folding this silverware real quick," Tamra said. "I'm sure you know how."

Emira said, "Sure," but this all felt very strange. Not only did she not know how to fold silverware into napkins, but the pile of hand towels seemed careless in a way that didn't match Mrs. Chamberlain. Mrs. Chamberlain definitely would have completed this task before guests arrived. Had Tamra unassembled them just so she and Emira could have this moment? Weren't they all about to have dinner together anyway? Emira looked down and she was almost startled to find her own olive green dress, instead of the oversized white polo she wore every Monday, Wednesday, and Friday.

Tamra laid the knife down first, and Emira copied her steps. After completing the first roll of silverware and tossing it into a wicker basket, Tamra reached over and gently tugged the bottom of Emira's braid. "So what's up underneath here, huh? I'm guessing you're afraid to go natural."

"Oh." Emira laughed, more out of discomfort than indifference. She'd been to several events where another black party guest was foisted on her by a well-meaning but ignorant host, but Tamra appeared to be conducting this interaction on her own. It reminded Emira of the one time she'd watched an episode of *The Bachelorette* at Shaunie's apartment. Four times she had to witness "hometown dates" in which the father of a white woman stood up at a staged dinner table and asked the Bachelor if they could have a man-to-man chat. Each time Emira cringed more than the last. "I don't know," Emira said. "I like it long, I guess."

"Wanna know what I use on my girls' hair?" Tamra stood up straight and counted the ingredients on her fingers. "I put coconut oil, water, and grapeseed oil in a spray jar, comb it out once a week, and honestly, that's all you need. How long is your real hair, honey?"

Emira almost flinched. She was suddenly so grateful to need both of her hands as she tucked a corner of a napkin into a crooked fold. She could already hear Zara's response to this question, which would be a wide-eyed, *She asked you* what? "Umm." Emira kept her brown eyes low. "Like, chin length maybe."

"Okay, that's something!" Tamra congratulated her. "I can definitely see you with some curls, girl."

"Memmy?" Imani appeared at the top of the stairs and Emira felt her breath come back into her shoulders. She turned to the little girl and said, "Hey there, I haven't met you yet." Emira continued to question Imani about being a big sister until all the silverware was wrapped.

When Emira came back downstairs she set the basket of silverware on the table and found Kelley on his way to the bathroom. "Sorry, that was weird," she whispered. "Are you okay?"

Kelley said, "Mm-hmm," and then, "I need you to check your

phone," before he slid into the bathroom and closed the door behind him.

Briar intercepted Emira in the foyer and Emira swung her up onto her hip. She kept her there as she snuck away to the front vestibule, moving coats and scarves aside to dig into her purse.

"Prudence has a big cat," Briar said.

"Yeah?" Emira clicked into her messages. "What's its name?"

There were three texts from Kelley on her phone, and she read them as Briar explained that cats don't pick their own names, and that the mama gets to pick.

The first message from Kelley said, Your boss was my high school girlfriend.

The second said, The one who only flew first class.

The third said, I DON'T WANT TO BE HERE ANYMORE.

Fifteen

Jodi was meant to sit next to her daughter Prudence, but Prudence had quickly remembered her obsession with a now very tipsy Rachel and begged her mother to switch. Peter and Catherine settled in at the head of the table, next to Walter and Payne. Next to Alix, Briar fiddled with the strap that buckled her into her booster seat. Across from Alix, Emira reached forward and touched a hideously sparkled pumpkin that read *Give Thanks!* in gold around its plastic body. "This is all so nice," she said.

"Oh. It's not . . ." Alix threw her hair behind her shoulders as she sat down. She tried to explain, but like everything else she'd said in the last hour it was more for Kelley than anyone else, which meant she couldn't find her words. Kelley took his seat next to Emira and winked at Briar in front of him. "Well, it was kind of a joke," Alix said. "But it's silly, though—"

"She's right, A." Jodi stepped in and saved her. "This is absolutely lovely. Pru?" Jodi looked to her left and squared her daughter's face.

"This is a *very* special treat that you are sitting next to Miss Rachel, so you need to behave, okay?"

Prudence did the same sneaky face she always did when Jodi alluded to such a thing as consequences. Rachel high-fived Prudence and said, "Us single ladies will be fine over here, right, Cleo?"

Two-year-old Cleo shook her head. "No, thank you."

Peter looked over at Alix but said to the entire group, "Should we say grace of some kind?"

Walter raised his chin at his daughter from the other side of the table. "Pru knows a prayer, don't you, Pru?"

Jodi mumbled, "Oh, God."

"That's perfect," Alix said. "Do you wanna help us out?"

Prudence looked around the table as if she were about to execute a very rude and smelly prank. She folded her hands on the table and giggled to herself. "For food and health and happy days, receive our gratitude and praise. And when we serve others may we, repay our debt of love to thee. Amen."

The adults at the table said, "Amen," and Walter echoed, "That's fantastic, kiddo."

Tamra leaned forward. "They taught her that at preschool?"

Jodi reached for a pot of sweet potatoes. "Don't even get me started."

Alix encouraged everyone to dig in, and those wonderful jingles of dinnerware hitting plates and porcelain started to drift up toward the ceiling.

Everything *sounded* like the Thanksgiving she wanted, which made the evening even more eerie. The guests looked festive and warm under the glow of the chandelier. The snow swirled effortlessly behind the front window panes. And the front hall of her home had switched to a dining room quite easily; it smelled like a mix of berries, brown sugar, baked crusts, and burning flames. Briar pointed to every item of food that Alix put on her plate and asked, "Mama? Mama, is dis hot?" Payne stood on Walter's knee and bounced adorably with a binky in his hand. Rachel applied strawberry ChapStick to Prudence's little lips, to which Jodi prompted, "What do you say, Pru?" Tamra replied to Imani's interest in this activity by raising her eyebrows and saying, "Don't even think about it." Everything sounded so homey and sweet and domestic, but across from Alix was her beloved babysitter, Emira, with what seemed from above the table like Kelley Copeland's hand on her left knee. As Alix spooned asparagus for Briar, she tried not to look at Emira while wondering, *How much do you know?* In a lull, Peter looked over to Emira and Kelley and asked, "So how did you two meet?"

Alix watched Kelley and Emira wait for the other one to answer, and this private language between them made her writhe in her seat. "They met on the train, honey." She said this as she cut Briar's turkey. "Isn't that right?"

"Ummm . . ." Kelley reached for his glass of wine and then, at the last second, grabbed his water. "That is . . . incorrect."

"Well." Emira looked at him. "Not entirely, though."

"Uh-ohhh," Walter boomed. "What's the real story then, Kelley? Come on, now. Let's have it."

At the other end of the table, Prudence blew bubbles into a plastic cup of milk. Jodi eyed her and whispered, "Prudence? That's one."

"I don't . . . uhh . . ." Kelley looked unbearably cute as he struggled, and Alix had to look into her lap. "I don't know if it's appropriate."

"Ohmygod," Rachel said. "They had a one-night stand." This seemed to please her greatly, and the fact that she sat next to two four-year-olds and across from a two-year-old did not interfere with her excitement. "Do not be shy, girl. We've all been there. These two met on a one-night stand"—she pointed a fork at Walter and Jodi—"and look at them now."

Around a cheekful of mashed potatoes, Jodi said, "Really, Rach?" as Walter said, "Hear, hear!"

"We didn't have a one-night stand," Kelley said. Alix swallowed her food. She watched Kelley look at Emira. Emira examined the details of her plate. Kelley stopped cutting into a turkey leg to say, "I met Emira at Market Depot, when she was being held by the police."

Alix's mouth cupped open and she quickly closed it. The table collectively took in this information as Prudence held up a marshmallow that was melted to black on one side. Prudence showed it to Imani and whispered, "This looks like a caca doo-doo."

Tamra leaned forward to see around Emira to Kelley. "You were there?"

"Yeah, I saw what was happening and I pulled out my phone."

"Wait a second, you're kidding." Peter sat back in his chair. In his left arm, Catherine started to wake up. "I remember you now."

Rachel snorted and said, "Whoops."

"Sorry, yeah," Kelley said to Peter. "I didn't expect you to remember me. You definitely had other things to worry about."

"You had your phone up," Peter remembered, "and you were recording."

"There's a video?" Tamra asked. She looked to Alix with a face that said, *I knew it.*

"Well, yes, but that's Emira's property now. Sorry." Kelley half laughed. "This isn't exactly Thanksgiving conversation. I probably should have said we met on Tinder or something. I'm sorry." This time he apologized to Emira.

Alix stared across the table at her sitter, feeling as if she'd been very publicly uninvited to a gathering that she herself had organized. The betrayal Alix felt (*Why wouldn't you just tell me where you really met? Why would you say the train?*) was quickly replaced by a new backstabbing confusion (*Why* did *you call Peter that night? Why wouldn't you just call me?*).

Emira adjusted her earring and picked her fork up again. "No, it's fine. We *did* meet for real on the train a few days later, though," she promised. "And then we just . . . kept seeing each other."

"Well, Jesus, Kelley. I'm glad you're here," Peter said. "And I'm glad that something good came out of that night. Emira, you're a saint for not suing that entire franchise. Which you could definitely do if there's a video."

Walter raised his glass to himself. "Abso-friggin-lutely."

"Oh, yeah no." Emira shook her head. "No, I would die if that video got out. I haven't even watched it."

"I'd be the same way," Jodi said.

"But umm . . ." Emira pivoted. "How did you guys meet, Mrs. Chamberlain? I guess I've never asked."

"You mean," Peter said, "how did Alix pursue me at the most disgusting bar I've ever been to?"

Alix forced a laugh. "*Pursue* is generous."

"Mama," Briar said, "I want to open the pie."

Alix shushed her. "Pie is for later."

Peter went on to tell a story that Alix had heard many times but never really annoyed her until now. The whole evening she found herself falling in and out of love with her husband quite abruptly, and through his account of how they met, she was both pleased that he depicted Alix as *stunning*, waving and buying him a beer from across a bar, and irked that he mentioned her being so nervous that she drank the beer herself. With Kelley sitting so close to her, Alix continued to switch from offense to defense. When Peter finished his story, she thought, *That's right, Kelley. I drink beer now. With my husband, who I've had sex with more than one time.*

Tamra looked to Alix and asked, "Is that when you were working at Hunter?"

"Yes, it was." Alix nodded. She wanted to say something about the obnoxious dollar drink specials this bar had provided, and how appreciated these specials were because she was making less than forty grand at the time, but Kelley seemingly took her tiny pause as an opportunity to ask, rather loudly, "And what do you do now, Alex? Emira said you're writing a history book. Is that right?"

Rachel said, "A *history* book?" as Peter said, "Now *that's* being generous."

Emira's eyes went small as she looked up at Alix.

Alix's face and neck turned hot against the sweater she now wished she had changed out of. She waved her head side to side and took up her glass of wine. "Bri, sit up my love," she said. "Well, it's umm"—she took a sip—"it's *my* little history." On *my*, she placed a hand to her chest, and it reminded her of hugging Emira the morning after Market Depot, and how Emira just sort of leaned in as if she'd had trouble hearing, instead of just hugging her back. "I have a book coming out with HarperCollins, and it'll have the best letters I've written and received since I started my business."

"That's really only half of it." Tamra turned to Emira as she went on. "I'm sure you've seen her Instagram and all the things she has her hands in."

"Oh, no." Emira smiled. "I don't have Instagram."

"Girl!" Tamra feigned dramatic shock. "We have got to get you caught up!"

"You don't have Instagram?" Next to Alix, Jodi's amazement was more genuine. "That's amazing. Even Prudence has one."

Emira said, "Really?"

"Well, I run it, and it's private," Jodi assured her, "but it keeps our distant family members very happy."

"So it's like a history of your business?" Kelley wouldn't let it go. Alix knew exactly what he was doing, but how could she fight him at the dinner table, in front of her friends and in front of Emira?

"Mm-hmm," she said. "Exactly."

"And when did it start?"

"Well . . . I started my business in 2009, so—"

"Oh wow, okay." Kelley smiled across the table. "That's a brief history."

"Wait, when did we all meet?" Jodi stepped in. "2011?"

"Rachel, I can't believe you were the *experienced* parent back then," Tamra said.

"Taught you bitches everything I know," Rachel said.

Imani and Cleo looked at their mother, seeking corroboration that a bad word had been said. Tamra shook her head in confirmation and put a finger to lips.

"You know what?" Peter said. "I want to make a toast."

Alix thought both *Oh Jesus* and *Thank God*. Peter was so good at making things easy and sociable but only in a way that made it seem like a TV show was ending. With all 141 pounds of her being, Alix wished she could just turn this night off.

"I know it wasn't easy for Alix to leave you ladies," Peter said. "And believe it or not, I miss you all very much too. As Alix writes her book and her business continues to grow, I've seen how much she's come to lean on you, how much you encourage her, and how much easier you make her life. And Emira, that includes you now too. I'm very happy, or should I say *thankful*, to be outnumbered by so many amazing women tonight. So here's to you."

Everyone raised their glasses and said cheers. Briar managed to get a green bean on her fork by herself. When she held it up and showed it to Walter, he said, "That's tremendous."

Sixteen

After Peter made a toast that made Emira so embarrassed she could barely speak, Peter handed Catherine over to Mrs. Chamberlain and the table broke off into smaller conversations. Walter asked Kelley what the heck net neutrality was anyway. Jodi said, "I can't believe how much she looks like you," and Mrs. Chamberlain said, "You should see our baby pictures side by side." Across from Kelley, Briar said to no one, "My tummy doesn't like that."

Twice during dinner Kelley had squeezed Emira's knee, but she hadn't known what he was saying by it; they were still too new. Was he mad that she hadn't filled him in on how she'd said they met, the lie she completely forgot that she'd told? Did he think Mrs. Chamberlain was lying when she said they'd met on the train, to cover up that awful night altogether? Was that why he was being so rude about her job and her book? And why would Mrs. Chamberlain tell her it was a history book when it obviously fucking wasn't? When Mrs. Chamberlain ran out the door on Mondays, Wednesdays, and Fridays, Emira imagined her going to the library and laying out big, dusty reference books and Post-it notes and maybe even using a magnifying glass. But a book about letter writing? Like—calligraphy and shit? It sounded like the kind of book you saw in the sale section at Barnes & Noble, or in the waiting line when you were shopping at Michaels. But Emira couldn't wrap her head around this, or the impossible fact that Kelley and Mrs. Chamberlain had once dated each other, let alone known each other out of the context of Emira, because sitting to her right, Tamra began to relentlessly ask questions about Emira's plans for her career and for the rest of her life.

"So you went to Temple . . ." Tamra said.

"Uh-huh."

"And then you took some typing classes."

"Yeah, that's my other job."

"Well, if you're thinking of grad school it's actually not too late to apply for next fall."

Had someone told Tamra that Emira wanted to go to grad school? Because no one had told Emira. She'd gone to undergraduate school to figure out what she wanted to do . . . wasn't graduate school for the students who had succeeded? Emira's eyes went from Briar, who had turned strangely quiet, to Prudence, who was squeezing the sides of Imani's face. Imani was giggling in awe at Prudence the way Emira would have when she was little, when she was still quite bemused by what white girls got away with. Jodi was saying, "Would you like it if I did that to your face?" and Prudence was saying, "Yes, I would."

"What was your GPA at Temple?" Tamra asked.

"Oh . . . not awesome," Emira said. She set her fork and knife at the side of her plate. "Like, a 3.1."

"Hmmm, okay, okay." Tamra nodded slowly. "So grad school may be out. But you know what, Emira? There are plenty of other options that will surprise you. In fact, my sister-in-law went to a certificate program for hotel management, and now she has a five-bedroom house and makes six figures, in *Sacramento*. Can you believe that?"

Briar hiccuped once and her cheeks turned red.

"Yeah, that's crazy . . ." Emira said. She wiped her hands on the napkin in her lap and said across the table, "Is Briar okay?"

But Mrs. Chamberlain was passing Catherine to Jodi, and they were trying to get her to say hi once again. On the other side of Emira, Walter, Kelley, and Peter were discussing the new Penn State football coach and his six-year contract. And as Briar's stare became more glazed and far away, Emira began to feel the way she had on the night she and Briar went to Market Depot, very much together but also brutally alone. Emira said, "B, are you okay?" Briar tapped her mother's arm. "I want Mama," she said.

"Mama's talking, Bri, I still see carrots on your plate." Mrs. Chamberlain turned back to Catherine and said, "Come on, sweetheart. Can you say hi?"

Tamra leaned over even closer to Emira. "I don't know if you know this, but Alix has a lot of pull. So does Peter, in fact." She reached over with long fingers and laid them on Emira's arm. "They *love* you," she said. "I'm sure they would help you get into any program you wanted, or change up your schedule to fit in an internship or classes, or whatever you were looking to get into. How old are you, honey?"

Briar hiccuped again. Emira said, "I'm twenty-five."

"Okay. We gotta hustle, don't we? What's the big goal for you?"

"Umm . . ." Emira readjusted in her seat. She took the clasp of her necklace from the space above her sternum and returned it to its place behind her neck. "I'm not really sure."

"Come on, now," Tamra pressed. Across the table, Briar's face looked like she was both falling asleep and ready to panic. "If you could wake up tomorrow," Tamra said, "and do anything you wanted, what would that something be?"

Next to Emira, Walter said, "He's gonna have to do better than that for a championship." Rachel looked at Catherine and said, "Hi, mini Alix." Jodi shushed Prudence and said, "Prudence? That's two," and Emira realized that if she'd answered Tamra's question truthfully, no one would have heard her. She could have placed a sweet hand underneath her chin and said, *If I had a "big goal," do you really think I'd be sitting at this fucking table right now?* But just then Briar started to gag. And when Emira grabbed what she knew was a very expensive napkin and dove across the table to cover the toddler's mouth, Jodi was the first to notice and scream.

Seventeen

Years ago, in Alex Murphy's teenage bedroom, with the door closed, Kelley did all of these things he'd clearly been told to do by an older brother or a more experienced friend, but this obvious instruction didn't take away from the wildly flattering fact that he was doing these things to her. Kelley made a grand presentation of a recently purchased condom. He asked her if it hurt and if she was okay. He even asked if they should put down a towel since her bedspread was so nice. The whole thing lasted about two songs ("A Long December" and "Colorblind"), but Alex had been so taken with Kelley that she breathed a sigh of relief and gratitude. *No matter what happens*, she told herself, *I'll never mind remembering this*. It wasn't like she thought they'd marry, but the infatuation was dangerous and heavy.

Now, in the comfort of her adult home, it seemed that the infatuation had never really ended. Alix couldn't tell if it had started up again, or if it had only become dormant by means of time and space.

Alix watched Jodi put her hands to her mouth. Emira's body was soaring across the table both in slow motion and also with a quickness that made Alix jump in her seat. Even slower was Kelley's rise as he stood up from the table and swung his arm around Emira's waist, inches above pots of almost-gone butternut squash and a platter of lukewarm dark meat. In the shuffle, Alix couldn't properly collect the fact that her child was throwing up at the dinner table. She could only stare at the same hand that used to hold the underside of her jaw after varsity games and coed scrimmages. It had only been a few months, but at one time in her life, Kelley made Alix so wonderfully nervous, and he used his hands to steady her. "Hey hey hey." He'd once said this outside the girls' locker room. "You gotta be still and let me like you a little bit."

And now his hands were wrapped around Emira in Alix's house on Thanksgiving Day. Alix had the sudden urge to remove Kelley's hands from Emira's hips, and not just because of the sexual familiarity that they displayed. In the same funny muscle memory that makes you take out your metro card to open your front door, or call your third-grade teacher *Mom*, Alix found herself ready to slap Kelley's wrists away from her sitter. In the same voice and motion she used almost every day, she felt herself almost say, *No no no. Don't touch. That's Mama's.*

Jodi squeezed Alix's arm so hard that it was clear that it wasn't the first time. Alix was suddenly back in the room as Briar started to cry. For a moment, when Jodi said, "Alix-honey, grab your girl," Alix thought she was referring to Emira.

Eighteen

Briar's face pinched together underneath the vomit-filled napkin, and it reminded Emira that the little girl rarely cried. Emira's heart raced from diving over the table, from almost falling on top of it until Kelley caught her in his massive hands, and then from seeing a tiny face at the other side begin to moan in shock and discomfiture. Emira cupped the vomit in the napkin and brought it from Briar's chin upward past her nose. With nothing in front of her face, the three-year-old began to scream.

Tamra said, "Oh no," and Peter ran to get a towel and Prudence said, "Eww!" and Rachel laughed. "Party foul."

Mrs. Chamberlain finally blinked. "Oh God."

She went to pick Briar up, but Emira stopped her. "Actually, can you just unbuckle her? I'll grab her." Emira said this with such urgency that Mrs. Chamberlain obeyed. Emira said, "B, stand up for me," and she swung the toddler into her arms, Briar's face dripping with snot and tears.

Mrs. Chamberlain said, "Oh no, Emira, you don't have to do that—"

"No, it's okay, I got her." Emira ascended the stairs and passed Peter and a bartender carrying paper towels and cleaning bottles in their hands. When she made it to the kitchen, she heard Walter say, "That was incredible!"

In the upstairs bathroom, Emira sat Briar down on the toilet seat and closed the door behind her. Briar did that nervous and uneven breathing Emira saw other children do when they skinned their knees or popped their balloons. It was alarming to know that this type of crying had been inside Briar all along, that she'd always been capable of it and just chosen not to.

"Hey." Emira took a washcloth and began to wet it with warm water from the sink. "Hey, mama, it's okay. Look at me." She wiped Briar's mouth and neck as Briar gasped for air so hard her whole body trembled every few seconds. "I'm sorry, big girl. That's no fun to throw up. But hey, I think I caught it all. Your dress is still clean."

Briar started to whimper as she touched her dress at the hem. "These is itchy," she said.

"Yeah." Emira took Briar's fingers and wiped each one down with the towel. "This dress isn't really my favorite either."

"I don't—I don't like . . ." Briar calmed herself enough to point at the ceiling with her free hand and say, "I don't like when Catherine bees the favorite."

Emira stopped. She hung the washcloth on the side of the sink and sat back on her heels. "What did you say?"

"I don't—I don't like when Catherine bees the littlest favorite to Mama. I don't like that." Briar had stopped crying and she said this with a calm and specific certainty, both that she had explained it correctly and that this was in fact how she felt.

Emira pressed her lips together. "B, you know what?" As she for-mulated her words, Emira held Briar's knees in both of her hands and thought, *This is the littlest your knees will ever be.* "You can have . . . favorite ice cream. Or favorite cereal. But guess what? When you have a family, everyone is the same. Do you have a family?"

Briar put her fingers in her mouth. "Yesh."

"Do you have a mama?"

"Yesh."

"And a dada?"

"Yesh."

"And a sister?"

"Yesh."

"Exactly, that's your family. And in families, everyone is *always* the same."

Briar touched her shoulders. "How come?"

"Well . . ."

In Emira's family, Justyne was so obviously the favorite, but Emira was her brother's favorite and so it seemed to even out. Her mother favored Alfie when it came to Christmas gifts, and her father favored Emira when it came to birthdays and phone calls. Emira didn't figure this out until high school, but Briar was doing so at the tender age of three. Emira looked at the little person on the toilet and felt as if she were pushing an enormous boat out into the ocean. She slumped as if the situation were completely out of her hands and said, "'Cause that's what family means. Family means no favorites."

Mr. Chamberlain knocked twice and the cracked door swung open. When Briar saw her father she frowned and said, "Hi."

By the time Emira came back downstairs, the bartenders were clearing away plates and everyone was gathering in the living room for dessert. Kelley made a very theatrical show of putting his own plate into the sink upstairs, and helping the two hired women push the dining room chairs back underneath the table. A few bites into a sugary strawberry-rhubarb pie, Prudence began to have a breakdown about *needing* more whipped cream (this marked the third time, in Emira's opinion, that Prudence had reached number three). Cleo started to cry as well, and then Rachel stood to slip on her jacket. Rachel explained that she was meeting a man-friend in town and would be back in a few hours. She tapped Briar on the nose and said, "I'm off like a prom dress," before heading for the door. Emira took the moment to squeeze Kelley's arm. "We should probably get going, too."

After awkward and stunted good-byes inside the Chamberlain house, Emira had all those feelings of leaving a movie theater and realizing that it was dark outside and that it had been for some time. The snow crunched underneath her feet as she stood next to Kelley and waited for their Uber. In a pink T-shirt and white bedtime leggings, Briar waved from Peter's arms at the top of the stoop. Emira waved back and mouthed, *Bye, pickle.* Inside the Uber, Kelley and Emira didn't speak.

Kelley stared out the window and rubbed his chin. As the silence settled in, Kelley started to remind Emira of the type of person on the train who cussed out loud when there was a delay. There was always that one passenger who seemed to believe that the train had been delayed only for them, as if no one else was inconvenienced and late. And as time went on, they became angrier at the fact that they couldn't speak to a manager, rather than bothered by the delay itself. The car rolled along in the glittery snow, and for the first time since they'd been dating, Emira felt that Kelley was acting particularly white.

Before they reached his apartment, Kelley told the driver that he could stop on the block before his street. He said to Emira, "I need one last drink," and reached to open the car door.

Emira followed Kelley into the kind of bar that Shaunie would have been tickled by, particularly at nine p.m. on Thanksgiving Day. There were three white men with gray and black beards seated in the center of the dimly lit bar, and a vacant pool table in a wood-paneled back room. One man was eating alone—chicken and something green—as he kept his eyes on the TV screen attached to the wall above the cash register. On the long wall opposite were pictures of John Wayne, Pennsylvania license plates, and other sepia-colored cowboys. Emira could hear low folk music, and just above it, a referee from the large television screen blowing a whistle and throwing a yellow flag. She took her coat off and hung it up next to a longhorn skull mounted on the wall.

On top of a bar stool, Kelley ordered a beer. Emira declined. She wanted to go back to his apartment and back to Kelley's bed because the idea of laughing away the awkwardness of the evening still didn't seem completely far-fetched. It wasn't that Emira *wasn't* bothered by the night's disclosure, but—she thought this as Kelley kicked one boot up on the footrest and kept the other balanced on the soiled floor—at the end of the day, what could she, or anyone, really do about the situation? High school was a *long* time ago, even for some-one you've slept with. In college, when Emira learned that she'd once slept with her current boyfriend's new roommate, Shaunie had gasped and said, "What are you gonna do?" Emira had laughed and said, "Probably just keep living my life." Josefa had said, "Amen."

So Emira stayed standing, which put them at eye level, a dynamic she loved. She put her hands behind her back and hooked her fingers together, knowing she had one shot to turn this night around. In an attempt that was dumb but still charmingly dadlike, Emira said, "At least the food was good?"

Kelley's face stayed the same.

"Emira, I'm not trying to be dramatic . . . but there's no way you can keep working for Alex."

Emira couldn't help but laugh. She waited for his face to break, but when it didn't, she placed her hands against the side of the bar. "Okay, Kelley, come on. Yeah, that was extremely awkward and it's pretty weird and gross that you used to date my boss, but that was *high school*. You expect me to quit my job over it?"

"This isn't just . . . thank you, sorry." Kelley said this as the bartender dropped off his beer. Kelley reached back for his wallet. "This isn't just an ex-girlfriend. Alex Murphy is . . . she's more than just a loss-of-innocence moment. She's a *bad* person."

"But I don't work for *Alex Murphy*." Emira took her purse off her shoulder and hung it on a hook underneath the bar. "I work for Mrs. Chamberlain. And you're acting like you guys still talk or something."

The idea of Kelley still hung up on Mrs. Chamberlain was slightly entertaining. Mrs. Chamberlain—at her core—was such a *mom*. She said things like *Look at Mama when I'm talking to you*, and, *Just one more bite, lovey*. She bought nonfiction books and used the dust jacket as a bookmark. She ordered diapers in bulk, and when she thought she was alone, she put her headphones on and laughed out loud as she watched clips from *The Ellen Show* on her iPad. Emira could recognize the fact that Kelley and Mrs. Chamberlain were only a year apart in age, but not to the extent that it put them in the same league of parenthood. Kelley owned nice things, but owning a baby was next level. Emira tried to keep her voice even as she said, "I don't understand why you care so much."

"I *don't* care so much. Okay, listen . . ." Kelley sipped the top layer of his beer and bent his head lower to speak to her. "Emira . . . the fact that Alex sent you to a grocery store with her kid at eleven p.m.

makes a lot more sense now. You're not the first black woman Alex has hired to work for her family, and you probably won't be the last."

"Okay . . . ?" Emira sat down. She didn't mean to sound flippant, but she doubted that Kelley could really tell her anything she didn't already know. Emira had met several "Mrs. Chamberlains" before. They were all rich and overly nice and particularly lovely to the people who served them. Emira knew that Mrs. Chamberlain wanted a friendship, but she also knew that Mrs. Chamberlain would never display the same efforts of kindness with her friends as she did with Emira: "accidentally" ordering two salads and offering one to Emira, or sending her home with a bag filled with frozen dinners and soups. It wasn't that Emira didn't understand the racially charged history that Kelley was alluding to, but she couldn't help but think that if she weren't working for *this* Mrs. Chamberlain, she'd probably be working for another one.

Kelley laced his fingers in his lap. "I didn't tell you this before because . . . I don't know. We were just dating and I didn't want you to think I was trying to be woke or whatever, but in high school . . . Alex used to live in a legit mansion. It was insane. Some shitty stuff happened where she wrote me a letter that got into the wrong hands, and this group of kids found out about where she lived. They tried to go swimming at her house because it was honestly a country club, but Alex called the cops. And this black kid named Robbie, who I'm still friends with, ended up getting arrested. He lost his scholarship. He had to go to community college for a year. She completely altered the course of his life."

Emira bit the side of her nail. "You were there when this happened?"

"Yeah, we were dating. Until this went down," Kelley said. "I told her not to call the police. Like—come on, a bunch of black kids on the property and a white girl calls the cops? It was obvious what would happen, but she tried to make it seem like she was protecting the black housekeeper her family employed." Kelley stopped and took another sip of his beer. "She acted like she was so embarrassed of her wealth, but now she's still living the same way she did then, and she's still hiring black women to take care of her family. And I was an idiot at the time. I thought like—*Oh sweet, your house has a movie theater and this woman makes you whatever dinner you want.* But looking back, it was super creepy. Alex hung all over this woman and acted like they were best friends. This woman even did her hair before school. Alex completely gets off on either having black people work for her or calling the cops on them. I can't . . . Emira, you can't be one of her people."

Emira crossed her legs. "Kelley . . . I don't know what to say. It's a job. Briar hangs on me all the time. And I comb her hair every time I see her."

"Alex was a senior in high school. She wasn't a baby."

"But . . . I don't know. I know it's weird"—she tried to explain—"but people do pay other people to act like part of the family. That doesn't mean it's not a transaction."

"Emira, this was different. The woman who worked for them? They made her wear a *uniform*. At first I just thought she wore the same polo a lot, but then I saw that it said *Murphy* on it and I was like . . ."

Emira couldn't keep it in. When Kelley said the word *polo*, she dropped her eyes. She let out a sound that was very Mrs. Chamberlain–like in pitch, and it sounded like a very curious "Huh."

"Wait . . ." Kelley lifted his hands and rested his palms at the base of his hairline. He looked like he was watching the end of a very close game. "Emira," he said. "Don't tell me she makes you wear a uniform."

Emira looked up at the water-stained ceiling. She raised her shoulders and said, "Well, she doesn't *make* me do anything."

"Goddammit, Emira!"

Emira gripped the sides of her chair and looked at the other end of the bar. Out of everything that had happened that evening, this reaction stunned Emira the most. She wanted to shake him and say, *No no no. You're* Kelley, *remember? You think videos of dogs who can't catch anything are hilarious. You take pictures of mirrors you see on the street, and send them to me with the caption, "Hey, A-Mira." You still put a glass of water by my side of the bed even though I've never drunk from it. Not even once.* But here he was behaving as if they were alone, in the type of bar that Kelley should have checked in with her about before sitting and ordering a drink. "You need to calm the fuck down," she hissed.

"You have to quit," he said. "You have to. You cannot work there. Holy shit, how did this happen?"

"Okay . . . I'm a *babysitter*." Emira scooted up on her seat to speak closer to him, hoping to lower his volume with her private proximity. "I wear a different shirt at work because we paint and color and go to the park and shit. It's just so I don't get my clothes messy, that's it. This is nothing like the house you went to in high school."

"Oh, right." Kelley had a childish glare when he asked, "So have you ever *not* worn it?"

Emira closed her mouth.

"Do the shirts say *your* name on them? Or hers?"

In a small voice Emira said, "I feel like you're being kind of a dick right now."

"This is *not* okay." Kelley hit his fingers against the bar top on *not* and *okay*. The brown liquid in his glass trembled twice. "This isn't me having some unresolved high school crush or grudge. Alex does this.

She uses black employees as an excuse for her own actions. Not only is she a bad person, but it's infuriating because you're incredible with children! You should get to wear your own clothes with people who deserve you. And I know I said I'd drop it but I swear to God, if you released that video from the grocery store—"

"Kelley? Back up." Emira said his name the way she said Briar's when the little girl wanted to open the trash can and look, just for a second. "Now you wanna use this video to shame Mrs. Chamberlain?"

"Alex shouldn't be able to get away with this shit. And you would probably get nanny offers from the richest families in Philadelphia."

"Cool, that would literally only make you happy. You do realize they'd pay me the same?"

"Then tell me what I need to do!"

"Kelley, ohmygod."

"If it's money or a job or if you need to live with me for a bit, whatever." He listed these options on his fingers. "Tell me what I need to say to get you to leave."

"I feel like leaving this fucking bar right now." Emira grabbed her purse.

"Emira. Don't."

Her heels clicked as she went for her coat. Emira heard Kelley's stool move as he did, and then his voice behind her. "Wait wait wait, talk to me."

She opened the door to the bar vestibule, much like the one at the front of the Chamberlain house, but this one was dark and smelled like stale smoke and sweaty shoes. The door outside was heavy and cold as she pushed herself into it. A gust of wind and snow fought her from the other side, and the door closed shut against her shoulder. Emira said, "Fuck."

The door behind Kelley closed and then it was just the two of them in this tiny space. "Hey." He held two fingers to the bridge of his nose as if he were checking it for a break. "Hear me out here. I don't want to fight. All I'm saying is that you should—"

"Okay, first of all?" Emira turned to him. She threw her coat over her arm and held it close. "You don't get to tell me where I should and shouldn't work. You literally have a cafeteria in your office. You wear T-shirts to work. And you have a *doorman*, Kelley, okay? So you can one thousand percent go fuck yourself. The fact that you think you're better than *A-leeks* or Alex or whatever is a joke. You will never have to even consider working somewhere that requires a uniform, so you can chill the fuck out about how I choose to make my living. And second of all? You were so fucking rude in there! At a Thanksgiving *dinner*!"

Kelley leaned up against the wall behind him and closed his mouth. Emira wasn't finished, and she felt she was finding her thoughts and recollection of the evening as the words and cold found her body. "You're not better than anyone," she said, "when you hang up your own coat and take your plate to the trash. I've been those girls helping out tonight. I fucking *am* those girls helping out tonight, and you're not making anything easier by giving them less to do. It's like eating everything on your plate 'cause you think someone else won't go hungry if you don't. You're not helping anyone but yourself. But that's not even the half of it. You're not seeing the whole situation for what it is. Of *course* I want a new job. I'd *love* to make real money and not have spit-up on all my clothes. But I can't . . ." Emira thought, *Oh God*. She did what Shaunie called "the ugly cry lip" and looked down to her boots. The toes were wet from melted snow. "I can't just fucking leave her," she said.

Kelley closed his eyes for a full two seconds, as if he'd been punched in the stomach, and had also seen it coming.

"For twenty-one hours a week, Briar gets to matter to someone and you want me to just pick up and leave? When would I ever see her if . . . It's not that simple." Her voice cracked again. Emira shook her head and crossed one knee over the other. They stood there like that for what seemed like a long time.

"I messed up," Kelley said. "I'm not—I wasn't trying to . . . even though it's exactly what I did, I'm not trying . . . Emira, look at me. I more than just like you."

With her coat pressed into her gut, Emira stood frozen against the door and felt her heart beat into it. She said, "Okay."

Kelley pressed his lips together. He stuck his hands in his pockets and bent slightly to meet her eyes. "Do you get what I mean by that?"

Emira nodded and looked back to her shoes. She wiped her eye with her pinky finger, looked up, and said, "Fuck."

An hour later, Emira sat in Kelley's bed. In the living room, Kelley Skyped with his family in Florida and she listened to the way his voice changed from parents to siblings to grandparents to nephew, and then to a very old dog who wandered into frame. Emira grabbed her phone and texted a list to herself. When she heard Kelley say good-bye, she walked with the lit-up screen into the living room. It was dark and the snow sent spots from outside the window over her bare feet.

"I have things to say."

Kelley closed his laptop and swiveled his chair to face her. Emira stood pantless and held her phone in both hands.

"I know I have to quit," she said. "I know that I can't stay there, and that . . . raising Briar isn't my job. But I just need to do it on my own terms. I turn twenty-six next week." Emira grinned sadly. "And . . . I'm gonna be kicked off my parents' health insurance. I've known for a while that this wasn't exactly sustainable, but I just . . . yeah, I need to figure it out on my own."

"I completely understand," he said. "And I didn't forget your birthday."

"I'm not done yet," Emira stopped him. She looked back to her phone. "Number two. You gotta stop bringing up that tape from Market Depot."

Kelley placed his elbows on the desk behind him.

"Like . . . I get it," Emira said. "You have a weirdly large amount of black friends, you saw Kendrick Lamar in concert, and now you have a black girlfriend . . . great. But I need you to get that like . . . being angry and yelling in a store means something different for me than it would for you, even though I was in the right. And I get that you wanna stick it to Mrs. Chamberlain or whatever to avenge your high school friend, but her life wouldn't change at all. Mine would. And I don't want anyone seeing it, especially as I start to look for a job."

Kelley nodded in long, slow dips. "Okay . . . I don't exactly agree," he warned. "I remember that night very well, and I really thought you kept your cool much more than anyone would expect . . . but I also respect that. And I won't bring it up again."

"You promise?"

"I promise."

"Okay, and last thing . . . ?" Emira put a hand to her neck. "You can't take me to bars like that anymore."

Kelley squinted. Then he tipped his head back, and she watched him appear to realize what he'd done, and why she was bringing it up now. "Okay . . . that was another mistake. But if it makes a difference, I've been there twice before, and I wouldn't have taken you some-where uncomfortable on purpose."

"Well, yeah, but, that's the point. You think it's comfortable because it's always been that way for *you*."

Emira and Kelley talked about race very little because it always seemed like they were doing it already. When she really considered a life with him, a real life, a joint-bank-account-emergency-contact-both-names-on-the-lease life, Emira almost wanted to roll her eyes and ask, *Are we really gonna do this? How are you gonna tell your parents? If I'd walked in here when they were still on the screen, how would you have introduced me? Are you gonna take our son to get his hair done? Who's gonna teach him that it doesn't matter what his friends do, that he can't stand too close to white women when he's on the train or in an elevator? That he should slowly and noticeably put his keys on the roof as soon as he gets pulled over? Or that there are times our daughter should stand up for herself, and times to pretend it was a joke that she didn't quite catch. Or that when white people compliment her ("She's so professional. She's always on time"), it doesn't always feel good, because sometimes people are gonna be surprised by the fact that she showed up, rather than the fact that she had something to say when she did.*

"I don't know . . ." Emira struggled. "Lemme try to say this. You get real fired up when we talk about that night at Market Depot. But I don't need you to be mad that it happened. I need you to be mad that it just like . . . happens. I'm also not asking you to boycott places or anything. Mrs. Chamberlain makes a big deal about not going to Market Depot anymore and it's like umm, okay, the other stores are mad far, but it's your life. But it's the same thing for you. Like—I don't want you to change your life because of me. If you wanna go to that bar without me, whatever. Just try to remember that we have different experiences. John Wayne said a lot of fucked-up shit and I'd rather not stare at his face while I have a drink."

Kelley poked his lips out in a way that let her know he wouldn't forget. "I can be better about that."

"Okay."

"Can I also just say . . ." Kelley added, "I wasn't trying to act like you can't get a new job on your own. I know you can."

"I know . . . well, ha, we'll see. Maybe I *will* need your help in case Mrs. Chamberlain fires me or whatever." Emira shook her head and clicked her phone to dark. "Which she better not. I'm babysitting every day next week 'cause she'll be out of town till Friday and I need that money like, yesterday."

"Emira. If I know anything about Alex, it's that she definitely won't fire you."

"She might if she's as bothered by us dating as you were."

"No way," Kelley said. "She would never fire you because it would say more about her than it would about you. Not to mention, now she knows there's a video of you being mistreated because of where she sent you."

"Kelley, she's sent me there about a hundred times. It may have even been my idea. I'm sorry, but I think you're the only one who sees it that way."

"Okay, fine. But listen, I obviously think you should start looking in the New Year, but for now, your job is safe. If I were you, I'd take the money and show that kid a really good time before you leave."

Emira crossed her arms over her chest and stared at the floor. She pictured Briar, hiccuping with each breath, and the way she always pointed to the ceiling when she was about to say something true. Emira pointed her toe on the dark wood floor and said, "That's an interesting way of looking at it."

Kelley swiveled his chair from left to right for a moment. "Do you . . . wanna talk about what I said to you in the bar?"

Emira bit her bottom lip. Kelley made her feel both extremely grown up and consumed with infantile reactions. Her heart could barely handle him remembering her birthday; she wasn't going to touch the L-word today. "Ummm, nope." She smiled. "I had three things on my list. So I'm good."

Nineteen

On Friday morning, Alix woke up before her husband. There was a part of her that marveled that he was still there, in their bed, in their home, as if the previous night's rift of turbulent envy could have deleted Peter from the equation that was her life. But there he was, very asleep, his face unknowing as it grazed the inside of his armpit. Alix rolled over and stared at her night table piled with books, her iPad, a gold lamp, and a picture of Briar and Catherine in bathing suits, eating watermelon with their hands. Catherine was in a yellow one-piece, but she was too little to sit up on her own, so Peter's arms were holding her up, his biceps cut off by the frame. Alix's children looked unbelievably small and innocent, pictured above her resting iPad, particularly because the night before, after her family was asleep, Alix had taken the tablet into the bathroom where she stayed for two hours to search, scroll, and stare at any image of Kelley Copeland she could find.

His Facebook. His Instagram. His LinkedIn. His workplace. When Alix discovered he didn't have a Twitter account, she crept back out to her bedroom to retrieve her phone so she could thumb through Venmo and try to find his transactions. Alix could remember when Facebook came out with a photo feature—it was 2005—and that was probably the last time she'd gone this hard. But ten years later there was much to behold. Despite what he'd said to her when he'd stepped into her home, it was Kelley who hadn't changed a bit.

Between pictures from European trips and holiday parties, Alix located all of Kelley's ex-girlfriends, and—surprise, surprise—none of them were white. Alix wasn't sure if any of them identified as black (one of them had a black father but this was all she could confirm)— however, they were all ethnically ambiguous looking with names like Tierra and Christina, Jasmine and Gabi. They had light brown skin and curly dark hair or dramatic widow's peaks and Spanish last names. They went to Black Lives Matter marches and worked for nonprofit start-ups. They did skin care tutorials on Instagram with quirky music in the background. All of Kelley's exes started their days with intricate smoothie recipes—Alix thought, *Is this a thing?*—and Alix dug deep enough to see that Kelley had referred to two of them as queens (once in 2014, *This queen*, and once in 2012, *Hey Queen*). Of *course* Kelley was excited to now be dating Emira.

But these girls were different than Emira. They had big passions and light brown skin and punchy, colorful blogs with punny titles. They had decent jobs and vacation photos and one had a few thousand Instagram followers. If Kelley had left these women in the same way he'd left Alix—ruining her reputation, choosing strangers over her, publicly breaking up with her with a horribly pretentious line—they had obviously and easily bounced back. But Emira was different. Alix couldn't quite explain it, but Emira was different in the same way Claudette had been different; they were extremely special people and while no one deserved poor treatment, they deserved it even less.

Back in high school, Kelley wanted status, and at Alix's expense, that's what he'd got. But what did Kelley think he was getting from Emira? How many times had he proudly told the story of how they met? Acting performatively flustered and suggesting that he shouldn't have? As she sat on the ledge of her bathtub, Alix's iPad became so warm that it started to burn her legs.

Alix reached to the side of the tub and picked up her phone. She texted the girls that she wanted to meet at ten a.m., not eleven. She took her iPad and went to the restaurant's website, moving their reservation up one hour.

———————

"I'm furious." Alix slumped. Across the table and over plates filled with brunch specials, Jodi held her coffee in both hands. To Alix's left, Rachel broke a yolk open and it ran onto a bed of greens. To her right, Tamra salted her eggs, but she kept her eyes raised and focused on Alix. "I hate that I'm completely shocked," Alix said, "and that I'm not surprised."

Tamra laughed bitterly as she set the saltshaker down. "This all makes a whole lot more sense now. I knew there was something off about him."

"Alix, don't be mad at me," Jodi said carefully. "But I'm having a hard time understanding. If anyone did what he did to me—telling awful kids where I live and putting people I love at risk—I would be furious too. But you're also saying that he's the opposite of racist? That he likes black people too much?"

"Alix is saying"—Tamra stepped in—"that Kelley is one of those white guys who not only goes out of his way to date black women but *only* wants to date black women."

With kale in her cheek, Rachel chewed and said, "That's racist."

"It completely fetishizes black people in a terrible way," Tamra went on. "It makes it seem like we're all the same, as if we can't contain multitudes of personalities and traits and differences. And people like that think that it says something good about them, that they're so brave and unique that they would even *dare* to date black women. Like they're some kind of martyr."

Alix nodded so vigorously that the table lightly shook. "This is what he does," she said. "In high school it was the black athletes. According to his Facebook it's now black women. And if he's still surrounding himself with black people just so he can feel good about himself, I couldn't care less . . . but now Emira is on the other side of it. And this doesn't even touch on what he did to me back then."

"Okay. I get it now. No wonder you were so upset last night!" Jodi cut into her hash browns. "Here I was thinking you still carried a flame for him, which I wouldn't judge you for either, but this takes it to a whole new level."

"No no, it's nothing like that. God, no," Alix said. "For the record, this has *nothing* to do with me dating Kelley Copeland." She said his name as if it were a myth or fickle philosophy, something to put air quotes around. "But I do care about my sitter. This guy completely ruined my high school experience, and I don't trust him as far as I can spit. And I know, I *know* people change . . . but when he showed up yesterday . . . I don't know. At first I thought, 'How are you here?' And then I thought, 'What do you want with my sitter?'"

Jodi placed a hand to her cheek. Rachel looked up from her plate and said, "I just got chills."

Tamra removed a bag of mint tea from her mug. "This is *not* good."

"It makes my skin crawl," Alix said. "And I can only imagine what he's told her about me."

"I'm playing devil's advocate here . . ." It was clear Jodi still didn't completely understand, but Alix appreciated her dedication to the topic at hand. "But is there a chance that while he may have a fetish, that fetish may have grown into something more serious? People do change, right? And call me crazy . . . but it seemed like he really liked her."

This observation made Alix's ears burn.

"Well, there are plenty of misogynists out there who are obsessed with a certain type of woman," Tamra said. "Despite the fact that they use women to validate themselves, they think they aren't sexist because they love to objectify women so much. And you're right. People do change . . . but it's not like he was twelve."

"But even so, what can we do about it?" Rachel, as usual, bent the conversation into another direction. "Because think about it. How difficult is it to tell someone, 'Hey, your boyfriend likes you for the wrong reasons?' If someone told me that I'd be like, 'No he doesn't. Mind your business.' It's not like Alix can tell her to *not* be with him." Then Rachel added this as if it were an unfortunate fact: "Emira *is* a grown woman."

"But she's *not*, though! She's . . ." This outburst surprised Alix as much as it seemed to surprise her friends. Her face suddenly felt hot as she remembered Kelley's hands on Emira's backside. The text he'd sent her. *Is basketball something you'd be interested in?* The way he'd turned to her when the video was mentioned. *That's Emira's property now.* "Emira is still *so* young," she said, and with this, Alix felt her eyes begin to water. When she let her voice crack to say, "What the fuck is he doing with her?" a tear dropped into her napkin. The idea of Kelley truly having feelings for Emira seemed slightly worse than him using her for his own gain. Just the thought of it put a sharp buzzing sound into her head. Alix also realized that sitting here at brunch with her girlfriends, with a legitimate excuse to discuss Kelley Copeland, might have been the happiest she'd felt since she moved to Philadelphia.

Tamra put her napkin at the side of her plate and touched Alix's back. "Let's go outside," she said. She scooted her chair back. "Come on, let's get some fresh air."

Out front were a dozen or so Philadelphians in down parkas and boots, bouncing with their hands in pockets as they waited for their names to be called. It reminded Alix of New York and she thought, *One more day and you'll be there.* She and Tamra walked down the street and stood underneath a drippy bridge passover. Snow and ice dropped down and collected in puddles on the asphalt. Tamra's boots echoed as they hit the concrete.

"I'm sorry. I'm okay. I'm fine." A breeze whipped Alix's hair into her mouth and she pulled it out with two fingers. "I'm just scared for her. He was a bad guy back then, and now that we're older I don't trust him even more."

"Then I think you need to tell her," Tamra said. "Don't tell her about what he did to you because that needs to stay separate. And if you tell her about the letter and that night, the rest of it will come out like you're still trying to punish him. But tell her what you know about his dating record, and that he's been like this for some time. Just be honest with her and say, 'If it were me, I'd want to know.'"

"Would *you* want to know?" Alix felt certain that Tamra knew what she meant by this question. That as her closest friend, her word already carried a massive amount of weight, but as a black woman, in this scenario, Tamra's outlook would dictate the moves Alix made next.

Tamra twisted her lips to the side. "I think this is less about what *I* would want to know, and more about if *Emira* should know. And

Alix . . ." Tamra shook her head. She breathed deep as if she'd just climbed a ladder to a rewarding rooftop view. "I think you're the best thing that ever happened to that girl. You should step into her life in any way you can."

Alix stuck her hands into both of her front pockets. "What do you mean?"

"Well . . ." Tamra stood with a face that seemed to be asking, *Do you want the good news first or the bad news?* She zipped up her jacket high against her neck. "I like Emira. A lot. I actually think it's quite lovely how she and Briar complement each other. It's incredibly sweet to watch."

For a moment, Alix couldn't tell if this was a slight to Emira, Briar, or both.

"But," Tamra said slowly, "that girl is very lost. She's twenty-five years old and she has no idea what she wants or how to get it. She doesn't have the motivation to maintain a real career the way our girls will have, which is probably not her fault but it doesn't make it less true. What I'm saying is . . . there are a lot of jerks like Kelley out there, but when they get hold of girls like Emira? Someone who's still trying to figure herself out? That's when I start to really worry. And the more that I think about it, it makes a lot sense she ended up with a guy like this. He's looking to validate himself through someone else. She hasn't caught on because she doesn't know who she is."

Alix shook her head and brought a hand up to her face. Her voice split again as she asked, "What am I gonna do?" The tears came so easily that through her sobs, Alix thought, *Thank God*. It felt like Emira really was hers. And that Alix's intentions must be good after all.

"Sweetie, hey." Tamra hugged her from the side. "Look at me. This will be fine. It's only been a few months and there's no ring on her finger. Emira is so lucky to have you worrying about her . . . but you gotta take care of yourself too."

"Oh, I'm fine, though. I'm fine." Alix took a tissue out of her pocket and swiped it underneath her nose.

"Alix. I'm gonna say something to you and I don't want you to take this the wrong way." Tamra stepped in front of her and held her elbows. "When you were in New York you were *Go go go*, all the time. You can't expect to feel like yourself when things have slowed down as much as they have."

Alix looked back to the awning of the restaurant as her eyes filled with tears again. She both hated and loved Tamra for bringing her lack of fulfillment into a harsh light. "But what am I supposed to do?" Her voice went into a tragic falsetto and she took her volume down even lower. "Peter is so supportive and the fact is, I *do* work from home. I thought the Clinton campaign would want me more, but this event next week is the only event I've had in months. I used to have my team, and my phone used to be blowing up all the time . . . and I know it's because I had a baby. I know. And I'm so glad because she's so perfect. But now I don't even know how to *begin* to have the same life I had while I'm living here."

Tamra pulled out her phone. "Let me work on this."

Alix sniffed into her tissue and from underneath it she asked, "What are you doing?"

"We need to get you back in the city." Tamra continued to type an email, most likely to herself because she did this all the time, and said, "Gimme two seconds," as Alix waited. "I know a woman who is looking for someone to facilitate a class on Tuesday nights at the New School. You'd actually be perfect and I can't believe I didn't think of it sooner."

"Tam, no. I can't leave Peter like that. He's doing so well and this was always the plan. This was what we agreed to."

"Then *use Emira*." Tamra said this slowly and like a song. "No one said you couldn't come to the city once or twice a week. You and Emira? You two need each other. I feel very strongly about this. You need a release, you need to get back on top of your business, and Emira? The more time she's spending in your house, the better. Let me help you fix this."

Tamra breathed into her ample chest and it almost felt like she was taking a breath for the both of them. Alix knew then that she was done crying and ready to put her feelings into action. This moment, *this* was why she had missed her friends so much. They knew how to bring her back to herself. "Thank you," she said.

"You don't have to thank me for anything. Now listen." Tamra put her cell phone in her pocket and grinned. "We're gonna go back in there and order some mimosas. We're gonna get you back in the city and feeling like yourself. And when you get back, you're gonna tell your sitter what you know, and do whatever you can to protect her."

Twenty

On Monday morning, the Chamberlain house was empty and charged with possibilities. Mrs. Chamberlain and Catherine were another state away, and after standing in the heat of Peter's gratitude for coming to Thanksgiving, and for looking after Briar so much this week, Emira sat next to Briar's big-girl seat. In her hand she held the forty dollars that Peter had left on the countertop. Emira leaned in to the three-year-old and said, "You wanna do something special today?"

Emira took Briar on the train for the first time and they rode between passengers with bags of presents and gift wrap and bows. On the street they held hands and walked two more blocks, until Emira opened the door to the House of Tea. Beneath a wall of hundreds of teas from all over the world, at a tiny table for two, Emira asked the waitress to bring out an arrangement of different tea bags but no mugs (the waitress said, "Umm, das weird, but okay"). For over an hour, in a puffy purple jacket and rain boots, Briar arranged the teas in an order that made sense to her, across the table and on top of her legs. "This is the baby tea." Briar introduced a packet of English Breakfast. "No, no, you have to wait," she told a decaf cinnamon spice. "And you have to go in the potty like a big girl." Emira sipped an iced water and watched.

Tuesday was for sledding. After several trips up and down a snowy and slight hill—Briar expelling a happy screech the entire way down—the little girl fell asleep over a Dixie cup of hot chocolate that Emira poured from a thermos in her purse. Emira woke her up to make a snow angel, which was very cute but not as fun. Briar lay in the snow with a confused expression and said, "Mira, this isn't a bedtime party, okay?" She insisted on pulling the sled for the entire walk home.

On Wednesday, Briar and Emira went to the mall located next to the hospital where Zara worked. In her scrubs and holding a plastic Subway sandwich bag, Zara ran to the front of the Santa Claus line, where Emira and Briar stood. As Zara stepped over a plush velvet rope, she grinned at Emira and said, "You are so stupid right now." They walked away with three different card holders that read *Santa and Me!* in red across the top. One photo showed Santa and Briar midsneeze; one was with Santa, Emira, and Briar, all of whom were magically smiling; and one featured Emira, Zara, and Santa. Next to Santa's lap, Emira crossed her legs and put her hands in her hair, a doe-eyed expression on her face. With her back to the camera, Zara squatted in front of Santa with her hands on her knees, and her face turned profile (when Zara Instagrammed the photo, the caption read, *Ho Ho Ho, Up To Snow Good*). Briar's head could be seen in the corner as she waited and asked an elf if she felt scared of Santa sometimes.

And on Thursday, Emira took Briar to Camden, New Jersey. By then, she didn't even think to ask. She and Briar were a unit, Mrs. Chamberlain wasn't there, and Briar fucking loved fish. At Adventure

Aquarium, Briar struggled to keep her mouth closed because so much wonderment kept spilling out. Emira was reminded of the insanity of being a child: seeing all the things you learned about in books as actual breathing creatures, swimming right in front of your face. Briar marveled at hippos and sharks and penguins and turtles. And somehow, magically, Santa made an appearance at the aquarium to say hello and talk about recycling. Emira told Briar to whisper as she asked over and over, "Who picks Santa up from the mall?"

In a reflecting blue hallway of glass and water, Emira and Briar walked beneath angelfish and guppies, eels and bottom-feeding sharks. Briar stood at one side and tapped the glass lightly with her hands, her little fingers in front of neon algae and rocks. "Mira, yes yes yes." Emira bent down next to her.

"Hey, you. Pickle-head," she said. "Hey, I love you."

Briar laughed from her nose—it almost seemed as if she were trying to blow something out of it—and she put her cheek on Emira's shoulder. Just then, the lights went off in their end of the aquarium to signal that closing time was near. Briar screamed out, "Mira, I can't find me!" Emira held her closer and said, "I still see you." The lights came back on.

The bus got them home by six p.m. and Briar looked sleepy, which meant Emira had to hustle. She liked having dinner on the table by six fifteen, so that Briar could avoid a second wind before bath time at six forty-five. Emira cooked scrambled eggs and toast. She used a fork to smash half an avocado onto the bread while Briar sang to herself from the kitchen floor, occasionally sniffing a sticker on her shirt (Emira didn't have the heart to tell her that it was not the kind that smells). In the last section of Briar's divided plate, Emira placed bright orange pieces of a peach. For maybe the two hundredth time, the two girls sat side by side at the kitchen table.

Emira checked the clock on the microwave—it read 6:46 p.m.—and as she reached to remove the Velcro at the back of Briar's bib, she caught herself thinking, *Wait a second. I don't want to give this part up either.*

On her own and at her best, Briar was odd and charming, filled with intelligence and humor. But there was something about the actual work, the practice of caring for a small unstructured person, that left Emira feeling smart and in control. There was the gratifying reflex of being good at your job, and even better was the delightful good fortune of having a job you wanted to be good at. Without Briar, there were all these markers of time that would come to mean nothing. Was Emira just supposed to exist on her own at six forty-five? Knowing that somewhere else it was Briar's bathtime? One day, when Emira would say good-bye to Briar, she'd also leave the joy of having somewhere to be, the satisfaction of understanding the rules, the comfort of knowing what's coming next, and the privilege of finding a home within yourself.

Emira loved the ease in which she could lose herself in the rhythm of childcare. She didn't have to worry about having interesting hobbies. The fact that she still slept on a twin bed meant nothing to Briar or any of their plans. Every day with Briar was a tiny victory that Emira didn't want to give up. Seven o'clock was always a win. Here's your kid. She's happy and alive.

PART FOUR

Twenty-one

The moment Alix returned home from New York City she put Catherine down for a nap, set Briar up with the iPad, and quickly fucked her husband in the third-floor bathroom. Peter had his work clothes on and his face revealed a miraculous elation in the mirror as his belt buckle jingled across Alix's hamstring. Alix had squeezed in a trim and blowout that morning in Manhattan before she boarded the train, and she liked watching her blond hair bounce as Peter plunged in from behind. They finished seconds before they heard Emira arrive and close the front door, which made Alix grin and hold her finger to her lips.

New York was like an ex who had worked out all summer. Alix had spent the last five days running through the city with Rachel, Jodi, and Tamra—sometimes just with Catherine—to all her favorite spots. She ate ice cream in a cone on 7th Street, standing under a lamppost in the snow. She bought Catherine a flowered beanie. And she wore heels for the first time in ten months when she attended an event for the Clinton campaign. Hillary Clinton herself wasn't there, but hundreds of sharp, smart, and sexy women were. By the time her train pulled back into the 30th Street Station, she had an email in her inbox from a professor in communications at the New School: *We'd love to talk about the upcoming semester. Let's schedule a chat soon!* Alix quickly responded, and then continued captioning future Instagram photos she'd taken in the city. She now had enough content for weeks to continue pretending that she still lived there.

"Hi!" With her pants back on, Alix jogged down the stairs and reveled in the flicks of fresh blond ends on her shoulders. Next to the kitchen table, Emira was kneeling in front of Briar, and Alix's chest seemed to expand all the way up to her eyes. Oh, how she had missed both of them! Her chatty and nervous daughter, and the quiet, thoughtful person she paid to love her. It was enchanting to see that nothing had really changed. Briar still needed help putting her mittens on her hands. Emira still wore pilled neon socks below her black leggings. "I can't believe I haven't seen you in a week!"

Emira said, "I know, welcome back," as Peter came downstairs. He slipped a jacket over his shoulders as he kissed Alix and Briar. Then he was gone and it was just the three of them.

"Have you guys been having fun?"

"Yeah," Emira said. "Same ol' stuff, I guess."

Alix turned to retrieve her coffee from the counter. With the cup in her hands she turned back around, tucked her hair behind her ear, and said, "Emira."

New York City had reminded Alix that if she could talk to more than four hundred women about asking for a promotion, she could definitely talk to Emira about Kelley Copeland. The past five days had reaffirmed the confidence she had in herself, as well as providing clarity about this conversation. It would be much simpler than she had imagined. She wouldn't be pushy. She'd stick to the facts. And she wouldn't expect Emira to do something right away. Alix had once been twenty-five herself, and all this time later, she could still remember the Kelley Copeland effect well. Regardless, Alix would protect her sitter. Thanksgiving was meant to mark a shift in their relationship, and her desire for this hadn't changed. She would step in to be an advocate in Emira Tucker's life, and not just on Mondays, Wednesdays, and Fridays. Alix smiled into the side of her cup. "Do you want to talk for a minute?"

"Ummm, sure?" Emira stood up from the floor. "Well, I was actually thinking of changing it up today and taking Briar to a movie."

"A movie!" Alix made a face at her daughter. "That's so exciting."

"How come these has fingers . . ." Briar said, pointing to Emira's gloves, "and mine has no fingers?"

"Because yours are mittens. They're very warm."

"Well, I'll warn you that her attention span isn't great," Alix said. "I can't imagine her sitting still in a theater for too long."

"Oh, yeah, it's the midday mommy-and-me one you suggested a long time ago. So the lights will be on and she can move around or whatever."

"Neat!" Had Alix really just said *neat*? Alix kept her smile broad, but inside she was wondering, *How are we talking about movie showtimes right now?* Emira and Briar needed to stay inside the house. Alix had put Catherine down early for this reason: she and Emira had a lot to discuss. "I've been meaning to try that out," she said. "It might just be on Tuesdays, though. But you know what—I can just give you the Amazon password if you guys want to snuggle up and do a movie here instead—"

"Can I just check and see?"

Emira always asked Alix if she could use the computer (*Can I make sure my train is still running? Can I check to see if it's going to rain?*), but now, Alix watched her sitter shake the mouse and hit the keyboard with such familiarity that it made Alix's head tilt hard to one side. Emira made two more clicks. "Perfect," she said. "It starts at twelve forty-five."

"Oh, great."

"I'm just gonna email the address to myself really quick."

"Mama?" Briar called, holding her blond ponytail in her hands. "Some fishes has no feet or tails? And that's . . . that's just how they are."

"That's very true," Alix said. "Emira, that sounds great. I think it'll be really fun. But do you mind if we talk for a second?"

Alix watched Emira click Send on an email before she turned around. "Sure, what's up?"

This return made Alix fold her arms in a protective response. How had this gotten so far away from her? Was this what it would be like to have a teenager some day? Someone dying to leave your space but also making it feel like it wasn't yours?

"Well . . . let me get straight to it," Alix said. She delivered this with a light laugh at the end that made her cringe. She took another breath and placed her coffee on the counter to create a moment between Emira's movie plans and the news she'd been practicing the delivery of for the past seven days. "We had a such a nice time at Thanksgiving, and we were so glad you guys came. But . . . I'm sure it was a little odd for you as well. First and foremost? Thank you for being such a superwoman that night. I know I said it before, but once again, you completely saved us."

"Oh, of course," Emira said. She looked at Briar and said, "It's no fun to be sick."

Briar turned grave and told Emira, "I threw up." Emira nodded and said, "I remember."

"And second . . ." Alix displayed both her palms. "I don't want you to feel awkward *at all* about the fact that Kelley and I dated each other way back when."

Emira laughed. "Well, sure." For a moment she looked out to the wall of windows and put her hands into her puffy vest pockets. "It was like . . . high school, right?"

This rebuttal felt like Emira had taken an unprompted guess at Alix's age and overshot the number by too many years. At her feet, Briar hopped on one foot and said, "Mama? Bees don't like when you do gymnastics on they's heads."

"Exactly, yes," Alix recovered. "I'm just making sure. But . . . well, Emira, will you sit down for a second?"

Alix picked Briar up into her arms and sat at the kitchen table; the toddler began to play with a frayed string on her mittens. Emira said, "Okay . . ." and half sat into the next chair over. She kept her posture upright, as if she were afraid the chair had recently been painted and she wasn't sure if it had dried.

"Alright, so . . ." Alix said. "I think you guys seem very happy together, and if you're happy, I'm happy . . ."

"If you're happy and you know it?" Briar declared. "Then row row row your boat to the store."

"The Kelley I knew way back when, well . . ." Alix sighed with the weight of unfortunate news. "Well, he wasn't very nice."

Alix had the floor again. She could feel Emira leaning in to her words and her bored resistance fading into mild intrigue, which was a lot coming from Emira. "Emira, you're so smart," Alix went on, "and I know that you know what you want out of a relationship more than anyone else, and I also know that people can change. I just . . ." Alix ruffled Briar's hair and kissed the back of her head. "I wouldn't feel right not letting you know about my experience with Kelley, especially when I think the same issues may come up in yours."

"I mean . . ." Emira crossed her legs and folded her hands in between her thighs. "I know you guys didn't have the best breakup . . . I don't know details or anything, but that's cool. It happens."

Ahhh, so he hasn't told you, Alix thought. *Of course he hasn't, because he knows he was wrong.* "Well, I wish that were the bulk of it," she said. "Kelley and I . . . we didn't date long, but . . . if I can be really candid about this . . . I had some issues with Kelley not respecting my privacy, which led to a lot of harassment from other classmates on my end. But more importantly, and why this may involve you, it was fairly common knowledge that Kelley had a habit of fetishizing African American people and culture. I won't get into the details . . . but I'd be so completely crushed if Kelley ever used you in the same way."

Alix's delivery had arrived in the light tone she'd mentally practiced in cab rides, in the shower, and while she applied her mascara over the past week. She was merely supplying information for Emira's benefit, not anyone else's, and she'd said the words *African American* and *culture* without lowering her volume to a suburban hush. And yes, she remembered Tamra's advice to not bring up what Kelley had done with her letter, but she didn't say Alix couldn't allude to the fact that he'd done something terrible. Alix expected Emira to pry—that was what Alix would have done—into what Kelley had done or said, and when. But Emira kept her hands between her legs. She swung her hair onto her back and said, "This was all like . . . sixteen years ago, right?"

"God, was it that long ago?" Alix laughed. It was fifteen years ago, but okay. "I know, it's a lifetime ago. I'm also saying this to let you know why I may have come off as rude when I first saw him at the door." Alix pivoted. "At first I was just so stunned to see him at all. But knowing him as well as I did, I became a little concerned about his reasons for dating you."

Emira flinched and looked at the floor. "I don't know. I think I'm like . . . pretty chill and dateable."

"Oh, Emira. No no no. That's not what I meant at all." Alix used her right hand to shake her fingers and waft her words out of the air. The *fuck fuck fuck* feeling from Thanksgiving was once again pungent in her home and her stomach. "There's no doubt in my mind that he's smitten with you. But I'm just making sure it's for all the right reasons."

"I see . . ." Emira sighed. "Well, I definitely know what you're talking about. And I've met guys who are like that, but I haven't really seen that with Kelley so far? So yeah, I don't know. I also did some really dumb things when I was in high school. Like, okay—this is really embarrassing, but I definitely thought that Asian people were just smarter. And I definitely used to say things like, 'That's so gay.' And both of those things are so offensive and awful, and now I can't believe I ever talked like that. So yeah. I really appreciate you telling me, but it would feel weird to make it a thing now when it hasn't been a problem."

Alix had definitely described things as *gay* in high school, too. She used the word *Oriental* until she was in college, and only stopped because a roommate told her to. And there was a point in time when—if someone was described as Indian—Alix thought it was funny to say, "Dot or feather?" But this was different, how did Emira not see that? Kelley had a penchant for othering black culture that had started in high school and *continued* to develop in adulthood. He still didn't think that what he was doing was wrong. What had Kelley told Emira to make her reject this information? In high school, Kelley's admiration for Robbie and his friends had been so palpable and excruciating. Had he been fetishizing black people for so long that he finally became believable? Alix knew she was doing *the right thing*, but she somehow felt the same way she had when her roommate had looked at her over a cup of noodles to say, "Dude, you can't say Oriental unless you're talking about a rug."

Alix said, "Totally," and she hugged Briar closer. "This is exactly what I wanted to hear. If it hasn't been a problem, then, wonderful. I just wanted to—"

"Sorry." Emira bit the side of her bottom lip and took her phone out of her pocket. Looking down at it she said, "The theater only has one showing today and I just wanna make sure we don't miss it."

"Oh, of course!" Alix placed Briar on the ground. She stood and immediately felt dazed and dehydrated. Briar sang, "Ella-meno-peeee," as Alix took her phone from the counter thinking, *How did I . . . What did she . . . What the fuck just happened?*

"But you're cool with it, though?" Emira stood too. She took a second and balanced her knee against the seat of the chair as Briar performed deep squats underneath the table. "I do realize that it's extremely random and weird. I'm just making sure . . . you're good with it, right?"

For a second Alix thought, *If I said no, would you really stop dating him?* But she shook her head violently and said, "Oh, a hundred percent!"

"Mira, look!" Briar reached her hand out from under the table. "Is dis my knuckles?"

"Kind of. Your knuckles are right there."

Alix bent and kissed Briar's cheeks. "You guys have so much fun!"

Emira slipped her jacket on, but she didn't leave. Alix stood at the other end of the table and refreshed her Instagram for the third time in the last ten seconds. Emira kept standing. Alix finally looked up.

"Sorry . . ." Emira said. "Peter would just leave cash on the counter."

Moments later, as Alix stood in the window and watched her sitter walk hand in hand with her firstborn child and thirty dollars in her pocket, she slipped her jacket over her back. She applied lipstick in the girls' bathroom above the child-sized toothbrushes, toothpaste, and baby lotion. She pushed her hair in front of her shoulders, and then she walked out the front door with just her keys and her phone.

It was as if she'd taken a breath at the front stoop and landed herself on the snowy sidewalk, her gloves on and booties tapping beneath her. The last time she'd come from New York, Philadelphia all looked the same, but now she knew her way around. It was twelve sixteen p.m., just enough time to get there. She'd looked at Emira's text messages enough to know where he worked and what time he went to lunch (Rittenhouse Square, twelve thirty p.m.).

There were several twenty- and thirty-somethings in button-downs and peacoats walking in groups and carrying brown to-go bags. The sidewalk was huge here in front of the colossal buildings, and Alix watched people pass as she leaned back against a fountain that was frozen over with ice and grime. For a moment she prepared herself to go inside the office and ask to speak with him right there. It would probably be one of those stupid modern offices with brightly painted walls and an open seating plan, and they wouldn't get much privacy but she could make it happen. And maybe the shock of her presence, and the calmness she'd deploy, would be enough to let Kelley know that he'd been caught. But it wasn't long before she saw him. He wasn't exiting his place of work but coming toward it, and fast. Alix's gut twisted inside her and she felt the urge to shield it in the same way she had when she was pregnant. Instead she straightened and stood. She kept her hands coolly in her pockets as she walked.

Kelley wore slate-colored pants, a black coat, and something adorably chambray underneath. He walked with two black men, also informally but expensively dressed, and Alix smirked, thinking, *Oh, you're good*. If Kelley felt better about himself by surrounding himself with unknowing human beings, then fine. But he wasn't going to do that with Emira.

Kelley and the men next to him were holding plastic containers with colorful build-your-own salads and forks inside. He finally noticed her, and for the second time that day, Alix felt as if she were the mother of teenagers. She watched him register her presence and slip into what looked like shameful shock. His entire body seemed to be saying, *Mom, what are you doing here? I'm with my friends. Go home.* He slowed his pace and Alix clipped toward him.

"Whoa. What are you—"

"I need to talk to you. Right now."

The two men next to Kelley took a step back from her as if she were contagious.

Alix pointed to a building next door. "Let's go in there."

Inside a building lined with windows, there was a double escalator that led up to a hallway of shiny elevators, and to the side of it, a dozen tables and a café were set up on the lobby floor. The whole place glowed and echoed in blue. A ginormous and hideous Jeff Koons piece dangled from the ceiling, spewing holiday cheer over the white tile. Alix found an open seat for two, and Kelley pulled out the chair across from her. She took her gloves off finger by finger and told herself to breathe.

"What's up, Alex?" Kelley sat down so carefully that it hurt, as if he were afraid to make any sudden movements. "How did you know where I worked?"

"Hi, guys!" A pixie-haired woman appeared next to their table. "So this is sparkling water and this one is flat. Your waiter will be here in a—"

"We aren't staying, sorry," Kelley stopped her.

She said, "Okay!" with the same inflection, but still placed the glasses on the table and left.

"You're honestly asking why I'm here right now?" Alix's stage presence kicked in and her voice came out smooth and smart. Inside, however, she was absolutely panicking. Had she really just decided to see Kelley and done so within twenty minutes? Maybe it had been a mistake, but she was here now, and he was waiting for her to continue. "I'm here because I'm *concerned*, Kelley," she said. She enunciated the word *concerned* as if it were an idea he may or may not be familiar with.

"*You're* concerned? Wow." Kelley laughed. "I'd love to hear more about why you're concerned."

God, he was cute. Even when he was being a dick. Had he been this cute at Thanksgiving? There were tiny flecks of brilliant gray hair in places at his temples that she hadn't noticed before. Alix swallowed and focused on the bubbly water in front of her. "I don't think it's fair of you to start dating my sitter and expect me to be quiet about it."

"Alex, come on." Kelley put his boxed salad on the table. "I don't love that she's working for you either. But the fact is that you and I dated more than a *decade* ago and she's gotta make her own—"

"Oh God, this has nothing to do with us *dating*, so get over yourself." The opportunity to say this to Kelley, to put air quotes on the word *dating*, with her hair blown out and her body six pounds from her pre-baby weight—Alix could practically taste it and the words were salty and warm. "Actually, I *wish* it had to do with you and I dating. You and I could have absolutely dated and broken up like normal people. That would have been great. But because you didn't believe in the concept of privacy, and because you saw black athletes as your ticket to popularity, I can't help but have an opinion on you filming Emira in a grocery store, and then deciding you should date her."

Kelley looked at her as if he possibly smelled fire. "Alex, what are you saying right now?"

"I'm not finished." Alix held up a flat hand in the air. "If you think I'm going to sit back while you try to look cool with someone who is like family to me, then you're crazy." Alix took a second to pause for effect. "If you're still okay fetishizing black people like you did in high school, fine. Just don't pull that shit with my sitter."

Alix watched Kelley take this in. She was furious, but she couldn't stop focusing on how attractive his face was when he was confused. How could she hate someone so much and also want him to think she was sexy? In this garish thing that was apparently a restaurant? At that moment, another waiter came by and dropped off menus. When he asked if they wanted to start with an appetizer, Kelley barked, "We're *not* together," and the waiter said, "Okaayy."

Once the waiter retreated, Kelley pressed his hands to the edge of the table and blew out through his mouth. "Okay, let's back up because there's a lot to unpack here."

For some reason this phrase made Alix want to throw the bubbling water across the room. She crossed her legs and watched Kelley prepare to speak as he ran his tongue over his front teeth.

"You didn't have the best senior year, and that obviously still affects you. But at the end of the day, I broke up with you." As he said this, he rested his palms upward on the table. "That's it."

Alix shook her head. "This has nothing to do with—"

Kelley cut her off with, "Let me finish. I broke up with you. That's all. And I'm sure you've broken up with people too, and you understand how it works by now. It's not easy for anyone involved."

Alix's mind couldn't land on what he was saying. It was all so loaded—she knew she'd analyze every bit of it later—but this seemed to block her from retaining any of the information. On one hand he looked exhausted, not angry, which made her want to throw up into the stretch of her scarf. On the other hand, he assumed she'd broken up with people? More than one? Did this mean that he still found her attractive? Was it a completely inappropriate time to clarify, *So you still think I'm pretty?*

"That's the only crime I've done against you," Kelley went on. "I know you disagree with me on that, and I don't understand why, all this time later, you can't consider that maybe you didn't have to call the cops that night?" Kelley proposed. "But as for you and me, I was seventeen and we broke up."

Alix looked up at the reflective glassy ceiling. "Again. I came here to talk about Emira."

"Okay, fine. As far as Emira goes . . ." Kelley stared at the table as if he were still trying to piece everything together. "I mean, honestly I'm shocked that the word *fetishizing* is even in your vocabulary . . . but Alex, I'm in love with Emira."

This comment felt like he'd reached in her chest and shooed her heart as if it were a bug that had landed too close.

"And sure," Kelley said. "I probably thought the black kids in high school were much cooler than the white ones. I don't think I was the only kid who thought athletes and rappers and rich kids, including yourself, were cooler than everyone else. But Robbie and I are still friends. I was in his fucking wedding. It doesn't matter how we became friends. And it doesn't matter how I met Emira either."

Alix hated herself for her immediate thought, which was *What wedding!? Why didn't I see the pictures? Ohmygod, did Robbie block me?*

"And in my relationship with Emira?" Kelley widened his eyes. "No one is being used for anything. And more importantly, Emira is an adult. So maybe you don't like it, but it shouldn't be any *concern* of yours who she chooses to spend her time with." Alix froze as Kelley put air quotes over the word *concern*.

Alix wanted to scream and she wanted her voice to echo up into the gaudy and pretentious space. *How dare you be diplomatic about this?!* she thought. *I get it, we're through, but don't date my fucking babysitter. And don't act like I'm crazy. We were in love with each other. How else was I supposed to react? And how else was I supposed to see you again?* The more Kelley had gone on, the calmer he got, and the more it seemed like he was slipping away. Alix wanted him to hear the things she wasn't saying, but she also refused to go home on good terms with this person who'd ruined her senior summer. New York City was still in her veins. Alix knew her hair and skin looked amazing. If Kelley thought he could leave this table without any repercussions, if Emira thought she could just ask for cash and call Peter by his first name, then they both had greatly underestimated her.

"So what I'm hearing is . . ." Alix grinned. "That you haven't told Emira exactly what you did to me?"

Kelley put his forehead to his hands and said, "Jesus, Alex. I didn't *do* anything to you—"

"You can believe whatever you want," she said. "But Emira has a right to know who she's really dating. And if you don't tell her about what you did to me, about everything that led to your best friend Robbie getting arrested, then I absolutely will."

Kelley choked out a laugh. Had Alix gone too far? Tamra had told Alix to not tell Emira what he'd done, but she didn't say that Alix couldn't get Kelley to tell Emira himself.

"Alex . . ." Kelley sighed. "You came down here leading with the fact that you think I'm using Emira. But now it's about a letter that I never even received?"

"They are *related*," Alix said through gritted teeth. "If it doesn't matter and you didn't do anything wrong, why haven't you told her what you did to me?"

"Why haven't you told her what *you* did to Robbie?"

"All *I* did was protect my sister and my sitter."

"Ohmygod, Alex. You're still doing this? 'I need to protect my black babysitter'? Just so you know, Robbie is still five-foot-five and—"

"You know what?" Alix cut him off. "How about you tell Emira what happened, how Robbie just happened to know where I lived and the code to my house, and let her decide for herself. Since she's so grown up and mature I'm sure she can make up her mind."

Kelley kept his head low but raised his eyes to say, "If this is you making a dig at her age, I'd be happy to discuss the gap between you and your husband."

Alix thought, *Motherfucker*. She often forgot that just because Peter looked young for his age, it didn't mean that he looked young. But she wouldn't be derailed. "Emira deserves to know who she's dating."

"No, you know what, Alex?" Kelley leaned forward with one arm on the table. "Emira deserves a job where she gets to wear her own fucking clothes. How about you start with that?"

Alix sat back. She felt the puffs in her jacket squish and deflate with a tiny whistle. "Excuse me?"

"You act like what happened to you was worse than what happened to Robbie, even though—let's not even go there. If you love Emira so much, then let her wear what she wants," Kelley jeered. "I'm sure I didn't handle things well back in high school. I was seventeen, I was an idiot. But at least I'm not *still* requiring a uniform for someone who works for me so I can pretend like I own them."

"Ohmygod!" Alix formed fists with both hands on the table. "You have no idea what you're talking about. She asked! I lent her a shirt!"

"You lend her the same shirt? Every day? In the business we call that a uniform."

"You are so completely out of line." Alix had started her day in Manhattan, ready to tell Kelley, *I know who you really are*. But now she sat in Philadelphia, participating in a losing game called "Which One of Us Is Actually More Racist?" Alix cracked her neck to the side and pointed her hands like daggers on top of the table. "Emira is part of our family. We've never forced her to do anything she doesn't want to do. I've known her for longer than you have, and I'm ready to do whatever it takes to protect her."

"This is fucking rich. You're unbelievable."

"I'm not joking, Kelley. If you don't—"

"Alex, listen to yourself!" Kelley screamed this in a whisper. "You are the same person you were in high school. God, I saw you on Thanksgiving and I thought, how the fuck did this happen? But of *course* this happened. Of course you're hiring black people to raise your children and putting your family crest on them. Just like your parents, who you were *so* ashamed of. And of course you sent Emira to a super-white grocery store, at midnight, and expected everything to be okay."

"Ha!" Alix tipped her head back. "So now you're blaming me for the police interrogating Emira? *That's* hysterical."

"Why's that?"

"Because she wouldn't have gotten in trouble that night if she'd been wearing a uniform, now would she?"

Alix watched Kelley do a thing with his jaw, as if he were trying to catch a kernel of popcorn in the air. Her heart rate somehow tripled and she wanted to hold her hands up to her face. If she had said what she was thinking, it would be clipped segments of *Wait, what I meant . . . the thing is . . . okay but you said . . . that didn't come out right.*

Kelley stood and dug into his jacket pocket. "Tell Emira whatever you want."

"Kelley, wait."

He threw two dollars on top of the table.

"Kelley." Alix stayed seated, hoping her resilience would make it impossible for him to go. "We . . . Emira has become very important to us and—"

"Yeah, you guys are like family, right?" Kelley picked his salad up from the table. "Is that why you're making her work on her birthday? Have a nice life, Alex."

———

Alix wished to God she had thought to bring her headphones, but she also knew that any song that she played to get Kelley out of her head would make her think of him for the rest of her life. Quick crunches of snow brought her home and up to the front door. She slipped herself in and locked it tight.

She went straight to the kitchen computer and thought, *Maybe one of the women from the campaign reached out. Maybe that one nice woman wrote me while I was gone.* Alix didn't have to be best friends with her babysitter. She just needed her family and her career. Her breathing had barely slowed as she clicked the email icon at the bottom of her computer screen. It flashed red with four new messages.

Between a SoulCycle promo and a sale notification for Madewell jeans, the name of Alix's editor flashed twice. Alix whispered, "Shit." She was so fucking late with the manuscript. But according to Rachel, this happened all the time and agents scheduled and prepared for their authors to ask for extensions. And Alix just had a baby, what did everyone expect?

The first email subject line read *Are you in NYC???*

Shit, she thought again. This was why social media was awful sometimes. Should she have blocked her editor? No, that would be weird, wouldn't it? *What the fuck is Kelley going to tell Emira? Don't think about it. Just read the email.*

> Alix!
>
> I saw that you and your babe were in Prospect Park! So fun! I know it's the holiday but I'd love to catch up, especially if you need an extension? Let me know if I missed an email or attachment with your first 50 pages. Xoxo Maura.

Okay, that wasn't so bad. Alix would write back saying that it was such a blur, that it was a lot of family time, and she would send over her first fifty pages ASAP. She just had to write them first. No big deal. Of course she'd planned to write them in all her favorite cafés and restaurants in New York City, but she'd been busy Googling Kelley. And his family. And their mutual friends from high school. And she was on vacation.

But then Alix scrolled to Maura's second email, which was sent an hour after the first.

> Hellooo? Alix love, let's schedule a chat. I'm getting concerned that I haven't seen any work from you, especially since most of the work in this case is already done. I know writing a book is quite a feat, especially with two little ones, but I want to make sure we're on the same page (oh God, what a bad pun) before we move forward. I'd hate to have to amend our contract but I want to do what's best for both of us here. Let's talk soon. Maura.

Amend our contract? Could they take her advance away? What if she'd already spent it? This slap on the wrist from Maura felt like Alix's mother had caught her drinking wine coolers in someone else's car, opened the passenger-side door, and said, "Alex. Let's go." How fast could she write fifty pages? Or thirty? Hadn't she had an outline for all of this? This was supposed to be easy and fun! *What was Kelley telling Emira?!*

And that was when she heard it. With her palm pressed to her chin as she leaned against the standing desk, Alix heard Catherine emit an annoyed drip of baby sounds. Alix turned to the counter and seized the black-and-white baby monitor screen. There was Catherine in her crib. Kicking in her sleep sack.

It was as if all her organs rushed up and squeezed into the space around her ears. *But wasn't Peter just . . . How did I . . . But I thought Emira had . . . She couldn't have been . . .* Alix ran and opened the girls' bedroom door, and there was Catherine, who, now startled from the door opening so quickly, started to cry. Alix swooped her into her arms and held her against her beating chest. Had she been screaming or crying? Had she accidentally swallowed something? Did the neighbors hear her cry? Was she completely traumatized? Alix had left her daughter at home. Alone. *What if something had happened?!*

You never leave a baby. It's unlikely something will happen to it, but what about to you? Alix could barely remember walking home. What if she'd been hit by a car? What if she'd had a seizure and was left unconscious? Emira and Briar would be at a movie and God knows where else for hours, and Catherine would just be by herself in a fleece zip-up sack? How could she forget a person who'd been strapped to her for the past five days? What would she have said? Had Kelley really made her forget her own baby? Her brand-new baby, who already looked like a replica of herself? When was the last time Alix had cried this hard? Probably when Kelley broke up with her. Alix pressed her hand against her mouth and said, "I'm so sorry," into it. Catherine calmed and waahh'd softly into her ear.

Alix bounced Catherine in her arms as she walked into the kitchen and around the table. On her third rotation, she glanced at her computer screen and caught sight of the word *Inbox* on a tab she hadn't opened. It was followed by *EmiraCTucker@* before it was cut off. Alix slid Catherine into her right arm.

It was just so easy to type his name. After *Kell* it came right up. It was even easier to find the attachment dated *September2015*; it was the first and only email they'd ever exchanged. And once it was downloaded, Alix dragged it into a folder marked *Spring Blog Posts* that she hadn't used since last spring. Without watching the video, Alix quickly emailed it to herself as well—now she had it twice—and then she erased the email in the Sent folder and logged out of Emira's email. Alix cleared her browser's history and put in two new searches before she left the computer—*winter toddler crafts* and *organic teething bars*—and then she reached for her phone.

"Hi, Laney, are you busy right now?" Alix sniffed audibly and let her voice shake as she greeted Peter's co-host. She kissed her daughter's cheek and continued to bounce her. "Well, I might need your help . . . but can you keep a secret?"

Twenty-two

Under peach neon signs and acrylic palm tree leaves, Emira sat with a plastic tiara on her head in a plunging black dress and sheer black tights. The implication that this was Emira's "favorite place" only slightly bothered her. Yes, the DJ was lit and played the best reggaeton in her opinion, but much like baking brownies and matinee movie showtimes and boxed wine that you kept in the refrigerator, Emira loved Tropicana 187 because of the low prices (two for ones, ladies' night specials, three-dollar beers, six-dollar palomas). It wasn't half as fancy as the places Zara, Josefa, and Shaunie had picked for their birthdays, but the drinks and the night were aggressively sweet.

In a red and squishy booth, Emira's three friends sat around her in tight dresses and heavy bronzer. The table was covered in piña coladas, fish tacos, pineapple salsa, and pulled jerk chicken. Everything reeked of sugary mai tais and fried coconut shrimp, and every song that came on was another killer. As she opened her last birthday present, a new phone cover to replace her faded and cracked one,

Emira unstuck her heel from the floor and said, "Ohmy*god*, thank you, Z." She began to rip the packaging open using the side of her black nail.

"Yeah we can't have you carrying this around anymore." Zara grabbed Emira's phone and began to remove the worn, pink rubber casing. "Ohmygod, this thing is so tired and done. It wasn't doing anything for our brand."

Zara applied the new, matte-finished gold casing onto Emira's phone. Emira placed her other gifts into one bag (metallic earbuds and an iTunes gift card from Josefa, two silky "interview shirts" from Shaunie) and announced to the group, "The next round is on me."

Josefa removed her straw from her lips and dipped her head so hard that her ponytail swung. "Excuse me? Did you just have a stroke?"

Shaunie laughed and wiped the side of her mouth with a napkin. "But Mira, it's *your* birthday!"

"Nah, I wanna do this real quick." Emira got the attention of a waiter and ordered four tequila shots. They arrived with a coppery glaze of sugar and pineapple slices around the rims.

"Okay . . ." Emira watched her girlfriends hold their shots up and lick the excess from their fingers. For a moment, she felt the way she did when Briar saw a picture of a flower, sniffed it, and said, "Delicious," but she pushed these feelings aside so that she could speak. She sat up and raised her voice above the bass and steel drums.

"Sooo I've been a little cranky and like . . . broke these past few months. And I really appreciate you tolerating me. Next year is gonna be different and I'm really thankful for you guys helping me get my shit together. Sefa, thank you for helping me print out my résumé on *nice* paper."

"*Nice* paper, yasss *mija*." Josefa snapped her fingers four times.

"Shaunie." Emira turned to her. "Thank you for emailing me about new jobs. Every day. Multiple times a day . . . can't wait to unsubscribe."

"You said you wanted help!"

"And Zara, thanks for helping me write stupid-ass cover letters and making me not sound like an idiot." Emira leaned into her friend. "And thanks to you ladies . . . I officially have an interview next week."

Zara and Josefa together said, "Ayyeee!" Shaunie appeared overjoyed at this news and also devastated that both of her hands weren't available for clapping. "Ohmygod, yay! Emira, that's amazing!"

"Okay, okay, that's it, though. No more work talk." Emira held her drink up. The girls followed suit.

"To Mira being all professional and shit in 2016," Zara said. "Cheers, bisshhh. Happy birthday."

Emira touched her chest as she tipped the glass back. Josefa pulled out her phone and said, "Mira, smile." Emira pursed her lips. "Oh, that's cute." Josefa examined it. "That's *real* cute. I'm posting this."

Earlier that day, when Emira returned to drop Briar at home, she didn't give Mrs. Chamberlain the fifteen dollars remaining in her jacket pocket. She'd spent $6.50 on a movie ticket for herself (Briar's ticket ended up being free), five dollars on a small popcorn, and then $2.25 on a red velvet cupcake. She and Briar split the treat sitting across from each other in a bakery filled with white people and pictures of vintage chickens framed on the walls.

"Hey, B. Guess what?" Emira said in between two licks of frosting. "It's my birthday today."

Briar seemed both charmed and unsurprised by this information. "Okay. Then you . . . you a big girl now."

"I *am* a big girl."

"Good job, Mira."

Emira said, "Thank you."

Emira *had* done a good job. That week, she'd spent her days giving Briar the time of her life, taking her to new places (she was fairly certain that Briar had never even heard of a mall), and teaching her what the words *curious*, *alarm*, and *dimple* meant. At night, she Googled childcare and administrative positions, sent out six résumés, and dropped off two more. Emira's upcoming interview was for a full-time childcare manager position at Body World Fitness down in Point Breeze. She didn't mention to her friends that the pay was shitty, four dollars an hour less than she was making now. And she didn't mention the quick onset of depression she'd felt when she dropped her résumé off at the colorful but faded room that smelled of sanitizer and spit-up. (One of the workers there, a girl a few years younger than Emira, had run to catch up with a mom and son, saying, "He forgot his cup!" while laughing. There was something about the way she trotted and held the dirty sippy cup that made Emira surprisingly sad.) But when she got the call back later that day, she said she was very interested in the job and would love to come in for an interview next week. Emira couldn't wait to tell Kelley. Kelley who'd sent flowers to her apartment that morning, who texted happy birthday at midnight the night before, who was working late but would arrive later for drinks and dancing.

After dinner, the girls made their way to the windowless bar downstairs. Shaunie's friends from Sony piled in, a few of Josefa's classmates stopped by, some girls they all went to Temple with came through, and none of Zara's co-workers showed up. When Emira told Zara she was welcome to invite them, Zara had said, "Ew, no. I work with them—please. But tell Kelley to bring that guy with the fade."

Kelley did bring the guy with the fade and two others. Emira was three drinks deep and sitting atop a bar stool when he walked in. It all seemed extremely funny and miraculous. *I have a boyfriend? On my birthday? And he's white? Oops! Okay!* Kelley inched through a crowd of bodies, and while still sideways, he looked at her and said, "Hey, pretty."

Emira grinned into their kiss. "It's my birthday."

"Oh, for real? That's crazy. Happy birthday," Kelley said casually. "How was . . . how are you? How was work?"

"Good." Emira set her empty glass on the bar and swiveled back around to face him. "We saw a movie. And then we saw another movie. And then we got a cupcake."

"*Two* movies?" Kelley said this with the goofy trepidation of a father who worried that someone was having too much fun.

"The theater was empty and we just talked the whole time." It had been so special. Briar looked unusually tiny in the movie theater seat. When the previews started, she'd covered both her ears and looked to Emira as if she'd forgotten to lock the front door. But she eased into it quickly, and halfway into the first film, she patted Emira's thigh and whispered, "I sit here with you now shhh."

"Is that why you didn't call me back, miss?"

"Oh, my bad." Emira touched her neck. "Sorry, I try not to have my phone out when I'm with her. And then I was in a rush to get out of there and get to Shaunie's . . . ohmygod, which reminds me"— Emira felt it in her chattiness that she was drunk, but she couldn't help herself from telling him immediately—"your high school sweetheart was back on her bullshit today."

Kelley nodded and placed both his hands in his front pockets. "Yeah, I wanna talk about that, and a lot of other things, but this may not be the place . . ."

"Oh no, I can tell you," Emira said. "It was just super awkward. I came in and she was like, 'I just wanna tell you that I don't mind you dating Kelley at *all*.'" Emira made her voice soft and urgent when imitating Mrs. Chamberlain. "I was like, 'Ummm, I didn't ask you but okay.' She tried to tell me that you were trouble in high school and I was like, 'First of all, that was so long ago. And second, I'm about to interview somewhere else so let's not get into this.'"

"Wait, what?" Kelley stopped her. "You're interviewing somewhere else?"

"I forgot to tell you!" Emira raised her hands up by her cheeks. "I have an interview on Monday!"

Emira tried to sound more excited than she felt. But it seemed worth it to add a little excitement when Kelley said, "No way! Emira, that's great!"

"It's a daycare managing position and I might not even get it. But yeah, it's got benefits and everything."

"Oh geez, I forgot. You're twenty-six today." Kelley touched both of her shoulders as if they might break any second. "Should we get you a helmet for while you're uninsured?"

She shoved him. "Imma be fine. I got like, thirty days or something."

"Hey, congrats," he told her. "And you're only just starting to look, so this is really great . . ." Kelley's mouth hung open with something else he wanted to say, and Emira thought, *Yeah, I more than like you too.* "Hey, don't go home with your girls tonight. Stay with me."

"Yeah?"

"Yeah," he said. "I have some stuff to tell you later, but not now."

"Good stuff?"

"Umm . . ." Kelley poked out his lips in a way that delighted and gutted her. He raised his eyebrows and said, "Interesting stuff . . . ? But it's your birthday. Lemme buy you a drink."

Minutes later, Zara, Josefa, and Shaunie descended on Kelley with *hiiiii*'s and side hugs. Zara pointed to the gold-cased phone in Emira's hand and said, "Did you see that I upgraded your girl?" Kelley laughed and said, "Damn. So much better." Emira said, "You guys are rude," and Zara matched her expression and said, "Sorry that we care about you."

"Kelley, Mira is blowin' up my Insta right now." Josefa's phone was still in front of her face. "She just got one hundred and fifty likes in like two hours."

"Okay, *that's* what we should have gotten you for your birthday," Shaunie said. "An Instagram account."

Zara said, "What kinda cheap-ass present is that?"

"It's a *thoughtful* present for *memories*."

"Literally no one uses it for memories."

"Hey, this round is on me," Kelley announced to the group. He asked for any requests and Zara and Shaunie shouted, *"Champagne!"*

"You'll drink champagne, right?" Shaunie asked Emira. "It's your birthday, you don't have a choice."

Emira didn't have a choice, but Josefa declined. Without looking up, she said, "Imma skip this round," and kept scrolling in her phone.

Shaunie insisted on taking a picture of Emira and Kelley squished in next to the bar top. Then she filmed an anticlimactic bottle popping from a bored bartender and the equal distribution into three glasses. Josefa called over, "Z, come here real quick," and Zara took her champagne and moved down the bar.

"This was so nice. Thank you, Kelley," Shaunie said. "Have you met my boyfriend? He's coming tonight and you need to meet him."

"Have I met him? I don't think so, I'd love to."

Emira mouthed, *No, you would not,* behind Shaunie's head, but then Zara grabbed her arm and said, "Emira, you're bleeding!"

Emira said, "What?" and Shaunie said, "Oh no!"

Josefa squared her face with Emira's and said, "Let's go to the bathroom right now and take care of it."

Kelley, opening up a tab with the bartender, bent his head back at them. "Are you okay?"

"She's fine, I'm a nurse!" Zara pulled Emira's arm harder. "We'll be right back!"

Emira allowed Josefa and Zara to pull and push her toward the bathroom. She said, "Girl, watch it," as Zara shoved her and Shaunie into the handicap stall. Josefa locked the door behind them. Emira looked down at her arm and saw that there was no trace of blood. She blinked four times in succession and thought, *Woof, I must be faded.*

"I don't see anything."

"You're fine." Josefa pulled out her phone.

"Wait, what?" In Shaunie's left hand was a Band-Aid and in her right was a travel-sized tube of Neosporin. Zara said, "The fuck are you doing?" Shaunie said, "I thought you said blood?"

Emira stopped all of them with, "K, what is this right now?"

Shaunie returned her first-aid items to her purse. Zara and Josefa exchanged a look that made Emira quite furious. Josefa crossed one arm over her chest.

"Guys, what the fuck?" Emira asked again. "This isn't cute. Kelley just got here."

"Okay," Zara said. "Did you share that video?"

Something fat and round formed at the back of her throat. Emira knew what video Zara was referring to, but she found herself stalling and saying, "What video?"

"Don't freak out." Josefa appeared ready to confess but couldn't look Emira in the eye. She tapped and scrolled with white nails as she spoke. "Someone commented on my photo of you and was like, 'Is that the black girl from the grocery store video?' And I was like, 'What?' So I Googled *black girl grocery store video* and . . . this came up."

Emira snatched Josefa's phone and her mouth dropped into an impossible O. Through the haze of three and a half drinks, Emira watched herself on the screen, saying to the camera, "Ohmygod, can you step off?" in the poultry section of Market Depot. She couldn't see Briar, but she could see a little stick of blond hair at the bottom of the frame. The sight of it chipped the side of her heart.

"No no no no no." Emira found herself backed up against the filthy stall wall covered in stickers and Sharpie and names and numbers. Her eyes and chest immediately felt sober but it was taking her limbs and hips longer to catch up. There was part of her that hadn't reached *How did this happen?!* and was still amazed by the technology that put her in this bathroom and on the screen simultaneously. As if from another universe, Emira heard her voice again. Zara had pulled out her phone and was playing the video for Shaunie. "Okay, umm . . ." Shaunie said. "Emira, don't panic."

"But there's no way . . ." Emira whispered. "What is this even? Who *has* this?!"

"Yeah, what is this site?" Shaunie's tone implied that this whole situation was actually a prank, that someone was just being very silly. "This doesn't look like a legit site. Maybe it's the only one."

Zara and Josefa exchanged another look that made Emira want to smash the phone into the piles of soggy toilet paper on the floor. "What!" she demanded. Her fingers were shaking now. "Tell me who else has this!"

"Girl, it's on Twitter," Josefa said. "So like . . . everyone has it."

"Excuse me?"

Josefa reached for her phone, went back a page, and returned the screen to Emira. Emira didn't have a Twitter account, so she tried to swipe left and right. All three of her friends said, "Scroll down."

There it all was. *Black Girl Almost Gets Arrested for Babysitting. Black Girl Destroys Security Guard Who Accuses Her of Kidnapping. Just Another Black Girl Trying To Do Her Job and Getting in Trouble for It. Philadelphia Babysitter Accused of Kidnapping. #BelieveBlackWomen. #AreWeFreeToGo. Sassy Black Woman Lets Security Guard Have It.* There was one clip from the video that had been cut and used over and over again with words typed overhead. Beneath captions like *When TSA tells me my bag is too big, When they tell me the bathroom is for customers only, When they tell me I can only bring six items into the fitting room*, there was Emira yelling, "You're not even a real cop, so you back up, son!" Emira touched the stall wall and said, "I need to sit down."

"Ew, no no no no." Shaunie took her by the elbow. "You can't sit in here. Just lean against me." Josefa took her phone out of Emira's hand and Shaunie blew cool air against her neck.

Everything seemed to blur over with a deep film. Emira was in this disgusting bathroom, but she was also back in the freezer aisle of Market Depot. But she was also in the Chamberlain bathroom where she gave Briar a bath, and then in Briar's bedroom as she put her down for a nap. "I think I'm gonna be sick," she said.

Josefa came in close. "Mira, who did this?"

Zara stepped in too. "Who the fuck did you send this to?"

"I don't . . ." Emira's lips crushed together. "I'm the only one who has this."

"Did someone steal your phone?"

Emira shook her head at Josefa. She reached into her crossbody bag and held up her phone in its new gold case; the unmarked plastic made her want to cry. When she glanced at her screen, there were twelve new texts and four missed calls, and the previews of these texts went back and forth between Happy Birthday! and Emira is this you? There was a message from her mother that said, Emira call us ASAP. Another from her sister said, Why aren't you answering your phone?! Emira placed her head against the wall and inhaled. "Ohmygod."

"Girl, you need to focus," Josefa said. "Look at me. Did your phone get hacked?"

"How would I even know that?"

Zara put her hands on her hips and stood with her heels shoulder-width apart. More to herself than anyone else, she said, "She would know if she got hacked."

"Did you send the video to anyone?" Josefa kept pressing. "Is it on the cloud? Or on a drive or a shared folder?"

"I don't . . ." A tear formed at the corner of Emira's left eye. "I don't even know what that means. No . . . no one has it but me."

"Except for Kelley though, right?" Zara said louder. "Didn't Kelley take this on his phone?"

This stopped Josefa's questions, and all other conversation. Emira looked up to see Shaunie, Zara, and Josefa waiting for her to answer.

For possibly the first time, Emira felt truly judged by her friends. She didn't doubt Kelley because, why should she? Instead, she felt her friends doubted her. And there were plenty of reasons to doubt her—she was terrible with money and she'd never had a real job and her life was stuck in a postcollege mess—but Kelley was different. Maybe Emira didn't have a work phone or paid vacation days or an email ending in *.edu*, but she did have a trustworthy boyfriend who remembered her birthday and played basketball on Tuesdays and always bought her and her girlfriends drinks, which Shaunie still held in her hands. In a voice she didn't recognize, Emira said, "Kelley doesn't have it."

"Are you sure?" Zara asked.

"He deleted it that night."

"You're positive?"

"I know he did. I *watched* him. I even looked in his photos to see if it was there."

Josefa matched Zara and put a hand on her hip. "Did you watch him delete it from his Sent folder too?"

From the bathroom stall, Emira heard a group of girls scream with recognition and joy on the dance floor. One voice said, "When did you get back?" and someone else said, "Girl, you look good!"

"Emira," Josefa shouted. "Did he delete it from his Sent folder? Did you make sure?"

"Of course I didn't *make sure*, okay?" Emira felt her cheeks prepare themselves for tears. "I was a fucking mess that night, but that doesn't mean he has it."

"Guys, Kelley would never," Shaunie agreed. "Maybe he just forgot and maybe *he* got hacked and then—"

"But doesn't he work in tech?" Josefa crossed her arms. "You're telling me that he took this video, showed you that it wasn't in his photos, and that was that? It could have been in a *million* other places. Doesn't Kelley work on iPhones for a living?"

Emira said, "Josefa . . ." and it might have been the first time she'd said her full name since they were students at Temple. When Emira looked back at Zara, she knew it was too late. They exchanged quick glances loaded with information (*Don't do this to me. If you don't I will.*)

before Zara flipped the latch on the swinging door and let herself out of the stall. Emira yelled, "Z, *stop!*" as Josefa darted behind her.

The music was louder now and a few clumps of people were dancing out on the floor. Kelley was still at the bar but joined by two friends. Zara touched his arm and said, "Hey, I lost my phone. Can you call it real quick?"

Kelley reached into his pocket. "Sure, what's your number?"

Emira stepped up next to her and whispered, "Zara, stop."

One of Kelley's friends said, "Hey, happy birthday," and another said, "You lost your phone? Is it that one on the bar?" Neither Zara nor Emira answered. As soon as Kelley typed in his four-digit code, Zara snatched the device and turned her back to his face. With his fingers still curled around an imaginary cell, Kelley said, "Zara, what the fuck?"

Josefa stepped between them, holding a hand up to Kelley. "Hey, it's cool. Just chill out for a second."

Kelley said, "What?" and looked to Emira. She held her breath, feeling everything inside her bubble and churn. She'd left the bar sipping champagne and turning twenty-six. She'd returned looking more like the enraged woman in the video that was currently hemorrhaging across the Internet. Standing there, drunk and confused, Emira thought, *He wouldn't*, but then she thought, *Jesus, please no.* She tried to mentally figure out what was on his phone before Zara could, but her mind was a choppy mix of segments that somehow flowed together: Kelley telling her she should write an op-ed. Kelley telling her she could work for the richest family in Philadelphia. Kelley saying, *Don't you wanna get him fired? Alex shouldn't be able to get away with this shit.* And for some reason, Briar was in the mix too, holding her hand in the movie theater that day, and saying, "You're just a little turkey, hello."

Kelley looked from Josefa to Shaunie to Emira. He licked his lips and said, "What the fuck is going on?"

"Just give her a second," Josefa said. Half of her body leaned to see his screen as Zara searched. Her other arm stretched out in front of Emira's body as if they were driving and Emira was the passenger, seconds after an abrupt stop.

Shaunie squeezed Emira's arm behind her. She looked at the floor and said, "Mira, just ask him."

"Ask me what?" Kelley demanded. "Can I have my phone, please? What is going on?"

"Did you . . ." Emira looked to the ceiling. "Did you share that video?"

She saw him have the same recognition she'd had; remind himself that there was only one video that mattered. To make matters worse, Kelley answered, "No," but then, "What video?" One of Kelley's friends laughed and stood with his drink. "Kelley's got all kinds of drama today." He stepped past Emira and the other man followed.

"The video from the night we met." Emira said this with more volume and charge. "Did you share the video from the night we met?"

"Of course I didn't. I deleted it that night."

"Are you sure?"

"Yes!"

Josefa clicked into her own phone and held the screen toward Kelley. "So why is it going viral right now?"

"Whoa whoa whoa, what is that?" Kelley squinted into the light. "Jesus Christ, how . . . When did this happen?"

"So you don't have the video at all?" Shaunie was still speaking very calmly. "Not on your phone or your computer or anywhere else?"

"No way, I've never even watched it back. Emira, fuck." Kelley gently lowered Josefa's arm so he could step closer. "I wouldn't . . . I wouldn't do this."

Emira breathed. "You deleted it?"

"Yes."

Zara bent her head around Josefa's. "You don't have it anywhere?"

"Absolutely not."

"K, then what's this?" Zara flipped his phone around to face the group. There, on Kelley's phone, was Emira blocking her face. For the third time that night, Emira heard how her voice sounded when she was tired and scared, saying, "Can you step off?" Hearing it for the third time, it was like listening to yourself leave a drunk voicemail, or continuing to sing a song after someone turns the radio off. Zara clicked out of the video, and there was Kelley's Sent folder. When Emira looked back up at Kelley, she thought, *This was just getting good*.

"Fuck you," she whispered.

"No no no. Emira, wait."

The next moments came together in an organized mess consisting of the logistics of leaving Tropicana 187 and the politics of breaking up. Zara told Shaunie to grab Emira's stuff and then Josefa declared that she was getting an Uber. Kelley kept begging Emira to stop, to listen to him, to look at his face, but Zara grabbed onto Emira's hand and steered her through the crowd in a way that felt young and reminded her of college. Somehow Shaunie appeared by the stairs to the street with Emira's coat and presents, like a boyfriend who had treated his partner to a shopping spree. Outside, it had started to snow.

My boyfriend leaked a video of me? Emira took a tighter grip of Zara's hand in the fresh layer of white. Kelley was still behind her and saying, "Emira, wait," to which Zara responded, "You need to back up 'cause I am not the one right now." Josefa stepped into the street first. A car drove up and asked her, "Hey, are you Molly?" to which she responded, "Do I look like a Molly? Get the fuck outta here."

Does he really more than like me? Emira made it to the asphalt. *Did he more than like me when he sent it? Am I a fucking idiot? Who has seen it? Ohmygod.* The thought of Mrs. Chamberlain seeing the video sent a bolt of disgust through Emira's spine and it landed in between the blades of her shoulders. *"I'm making money right now, and I bet I'm making more than you." "He's an old white guy so I'm sure everyone will feel better." "The fuck are you doing? Don't touch me!"* This would be the Emira that existed when Mrs. Chamberlain left her house and children. As Kelley stepped into the street and begged, "Emira, just talk to me, please don't do this," Emira looked at him and wondered, *Will I say good-bye to Briar on terms that aren't mine?*

"Sefa, Imma need an ETA," Zara called.

"Derrek and his Honda are two minutes away."

"Emira, look at me! I didn't fucking do this!" Kelley said.

"Ohmygod Kelley, stop!" Emira was shivering in the snow as she finally spoke. Shaunie tried to put her jacket on her shoulders, but Emira waved it off. "Literally no one else wanted this but you."

"Me wanting that and actually sharing a video are two completely different things."

"Cool, but you still wanted me to share it, right?" When Kelley said nothing, Emira kept going. "Exactly. You want me to be a completely different person. Like . . . you hate that I live in Kensington and you've never even been to my apartment."

"Whoa whoa whoa, you never invite me!"

"You make jokes about me not having health insurance when I'm obviously fucking trying."

"That's not true. *You* make jokes about it!"

"You hate that I babysit for a living, which is fine, it's whatever. But it'd also be easier if you'd just fucking admit it."

Kelley dropped his arms to his sides. "Emira, the only person who hates that you still babysit is you."

Emira took two steps back.

There was a time when she would have accepted this statement from Zara, maybe Kelley if they'd been dating a little bit longer and if she'd been drinking a little bit less. But Zara would have never used the word *still*, highlighting the fact that yes, Emira was a bit late to adulthood, that she should have moved on to something else, and that she currently held a job that thirteen-year-olds were trusted to do. Underneath a patina of tequila and champagne, seeing herself pull her skirt down on tape, and watching it happen via Kelley's Sent folder, Emira could see nothing else but Kelley's doorman, the free basketball tickets he got from work, and the time he said the N-word in front of her, which suddenly didn't seem so banal. Emira looked Kelley up and down. She stuck out her lips and said, "Cool."

"Wait, I don't—this is . . ." Kelley blew through his lips. "Emira, I swear to God I didn't do this . . . but I do think Alex did."

Emira laughed and said, "Ohmygod," as Zara pulled her toward Derrek's approaching Honda. Shaunie hopped in the front seat of the SUV and Josefa went around to the other side.

"I'm not kidding, Emira. She did this. I don't know how, but she came to my work and she—"

"Ohmygod! You have to stop! You two are obsessed with each other and it's so fucking stupid. Actually, you know what? You obviously wanna be with someone who has lots of money and a great job and a book deal, so you might as well just date her again." Once she was inside the car, Zara reached over her lap and pulled the back door shut.

In the backseat, Emira held both sides of her face. Zara put her seat belt on, Shaunie placed a coat on her legs, and Josefa said, "Gimme your phone." By the time they reached Shaunie's apartment, Emira had two missed calls from Kelley, though the new contact name in her phone read Don't Answer.

Twenty-three

On Saturday afternoon, Alix struggled to find a walking speed that fell somewhere between feeling safe and looking offensively scared. For all she knew, Emira had moved out of this apartment, and the address she'd put on her résumé belonged to someone else. But Alix hadn't called because she didn't want Emira to reject her visit. She asked the cab driver to drop her off two blocks away.

Alix liked taking the scooter instead of the stroller because leaving the former somewhere by accident didn't mean losing thirteen hundred dollars (and she could potentially use it as a weapon). With Catherine strapped to her front, Alix held the handlebars as Briar stood on the lime green children's scooter with an unnecessary but adorable helmet strapped to her head. Alix guided Briar with one hand and held her phone in the other as she used Google Maps to navigate past apartment buildings built on top of one another with white bars in front of windows, some of which had cats perched behind them. Emira's apartment building—two satellite dishes were attached to the side of it—was across the street from a basketball court currently covered in a thin layer of snow. Alix lifted Briar and her scooter onto the front step with her left hand and hip. She pressed the button labeled apartment 5B.

"Hello?"

This was definitely Emira's voice, and not on a good day. Alix pushed forward and placed her mouth closer to the intercom.

"Emira? It's Alix. Hi. It's Mrs. Chamberlain."

"Ummm . . . Hi?"

An older black man passed by on the sidewalk with his hands in his jacket pockets. He glanced up from underneath a blue baseball hat and looked at Alix as if she were lost. Briar pointed directly at him and said, "That man is driving the train."

"Honey, shh. Emira, I know this is strange," Alix said. "We just wanted to drop off something for you and . . . just say hi."

Briar kept her eyes on the man and shouted, "Choo choo!"

Under a dense static, Emira said, "Wait . . . is Briar there with you?"

The man was almost at the next street, but Briar cupped her arms around her mouth to yell, "Stand clear of the closing doors, peas!"

"Briar is here and she's making lots of friends," Alix said. "But do you have a mailbox? I can just leave this inside the door."

"No no, I'll come down. Just a second."

The fuzzy connection clicked off and Alix stood up straight.

Briar gave up on the train conductor and looked up at her mother. "Mama? Mama, what . . . what is this right here?" She touched the front door three times with her palm.

Alix licked her thumb and swiped dried yogurt off Briar's lips. "This," she said, "is a little adventure, okay?" She took out antibacterial gel and rubbed Briar's hands, then her own.

Through the window in the door, Alix saw champagne-pink

terry-cloth sweatpants come down the stairs first, and then the rest of Emira appeared. Her hair had been pulled up into a black silk wrap that came up together in a bun on top of her head. Emira had a T-shirt on underneath a denim jacket, which seemed like an odd choice of clothes for a weekend at home, but then again, this wasn't just any weekend. There was no makeup on her face. Emira's eyelids were swollen and soft.

"Hey."

"I'm so sorry to surprise you. Hi."

Briar looked up and pointed. "Mira has no hair."

"Well, hi." Emira smiled. "I still have hair. I just wrapped it up."

"I know this is crazy." Alix raised one hand in the air as if she were swearing on a Bible. "And if you're busy, we don't have to—"

"No no, come on in. I am four flights up, though."

"Not a problem. Can I leave this down here?"

"Ummm . . ." Emira bit the side of her thumbnail and stared at the scooter. "I mean, I wouldn't. But that's up to you."

The stairwell smelled like dust and mold, but when they made it to the fifth floor, Alix could start to smell Emira. Nail polish, lemon, the artificial trace of coconut, and wet grass. When Emira pushed her front door open and revealed her apartment, Alix thought, *Okay, phew, I can do this*, and then, *Oh man, this is depressing*.

Emira's apartment looked like one of those graduate college dormitories where all the rooms are exactly the same, except the corner ones are slightly bigger, or maybe they have one extra window. The hallway and kitchen floor were cased in puckered linoleum that was meant to resemble wood. On top of the refrigerator was a bright red microwave, and Bed Bath & Beyond coupons were stuck to the refrigerator door. There were two bedroom doors off the carpeted living room, and Alix could tell that one was very much Emira's.

There were pictures of brown girls on a corkboard, and hanging on one of the pushpins were the black cat ears from Halloween. There was a tall plastic shelving unit with unfolded black clothing inside, a paisley quilt on the unmade bed with a sad black dress crumpled on top, and a pink bowl on the floor next to the bed that held a shallow pool of sugary milk. The living room had a television, a black IKEA coffee table, a black butterfly chair, and a purple futon couch with an ill-fitting cover sheet. (Alix had once written a blog post that was a letter addressed to futons. In this letter she referred to futons being the biggest furniture hoax of her generation, and called them "glorified bean bags on a rickety but colorful frame." This unsent letter was meant to be funny, but seeing Emira's living room setup made Alix feel like a bully.)

But when she sat down on Emira's couch, Alix spotted something else. On the wall opposite the futon was a ten-gallon fish tank on the floor. There was no lid on top, and there were no fish, but there were about a dozen potted plants—ferns, palms, snake and spider plants—and their green leaves shot up and over the sides. It was completely unexpected, and Alix was grateful that Briar raced to it, so she could figure out how both a lumpy futon couch and this lovely aquarium could exist in the same space.

"Can I get you some water?"

"That would be great. Thank you. Briar, don't touch, lovey. You wanna take your helmet off?"

Briar said, "Nokanku," and pointed to the fish tank. "They's no fish in here."

"But look at all those pretty plants, honey." Alix removed the straps to the Babybjörn and slid Catherine to a horizontal position, her little head on Alix's knees. "Emira, that is such a clever idea."

"Oh." Emira closed the freezer door. "Well, the tenants before us left it here. And it was too heavy to move downstairs . . . so yeah. That's what that is now." Emira broke up the ice cubes in a blue plastic ice tray and filled a glass with water from the sink.

"Why . . . why they's no fish in here?" Briar asked. Emira delivered the glass of water to the coffee table and sat in the butterfly chair.

"It's just for plants, girlfriend. I know that's kinda funny," Emira said. "But I think there used to be fish in there."

While Emira explained this to Briar, Alix got to peek into the bathroom door off the kitchen. There were four damp and colorful bras hanging across the shower rod and Alix thought, *Okay, that's why you're wearing a jean jacket. I get it.* Washing her bras also seemed like something Alix would do if Alix were very restless and upset. One of the bras dripped twice on the shower curtain, and for some reason, this made Alix quite certain that Emira and Kelley were no longer together.

"So, I hope we didn't startle you too much," Alix said. Catherine was taking in the new ceiling and saying *dadada.* "But I just wanted to drop by and—"

"No, yeah. Umm . . ." Emira cut in. She leaned forward and put her elbows on her knees. "Sorry . . . can I talk first?"

Alix lifted Catherine to her shoulder and crossed her long legs. She noticed a Netflix DVD envelope on the bottom shelf of the coffee table, and this, combined with Emira's request to speak first, filled her with affection. *I love this girl,* Alix thought. *She actually still gets the DVDs? What movie is that?* The Devil Wears Prada? *Jesus Christ, I love this girl. Emira and I will be okay.* "Of course you can speak first," she said.

"So umm . . . I'm sure you saw that video 'cause . . . like, everyone did," Emira said. "But just so you know, I definitely don't usually talk that way in front of Briar. I mean—I obviously say things around my friends or whatever but never in front of Briar and that was honestly the only time. I was just super freaked out that they would take her away from me or something and so I yelled and said some things that weren't child-friendly."

Briar reached underneath the coffee table and pulled out a red water bottle that said *Temple* in white letters. "I open dis," she said.

Alix said, "Briar, no no."

Emira waved her hand. "Oh, it's empty, she can play with it. But yeah . . . obviously you're here so maybe your mind is made up and I get that." Emira folded her hands between her knees. "I just wanted to say my piece of it and umm . . . yeah, I guess that's it."

The night before, Alix watched the video on her iPad five times, sitting on the bathtub as Peter slept, just after receiving a text from Laney that read, "It's up." Each time, it was like she was meeting Emira all over again. She'd never seen her sitter talk so much and she'd never realized how pretty she was and she'd never seen Emira so bright and quick. Alix knew the ending. She knew that everything eventually turned out alright. But watching the events play out and listening to Emira's voice change over into fear made her heart beat as if she were watching a horror movie. Alix found herself thinking, *Yes, Emira. Tell him*, and *Watch out, he's right behind you!* But mostly she just thought, *Ohmygod, was that only a few months ago? How in the world was Briar so teeny?*

Most of the content on Twitter and trashy websites was praise for Emira's behavior, but some of it got off course. This seemed to be the content that Emira considered when recalling her behavior on that September night.

Why wouldn't she just let the cop talk to the kid's dad? That's technically resisting.

Sorry, but she does NOT look like a babysitter.

If she acts that way in front of a camera, I wonder what she's saying to the kid when no one's around.

But Alix felt the same way seeing Emira say these things as she did when she caught the foul lyrics of a song on her phone: delighted and intrigued. Alix was never more frightened of Briar acting like Emira than she was of Briar acting like her. Did she want Briar to act like Emira? In her better moments, sure. More importantly, did she want a babysitter who was capable of standing up for herself? Alix thought, *One hundred percent.* She folded her lips together and bounced Catherine on her shoulder. "Emira," she said. "Did you think Peter and I would be mad at you?"

Emira looked up and patted the back of her head. It was clear she had been crying for some time. "Well, I feel bad for calling Peter an old man because he's always been nice to me and he's not even that old."

Alix couldn't help but laugh as she pulled Catherine's sock farther up her ankle. "He would appreciate you saying that but it's honestly not necessary. Well, first of all . . . I know we've had our moments, you and I. But Emira, I feel very strongly that I know where your heart is. Peter and I are so grateful that you care about our children and that you're there to protect them when we can't. And I appreciate your protectiveness over the girls as much as I appreciate your privacy as a person, so I can't imagine what you're going through right now."

Emira crossed one leg over the other and said, "It is what it is."

"Well, we are definitely not mad at you," Alix said. "We're the exact opposite. We're so impressed with how you reacted that evening, and so grateful that you came into our lives . . . and for the record, I've definitely said plenty of things in front of them that are not child-friendly, so please don't stress out about that. Okay . . ." Alix reached for her purse at the other end of the couch and set it down between her ankles. "I have a lot to say right now, so just bear with me. Briar my love, come here."

Briar looked up and pushed her helmet back onto her skull. Alix held Catherine with one hand and dug into her purse with the other. She pulled out a small, wrapped square gift with red and white twine tied on top. "That's for Emira, remember? Go ahead and give it to her."

Emira said, "What's this?"

Briar took the gift in her hands and made her way to Emira. "I want . . . I want to open dis. I do it."

Alix said, "That's for Emira, lovey," and Emira said, "How about you help me?"

Alix watched Briar and Emira open up the small package to reveal a pocket calendar with a painted floral theme for the year 2016. Emira's eyes went wide in confusion, but she still said, "Oh, thank you."

Alix brushed Catherine's hair with her fingertips and said, "Why don't you look inside."

That morning, Alix had written the name *EMIRA* on all the Mondays, Tuesdays, Wednesdays, and Fridays in the first six months of the calendar. She watched Emira flip the page open to the month of January, as Briar pointed at the picture of the featured flower and said, "I smell dis right now." Emira flipped to February, seemingly waiting for something to pop out.

"Emira, this is my very bad way . . ." Alix started, "of asking you to do more hours with us."

Emira flipped to March. "I'm not sure what you mean."

Briar tapped her helmet. "Mama, I want dis off."

"Come here and I'll help you." Alix looked at Emira and smiled. "So . . . Mama got a very cool opportunity, right?" With one hand she released Briar's helmet. "And it looks like I'll be facilitating a class at the New School for the upcoming semester. And it's every Tuesday evening, but the girls obviously can't come with me, so . . . we'd love for them to be with you. So! It would be . . ." Alix held up a pointer finger to count. "Monday, regular hours, twelve to seven. Tuesday you'd come in at noon and spend the night till noon the next day— we'd make the guest room perfect for you and make sure you're all set up—and then regular hours on Friday from twelve to seven."

Emira appeared so stunned by this proposed schedule that she began to hold the calendar as if she'd learned it was quite expensive, and she didn't want her fingerprints to prove that she'd come in contact. "Wow," she said.

"Now, I know you have another typing job you do on the days that you're not with us, and I don't know how attached you are to it . . . Briar lovey, helmet straps are very dirty and not for your mouth, okay? But yes, we'd obviously make this a full-time job since you'd be giving your other position up. This would put you at thirty-eight hours a week, but we'd bump you up to forty just in case a train is running late one day or what have you. And that way we'd be able to include health insurance and vacation days and all of that good stuff . . . And I didn't mark up summer only because I know you'll probably go home at some point, and we can work around all that . . ." Alix sighed and smiled; her shoulders went down about two inches. "I did write all of this down for you because I know it's a lot," she said. "And you don't have to let us know right away, but maybe for now, if you can think of any questions you might . . . oh no . . . Emira, honey, are you okay?"

In the most uncomfortable and cheap-looking chair Alix had ever seen, Emira put her hands to her face and cried. There were no tissues on the coffee table (just two remotes and a tube of something called

Baby Lips), so Alix carried Catherine to the bathroom and grabbed a roll of toilet paper. With Catherine at her chest, Alix kneeled in front of Emira, and when she put a clump of the tissues into Emira's hand, she let her own hand linger.

"You're having such a time right now and I'm laying all this stuff on you, I'm so sorry." Emira had such a sweetly embarrassing and mushy crying face that Alix felt that she too might turn teary. "I thought it might all be perfect timing but maybe we should deal with this video first and then we can start to think about next . . ."

But Emira shook her head, almost as if she were both happy and spent, and said, "No, I'm sorry, yeah. Yeah, that sounds really good."

"Really?!" Alix didn't mean to say it so loud. She placed a hand over her mouth, as she felt certain that Emira's neighbors had heard her through the popcorn-textured stucco walls. "Yes? Ohmygod, we'd be so happy, are you sure?"

"Oh yeah, for sure." Emira laughed. "Yeah, I'd ummm . . . I'd definitely like to up my hours."

"Oh God, that's amazing news! Okay. Okay." Alix beamed. "Bri, lovey, guess what?" Briar was unsuccessfully trying to buckle her helmet to the widest part of her stomach. "Bri, you and Emira are gonna do sleepovers next year. Isn't that so special?"

"Mira?" Briar picked up the Temple water bottle and brought it to Emira. "Mira, let's put . . . let's put raisins in here and we save them for later, okay?"

Emira said, "That's a pretty good idea."

Alix sat back on her heels. "Okay, so yes. In the New Year?"

Emira wiped her eyes with her pinkies and said, "Yeah, that's perfect."

"I promise we'll iron out all the details and get everything set before then. But I do want to mention one last thing."

But there were so many things Alix wanted to mention. She couldn't wait to reach a point in their relationship where she wouldn't have to sit on opportunities for growth that Emira would hopefully carry with her for the rest of her life. *This video you're embarrassed of?* Alix wanted to tell her, *It's honestly not that bad, and it shows how much you love my kid. And this water bottle you've been using? It might give you cancer so let's get you a new one made with glass or stainless steel. And this thing you did by accident? With the plants and the aquarium? It's so, so lovely and your instincts were spot on. And I know that a couch is a huge investment but it's one of those things you'll want to spend money on. And these are the staple items you want to have in your closet. And this is a meal that looks fancy but it's really not. And this is how to crack an egg with one hand; you practice with a quarter and two Ping-Pong balls.* This was not the time to share these things, but with Emira working full-time, Alix would definitely get her chance.

"If it's all too fresh to talk about, just tell me," Alix said. "But Peter and I want to help you out with this video."

Once again, Emira said yes.

———

And so on Monday morning, Laney Thacker and her camera crew arrived at the Chamberlain house at seven a.m. Tamra took the train in and arrived with coffee and croissants. Emira entered with Zara shortly after, holding two dresses in the colors Laney recommended (mint and cobalt blue). Her hair was straightened and curled in a way Alix had never seen before, and she'd ditched the chunky eyeliner. A simple gold necklace sat on her chest, and when Alix saw it, she thought, *Good girl.*

As Alix prepared for her first appearance on the local news, buttoning her dusty-rose blouse in the mirror, she looked at Tamra for a final confirmation. "I did the right thing, right?" she whispered. She pushed her hair in front of her shoulders. "Sorry, just . . . just tell me that I did the right thing."

Tamra's eyes went small in an exaggerated and confident expression. "Oh girl, yes," she said. "One hundred percent. This is probably the best thing to ever happen to Emira."

Twenty-four

When Mrs. Chamberlain opened her front door, Emira heard Zara whisper, "Oh shit, okay." On top of the grandness of the Chamberlain home, which had once shocked Emira as well, there were lights and cameras set up inside the living room along with glass vases of pink hydrangeas on the side tables.

"Hi, sweetie. Are you awake yet? We have lots of coffee if not. Hi, Zara. Nice to see you again." Mrs. Chamberlain looked sharp and awake. The *sweetie* caught her off guard, but they were fresh off a hard weekend, and Emira told herself that Mrs. Chamberlain's warmth would become more natural. Emira and Zara held Dunkin' Donuts coffees in their hands, but Zara put hers down and accepted a cold brew from Tamra.

Laney Thacker welcomed Emira into the living room. She gave Emira a hug with her arms overly stretched in front of her body and a white napkin tucked into her collar, so as to not get makeup on her dress. Then she said, "Lovely," as she took Emira's dresses from her; she held one in each hand. "We're gonna go with this one." She raised the bright, cobalt blue. "Just a little pink on your lips and a super-clean finish on your cheeks, okay?"

"Emira, the girls' bathroom is all yours," Alix said.

Laney nodded as if she'd been part of this decision. "Let's meet back in twenty and we'll be on at nine, superstar."

Emira tried to match their excitement. While she wanted to ask where Briar was—she was very curious to see what the little girl would be wearing—Emira took to the stairs with Zara. She would see Briar soon enough, and spend plenty of time with her in the near future.

Inside the children's bathroom, Emira sat on the toilet as Zara applied a finishing layer of powder on her cheeks. "So . . ." Zara whispered. Emira smelled the fancy cold brew on her breath. "They's some mad plantation vibes up in here."

"Aight, okay." Emira opened her eyes. She held up a compact and looked at her reflection. "Imma be spending a lot of time here, so chill. Can you get my edges a little bit?"

Zara tsked and said, "Where's your baby comb?"

Emira sat up to peek into her makeup bag. "It's not in there?" She took the bag from the sink and held it in her lap. After pushing filthy compacts and wands from side to side, she said, "It must be in my backpack," and looked up at Zara.

Zara poked out her lips. "Oh, it's like that."

"Can you just bring my whole bag up here?"

"Wowww, okay, okay." Zara reached for the door. To no one she said, "She think she cute now that she got a job but okay."

Emira called, "Thank you!" as Zara closed the door. Alone, she stood and looked into the mirror. There, above a bulk pack of wipes and a jar of baby powder, was the version of herself she'd much rather appear on camera than the one that was still making its way across Facebook and Twitter.

All weekend long, Emira couldn't help but Google comments and posts about the Market Depot video. In the midst of an onslaught of police brutality videos and Black Lives Matter marches, Emira's viral video was somehow . . . funny? Viewers and sharers of the video tacked it to their feeds with comments like, This is fucked up but I'm also dying laughing, and OMG, this girl is my hero. Someone had taken a screenshot of Emira yelling at the security guard with a hand to her hip, and they zoomed in on Briar's face looking helplessly at the camera. The caption read, *record scratch* Yep. That's me. You're probably wondering how I got in this position. People made comments like This baby is killing me and Baby girl has had enough and I'm ready for a spinoff with this kid and her sitter. The more it was shared, the lighter it seemed to be, which made the whole thing both better and worse.

Emira believed this light take was the consensus because of a few factors. First of all, no one got hurt. Briar was adorable and agreeable and bored with the situation, and Emira's quick retorts often masked her fear. This was a video about racism that you could watch without seeing any blood or ruining the rest of your day. Emira couldn't help but think of how the Internet would react if they knew she and Kelley were dating . . . *had* dated. (Emira ignored the four calls Kelley placed to her cell in the last two days. Zara answered his last attempt with, "Okay, so we've calmed down? But we aren't ready to speak to you yet. Please respect our transition.")

Kelley wasn't the only one calling. All weekend, Emira kept her phone on the charger because it buzzed every hour with requests for interviews and one appearance on a talk show called *The Real*. But Emira answered every call with the scripted phrases that Mrs.

Chamberlain left her with. "You tell everyone that you don't have a comment at this time, and that's all you have to say at the moment," she said. "We can turn this around, I promise you. We'll go in, clear up anything that may have been misconstrued, and you'll be out of the spotlight as fast as you were in it."

As it happened, Kelley was correct about the notoriety this video would bring, but on a much smaller scale than he most likely presumed. In the two days following the video, Emira received three voice mails offering employment. One was from an affluent black family in the city seeking a nanny for their three boys. One was from an online publication asking her to do a three-piece series on protecting the rights of caretakers in Philadelphia. And one was from her current employer, the Green Party office. Emira's Tuesday and Thursday supervisor, a woman named Beverly, phoned her cell three times and left two messages: "Let's talk about getting you in here more, okay?" After the ream of nice paper she'd spent her money on and the cover letters she'd spent her evenings writing, Emira was annoyed, rather than delighted, by the fact that a viral video seemed to make her more qualified than reference letters and a bachelor's degree. But that didn't matter anymore because she didn't need it. Emira's parents—who seemed most concerned with her outfit in the video—panicked at the assumption that she was both jobless and coatless. "Mom, it was back in September," Emira explained. "And I do have a job. I'm a nanny."

The Thanksgiving invitation didn't make her feel like family. What did was receiving a contract and 1095 tax form from Mrs. Chamberlain. In 2016, though Emira would technically be making less money per hour because of taxes, she'd still be making more money than she ever had in her life, almost $32K a year. She wouldn't be moving into Shaunie's old room, but if she was ever stopped by a security guard again, Emira could say she was a nanny without stumbling over a lie. She'd have a valid excuse not to go out because she'd be working twenty-four-hour shifts. And for Briar's future pre-school, her swimming classes at the YMCA, and fall ballet at Little Lulu's, Emira's name and number would be listed at the top of Briar's emergency contact list.

So on the brink of a new career and Internet persona, it seemed incredible, far-fetched, and slightly amusing when Zara returned with Emira's backpack, closed the door behind her, and whispered, "So, we got a problem." Zara dropped the backpack to the floor and pressed her lips together. She held her hands in prayer and placed her index fingers against her mouth.

Emira reached for her backpack and said, "I'm sure it just fell to the bottom."

But Zara didn't seem to hear her. With her right hand, Zara made a fist and pumped it in a small circle in the air. After she pressed her knuckles to her mouth she whispered, "Mira, I'm not playin'. Look at me." Zara took a breath and said, "You can't work here no more."

Emira laughed and stood with her edges toothbrush in her hand. She let her backpack fall against her ankles and leaned a hip against the counter. "Excuse me?"

"You need to listen to me right now."

"I *am*, what is wrong with you?"

"So I'm downstairs . . . kneeling down to get your heavy-ass back-pack, and I hear your boss go into the bathroom." Zara whispered this as she pointed down toward the floor, where just below them was the guest bathroom. "I'm getting your shit, and then I hear that woman ask if she'd done the right thing." Zara put aggressive air quotes over *the right thing*. "And then that Uncle Tom Tamra woman told her, 'one hundred percent,' and that this video is the best thing to ever happen to you."

Emira held the toothbrush in both hands and waved her thumb four times across the white and blue bristles. She set it down on the counter and it made a tiny click. "Okay, no . . . hold up." She brought her own voice down to match. "She probably means this news thing. Like—*this* video we're about to shoot." But as she said it, Emira realized that if that was what Mrs. Chamberlain meant, then that hurt all on its own. Emira was constantly pointing out the instability of her current situation, specifically so that other people didn't have to. The implications of Zara's allegation took their time to be hardened in her mind, and for the moment, all Emira could think was, *Mrs. Chamberlain was talking shit about me? I thought we had a deal.*

Zara shook her head and held up a pointer finger. "Nuh-uh, girl. You said *yes* to this news thing. You didn't say yes to the grocery store shit. That lady did something. Mira . . ." Zara trailed off as she stared into Emira's face. "That lady leaked your tape."

"Okay, no . . ." Emira was saying *no* to this accusation, but mostly she was saying *no* to the idea of having another conversation in which she had to examine who loved her least: Kelley or Mrs. Chamberlain. She crossed one arm and said, "Z, there's no way. How would she even get it?"

"I don't know," Zara said. "Do you leave your phone out?"

"Sure, but it's not like she has my code."

"Do you bring your laptop here?"

"I don't bring my laptop anywhere."

"Okay, do you check your email on her laptop?" Zara pointed to the bathroom door. "Or the big-ass computer out there in the kitchen?"

Emira placed one hand against her opposite shoulder. For about eight seconds, her face stiffened into a position of almost remembering a simple word she'd somehow forgotten midconversation. Her mind rounded to three days prior, the day she turned twenty-six, and how short she was with Mrs. Chamberlain in her kitchen. She'd logged into her Gmail to send herself an address, but she didn't remember logging out. She did remember peeking at the time on her phone to speed up the painfully practiced conversation that she didn't allow Mrs. Chamberlain to have. And she'd taken Mrs. Chamberlain's money and returned six hours later to drop off her child happy, sticky, and loved. Emira considered the fact that because she hadn't let Mrs. Chamberlain endorse or even entertain a breakup with Kelley, that the mother of two had potentially done this legwork on her own. But weren't they cool now? Wasn't that why Mrs. Chamberlain had hired her as a nanny? But wait, shit . . . was *this* the reason she'd hired her as a nanny? Emira breathed out through her nose. She suddenly remembered the first time she stayed late to have a drink with Mrs. Chamberlain. The expensive wine she'd received for free. She'd asked if Mrs. Chamberlain had an event coming up. Mrs. Chamberlain had winked and said, "When my book comes out, I will."

Emira looked up at Zara and whispered, "Fuck."

"Okay, we can talk about this later? But your understanding of technology is *truly* problematic."

"*You* told me that *Kelley* did it!" Emira shouted in a whisper. She reached forward and shoved Zara's shoulder harder than she meant to. "What the fuck was I supposed to think?"

Zara dramatically brought her body back to center. "Okay, listen, I fucked up." She held both her pointer fingers up as she explained. "I had way too many mojitos and maybe I jumped to things, but I was honestly just trying to protect you. And when you get a new man or go back to Kelley or whatever I swear to God I'll chill out but—"

"Shhh shh, it's fine it's fine." Emira stopped her. Not only was

Zara getting too loud but the sound of Kelley's name still stung. "Are you *sure* that's what she meant?"

"Deadass?" Zara looked up to the ceiling as if she were swearing to both Emira and to God. "That is what I heard her say, and that is how I heard her say it."

Emira and Zara stood still in the bright white bathroom. Zara bit her lip and said, "Girl, you can't work here." Emira raised her shoulders and—knowing it had all been too good to be true—released them and said, "I know."

"Okay, fuck it then," Zara said. She began putting Emira's makeup back into her travel bag. "Let's just leave. You don't owe her shit." A pencil shaving dropped out from an eye pencil sharpener, which Zara quickly scooped into the trash. It was as if she were trying to conceal the fact that she and Emira were ever there.

"Wait. Zara, stop." Emira gripped her friend's forearm. Her pulse quickened as the consequences jelled in her mind. "I won't have a job," she said. "It's not like I can put in my two weeks' notice. I can't not have a job."

Zara sucked her top lip. "Can you live off your typing job?"

"If I could do that, do you think I'd have this one?"

Zara went quiet in thought. She reached up and tapped her thumb to her mouth. "Okay. Then let's get you another job right quick."

"What?"

"We gettin' you a temp job," Zara decided. "It don't have to be perfect. It just needs to work right now. So who called you this weekend? You better not have told any of them no."

"I didn't," Emira said. Suddenly she was back to where she started. The idea of scouring the Internet and checking Craigslist and seeing disgusting children on the street and thinking, *Could I learn to love you?* put a twist inside her chest that brought her shoulders forward.

Emira took a deep breath. "Okay, umm . . . this family called and said they'd take me as a nanny."

"Nuh-uh." Zara wagged her pointer finger. "We ain't doin' this mammy shit no more. Next."

"There were stupid offers for essays that I could never write," Emira said. "And then my boss at the Green Party said she'd take me on for more hours."

"Your typing boss?"

"Yeah, but it'd be as a receptionist."

"Okay . . . ? Can you work there?"

Emira said, "Yes . . . ?" It would be boring but she could do it. And in that moment, what seemed like the biggest selling point was the fact that she wouldn't have to buy new clothes because everyone who worked there always wore jeans. "I mean, yeah, they're chill over there."

"Okay, perfect, that's all we need," Zara said. "It doesn't have to be forever. How much will they give you?"

"She didn't say."

Outside in the hallway, Laney called, "Five minutes to places, ladies!"

Zara said, "Get them on the phone."

Emira bent down to her backpack and retrieved her phone. At this point it was a relief to have someone telling her what to do. She stayed seated on the toilet as she tapped Beverly's office number, and the line began to ring as Zara continued to pack her makeup. "Don't say yes yet. Just ask for details." Zara zipped up Emira's makeup bag and threw it down to her backpack. "Just be cool," she told Emira. "We got this, don't stress."

On the fifth ring, she answered.

"Hi, Beverly? It's Emira." Emira tried to sound as natural as possible while whispering in the echoing space. "I got your message and I just wanted to talk about . . . your offer?"

Beverly explained that she just got into the office, and apologized if she sounded out of breath. She went on about how she had no idea what Emira had gone through, that it might be perfect timing, that the current front desk person would be going back to school and that they'd love to have her. Then Laney knocked on the door.

"Finishing touches in there?" she called.

Zara bolted for the doorknob. She stuck her face in the crack between the door and the wall and grinned, "Yep! Just one more minute!" before she closed it once again.

"Can you hang for two seconds?" Emira asked. She clicked her phone on mute. "They'll give me sixteen dollars an hour for thirty-five hours a week."

"Ooohh, nuh-uh nuh-uh." Zara shook her head and pulled out her own phone. "They fina do that so they don't have to give you benefits."

"Are you sure?"

"Go'n and ask her."

Emira's breath quickened within her rib cage as she clicked back into the call. "Sorry, Beverly?" she said. "Does that mean I wouldn't have health insurance?" Emira listened to Beverly confirm that it wouldn't. She looked back at Zara and mouthed, *Shit*.

"Okay, we gon' negotiate right now," Zara whispered. She knelt down in front of Emira and began to type furiously into her phone's calculator. "Tell her . . ." Zara held a hand up in the air as she formed her words. "Tell her that you're very interested in the position, and that you'd like to talk about including health coverage."

Emira slowly spoke these exact words into her cell's receiver.

"And," Zara whispered as she typed, "that you're willing to go down in rate."

Emira wanted to ask her friend, *Am I? Am I willing to go down in rate?* She currently made sixteen dollars an hour. And Briar wouldn't be there, so honestly, what was the point? Emira realized then that she never would have actually worked at Body World Fitness as a childcare manager, even if they had offered the position to her. She would have stayed with Briar for as long as the Chamberlains would have her. But Mrs. Chamberlain had finally gone too far and it was no longer a private matter. Emira heard Mrs. Chamberlain in the hallway say, "Are they almost done?" Emira repeated Zara's words verbatim. "I'm also willing to go down in rate."

In Emira's ear Beverly said, "Alright, let's chat about it . . . where could you meet us at?"

"Ummm . . ." Emira looked to Zara. "Where could I meet you at?"

Zara looked back down into her phone. "So if you go down to fourteen an hour," she whispered, "it's the same offer of 29K but with the addition of benefits."

"Okay, could you guys do . . ." Emira knew that her words did not match the professionalism of the situation, but she pushed past her novice and embarrassment and threw out the number. "Fourteen an hour?"

"Emira, hang on," Beverly said. Emira heard voices in the background before Beverly returned. "They're telling me that we can do thirteen an hour if we throw in benefits. I know that's rough, but if you stay on for six months, I'm sure I can get you more."

From the way she said this, Emira could gather that Beverly genuinely wanted her for the job, and that she'd offer more if she could. Emira's professionalism had dropped into necessity, and it was a strange relief to see that Beverly's had too. Emira covered the phone and said, "They can only do thirteen."

Zara twisted her lips. "Does that include dental?"

Emira winced. "That doesn't include dental, does it?" She listened to Beverly verify that it didn't, and shook her head at Zara. "How much is that?" Emira whispered.

Zara flipped the phone around and showed her the number $27,040: a few hundred dollars less than she was making now. Zara nodded and said, "Tell her yes." Emira hesitated and Zara reached out her hand. "Mira? It's just for now," she said. "This is a real-ass job. You want *this* on your résumé." Zara pointed to the phone at Emira's ear. "You don't want this." She pointed to the door behind her and shook her head. There was a fierce desperation in Zara's eyes, and it told Emira that her friend was worried for her, and that she had been for some time.

Just then, Mrs. Chamberlain knocked and said, "Hello?"

Into her phone, Emira said, "I'll take it."

As Zara zipped up Emira's backpack, Emira bent down onto her knees next to the toilet and cupped her hand around the mouthpiece ("Okay, thank you so much, Beverly . . . okay, thank you!"). The second she clicked Off and stood up straight, Zara opened the door and shielded herself behind it.

"You guys okay?" Mrs. Chamberlain peeked in the bathroom. "Oh, Emira. You look so pretty. We gotta hustle downstairs because they're about ready. You okay?"

Emira took a breath and said, "I'm great."

Laney appeared next to Mrs. Chamberlain, clapped in the space below her chin, and sang, "Places!"

Laney turned to go back downstairs, and when she did, Mrs. Chamberlain looked at Emira with a wide-eyed expression that said,

God, she's a lot, am I right? The quickness of it was so sharp and pointed, and the ease of it revealed years of practice. Emira swallowed as Mrs. Chamberlain playfully rolled her eyes before she followed Laney downstairs.

Zara slowly pushed the bathroom door closed once again to reveal a face of urgency. "If we gonna go? We gotta go right now."

But Mrs. Chamberlain's bite-sized dig at Laney set off something in Emira's blood and joints, and as she looked back into the mirror, Emira said, "No." She twisted her head from side to side to make sure her foundation blended properly across the arc of her jawline. She threw her hair behind her shoulders and checked the whiteness of her teeth. "I'm still gonna do it."

"Say what?!"

"Listen to me." Emira turned to her. "I'm doin' this thing, okay? But as soon as I give you a look, I want you to make a scene."

Zara shook her head in reluctance, obligation, and stoic confirmation. "Mira, don't play with me 'cause you know I'll start some shit."

"Do it. I'm serious," Emira promised. In the mirror she reached into the neck of her dress to hoist and center her breasts. "Just stay with me and when I tell you, I need you to start wildin' out. But girl, wait . . . ohmygod? I have benefits now?" Emira broke a smile. As Zara and Emira quietly jumped up and down, Emira suddenly realized that there would be a day, probably quite soon, when Briar would no longer remember her.

Twenty-five

That morning, Laney had been the first to arrive at the Chamberlain house. She was also the first person Alix directed her question to: "Did I do the right thing?"

With a face full of makeup at seven a.m., Laney took both of Alix's hands. "Honey," she said. "Listen to me. When I was a junior in high school, a soccer coach of mine got a bit too close to our center fielder, and performed in our locker room what I now know as second base. I knew it was wrong. Everyone on my team knew it was wrong. But this girl, Mona . . . Monica? Monica. Well, she said to keep quiet. And at the time, none of us knew what to do, so we didn't do anything. But I bet you that if Monica were here right now, she would wish that we had. Do you know what I'm sayin', Alix?"

Alix pressed her lips together and nodded. She tried to release her fingers from Laney's as she said, "Yeah. Totally."

Alix would wait to receive a better confirmation from Tamra. In the meantime, she tried to be thankful for Laney's discreet savvyness. Three days prior, Laney had quickly and successfully delivered the grocery store video into the wrong hands, and then swooped back in to land the first interview. "Everybody wins with this," Laney promised her. "Emira gets to clear her name. Peter's little mix-up will be smoothed over. And you'll get to come back into the spotlight a bit. And don't worry, I know exactly how to plug your book *without* plugging your book. You know what I mean."

And this was the moment when Alix realized that she'd have to live in Philadelphia both in the flesh and on the Internet. But really, it was about time. Alix had accepted the position at the New School; Emira had accepted her role as a full-time nanny; her editor, Maura, had accepted Alix's apology and the thirty pages she'd scrounged together over the weekend; and now it was time for Alix to accept that she no longer lived in Manhattan. Alix had somehow walked out of this Kelley Copeland mess unscathed, and her upcoming Philadelphia confession seemed to serve as a secret penance. As Emira and Zara finally emerged from the upstairs bathroom, Emira looking charming and nervous in a way Alix hadn't seen before, Alix felt prepared not only to represent the city of Philadelphia, but to let Emira represent her too.

As they walked, Zara and Emira swapped a precious exchange before Emira came into the living room and into the light. Laney said, "Let's have a look." Briar—in a dark purple wing-collared dress—pointed at Zara and told Emira, "That's your friend." Tamra squeezed Briar's hand and said, "That is Mira's friend. It's almost time for you to sit with them, okay?" Emira grinned at Briar and said, "Hey, big girl."

There were two cameramen and a sound guy set up in the center of the room. The television, an armchair, and two bins of children's toys were lined up along the wall behind them. Laney was at the helm. She circled the room as she double-checked all angles, numbers, and light sources. She showed no qualms with telling her team, "Nope, not good enough," and watching while they tried again. Alix felt naïve to see that Laney wasn't just a talking head on television but the executive producer of this upcoming segment that would be broadcast live on *WNFT Morning News*. In a bright green blouse that tied at the side of her neck, Laney stood in front of Alix and Emira and took them in. "Let's get Miss Briar in here too?" Laney called. With Catherine babbling in one arm, Tamra delivered Briar's hand to Alix. "Mama?" Briar pointed to one of the cameramen. "I want—I want . . . that man has glasses."

"So Emira, let's add the cream-colored cardigan on top, I think that'll look really nice," Laney said. "And Alix, let's get a little more powder right here on you. Just a tiny bit." Laney pointed with her pinkies to the space on the inside of her own eyelids.

Tamra called, "Got it," and went to receive a square of foundation. When Zara realized that the cardigan retrieval was in her purview, she mouthed, *Oh, das me, okay*, and jogged to retrieve it from the front vestibule. She tiptoed into the camera light and handed her friend the knitted sweater before backing out and leaning against the living room door frame.

Once Alix and Emira made the corrections, Laney told them to take a seat on the couch. Alix's house suddenly seemed like one large prop, and she wished she could go back and add Philadelphia-purchased touches that could make her feel more connected to the space. But now that Emira would be spending so much time here, Alix would have another reason to make it feel like home. Alix sat next to Emira on the couch as Laney straightened Briar's dress across Emira's knees. Briar pointed up at Emira and said, "You got sparklers on you face."

"Okay, ladies. Great." Laney sat in her own chair across from

Emira's end of the couch. "So it's just like we talked about. Keep your answers to one or two sentences long. Legs shut, eyes open. And don't be afraid to take your time. We've got a whole four minutes, okay? Bri, sweetie? Look up at me." Laney snapped her fingers twice in the air, and Briar looked at her as if she'd shouted this information. "So you gotta stay with Emira and be the big sister today, yes?" Laney nodded four times and answered the question for herself. "Yes, ma'am. Big sister. Garret, gimme an ETA?"

One of the cameramen took his face away from the equipment to adjust his headpiece and say, "We're on in two minutes." Alix reached over and squeezed the top of Emira's hand, grazing the sides of her daughter's knee. This was a first for her too. She'd never been on the local news. Much like Thanksgiving, Alix foresaw this four-minute segment as a moment that would unite her and Emira in a way that neither of them could ever take back. Alix felt woozy off how pretty Emira looked, how graciously she'd accepted Alix's advice all weekend, and how she was now in her home without being paid. Alix adjusted her posture one last time as Laney led the women in a silent group breath. "Just stay with me," Laney whispered, and smiled. "You're gonna hear Misty and Peter first and then I'll lead you in."

From the little black speaker balanced next to the sound man's feet, Alix heard a buzz and then the familiar sound of WNFT's theme music. The sound guy bent to turn up the volume and stood once again with the boom outstretched over their heads.

"Welcome back to WNFT. You're probably wondering where Laney is right now," Misty said, "and that leads us to our main story. It's not often that a segment hits this close to home, but this one is currently taking place *inside* Peter's home!" There was a pause, and while Alix couldn't see her husband, she imagined he was doing a sheepish but charming *what are ya gonna do* face while admitting guilt with a raised hand. Misty went on as Alix curved her tongue around her front teeth one last time. "This weekend, a video went viral which showed twenty-five-year-old Temple graduate Emira Tucker being accused of kidnapping by a security guard at Market Depot. Emira was not committing a crime—rather, she was babysitting. And Peter, I'll pass it on to you because you know Emira and the child in question quite well."

"That's correct." Peter let out a small laugh. "I'll let Emira speak for herself, as she can shed much more light on the situation than I can, but I would like to say this . . ."

At this moment, Briar looked up at Emira and said, "That's Dada." Emira nodded with a finger to her lips and whispered, "Shh." Briar put her own finger to her lips, looked at Alix, and with the same volume as before, she whispered, "I hear Dada."

"Before anything else, I'm a father," Peter confessed from the WNFT stage. Alix stared at her shoes as his voice came through the speaker. "My wife and I hired Emira last summer to watch over our children, and she's been with us ever since. We try to keep our girls out of the spotlight as much as possible, but on the night of September 19, that wasn't so easy. It's been a strange couple of days and my wife and I appreciate all the incoming support for our family, Emira included. Today, my wife, my oldest daughter, and our babysitter, Emira, are going to answer some questions about that night, and hopefully put the matter to bed."

"On September 19, a rock was thrown through the front window of the Chamberlain house." This was Laney's voice, prerecorded. When Laney heard the sound, she perked up in her seat and looked to Alix and Emira to mouth, *Here we go.* Alix couldn't remember if Emira knew if it was a rock or an egg, but Laney had assured her that a rock would read better and amplify a heightened sense of desperation from Peter and Alix, an obvious reason to reach out to a sitter. All this time later, it seemed almost silly that Alix's biggest concern for months was whether or not Emira knew why said rock/egg was thrown. But Alix told herself that it didn't matter, and to take a deep breath. *In four minutes*, she exhaled, *this will all be over.* Laney's recording went on.

"Peter and Alix Chamberlain quickly called Emira Tucker, their part-time babysitter, to take their toddler out of the house while they called the police, but Emira ran into a situation of her own. A Market Depot customer and security guard accused her of kidnapping three-year-old Briar, and refused to let her leave the store." The sound of Emira's voice radiated into the room through a small speaker, and Alix felt the sofa shift. Emira's entire body rose half an inch. Alix had seen the video enough times to know that while Emira said, "What crime is being committed right now? I'm *working*," she could be seen placing a hand to the side of Briar's head. Alix listened to the video skip to the part at the end where Peter jogged down an adjacent aisle and placed his hand on Emira's shoulder. She could tell that they had raised the volume on Peter's voice so that it could be properly heard by people other than the regular viewers. "Our correspondent Peter Chamberlain," Laney went on, "was called to the scene to set the record straight. Today we're sitting down with Emira Tucker, Alix Chamberlain, and the oldest Chamberlain daughter, Briar."

As Alix heard her own name, one of the cameramen looked up with bright eyes and began to dramatically count down from five with his right hand. Alix's pulse went into her ears, and her toes seemed to numb as she watched him go from three, to two, and then point directly at Laney.

"Alix, Emira, thank you for sitting down with us."

Emira nodded and Alix said, "Absolutely." Her voice came out a bit too eager. She sounded as if she were being interviewed for a job and not by the news. And so she tried to silently sit deeper and find her normal register. Briar, still hung up on the cameraman's sudden countdown, raised both her hands in the air and announced with an air of defensiveness, "I can count too."

"And thank *you*, Briar," Laney said. She gave a kind kids-say-the-darnedest-things expression, and then got right back to business. "Alix, let's start with you. Could you have ever foreseen this happening when you called Emira late that night?"

"Ohmygosh, not at all." Alix felt herself start to breathe. Laney was smooth and curious in a way that implied the four of them had never met, much less rehearsed. Her conviction made the room seem less staged, their words much less studied. "We were very new to the city and it seemed like a no-brainer to call Emira to see if she could help out. I think other parents can understand that life gets messy sometimes, and that the grocery store is typically an excellent place to kill time with a toddler."

"So, Emira." Laney turned thoughtful and grave. "You and Briar are at Market Depot. What happens next?"

Unprompted, Briar sadly put her hands to her cheeks and said, "What happen?" Alix smiled and smoothed Briar's hair down her back.

"Well . . . we were walking around and about to go look in the nut section . . ." Emira said this more to Briar than to Laney. "And then a security guard asked if she was my child."

As if Emira had just recited an ancient proverb, Laney put her elbow to her knee. She squinted, cocked her chin, and intoned, "Hmm."

"I told him that I was her babysitter, but he said that I didn't look like I'd been babysitting, and then he refused to let me leave."

"I think it's important to point out that Emira had been attending a birthday party, which she left to come and help us out." Alix transferred her hand from her daughter's back to Emira's shoulder. This remark had not been practiced, but the gesture came to her so naturally that she didn't want to stifle it. "And since it also seems to be a source of confusion, this video was taken way back in September. Emira was dressed very appropriately for the evening she planned on having."

"So I take it that this wasn't your typical babysitting outfit," Laney responded with a small laugh.

"Oh, yeah no," Emira said. She grinned at both Laney and Alix as she added, "I usually have, like, a babysitting uniform."

Alix inhaled quick and doubly. She looked into Laney's green eyes to ground her in the space, and she told herself, *Calm down. She means that figuratively. She means jeans or leggings.* Alix tightened her ankles against each other. *She chose you. Emira and Kelley are no longer together. Stay with it, Alix. You're almost there.*

"So this interrogation begins, they refuse to let you leave." Laney recounted the night's events. "What's going through your mind?"

Alix turned her head to face Emira straight on as Emira tried to find her words. She had already touched her once; she couldn't do it again. But she tried to give her space and positivity, thinking, *Come on Mira, you can do this.* Emira picked up Briar from under her armpits and readjusted her on her lap.

"Ummm, I felt pretty confused and upset?" Emira upspoke. "We weren't being loud or anything, so it was weird that they came over. And then I was just really afraid that they would take her away from me."

From Tamra's arms, Catherine let out a very cute yawn that was slightly audible. Tamra tiptoed over to where Zara leaned against the living room entrance in case the yawning continued and she needed to relocate. As Emira finished speaking, Briar looked at one of the cameramen and said, "I'm not a baby, okay?"

"Looking back on the accusations placed against you . . ." Laney said to regain the room, "Emira, do you feel that justice needs to be served in terminating the security guard's position?"

This was not a question they had rehearsed. Was that purposeful on Laney's end? Alix couldn't tell. She held her breath as she watched Emira secretly react to the surprise, recover, and deliver.

"Oh. No no." Emira shook her head casually as if she were refusing dessert after a large meal. "I was pretty upset, but now I'm more mad that this video got out without my permission. I didn't want that at all, and . . . umm, whoever released it obviously doesn't really care about consent. And I think that is . . . a pretty sad thing."

Alix's closed-mouthed and listening smile became taut and tired against her face. *There's no way*, she thought. *There's no way that anyone could know.* But even more important than this video and the way in which it found its way to the Internet was the fact that even if Kelley hadn't betrayed Emira's trust by now, it would only be a matter of time. Briar touched her toes and looked up at Emira. With a piqued interest she asked, "Somebody crying?"

"And Alix." Laney turned. Her voice had a slightly joyful lilt in it and Alix could tell she was preparing to conclude. "You're no stranger to women sticking up for themselves. Coincidentally, you've made a career out of it!"

"I have." Alix turned toward Laney as she spoke. Alix realized that this might be the one circumstance where she could freely admit that Emira meant the world to her, and she could say this without a cloud of reticence, or a concern that Emira was on the clock. "Emira embodies much of the spirit in my business LetHer Speak," she said. "Not only did she stick up for herself, but she listens to herself, and this is exactly the kind of person Peter and I want around our girls, especially at this important time of their lives."

"And I hear that Emira will be around a lot more often in the New Year?" Laney looked for confirmation from both Emira and Alix. "As you continue to write your first book?"

Alix chuckled. So Laney's plug wasn't as subtle as Alix had hoped for, but it made her feel more like a small-business owner than she had in months. "That's right," Alix said. "As I finish my book and go back to work, Emira will be joining us full-time. And honestly . . ." Alix looked at her daughter and said, "We couldn't be happier." Out of the corner of her eye, Alix watched Emira bite the side of her cheek.

"And lastly, Emira." Laney sighed. "Is there anything you'd like to add? Do you have any advice for other caretakers who might run into a similar situation?"

Emira's rehearsed answer included phrases such as, *to stick up for themselves*, *to hold their ground*, and *to always have their phones charged no matter what*. But when Emira began to nod very slowly and say, "Ummm, so the thing is . . ." Alix couldn't figure out how she planned on transitioning into a closing line.

"Well . . . no. I don't really have any advice because umm . . ." Emira exhaled upward and several strands of her bangs fluttered in her breath. "I will actually not be joining the Chamberlains full-time? Or like . . . at all."

Alix straightened her posture and inhaled through her nose. Her first thought was, *Oh no. She's confused.*

With sweet and encouraging eyes, Laney said, "Can you say more on that, Emira? Is there anything you've gathered from this that you'll bring into your new role?"

"Yeah, ummm." Emira dropped her head to the side, and this was when Alix recognized the Emira who had been coming to her home for months. The bored tilt in her voice. The cool air of annoyance. Alix's pulse began to tap her neck harder.

"So yeah, it's been fun?" Emira said to Laney. "But this video being released has definitely put some things in perspective and . . . due to some creative differences, I will no longer be working here. But you can find me at the front desk at the Green Party Philadelphia office because . . . yeah. That, that's where I'll be."

Alix's first instinct was to laugh. She let her lips creep beautifully over her teeth and put her hand on the couch in the space between her and Emira. "No, Emira." She grinned. "She's talking about you being our nanny next year."

"Mm-hmm. Yeah, I am too?" Emira lifted Briar and put her on the ground—an act with which both were so clearly familiar—and Alix froze in her seat. "Yeah, I'm not gonna do that," Emira clarified. "I'm gonna be working full-time with the Green Party instead."

Alix laughed again. She looked at Laney as if she were realizing in real time that an elaborate joke had been played, but Laney's face was stretched in bewilderment as well. "I'm sorry," Alix said, tucking her hair behind an ear. "What did you—"

"Well, the thing is . . ." Emira turned toward her. "Basically . . ." Her eyes came up to meet with Alix's. And for a second, Emira appeared as if she'd just remembered a dream she had the night before. "I just think it would be best if we went our separate ways and . . . that those paths never like . . . came back together."

It was as if Alix had floated out of her body and was watching herself from three feet above. The room suddenly reeked with the terror of a surprise party and the cameras seemed twice as large, sucking her into their dark round lenses. Emira had dropped the kind of punch line that evoked both petty embarrassment and screaming dread, and her inflection came as if she'd said, *Sorry, this seat is taken*. But the reference and the implication that yes, Emira and Kelley sat around laughing at new-money-trash Alex Murphy, that she was still a person that existed—it felt like the plot twist of a horror movie. Suddenly, the call was coming from inside the house. She was the one who had been dead the whole time. This was a dream within another dream. Out of the corner of her right twitching eye, Alix could see Tamra's hand go up to her mouth. She covered half of her face, but Alix could hear her say, "Ohmygod."

The cameras kept rolling.

Alix's nervous system told her to stay as still as she could, to try to keep smiling. She knew she looked like a three-year-old who had just been tapped on the shoulder in a friendly game of freeze-tag, excited but awkwardly unsure of how long they'd have to stay frozen. She opened her mouth to say something, anything, but her tongue felt stupidly huge.

"Okay, yeah, so thanks!" Emira said to the floor. She stood up and scooted between Alix's legs and the camera gear. Briar trotted after her and said, "Mira, way fo' me!" As Emira exited the living room, she and Zara exchanged another look, but this one prompted Zara to slip her phone into the waistband of her pants. Just as Emira left from sight, Zara jumped into frame.

"Yeah, das right!" Zara said to the camera behind Laney. "Home-girl is *out*, okay?! She ain't need this!" By *this*, Zara meant the white throw pillow Emira had been sitting against, which Zara flicked with a disinterested hand. "She wit' the Green Party now, nigga! She got *money!*" Zara began to dip her head at different angles in the camera lens, shouting and clapping on every syllable of "This is what democracy looks like!" As Catherine began to clap with Zara, a privately panicked Laney said to the camera, "Alix Chamberlain's book *To Whom It May Concern* will be out in May 2017. Back to you, Misty." In the space above her crotch, Laney did a manic signal for *cut*.

Twenty-six

Emira said, "B, come here real quick," but Briar was already on her heels. Zara's voice began to echo through the first floor of the Chamberlain house as Emira took Briar's hand, and for a moment she thought, *What if I just took you and walked out the door? How far would we get? Shaunie's apartment? Maybe Pittsburgh?* Instead, Emira hoisted Briar onto the toilet in the guest bathroom and closed the door behind her. She squatted and placed her hands on Briar's knees, but when she noticed her palms and pinkies were shaking, she placed them on the sides of the toilet.

"Hey. Look at me real quick." Briar swung her legs aggressively on the toilet seat, and the top of her shoes almost smacked Emira's chest. With one hand, Briar swiped at a shock of blond hair, which had fallen into her face. Emira felt her body begin to crack beneath the realization that the ponytails she gave Briar Chamberlain had always been tragically numbered. Briar looked up and pointed to Emira's necklace. "I want dis," she said. Emira thought, *Oh fuck, this is really it.*

"Hey," Emira whispered. "You know how I said you can't have favorites?"

Briar nodded. She agreed with this statement and waved a finger to say, "No no, that's not nice."

Outside, Zara could be heard shouting, "Whose streets?!" She clapped three times. "*Our* streets!" She clapped again.

"Okay, but guess what?" Emira smiled. "You're *my* favorite. No one else. Just you."

"Okay, Mira?" Briar's eyebrows suddenly appeared as if she had something very important to say. "Maybe?" She pointed at Emira's necklace again. "Maybe I keep dis for a little while."

Emira realized that Briar probably didn't know how to say good-bye because she'd never had to do it before. But whether she said good-bye or not, Briar was about to become a person who existed without Emira. She'd go to sleepovers with girls she met at school, and she'd have certain words that she'd always forget how to spell. She'd be a person who sometimes said things like, "Seriously?" or "That's *so* funny," and she'd ask a friend if this was her water or theirs. Briar would say good-bye in yearbook signatures and through heartbroken tears and through emails and over the phone. But she'd never say good-bye to Emira, which made it seem that Emira would never be completely free from her. For the rest of her life and for zero dollars an hour, Emira would always be Briar's sitter.

Outside, there was a shuffling of feet. Zara began performing an accelerated rendition of "We Shall Overcome" and she ended every verse with *Ayyeee*. Emira heard Tamra say, "Girl, get down from there!" and Zara yelled back, "I'm not resisting!" Laney asked everyone to please calm down as Catherine began to cry. Mrs. Chamberlain's voice said, "Where is Briar?"

Emira placed her head at the side of Briar's. She kissed her cheek and took in Briar's scent: baby soap, strawberries, and the tart sweetness of dried yogurt. She sat back on her heels. In what she hoped would be the saddest gesture of her twenties, Emira tickled the side of Briar's neck and said, "I'll see you later, okay?" Briar pursed her lips into a smile and dipped her chin into Emira's fingers. She raised her shoulders up next to her ears as if she didn't know the answer to a very darling and rhetorical question.

There were quick footsteps and then the bathroom door swung open. Zara was out of breath. She leaned over with her hands on her knees, and between dramatic exhales, she said, "K . . . they mad so . . ."

"Go get an Uber," Emira instructed. She kissed the top of Briar's little head, placed her on the ground, and told herself to get out of the house. When she turned to go, Zara's presence had been replaced by Mrs. Chamberlain's.

Mrs. Chamberlain's neck was blemished in red splotches of freckled skin. Her jaw was set strangely forward and only her bottom teeth were showing. She looked at Emira as if Emira were hours late, and she were waiting for her to deliver an apology. "Tamra?" she called. The sound of Tamra's socks could be heard on the tile as Catherine's uneven crying came closer. Once she had sufficient backup, Mrs. Chamberlain locked eyes with Emira again. From somewhere deep in her diaphragm, she said, "Emira? Get away from her."

Emira let an impressed expression slide over her face. This was really how Mrs. Chamberlain wanted to end it, by playing the matchless mom card that she always held so tightly to her chest. This was the most responsive reaction Mrs. Chamberlain had ever expressed concerning the whereabouts of her daughter, in what was, in Emira's opinion, the safest place Briar could ever be. *There's literally one thing I'm good at*, Emira thought, *and that's taking care of your daughter.* But still, Emira laughed once and said, "Okay."

Emira walked past her and Tamra swooped in on Briar as if Emira had just surrendered her last hostage. To her right, the front door was propped open by Zara and her shoe. Mrs. Chamberlain held her ground in the space in front of the guest bathroom, and from there she called Emira's name with a bold and bitchy authority. "Excuse me, Emira?" With both her hands on the vestibule door frame, Emira looked to the hooks on the wall and said, "Where's my backpack?" With her phone in her hands, Zara looked to the stairs behind Emira. She winced and said, "Uh-oh."

"Emira!"

Emira turned around to find Mrs. Chamberlain's hands in the air in front of her and her fingers splayed wide. Emira took a breath and walked past her to the stairs. She found herself gracelessly crouching down as if doing so would make her less likely to be seen, or as if she were walking in front of a large group of people watching a game on a television screen. Emira saw Tamra patting the back of Briar's head on the couch as Mrs. Chamberlain took the stairs after her. "Emira, stop," she said. Emira sped up. She heard Briar ask, "Where does Mira go now?"

She didn't stop until she spotted her backpack on the floor of the upstairs bathroom. She snatched the strap and stood up, swinging it onto her right shoulder, but Mrs. Chamberlain took advantage of her delay by securing her feet in front of the bathroom door. With her hair around her face and her chest growing pinker by the second, Mrs. Chamberlain closed her eyes and said, "Are you *kidding* me?"

Emira closed her mouth as Mrs. Chamberlain went on. "Emira,

this can't be real," she said. "Do you know what you just did? You just *humiliated* me and my *entire* business."

"Ummm . . ." Emira couldn't believe she was in another white space so soon, trying to keep her cool, and struggling to imply that she could honestly just go. Emira hoisted her backpack farther up on her shoulder. "I'm just grabbing my stuff," she said.

"Ohmygod, Emira!" Mrs. Chamberlain's hands were in front of her chest again, and she wrung them as if she were wringing a neck. "Do you think that looked good for you either? Did you *honestly* seek out the Green Party just to do this to me?"

Emira squinted in confusion. "Umm . . . no?"

"Oh, so I tell you that I'm working with the Clinton campaign and suddenly you want to quit and work for the *Green* Party?"

"No . . ."

"No?!"

"No," Emira said louder. "I've worked for them longer than I've worked for you."

In the most dramatic reaction Emira had ever seen in real life, Mrs. Chamberlain's eyes bulged as she said, *"What?"*

Emira thought about carefully pointing out that the things Mrs. Chamberlain seemed to care about most were whom Emira was dating, or what her favorite cocktail was, or what she was up to on a Friday night. But what was the point of having one more incident of trying to prove a point in the proximity of a three-year-old child who Emira more than liked. So instead, Emira said, "I'm just gonna go." She inhaled through gritted teeth as she inched past Mrs. Chamberlain and reached out to the stair banister.

"Emira, are you serious?!" Mrs. Chamberlain followed. Emira told herself not to trip as she gripped the railing and jogged down the steps. At the bottom, Laney stood by the front vestibule with one hand to the wall and one against her chest. When Emira reached the first floor, Mrs. Chamberlain yelled out, "Don't you dare walk out that door like this!" Standing in the vestibule doorway, Emira turned around.

"All of this was for *you*!" Mrs. Chamberlain cried. "We wanted to help you clear your name and you turn around and do this? Whatever Kelley said, I . . . Emira. Everything we've done was for you. *Everything*," she said. Her focused stare seemed to say, *I know you know what I did, and I also don't care.* "You might be too young to understand this right now, but we have always had your best interests at heart. Emira, we, we love you." Mrs. Chamberlain threw her hands up in surrender as she said this, as if loving Emira was despite her family's other best interests. "I don't . . ." She shook her head. "I don't know what to say."

Emira stared up at the foyer chandelier. In that moment, Mrs. Chamberlain going into her email and releasing a private video seemed like the least of her or Mrs. Chamberlain's problems. Emira understood that if Mrs. Chamberlain had a video of herself being mistreated, she'd want someone to release it for her too. There was no way of convincing Mrs. Chamberlain that what she had done had actually not been for Emira; however, this was a chance, Emira's last one, to suggest that Mrs. Chamberlain do something for someone else. Emira reached behind her back and secured the other strap onto her left arm. "Sooo . . . right now it's probably whatever 'cause she's only three?" she said. "But you gotta act like you like Briar once in a while. Before she like . . . really figures it out."

Mrs. Chamberlain put a hand to her sternum. Her collarbones became dangerously apparent as her neck curved; her posture stiffened into an awkward slant. She stared at Emira and said, "Excuse me?"

"I know I'm not a mom or whatever," Emira said, "But you gotta stop looking at her like you're just waiting for her to change, 'cause umm . . . It is what it is, you know? You're her mom."

Everyone in the room stopped speaking.

If someone had told Emira that she was bad at her job, she most likely would have done what she always did, laugh once and say *Okay*. She knew that she was an excellent typist, she was an even better babysitter, and she'd be secretly grateful that someone considered what she did a job, and not just a temporary side hustle. But Mrs. Chamberlain's stare went empty and embarrassed as if she'd been caught in the middle of the night, standing in front of the refrigerator, fork in hand and chocolate frosting on her face. Her lips smushed together underneath her nose and Emira thought, *Is she really gonna cry?* For a second, Emira tried to convince herself that what she'd said wasn't that bad, but merely necessary and hopefully constructive. But then she heard air being tightly sucked into Zara's mouth behind her. Zara finished this inhalation with a quiet, "Oop. There it is."

Outside the front door and down the porch steps, a car honked lightly.

"Sorry . . . this is weird." Emira exhaled. She sidestepped twice before she finally turned to walk out of the Chamberlain house one last time. She made it all the way to the front porch, but then she turned around. She leaned her body back into the vestibule and said, "Sorry, Laney," before she followed Zara to the passenger side of a silver Ford Focus. Zara opened the door and said, "You Darryl?"

The man nodded and the girls hopped into the backseat.

Twenty-seven

Alex Murphy was one of the two senior class representatives at William Massey High, which meant she delivered announcements at every other assembly and wore a Student Council polo on Fridays. But by graduation, it didn't feel like Alex had achieved anything from this title. High school felt much more like a bad dream. After becoming the reason that Robbie Cormier wouldn't be attending George Mason University on a volleyball scholarship, Alex spent the final days of her senior year finding notes attached to her back and textbooks that read *Thanks Narc* and *Richy Bitch*.

One of the student council's responsibilities was cleaning up after graduation. Alex begged her student council advisor to give her another task, to not require her presence with the rest of the group as they took down streamers and told one another they couldn't believe high school was over. Her advisor must have known what happened— everyone did—and so she gave Alex the easy, alternative job of cleaning out the senior-patio lockers. On the day after graduation, with a sullied rag and a bottle of surface cleaner, Alex started at the Z last names and worked backward toward the A's. Standing and cleaning the top lockers wasn't so bad. Kneeling on the concrete for the bottom ones, however, began to bruise her knees.

By the Johnson lockers she had to ask a maintenance worker for a new towel. And by the Garcias, she had filled up an entire trash can with leftover spiral notebooks, a few socks, magnetic mirrors, and candy wrappers. Alex threw away at least a dozen pocket-sized photos showing girls with corsages, two hands around their waists, or group pictures of soccer teams and exclusive lunch table attendants. The closer she got to Kelley Copeland's locker, the more Alex felt as if she were being watched. She began to feel unnatural in all her movements, as if she were pretending to read a magazine when she was really trying to overhear a conversation.

Alex popped Kelley's locker open. It was so vacant and sad. This was the locker she'd dropped several letters into, and Kelley didn't even have the decency to leave it dirty for this moment. She hadn't known what she expected to find, but the fact that it didn't really need cleaning felt like a backhanded compliment. Still, Alex cleaned out Kelley's locker as if it had a thin coat of high school wear and tear. Kelley's locker creaked all the way open as Alex began to clean the locker directly beneath it.

She started at the top and planned to work her way down, but Alex felt and heard the rag snag on something in the top corner. There was something paper and triangled squished in the metal plates in between this locker and Kelley's up above. With her fingernail underneath the rag, Alex bent farther on her knees and fingered the roof inside the locker, preparing herself for something foul to pop out like a forgotten sandwich bag or the hardened wings of something dead. But after one final swipe at what she thought was possibly a dirty magazine, hidden here for safekeeping, Alex gasped to see a flash of her own handwriting on folded loose-leaf paper fall out onto the ground in front of her knees. From the slot of space in between Kelley's locker and the locker beneath it were five of her letters. They were grimy and bent and yellowed, but even worse, they were still unopened and sealed with her cursive on the front reading *From A.M.* Alex gasped. She turned over her shoulder to find she was thankfully still alone, rapidly picked up her unopened letters, and stuffed them between her breasts and her bra. She quickly wiped the locker down and slammed it shut, which was when she saw another set of initials engraved into the rusty metal. In the top corner of the locker door Alex saw an R and a C. Just below Kelley's locker was Robbie Cormier's.

For weeks, Alex had been thinking of Kelley and mostly just wondering, *How could he do this?* As it happened, all this time, he actually hadn't.

But what did it matter now? The damage had been done. No matter what, students would call her names all summer, and Robbie's admission wouldn't be regranted. For a moment, Alex wondered if she should pull the letters out from her bra, or if they carried some dirt or muck that would make her skin break out. But once again, she looked over her shoulder and saw that no one was there. Alex was alone, and the one thing she still had was the freedom to follow the narrative that suited her best.

It would never be a relief to know that a locker malfunction was to blame for her demise, rather than Kelley Copeland himself. Believing that Kelley was the starting point of her adversity would always be easier than believing she'd simply slipped through an unlucky crack. This choice to believe otherwise, to pretend there weren't coffee-colored letters pressed into her chest, would keep her close to him, even if staying close to Kelley meant holding a grudge for something that he never did. And all summer long, as Alex rolled silverware and received lousy tips, it was easier doing it while mad at Kelley, rather than having no relation to him at all.

And by the time Alex moved to New York, it was like she didn't have to pretend.

Kelley was the guy who ruined her senior year, much in the same way that her name was spelled A-l-i-x.

Twenty-eight

t would be unfair to say that Emira Tucker stopped babysitting. She worked the front desk of the Green Party office but only for a total of five weeks. During a fund-raising event, Emira was refilling a large carafe of coffee when she saw a little boy place a handful of goldfish on a flimsy paper plate. "Hey," Emira said to him. "How about we put those in a cup instead?" This child belonged to the regional director of the U.S. Census Bureau, a six-foot-tall woman named Paula Christi, who watched on from afar. Paula hired Emira as an administrative assistant, and Emira proceeded to spend the majority of her twenty-sixth year in meeting rooms and black SUVs.

Emira booked Paula's appointments and ordered her lunches and stood backstage at panels and speeches. But she also rubbed the backs of Paula and other middle-aged adults as they cried and swore in private (she handed them tissues and told them it was okay). While her own news segment on WNFT was the gateway to the highest-paying position of her life (eighteen dollars an hour—she also received free lunch), Emira later found it funny that she once considered her four-minute segment on Philadelphia local news "a big deal." The interview cut just after Zara announced *Yeah, das right!* And aside from a few YouTube compilations of Local News Interviews Gone Wrong, no one Emira's age saw it. Not even Shaunie or Josefa; Emira made Zara swear.

Three days before Emira turned twenty-eight, her boss called her into her office. Emira sat down across from her and opened up her notebook, ready to take instructions or a lunch order, but Paula told her to put it away.

"You've been here for almost two years, yes?" Paula confirmed. After Emira nodded, she added, "When are you planning on leaving?"

Emira blinked three times and smiled. "Leaving?" she asked. Something Emira appreciated about Paula was her directness, but in moments like this, Emira was both grateful and afraid, because Paula always meant what she said. Emira squinted and asked, "Am I getting fired right now?"

"God, no. But Emira," she said, "I've never had an assistant who wanted to continue being my assistant for more than two years. Basically, if you stayed on for much longer, it would mean I'm doing something wrong."

Emira sat back and laughed. "Okay, well . . ." She looked at Paula's desk and a picture of her family. "I can't believe I'm saying this . . . but I actually think I'm okay."

Maybe she wasn't by her girlfriends' standards (Shaunie was engaged, Josefa was teaching at Drexel, Zara made enough money to get a two-bedroom apartment and pay rent for both her and her little sister), but Emira really *was* doing okay. She'd gone to Mexico for Zara's birthday, all five days. She'd stuck to her New Year's resolution to make her bed every day. She had a savings account, which she dipped into often, but not so much that it didn't exist. And she'd added two new recipes to her dinner circulation, both of which were Crock-Pot meals, but still. Emira also liked Paula and her kid. Her boss was fairly rude to everyone except for her, and Emira went to work feeling paid and protected.

But Paula seemed disappointed in Emira's contentment. "Good bosses shouldn't make you happy in a job that they wouldn't want to do themselves," she said. "It's my job to make you so miserable that you're forced into finding something that brings you joy, and then I help you seal the deal. So . . . your goal for the next year is to learn how to properly hate your job, and find something else that you wouldn't hate doing. Got it?"

Emira said, "Got it," and went back to her desk. She would stay on as Paula's assistant until Paula retired.

It would take Emira four more years to receive Shaunie's starting salary of $52K, but Emira came to know the rare relief of having a boss who was so consumed with her assistant's success that she was never derailed by the idea of being Emira's friend. That day, after she walked out of Paula's office, Emira went back to her desk and clicked an open window on her computer. She clicked Add to Cart and Check Out on a loveseat for her apartment, upon which she and Zara would spend an entire weekend painting their nails and watching two seasons of *America's Next Top Model*.

After her news segment, Emira didn't hear from Kelley for six whole days. She told herself that she and he were too different, that they drank too much when they were together, that she didn't know why she tried to date a white guy who lived in Fishtown anyway. Technically, Kelley had won. Emira very publicly stuck it to Mrs. Chamberlain with a remix of his breakup line, which, despite her paraphrasing, she thought he could use as an opening line if he decided to try calling her one more time. But when he did finally

contact her, one week after she quit, it was a clunky and trite text of
encouragement that Emira did not enjoy.

> Emira. Holy shit. I just saw your clip from the news.

> I know things are weird right now, but I'm so proud of you.

> I always knew you could do it.

Despite being more broke than she'd ever been in her life, and still
grieving the loss of Briar Chamberlain, this complimentary sentiment
promptly made it final: there was no way that she and Kelley would
ever recover from the acknowledgment that he'd been right about
Mrs. Chamberlain. Forming a relationship again would somehow
dictate that he could be right about everything else, when really, he
had a lot to learn. Emira never texted him again. His name in her
phone remained Don't Answer.

Emira did see Kelley again, but he didn't see her. On a Saturday
summer morning, when Emira was twenty-eight years old, she went
with Shaunie to a farmer's market at Clyde Park. The girls got sepa-
rated when Shaunie spotted a truck with kittens for adoption, and
Emira roamed the produce tables, taking in the smells and looking
for her friend. For a moment, Emira thought she spotted the back of
Shaunie. But she quickly realized that it couldn't have been Shaunie,
because this person was holding Kelley Copeland's hand. Next to a
table of soy candles and bottled honey, Kelley stood next to a light-
skinned black woman with fresh coils of dark hair. She turned and
Emira took her in. There were gladiator sandals on her feet, a small
gold septum ring in her nose, and a basket hanging on her arm filled
with root vegetables and essential oils.

"Babe, gimme two seconds," she said, touching Kelley's arm. "I'm gonna see if I can sign up to sell my shea butter here next week. Can you hold this real quick?"

Emira watched her hand Kelley a smoothie. When he accepted it he grinned and said, "Okay, miss."

In another lifetime, Emira would have texted Mrs. Chamberlain to let her know she'd run into Kelley. She would have typed, You won't believe who I saw, and Mrs. Chamberlain would have texted back, Tell me everything. Because even though Kelley been right about her, Alix had been right about him too. If things had gone differently, Emira would have also texted Mrs. Chamberlain a picture of her new couch, and Mrs. Chamberlain would have been ecstatic. Sometimes Emira thought that if she'd learned how to say Mrs. Chamberlain's first name, that maybe she would have calmed down a bit. But they hadn't gone differently. And like Emira, Mrs. Chamberlain was a grown human person with choices and decisions, and the funds to order sushi at least two times a week. Emira would think of Mrs. Chamberlain many times on election night, and pray that she had enough room in her heart for both a devastating failure and her firstborn child.

That same year, four months after she spotted Kelley, Emira walked to pick up a bridesmaid dress for what would become Shaunie's first wedding. It was three days till Halloween, but it was a weekend, and children walked the sidewalks in costumes and masks, pillowcases and buckets in their hands. There was a carnival in Rittenhouse Square, and along a brick ledge that bordered the sidewalk sat mini-pumpkins that had been decorated by what looked to be mini-hands. They were covered in glitter paint and feathers, and they were drying in the sun. Down at the far end of the four-foot-tall ledge, five-year-old Briar was dressed as a hamburger, reaching up on her tiptoes, and struggling to reach a pumpkin doused in green.

Emira whispered, "Fuck," and willed herself to keep walking.

"Mama? Mama, can you get mine for me?"

"Just a second, Bri," Mrs. Chamberlain said. At the other side of the sidewalk, wearing an expensive beanie, a khaki trench coat, and booties that had tassels on the backs, Mrs. Chamberlain was squatting in front of two-year-old Catherine. "This zipper is *stuck*, isn't it?" she said. Catherine yawned and licked a sucker.

Emira watched Briar come down off her tiptoes and take a look around. Behind her, two black nannies were pushing strollers with sleeping babies inside. Emira watched Briar go straight up to one, lift her hand, and pat the closest woman's thigh. "Excuse me, nice lady?" she asked. "Can you please help me reach my pumpkin?"

The nanny seemed greatly amused, as if she hadn't been called *nice lady* in years. She said, "Sure, which one is yours?" Emira wished that she'd walked up a little faster, that Briar could have called her the same name, that she could have talked to Briar without Mrs. Chamberlain, just one more time. And then she felt her heart crush even further into her stomach as Briar pointed up at a bright green pumpkin and said, "It's dis one."

Emira held her breath as she put her head down and walked around the nannies, Briar, Mrs. Chamberlain, and Catherine. She heard Briar tell the woman thank you, and Mrs. Chamberlain laugh and apologize for her daughter.

———

Deep into her thirties, Emira would wrestle with what to take from her time at the Chamberlain house. Some days she carried the sweet relief that Briar would learn to become a self-sufficient person. And some days, Emira would carry the dread that if Briar ever struggled to find herself, she'd probably just hire someone to do it for her.

Acknowledgments

My family, Ron, Jayne, and Sirandon Reid, have been a longtime source of support and encouragement. From *Goosebumps* to graduate school, thank you for keeping books in my hands, and allowing me to keep my bedroom door closed.

This novel came into being because of the razor-sharp eye and finishing power of my tireless agent, Claudia Ballard. Claudia, it has been a complete honor to see this project through with you, and it is a daily relief to be on your team. I'm so glad I met you first.

My editor, Sally Kim, inspires in me very cliché but nonetheless true sentiments such as *You're the one*! and *It was you all along!* Sally, I'm indebted to your dedication to every line of this book, your effortless congeniality, and your faithfully calming email response time.

WME and Putnam are filled with wonderful people who unabashedly geek out over characters and plots, and continue to make my life easier every day. The biggest thanks to this unparalleled team, including Alexis Welby, Ashley McClay, Emily Mlynek, Brennin Cummings, Jordan Aaronson, and Nishtha Patel. Elena Hershey and Ashley Hewlett, please never leave me. Anthony Ramondo and Christopher Lin, thank you immensely for clothing this novel so beautifully. Sylvie Rabineau, thank you for championing this book and advocating so smoothly on my behalf. Gaby Mongelli and Jessie Chasan-Taber, I adore working with you and I just think you're both so great.

I crafted the first chapters of this book in Arsaga's coffee shop in Fayetteville, Arkansas (the one on Church and Center), and I couldn't ask for a sunnier, quieter, more judgement-free zone. I completed this book at the Iowa Writers' Workshop by means of the most remarkable gift a writer can receive: inspired stretches of space and time. Thank you to the Truman Capote Foundation for granting me stability as I found my way through the snow and these pages. And thank you to two incredible professors, Paul Harding and Jess Walter, who continue to guide me toward the truth of my obsessions. It's a comfort to have your voices in my head, even when I am not in workshop.

Rachel Sherman's work in *Uneasy Street: Anxieties of Affluence* was a brilliant source of inspiration, not just for this novel, but for how I walk through life. Thank you for capturing a complicated human experience, for leading with empathy in your studies, and for leaning into the uncomfortableness of American capital. I'm so pleased to have your name bookend this novel.

Part of writing is often finding part-time jobs. I've been so fortunate to have bosses who were first to acknowledge that my position was a means to an end, as well as lovely coworkers who made the hours go by quicker. A huge thank-you to Ingrid Fetell Lee, Ty Tashiro, Sarah Cisneros, Meg Brossman, and a whole slew of people at IDEO New York. Thank you, Lindsey Peers, for being a great boss at the best job I've ever had. You facilitated a space where I learned to problem-solve like never before, and you developed in me a lasting appreciation for the mirth of being a child on your birthday. So many thanks to all the mothers who trusted me with their children, particularly Lauren Flink, Jean Newcomb, Kalpana David, Mary Minard, Karen Bergreen, and Ali Curtis.

Sue and Chuck Rosenberg were always enthusiastic readers, great email writers, and endlessly flexible.

Ted Thompson's notes on the first fifty pages were spot-on and honest. More importantly, they were kind enough to make me start over.

Deb West and Jan Zenisek kept me organized, and were always keen to celebrate the little moments.

My goal at Iowa was to find readers who I would keep far past graduation. This resulted in Melissa Mogollon, who spent hours in my living room ironing out backstory in exchange for Nodo sandwiches, and Isabel Henderson, who went line by line and downloaded the MTV channel so we could forget about writing. And in addition to letting me camp out in her kitchen for hours ("Am I being a bad host? Do you need more club soda?") Claire Lombardo supplied detailed track changes that I went back to when I was feeling low. I'm so appreciative of this feedback and these friendships. You are somehow even more than the reason I came. (Claire, I'll text you in five minutes.)

This novel also came to be by the support and humor of wonderful friends, and their unspoken agreement of mercy to forget the years of rough writing that preceded this one. I am so thankful for the friendships of those who believed in my writing even when I didn't. So many thanks to Mary Walters, Njoki Gitahi, Caleb Way, Karin Soukup, Loren Blackman, Darryl Gerlak, Holly Jones, and Alycia Davis.

The teams at the Hillman Grad Network and Sight Unseen Pictures challenge and excite me every day. So many thanks go to Lena Waithe, for her warmth as a teacher, quickness as a writer, and her incredible ability to shine while holding the door open for others. To Rachel Jacobs, for her ability to see outside of a story, her generous and undying patience, and all the times she answered texts and emails when she shouldn't have. And to Rishi Rajani for his attention to detail, his commitment to the spirit of this novel, and for the most genuine use of exclamation points I have ever encountered.

Christina DiGiacomo has read everything I have ever written and jumped up and down with me when a full-time job became available. I'm quite pleased that we decided to be best friends back in 2001.

And then, lastly, there's Nathan Rosenberg. Nate, it is an absolute privilege to call you my family. Maybe the best thing I've ever done was click Send.